A THOUSAND RECIPES FOR REVENGE

A THOUSAND RECIPES FOR REVENGE

BETH CATO

47NORTH

Text copyright © 2023 by Beth Cato
All rights reserved.

Published by 47North, Seattle

www.apub.com

Amazon, the Amazon logo, and 47North are trademarks of Amazon.com, Inc., or its affiliates.

ISBN-13: 9781662510281 (paperback)
ISBN-13: 9781662510298 (digital)

Cover design by Philip Pascuzzo
Cover image: © Steven Puetzer / Getty; © zoom-zoom / Getty;
© mxtama / Getty; © valeo5 / Getty; © DrPixel / Getty; © Difydave / Getty

Printed in the United States of America

With much gratitude for my agent, Rebecca Strauss

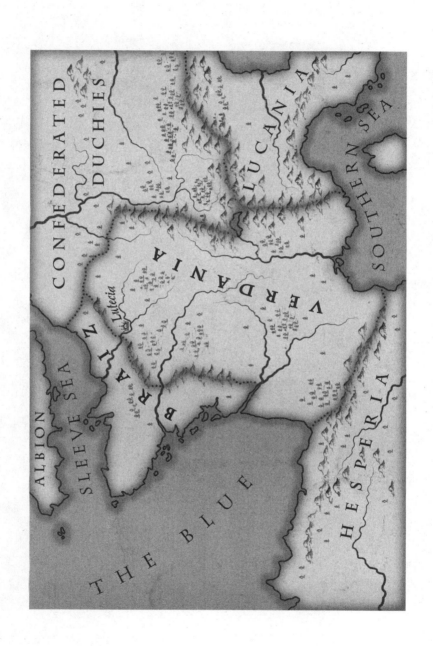

MAGIC AND THE FIVE GODS

The Five Gods have graced people with dominion over land and sea, and designated that which we may eat and be empowered by. Magical powers are imbued through food alone. To scorn what the Five have granted us is to be a guest insulting the host.

Rare family lines are blessed through their tongues with the ability to sense and understand food in ways that no others can. In Verdania, these people are called Chefs, trained from their youngest years to master cuisine through their heightened perception. Chefs take ingredients derived of divinely blessed flora and fauna and call upon the Gods to awaken the magical potential in the foods they prepare. In this, they serve the Gods and Gods-ordained rulers.

Among Chefs, a select few have empathetic talents; they can perceive food as others would taste it and customize dishes to their preferences, whether they work with ingredients common or magical. They can maximize flavor and magic to a degree beyond that of other Chefs and talented cooks.

Gyst, God of the Unseen and Unknown ✕

Overseer of fermentation, yeast, molds, even infections—things that often begin as or remain invisible or strangely small yet are powerful. Gyst feeds on secrets. Caves, cellars, and bakers' kitchens are his favored domains, as are any places shadowed and private, where privy details may be whispered for Gyst's ever-listening ears.

Hester, God of Hearth and Home 🔥

Hester is the warmth and coziness of home—but also an entity of crackling rage. After all, the same hearth fire that cooks meat to make it edible and delicious can also raze the building to the ground. Hester is fabled to have traversed Verdania with such regularity that her heavy tread created its ponds and lakes. Though Hester is worshipped the world over, Verdanians regard her as their home-born God and plead for her favor by throwing their choicest foods to the flames.

Lait, God of Milk and New Life

Loving and beloved matron of new mothers and infants, human and otherwise. Spring is her season, care and compassion her emphases. Around the world, Lait's Houses care for orphaned and abandoned children, and Lait blesses those who donate food, especially milk and cheese, to help those in need at her Houses and to the temple-kitchens known as pentads.

Melissa, God of All That Is Sweet

Sugar beets, honey, ripe fruits, and even a loved one's kisses are under Melissa's regard. Nobles enjoy confectionary delights that melt upon the tongue or marvel at sculpted sugar extraordinaires, but even the humblest of denizens can enjoy the harvest of the hive or hearken to the peals of so-named Melissa's bells, which celebrate special occasions in any town of considerable size.

Selland, God of Salt

A God fluid in nature, equally of the salty ocean and the briny wetland and the high-mountain cave crusted with crystalline deposits. Blustery coastal storms embody his might, as does the single pinch of salt that awakens the incredible flavors within a dish. The God of Salt asks for no offerings. No, Selland takes what Selland wants and is fickle with his favor, even to the seafaring people who hold him closest to their hearts.

CHAPTER ONE

ADA

Commoners believe that a Chef is best identified by their distinct uniform dress, but in all truth, the best way to recognize one is by how they dress a chicken.

—Excerpt from *Manual for Tour Chefs*

Adamantine Garland, in her sixteen years as a deserter from both Verdania's Chef Guild and army, had observed that rogue Chefs such as herself were usually caught after committing at least one of three critical errors: they either revealed their Chef skills to untrustworthy people, displayed kitchen intuition beyond the ability of mundane cooks, or were entrapped while utilizing illicit magical ingredients.

On the first count, she remained safe. Grand-mère was her only immediate confidante, and her continued mental degradation worried Ada like nothing else.

As to the second point, Ada had learned to grit her teeth and undersalt, overcook, and otherwise make food edible but unworthy of note. Even though she'd been a deserter for more than a decade, to perceive perfection and consciously keep beneath it irritated her like sand in a boot.

As to the third point, well, a full table of gendarmes currently sat in the dining room of the small inn where she labored. The police seemed to be more interested in the kitchen than their wine. Not a good sign. Ada, at least, hadn't forgotten the rigorous military training of her youth. She warily watched them through the serving hatch, her mien casual even as more sweat than usual rolled down her spine to soak the waistband of her breeches.

Five help her. She *knew* she shouldn't have gone to the Alley of Seasonings on Laitsday. Ada had conversed with several purveyors of black-market ingredients to get a sense of current prices and left feeling half-ill at the exorbitant numbers she'd been quoted. She'd need to save up for a month to buy even a handful of the awake oak flour that would help alleviate the worst of Grand-mère's symptoms. She'd thought she'd been careful when she went home afterward, too, but someone must have tracked her. Someone had informed the Guild prosecutors, who'd then sent the police.

If such a thing had happened even a year ago, Ada would have abandoned the kitchen to hastily pack up Grand-mère and their belongings to start anew elsewhere.

Nothing was so easy now. Even on good days, Grand-mère could get lost if she went farther than the privy. Hester, God of Hearth and Home, had blessed them with compassionate neighbors who stayed with Grand-mère while Ada worked. If they moved now, the change would leave Grand-mère all the more addled, and Ada would have no help while she was away.

If they were arrested, the Chef Guild wouldn't conscript Grand-mère again, as they would Ada. No, even as old and doddering as Grand-mère was, they'd swiftly deliver the most brutal punishment extended to any deserter-Chef: the public removal of her Five-blessed tongue.

Behind Ada, the inn's proprietor, Pascal, hummed to himself as he assisted her with prep work. The thud-thud-thud of his knife added rhythm to his song as she deliberated what to do.

She could try to make a run from the building, but she couldn't count on the gendarmes being completely inept. They must have additional police stationed in the back alley, probably in the company of a palace prosecutor. She considered the root vegetables in their iron pan. The pan itself would be a good, solid weapon if it came to a brawl. She couldn't help a small smile at the thought of a gendarme taking a scalding carrot to the eye.

But no. She needed to stay collected for now and hold off on any offensive measures with produce.

With a deft jerk of her wrist, she swirled the chopped vegetables through the nutty butter, then poured everything onto a ready tin platter. Without raising a sample to her lips, she perceived the tastes and textures. The rutabaga, turnip, beet, and celery root were tender inside, their outsides crisp and lacquered in butter churned fresh this morning from a farm just outside the city of Lutecia. The cows fed on early-spring clover, she detected, from fields along a creek that followed the southern highway. The clover there had a particular floral sweetness that she could also recognize in honey from the same vicinity.

Alongside the vegetables, she added a roasted chicken seasoned with tarragon, chervil, and parsley. The proper balance of herbs, however, would fail to redeem the scrawny bird. She knew how tough it would be to her teeth.

Perhaps the worst offense of all, though, was the dearth of salt across the whole dish. May Selland forgive her! She forced away her grimace as she carried the finished plate into the dining room.

It galled her to present such fare to anyone, but the subterfuge was necessary to make her look like a cook and not a Chef.

"Your meal, mesdemoiselles," Ada said, gaze humble as she set down the plate before two officers. The men at the other end of the table shared a platter of their own.

The nearest woman acknowledged Ada with a wave and didn't cease her conversation with her peer across the table. After a few seconds,

Ada's awareness of the dish shifted to perceive the food through the closest woman's tongue as she speared a beet nugget on the tip of her knife. The lack of salt wouldn't perturb the diner too much, but the herbal mélange would be strong for her preference.

Ada's perception faded as she backed away. Even now, with the peril involved, some small part of her wanted to whisk the plate away and return with food perfected to the woman's taste. Propaganda would say that such an urge—a calling—was Ada's responsibility as a Chef with a tongue blessed by the Five to serve her king and country. More than four decades of practical life experience, however, told Ada that this desire had nothing to do with a calling and everything to do with her own personal satisfaction in doing a job right.

She knew that she wasn't the only Chef who had difficulty with imperfection. That was why, whenever she spoke with other Chefs as she helped them desert, she made sure to bring up her own struggle to stay hidden.

It was truly for the best that most rogues were wise enough to leave the country.

"Officers," Ada murmured. She bowed to the entirety of the table. "Are you in need of more bread?"

A man grunted and shook his head, his mouth full. He should have put more butter on his piece. Across from him, a woman nodded. Plentiful dandruff flecked the shoulders of her navy-blue justaucorps, though the long uniform coat was otherwise pristine, the two rows of brass buttons down the front like shiny yet worn coins. The officers glanced at each other as if awaiting a signal.

"Go ahead and drink up," muttered a man. "Best get this done." That didn't bode well.

Ada pursed her lips in thought as she left the dining room. "Pascal!" she hissed.

His humming ceased the instant he saw the look on her face. "What?" he asked, setting his knife beside the beets. Chairs dragged on the floor in the next room.

"The gendarmes. Something's about to—"

"Oh no." Pascal seemed to wither. "They must be—oh, I forgot."

"What?" Ada asked sharply.

"Payment." He ended the word in a moan as boot steps shuddered through the wooden floorboards. Forgetting to pay graft to the police was like forgetting to wear trousers in public—anyone past a certain age knew such things needed to be done.

Ada moaned softly. The man had retained important facts about as well as a sieve ever since he'd been boxed in the head by an unruly customer some months earlier. Ada had tried to help him since then, but Pascal often didn't remember to ask for help.

"I'm sorry," he mumbled.

She could only give her head a slight shake. He didn't need to worry about her, not with the misery he was about to endure.

"Pascal Dupuis?" spoke up a gendarme behind her. "Step away from the knife."

Pascal turned the pale shade of finely sifted Lynette Valley flour. "How may I—"

"We've been made aware that you haven't paid your wine tariff. If you do not pay the tariff, you cannot sell wine," the officer continued. He jerked a hairy thumb toward the table they had just abandoned, their flagon and glasses now empty.

"I-I'm sorry! I can pay it now, and more, for your trouble! Vera!" he yelled, calling Ada by her fake name as he faced her. "Let's go into that new cask of the red! These officers need—"

"You don't know what we need." The speaker worked at a crumb stuck between his teeth. He pointed to Ada. "Stay put."

"Monsieur." She gazed down, playing jittery and shy, but she was more angry than anything. Pascal was a good sort. Bumbling and pleasant, generous enough to send leftover food to the nearest pentad several times a week. Kitchen-temples were always in desperate need of meals for the impoverished. If an inn guest or diner couldn't cover their bill, he always let them work off the debt through reasonable labor or barter. He didn't deserve this shakedown.

The officer slowly gazed around, clearly savoring the drama of the moment. "A payment as tardy as yours should be made into a lesson. We're shutting this place down, inn and all."

"No! No!" wailed Pascal. "What of the people who've let rooms? Please, please—"

"Stop whining," the leader continued in a bored tone, as if reciting from a letter already read a hundred times. "Your wine will be confiscated. Your establishment can open again after the tariff and additional fines are addressed."

"But my wine!" Pascal pressed his hands to his balding pate. "I'll get it back, yes?"

Ada flinched. He'd be lucky to get back half the casks in his cellar. They'd vanish, along with any police bookkeeping on the proper tally.

She wanted to argue, fight back, do *something*, but the only way she could really help Pascal right now would be if she had a bag of livre to pay his graft. She didn't.

To their credit, the officers didn't bother lying to Pascal, or answering him at all. Instead, two took Pascal by the elbows, dragging him from the kitchen with more roughness than necessary as he continued to sputter. A glance at the dining room confirmed that their guests had wisely evacuated the premises. One man lingered by the door, head tilted back as he finished off a flagon of wine, then exited with the crock still in hand. Better for him to enjoy it than these corrupt officers, she supposed.

One of the gendarmes approached Ada. With a trembling voice, Ada spoke first: "Mademoiselle, you're not taking me in, too, are you? I'm just the cook."

She studied Ada with pursed lips, assessing her monetary worth. "We're only here for Pascal Dupuis. You can go."

"Thank you, oh, thank you." She dipped her body in an exaggerated show of respect.

The officer sidestepped to the counter nearby and used a piece of bread to mop up drippings on a platter. Ada averted her gaze to hide her smile as the woman gagged. The officer had ingested a rather unhealthy amount of raw drippings from the recently cooked chicken, and oh, did it taste terrible. Ada perceived the room-temperature juice as if she'd been idiotic enough to eat it for herself, her stomach twinging with a warning of the cramping and suffering the woman would soon endure. Fortunately for Ada, her perception was over and done in a matter of seconds. What the woman would experience would last for hours.

Ada was one of few Chefs in Verdania with a tongue so profoundly blessed by Gyst, God of the Unseen and Unknown. For that reason, her value to the Guild and the Crown was beyond compare.

The nearby officer guzzled down wine, as if that would make everything better. Ada took advantage and hurriedly filled an empty flour bag with bread rounds, then filled another with raw vegetables. At least she and Grand-mère would have food for the coming days.

Ada slipped into the hallway and pulled her double-collared coat over her work smock. Head bowed, she confronted the chill of the alley. As she had anticipated, two additional gendarmes gabbed there—no crown prosecutor, though. Thank the Five she'd been wrong about that. The officers paused to consider her and her laden bags, then continued their conversation.

"I don't mind the extra shifts coming up," said one. "The prince gets bound to his dullard wife; I get extra livre to help feed the children. I vow, with spring nearly here, it's like they are growing along with—"

Ada hustled past them, breathing out warmth against the coarsely woven ratteen collar that flared around her jaw. The city had been buzzing like Melissa's blessed bees about Prince Rupert's impending nuptials, and every mention made her grimace as if beset with indigestion. The royal family could rot in a privy, far as she cared.

Actually, no. She corrected her vicious thought as she sprinted over horse manure and puddles to cross the avenue. She had no personal grudge against young Prince Rupert, but his father . . . ! If Gyst cursed King Caristo to a long, miserable decline by gangrene, she would raise a toast in gratitude.

Among Chefs existed a saying: "There are a thousand recipes for revenge, and every one of them tastes like scat." Ada disagreed. Anything could taste sweet with enough honey or sugar in the mix, even feces. Flavor was only one part of the equation. Digestion—that was what granted a person energy or illness, or endowed magic through epicurea.

Epicurea. Oh, Five help them. Ada would never be able to afford that awake oak flour now.

The injustice of Grand-mère's condition drove anger into her steps. It wasn't right for so brilliant and kind a woman to lose herself in such a way. Grand-mère had been nothing but loving and supportive of Ada her whole life. When Ada was a scared five-year-old dropped at her door, Grand-mère could've taken her to a Lait's House to join the other discarded children and orphans, but no. She'd accepted Ada, the get of her drunkard Chef son. Years later, Grand-mère had sobbed with both sadness and pride when Ada departed for her Chef apprenticeship. When, sixteen years ago, Ada had arrived at her door with a sore heart and milk-pained breasts, Grand-mère had listened to her ranting plan to go rogue and, after a moment of thought, nodded and said, "You won't make it alone. I'll go with you."

For a brief, blissful time in her youth, Ada had thought she could have it all. A husband. A baby. Maybe more babies. King Caristo had dashed those hopes like a porcelain vase dropped onto flagstones. Grand-mère was all she had now. Ada would find a way to continue caring for her. She had to.

Which restaurants might need a cook right now? Restaurants that weren't too busy or crowded or near avenues that were likewise busy or crowded? She needed someplace small but that would still enable a decent wage. Someplace she hadn't already worked at under one identity or another.

Ada kept to side streets and alleys wide enough to admit one wagon at a time. Fewer people traveled these ways. The bellowing of roving bread merchants and butchers was distant, echoing amid the canyons of two- and three-story buildings of wood and whitewashed walls. Harnesses jingled, wheels rattled, crisscrossed clotheslines above aflutter with their burdens.

The long walk passed quickly, her mind occupied as it was. Ada realized she was home only when she stood before the entrance to her hotel, blinking stupidly, as if the old building had spontaneously appeared before her. Two women from the hotel next door prattled on the sidewalk about how best to remove stains from swaddling clothes. Farther down, a man sat on a stoop and thumbed through cards as if in wait for someone.

Sighing, Ada started up the narrow stairwell. Her breaths came fast as she reached the third story. The wooden floor griped underfoot like a cat denied its dinner.

"Grand-mère! I'm here," she said as she entered their flat, then stopped. By the light of a single candle, a chair lay in shattered pieces before her.

She smelled blood.

"Grand-mère?" Ada softly closed the door. She set down her bags as she reached for the knife always sheathed at her belt. On light feet, she crept forward.

Someone breathed in the darkness at the far side of the room. Ada moved toward the sound. Cloth rustled closer. "Grand-mère?" she called again, knife at the ready.

A gray blur lunged at her with a subdued shriek. At the last second, Ada jerked the knife away, missing her grandmother's chest by inches.

Grand-mère, however, didn't utilize such restraint. Ada took a hand-chop to the side of her neck, followed promptly by a jab to her gut that was blunted by the thickness of her coat.

"Grand-mère! Stop, stop! It's me, Ada!"

Grand-mère froze, panting hard. "Ada?" she asked, squinting in the near darkness.

"Yes, it's me. What happened here? Let me get the candle. Why aren't there more lights? Where's Belda?"

Ada cringed as she kicked a chunk of wood, and then she kicked something more—a leg, clad in brown cloth. This wasn't the kind neighbor who often watched Grand-mère; Belda always wore her blue servant's garb.

"Belda?" Grand-mère sounded clueless and a little scared. "What happened, Ada?"

That's what Ada so desperately wanted to know, but she had to maintain the appearance of stoicism to help Grand-mère stay calmer. Evenings were always worse for her—Ada could scarcely imagine what this turmoil would do.

"Belda is the nice lady who brings you honey. Where is she?"

"Oh, her! Her son came down sick, I think? She had to rush off."

Under other circumstances, Ada would have been upset with Belda for leaving early, but maybe the woman had been spared something dreadful tonight. Ada grabbed the lit candlestick from the table and moved around the body on the floor. An unfamiliar man's body. His throat had been slashed beneath his bushy black beard.

She lifted the candle to check Grand-mère. Bright, fresh blood spattered her disarrayed clothes. "Are you hurt?"

"Hurt?" Grand-mère studied the blood on her clothes with fascination. "This? No, no. But that man." She pointed, her arm shaking. "He came here asking after you. He was *rude*." At that, she suddenly became more calculated and calm. With stocking toes, she nudged a wooden chunk on the floor—it was a jagged piece of chair, Ada realized. The sharp end was dark with blood.

"I killed him," Grand-mère said with a profound air of satisfaction.

CHAPTER TWO

ADA

To serve Verdania is to serve the Gods. In deserting your duties to the Five, you divorce yourself from all that is holy. Your tongue, the conduit to the divine, is therefore forfeit.

—Decree read before Verdanian rogue Chefs at trial

"You always were a stickler for proper manners," said Ada. "Was there only the one man, Grand-mère?" She used her candle to light a lantern. She was relieved to see no one else was in the room, dead or alive. Ada hadn't trusted Grand-mère to be correct as to whether Belda had left.

"He said he had a . . . a friend. Down on the street."

"A friend?" Ada had never been more frustrated by Grand-mère's slowing thought processes.

"Yes, that's right. He was going to wave to him from the window. I put a stop to that!"

"Did he say why they came for me?"

"He was surprised I was here! Ha! The unprepared buffoon."

That didn't answer the question.

Ada stepped closer to Grand-mère for a more thorough inspection. Grand-mère had dark-hued skin like Ada's, her eyes a woodsy hazel. Her shape had tended toward short and round, and in recent years she had begun to shrink, with her skin taking on a leathered, stretched appearance. Her long silver hair was braided and coiled up in buns, most of her head covered by a plain black cap.

"Your neck." Ada sheathed her knife and touched Grand-mère's face, angling her jaw upward to better see the ligature marks that formed a purpling collar on her saggy skin. "You said you weren't hurt!"

"Bah, I had worse in pentad drills, back in the day." She blew her lips in dismissal. Grand-mère had forgotten so many other things, and hadn't trained in years, but she apparently remembered how to handle herself in a scrap.

Ada realized she shouldn't be surprised. For everyone, pentads were places of spiritual and physical nourishment, but for Chefs they were also places of training in culinary and martial arts. Chefs were to stay in excellent physical condition in case they were summoned for military duty. Grand-mère had worked in the palace for most of her life, but even so, she'd been required to train at least three mornings a week, often doing repetitive drills. The body often remembered what the mind did not.

"This happened minutes ago," Ada stated. The color of the blood made that obvious. She dragged a trunk against the door to slow down any new assailants. "He was no burglar. Not a prosecutor either. This fellow looks like a mercenary scraped off the floor of a quayside tavern." She crouched to search him, her nose crinkling. "Well, for starters, he's been at the wine. He missed his mouth more than once. I can smell the liquor even through the blood."

"Are you suggesting," said Grand-mère in a tone of offense, "that I had an advantage over him only because—"

"Grand-mère, your skills would give you an advantage over him regardless of his state of inebriation," she was quick to say. Grand-mère released a mollified grunt. Ada peeled back his coat. "Rope," she muttered, finding the coiled length tied to his belt. "Was he supposed to take me somewhere?"

"Oh, I've remembered something important!" Grand-mère paused, face scrunching as she sought to hold on to the slippery thought. "He used your real name. Your full name. Adamantine Garland Corre."

The name speared Ada like a falling icicle. "Corre? You're sure?"

Grand-mère nodded with conviction.

Ada's heart pounded fast. Verdania had nullified her marriage sixteen years earlier—at the same time as the disbandment of the Thirty-Fifth Division, the war ending along with the alliance with Braiz. This man wasn't familiar, but thousands of soldiers had been beneath her command. If he was here for revenge, why now? And how had he found her?

She almost moaned aloud. Her venture to the Alley of Seasonings. She must have been recognized and tracked after all, only her whereabouts had been sold not to the Guild but to some other party.

She searched the dead man's pockets with new urgency, adding his few livre to her own. His knives she left. As a Chef and cook, she was particular, and these pieces were undeniably crude. A shame he had no pistol. She could use one about now.

Her fingertips discovered soft leather, tucked deep in a pocket, and her tongue tingled. She recognized the flavor of stone, as sure as if she'd licked a statue.

She recoiled like she'd touched fire.

"What? What is it?" her grandmother asked.

Ada's lips curled with disgust as she tugged out a pouch the depth of an adult thumb tip. "This held rupic powder." Some grit remained wedged within the seam of the bag, so little she hadn't sensed anything until she touched it.

"Rupic!" Grand-mère hissed. "If he was the one who ate it, the magic had already worn off." The man would have had stonelike skin and incredible strength otherwise. "How did someone like *him* get an ingredient that expensive and rare?"

"As payment, I imagine, though this was little more than a taste. A battlefield dose is apple size." Ada stood, letting the contaminated pouch fall to the floor. "I can only think of Mallory Valmont, but he can't be behind this. He must be dead."

Mallory Valmont. The Hero of the Thirty-Fifth. Her peer as an officer of the division. And, due to Ada's investigation, outed seventeen years ago as a murderer and cannibal, and sentenced to the mines of the notorious prison of Mont Annod. She'd never checked on his condition after that. There was no point.

"He couldn't have survived a year, certainly not seventeen," she continued. Though that was indeed the length of his sentence. Ada felt an eerie prickle down her spine.

"Someone could be acting on his behalf," Grand-mère said.

"Maybe. We need to know more." Ada discreetly peered out the wooden shutters. Full night had fallen. How long would the other brigand wait for his comrade? If he was the fellow playing cards, he'd seen Ada enter the building. "We need to go."

"Go? Where?" Grand-mère asked.

Ada pressed a hand to her white cap. "Away." Away from the flat where they'd lived the longest as deserters. Away from the stability Grand-mère so desperately needed—that Ada needed as well. They hadn't the livre to stay at a decent inn, and Grand-mère couldn't be out all night. Ada had taken care not to make friends in recent years, but she did have old ones.

Emone and Didina were in Lutecia. Emone, with certainty, would have room for them at her establishment, but the idea of showing up on her stoop like beggars was outright appalling. Ada had her pride. And she'd vanished for sixteen years. That would make for an awkward reunion.

If Ada had money, they could ride for Petry's hermitage in the wilderness; he was the next link on their chain to help rogue Chefs out of Verdania, and she communicated with him by letter on a regular basis.

But they had neither money nor horses, and the way was too far on foot for Grand-mère. Even Emone's shiny Golden Horse Inn, on the far side of the city, would be a terrible walk on a night as cold as this.

Which led her to a more accessible yet highly unwelcome option.

"We'll go to my mother's house," Ada said, feeling near ill with the words. "Only for tonight."

Grand-mère nodded in an airily innocent way. "I wonder how she and her husband are doing?"

"I'm sure she's the same as ever." Meaning selfish and pompous. Her husband would be the same as he'd been the past twenty years—dead, which Grand-mère knew in her better hours. "Change into something warmer." She motioned her grandmother toward her trunk.

Ada took a deep breath and considered what they might need to survive these next hours and days.

Food was foremost. Her time in the army had taught her to never trust food to be available when needed. In a leather knapsack that was probably as old as Hester, she packed up some of the bread and vegetables she'd brought, then added hulled oats, herbs, salt, and a cooking pot. A canteen for water and a second one on a strap, for Grand-mère.

"Shouldn't you change as well?" her grandmother asked as she tugged on a second layer of dress.

"No, but I'll bring more." She shoved clothes into her bag. "My cook's smock will enable us to walk through the palace quartier, though we dare not linger anywhere."

"The palace quartier!" Grand-mère paused. "Is that where she lives now? My oh my."

Grand-mère knew that already. "Not a half mile from the palace itself," Ada added. "Not that far from us either." They essentially lived in the gutter beneath the more grandiose districts of Lutecia.

Ada hadn't seen her mother in more than seventeen years, but she had monitored her whereabouts the way a wise person tracks a neighborhood stray dog with a propensity for mauling people. Fortunately,

Lutecia being a city of some seven hundred thousand people, this had been fairly safe to do from afar. Ada, working as a mere cook, would never be anywhere near where Maman might be.

One night. They needed refuge for one night, that was all. She would figure out a better course tomorrow.

Ada swung the knapsack onto her shoulders, cringing. Her army pack had weighed as much, back in the day, but she was twice as old.

"This is what we're going to do," she said. "We're going downstairs. You'll stay within the stairwell. I'll confront the man out there to see if he's a threat."

Grand-mère arched a silvery brow. "A direct confrontation? That sounds stupid."

"What, do you want me to kill him outright, without ascertaining if he's even involved?"

"It'd be tidier." She frowned at her bloodied clothes, folded and set on a wooden bench. "I need to wash these later."

Ada ignored the tangent. "If he is associated with our dead man, I'll question him. That's why I'm confronting him at all."

"What if he used rupic powder too? And it's still working?"

"Then you let me handle it." May the Five help her! "You wait for me, understand?"

"Fine, fine," Grand-mère grumbled.

An icy wind penetrated the stairwell and Ada's thoughts. If this man was using rupic too—what would that mean? What did any of this mean?

At the base of the stairs, Ada slipped off the bag and set it beside her grandmother, who lowered herself to sit on the bottom step. "I should be right back."

Grand-mère grunted. "Don't meet Gyst before I do."

"I'm not planning on it." But then, the God of Unknowns enjoyed creating and perpetuating mysteries—he unraveled plans like a cat with a string. Gyst had already surprised Ada on several occasions with physical encounters that, according to pentad doctrine, shouldn't even have been possible.

"If the man is trouble, a jab to the kidneys will do the trick." Grand-mère motioned with a hand. "Easy as bread."

Ada had to smile at the violent demonstration. "I remember that move too. Thank you." Grand-mère herself had taught it to Ada when she was about eight, before her own official training began a few years later.

Ada palmed her knife and, taking a deep breath, pushed open the door to the street.

The narrow lane lay in deep shadow, the only light coming from windows above. An off-key singing voice echoed between the buildings. Ada's eyes caught a tall, gray movement toward her. She didn't need to seek out the man after all.

"Hail, stranger! Do you—"

He clarified matters by blatantly unsheathing his knife, a stubby thing that reminded her of blades designed for breaking aged cheese into chunks.

"I been waiting for you," he growled. "You're coming with me." He stopped feet away, striking an arrogant stance as if he could intimidate her by size and demeanor.

Ada's tongue tingled, perceiving a rupic-like flavor of stone, but then it stiffened, followed by the rest of her body. Her heartbeat slowed, as if threatening to stop completely.

The effect lasted mere seconds, but she spent several more frozen in place in sheer horror. She was fortunate that the expression on her face seemed to have stopped the man in his tracks as well.

"What is it?" he asked.

"You ate stony owl gut?" she blurted out.

He blinked, wavering. "What? No! I had rupic!" He declared this with pride. For his ilk, trying such an ingredient would be a tavern bragging point for many a month.

"No. You didn't." She almost felt sorry for him. "Your comrade inside had a pouch with rupic in it, but the amount was so minuscule it did him no service. He's dead."

His jaw gaped. "No! He can't be!" He didn't act surprised that she spoke as would a Chef. He knew what she was.

Ada caught a whiff of his breath. "By the Five! You both pickled yourselves before setting out to do your dirty work." She paused, thinking. "Did your friend give you that epicurea? Was he trying to kill you?"

"No." He shook his head with such ferocity that he staggered to one side. "He's my comrade in arms. He'd do no such thing!"

"Then you're simply two idiots. Your drunken ways have killed you both." Ada shrugged. "But before you die, I'd like to know who hired you to kidnap me."

"I'm not dying today," he snarled. "You are!"

He lunged toward her with that knife of his, which would have been wonderful for up-close, repeated stabbing but lacked reach. Not that she could complain that much. She sidestepped and swept out her right leg, toppling him like a skittles pin. He smacked the cobbles with a surprised grunt.

"Who hired you?" she repeated. "You don't have much longer."

He wheezed as he rolled himself into a crouch. "I'm fine."

"Maybe it's a good thing you're as drunk as you are. You've numbed yourself. Do you even know what stony owl and rupic are, besides being rare and expensive?" She knew from experience that most people were aware of the more lurid ingredients but had little actual understanding of what they actually did. When he only managed to sputter, she continued, voice low to obscure her words from their gathering audience. "The stomach of stony owls will turn a person into stone. I don't think you're inebriated enough to eat such a thing raw. Did you, by chance, eat a meat pie a short while ago? The ingredient would've been mixed in with other offal."

The man became very quiet.

Epicurea was often referred to as an "ingredient," because that's what it needed to be—an ingredient prepared with other foods, in careful amounts, in order to be digestible and effective. It was like eating a handful of freshly ground pepper versus knowing how to season food with it, just so. Different digestive processes meant different spans of empowerment from person to person, much as satiation varied between people. As a Chef, however, Ada understood certain baselines.

She continued. "I've never known someone to willingly eat stony owl. These days, it's most known as an elaborate means of murder." Courtesy of Mallory Valmont. "Within hours of ingesting the epicurea, the victim begins turning to stone. That's where you are now. You're staggering, and not simply due to drunkenness. Your muscles are locking up. Soon, you won't be able to move at all."

He quivered. "But I thought—we thought—the rupic—"

"That's what you thought you ate, but that's what you're *becoming*," Ada said with patience. "When a person fully turns to stone—when they are dead—they are called 'rupic.' That statue, broken into pieces and ground down, is rupic powder. When *that* is ingested, the eater will gain temporary stonelike might without being killed outright."

Which was what her old comrade had done. Mallory had murdered his rivals, cannibalized them, and used the resultant magic to become a grand battlefield hero.

"Again I ask: Who hired you? Why did you come after me?"

The telltale wooden clatter of a shutter reminded her that this conflict was occurring in the street, with many witnesses about. These neighbors knew her by name and home. A fake name, and a place she could no longer call home, but still bothersome.

Also bothersome: Grand-mère had been left alone for far too long. Ada could only hope that she had stayed put.

Her assailant stood straighter, scowling again. "No. I still feel fine! I am fine! And if my crony is dead—well, the money we're due will be all mine then, eh?"

"Oh, you dunderheaded—" she began, but then dodged as he dived at her with urgent ferocity. He was trying to prove to himself that he was hale, she realized. His slashes were frenzied, chaotic. His knife tip caught her sleeve, tugging her arm to one side, but didn't come near to drawing blood. Dodging her kick, he tried to stab her left shoulder. She ducked, knocking him down with a hip thrust. He refused to stay down. He crouched, snarling, aiming for her legs.

He might not even remember who hired him at this point, so lost was he in his haze. Nor could she linger to interrogate him. Gendarmes didn't rush to this quartier, but they would come eventually, and onlookers might've heard words that would identify her as a Chef.

This needed to end.

Her left elbow clobbered him in the face with a mighty crunch of bone and cartilage as her right hand sliced upward, bringing her knife into his gut. He smacked the ground with a deflating groan, both hands to his bloodied torso. Gasps and whoops rang out around them. A few onlookers applauded.

"Gyst take you quickly," she murmured, motioning the God's X.

In the dark, she couldn't see the light of life leave the man's eyes, but she perceived the quick fade of epicurea as his body stopped processing him into stone.

She knelt beside him. After wiping her blade clean on his coat, she made a quick check of his person. She found a thin cord he'd have used to secure her. There was nothing else to explain who he was or who had sent him.

"You're learning the resolutions of all your mysteries right now," she muttered to him, "and compounded mine all the more."

She stood, sheathing her knife. "You a-right then?" called a fellow who lived in the hotel across the way. Murmured conversations surrounded Ada. Some twenty people had gathered. Coins jingled as livre exchanged hands. She didn't want to know how many people had bet against her survival.

"It's been a lousy day." Ada walked away.

Her bag still sat in the shadows. Grand-mère was gone. Ada hissed and spun around. A soft noise up the stairs drew her attention. She found Grand-mère a flight up, sitting in the blackness, humming to herself.

"Where did you go?" she asked Ada crossly.

"I was wondering where *you* went!" Ada said. Her heart was pounding harder from her grandmother's absence than from her fight. "Come along. We're going on a walk."

"At this time of night?"

Ada took her by the hand and guided her back downstairs. She hefted her bag. "Yes. It won't be that long."

"I hope not. It's about my bedtime." Grand-mère didn't even notice the crowd around the body. Their neighbors would be as useful as carrion crows, stripping anything of value before leaving the brigand to the police or the river.

"I know it is, Grand-mère," Ada said softly, her grip on her hand tender yet strong.

They kept to narrow lanes, passing merry drunks and mothers herding children and hoarse-voiced vendors trying to unload their last wares. Ada glanced back every so often. No one seemed to be following them. Grand-mère asked several times if they were done and if they could go home, but she soon became silent with cold and effort. She was dragging her feet by the time they reached the palace quartier with its stately white walls and tall, manicured trees. Ada wanted to feel relief as they approached Maman's estate, but instead, she was overwhelmed by a new sense of dread. Her mother would welcome them, but there would be conditions.

"One night, that's all," Ada whispered to herself as Grand-mère huddled closer to her, shivering. She tugged on the gatepost bell to send it clanging and waited for someone to admit them within the enclosure of iron and stone.

CHAPTER THREE

SOLENN

Select few can perceive as do Chefs, but one can still cultivate the senses as a discriminating gourmet. Wine is a good place to hone such skills. Learn to recognize the primary aromatics of the foundational grapes and the tertiary aromatics that develop through aging and means of storage. Can you discern oak? Butter? Minerality? How does the smell compare to the taste?

—Excerpt from *Book for Cooks to Excel as Do Chefs*

"What must you always remember?" Madame Brumal asked, hands on her hips as she stood back to scrutinize her young charge.

Solenn gritted her teeth. "To speak and act like a lady."

"Pin up that strand—yes, like that. I think that will do it," Madame Brumal said to the maid. Solenn's long black hair had been braided and coiled upward, ringlets teased free, the lot of it ornamented with diamonds and pearls in gold settings. Solenn thought it looked like a jewelry armoire had vomited atop her head. "That answer is incomplete, Princess."

"To speak and act like a *Verdanian* lady," she corrected. She had been primped for the past two hours. Sitting this long was unbearable unless she was on a horse.

"Mind your tone." Madame Brumal paced a crescent around Solenn. "You may go," she said to the maid with a flick of her fingers. Gaze low, the young woman curtsied.

"Thank you," mouthed Solenn. A small smile curved a corner of the woman's mouth as she scurried away.

"Not simply a Verdanian lady, not simply a noble, but soon a *princess* of Verdania. You must speak and act appropriately."

Meaning don't act like a princess from Braiz.

Of course a noblewoman of Verdania would advise such, firm in the belief of her own superiority. Solenn resisted the urge to sigh. She didn't need more criticism about her attitude or tone. "I can't see the clock from here, but surely it must be time." The windows had turned black as she idled. "Captain Corre must be wondering at the delay."

"The captain knows you must be perfect tonight when you are formally presented to your fiancé as his future bride."

"Yes, madame." Solenn yearned for the familiar maids she'd left behind in Braiz. Queen Roswita had insisted that Solenn accept a fully Verdanian staff upon her arrival. Madame Brumal *did* know the current fashions and mannerisms, Solenn had to grudgingly admit, but she also acted as if Solenn were completely ignorant. By Selland's rake! Erwan, her parents, and others had trained her for this possibility over the past five years. She wasn't *stupid*.

Solenn strode toward the door. Within just a few steps, her feet hurt. Her feet were too big for court standards, requiring shoes that were too small in size. They did appear nice with blue-dyed leather, shiny golden buckles, and the bright-red soles only nobles could wear, but Solenn was apparently in a quaint minority in her belief that prettiness mustn't equate with suffering.

"Look at me, Princess." Madame Brumal swooped close. "Oh, why must your skin be so dark? You look like you work in the sun!"

"Madame Brumal, my skin is fine." The even response emerged, reflexive from training and previous experience, but she inwardly seethed as Madame Brumal's words gouged like splinters. How *dare* this woman say such a thing to her, to anyone? She bit her lower lip to contain a retort. Solenn needed Madame Brumal's aid. She needed to play the Verdanian princess.

"Just a touch more powder would help." Madame Brumal's smile could only be described as patient and helpful.

"No, madame." If she bit her lip any harder, she'd draw blood.

"Very well, Princess." Madame Brumal sighed.

From a practical standpoint, more powder on Solenn's face meant her robe volante would need to be brushed off again, by which time her hair would need to be tweaked, and the whole vicious circle would repeat to infinity. It seemed that Madame Brumal wouldn't be satisfied until Solenn's face was as white as a baker's peel, which was infuriating and vile. The fact was, Solenn's skin *was* naturally darker and she *was* often in the sun back in Braiz. If Verdania had a problem with that, then she shouldn't be here at all! She could jump onto a horse and ride straight home.

Home. Solenn swallowed dryly. Lutecia, capital city of Verdania, was to be her home from now on.

Besides, Mamm had told her to expect judgment such as this here in Lutecia—they'd both experienced it in the Braizian court. Her mother's grandmother had come from Hesperia and introduced golden-hued skin to the family. Braizian court, like that of Lutecia, more resembled fresh cream. Solenn's deep-bronze tone stood out even against the complexions of her mother and cousins. In recent years she'd overheard snide comments that she looked like a laborer, that she'd be difficult to marry off. The insults had made her sob a few times, but her cousins and friends—quite a few people, really—had been enraged on her behalf and done all they could to bolster her confidence. The malicious whispers no longer made her cry. They made her *angry*.

Now here Solenn was, in the greatest marriage match of her generation, but under these circumstances, she took no pleasure in proving her critics wrong.

"I will not be detained further," Solenn said, assuming a regal tone as she continued toward the door. She would not leave this room coated like rising bread in a banneton. "I'm pleased with my appearance." In all truth, she was.

"I'm sorry, Princess Solenn." Madame Brumal seemed to realize that she had overstepped. "I'm nervous. I feel responsible for your presentation tonight."

"I appreciate your efforts, madame," Solenn said, to which Madame Brumal curtsied.

She then hurried past Solenn to open the door to reveal Erwan standing in wait, his hands tucked at his back in parade rest. At just shy of fifty, he had some silver to his hair and creases in his face.

"Princess Solenn." He wore a formal skirt, as would everyone tonight. The silk pleats swayed as he curtsied, the distinct Braizian blue looking as soft as rose petals. As he arose, she had to smile at the proud sparkle in his blue eyes. "You look beautiful."

"You told me the same earlier, when I wore my usual day suit," she griped in a low voice.

"It was true then as well. Fine work, Madame Brumal."

"Thank you, Captain Corre. Such work is easy with a young lady as fine and cultured as your Princess of Braiz." Solenn rolled her eyes as Madame Brumal drew behind them. Farther back followed five Braizian musketeers in formal regalia, their rapiers and other weapons absent as a public show of faith in their host.

Erwan raised a skeptical eyebrow that only Solenn could see. "Shall we go, oh fine and cultured one?"

"Shush, you," she whispered as she tried not to smile too widely and muss her cosmetics.

"Your preparations did take a long time," Erwan whispered. "I was starting to wonder if you had thumped her with a vase and tied together sheets to climb down from the balcony and make your escape."

"You knew I had done no such thing. You have guards stationed below my room. Nor would I abuse fine bedsheets. I'd have acquired good, stout rope from the stable if I had such intentions."

"Should we search your room?"

"You'd find nothing of the sort *now*, but if things go poorly tonight . . . well, you taught me to know where I've entered and five new ways to exit."

"I'm glad my lessons took heart," he said with soft pride.

Erwan knew Solenn better than anyone, even her parents, though they'd made an effort to be present and supportive of her despite their obligations to court and country. As far back as she could remember, Erwan had been her personal captain and guardian, her mentor, her friend.

Soon, though, she would be wed, and he'd return to Braiz. She'd be alone here in Lutecia.

No, not alone. Her fiancé wasn't a terrible sort, just . . . immature, fourteen compared to her sixteen. And surely she would make friends soon. She could start forming such connections at the fete for young courtiers tomorrow.

She must endure, for the sake of her people. Braiz needed this union.

"Princess!" Madame Brumal huffed slightly as she caught up with them. Solenn felt pinned between her and Erwan. "Remember the order of events. Circle the room and socialize. There is no strata divide tonight." At many events, provincial nobles were present but segregated. "When you are summoned, sit with Prince Rupert to share the wine. Be composed. Be polite." The woman's glare was severe, as if Solenn were predisposed to spilling her wine and slurping it from the floor.

"I understand, Madame Brumal. Thank you." The older woman nodded and retreated.

Verdanian musketeers flanked the path ahead, each genuflecting as she passed. "You can make it through this, Solenn," whispered Erwan as they entered the grand ballroom. With that, he drifted to the periphery of the room, where he and his company would monitor the proceedings.

She was alone for mere seconds before the court descended on her. Glittering, gibbering, everyone aswirl in enthusiasm and silken skirts. They reeked of scents that would be pleasant in reduced company but became a sensory assault when multiplied by a hundred—perfumes and scented body and hair powders plus the aromatic walking sticks that were in fashion, the odors so strong she could almost see them like clouds. Her nose threatened to dribble, and she delicately sniffled and hoped no one could hear her amid the cacophony. Her tongue even felt tingly. She hoped that wasn't some portent of illness. All she could do was smile and nod as if she could hear the introductions and platitudes, the faces around her a blur.

After some length of time, the crowd lessened. Drinks came out. People separated into merry clusters. Solenn began to breathe a bit easier. Faces became more distinct. In advance of her arrival, Erwan had utilized his knack for drawing to depict prominent people of court whom she needed to remember. Thanks to his tutelage, she continually surprised courtiers by greeting them by name.

Such details were important. In recent years, her parents' household had become the place of formal negotiations on behalf of her ruling grandparents. Solenn had regarded the constant stream of merchant lords and foreign dignitaries as exciting guests at first, then realized the act of negotiation was even more enticing. You had to know what someone wanted, and what they were willing to barter in order to get it—that is, if they were willing to barter at all.

"How are you doing, darling?" Queen Roswita swept through the crowd, the breadth of her panniers extending her hip width to that of four people. She resembled a mobile tapestry of colorful spring flowers against a backdrop of greenery. The revealed V shape of her stomacher was a riot of fine embroidery, the crisscrossed stays designed like verdant vines to lead the eye up to the exaggerated bounty of her bosom.

"I am well, Mère." Solenn had been told to refer to the queen as such, though it felt like a lie to call a stranger "Mother." She added, "Somewhat dizzied and dazzled, I must admit, but grateful for the kind welcome."

"Yes, you're not in poor Braiz anymore." Queen Roswita's grin was as tight as her bodice. Solenn smiled to hide her prickle of annoyance. Erwan had warned her of how Braiz was regarded abroad, but she had hoped better of Roswita, who decades ago had come here as a foreign bride from Grand Diot in the Confederated Duchies.

"I certainly am not in Braiz," Solenn said in an even tone.

"You'll soon sit down with Rupert. Incredible, to think of my little boy, almost married." She took a delicate sip of her drink. "But then, I came to Lutecia at age twelve for my own wedding, though I saw my husband little until he reached sixteen."

According to everything Solenn had heard, the royal couple still saw little of each other. She had caught only a few glimpses of King Caristo in the room tonight, his mistress and favorites in accompaniment.

"I'm glad I have a few years to get to know Rupert better before he comes of age, Mère," said Solenn.

Queen Roswita patted Solenn on the forearm and leaned closer to whisper, "You have plenty of other things to concern yourself with in the meantime. When that time does near, we'll talk more about the *expectations* upon you. You'll be ready. I'll make sure of it."

Roswita obviously intended to comfort her, but Solenn didn't need to be told of the technical intricacies of breeding. She knew enough to comprehend that it held no interest for her. Some of her mother's ladies-in-waiting had chortled when she'd stated this opinion and assured her that her attitude would change with time, but it hadn't.

"Thank you for your thoughtfulness," Solenn managed. Queen Roswita patted her again, as one does a well-behaved dog, and rustled onward.

A couple promptly stepped into the void left by the queen's departure. Their powdered faces looked somewhat . . . sparkly? The man's grayed mustache was thick enough to brush down muddy horses. In accordance with current fashion, he wore a rounded white wig atop the black-gray streaks of his natural hair, which was bound in a queue at his neck. The woman with him was significantly younger, her robe volante of a cut not unlike Solenn's, though in stripes of soft blue and green.

Solenn blinked as she recognized the man by Erwan's artwork. This was the Marquis de Dubray, recently returned from a stint as ambassador to Albion. He was a close compatriot of King Caristo's. Dubray's sole son and heir, Jicard, was intimate friends with Solenn's fiancé.

"Princess Solenn, good to make your direct acquaintance." As Marquis Dubray raised her hand to his lips, the cloying fragrance of roses prickled her nostrils.

She swore that she could almost *taste* it.

Caught off guard, she hesitated a moment more than appropriate before replying, "Likewise, Monsieur le Marquis." He arched an eyebrow as if impressed that she knew his identity. Solenn didn't know who the woman was, though. She certainly looked too young to have borne his teenage son. "Your necklace is lovely, mademoiselle," she added. "And what is your name?"

The woman touched the parallel rows of gold-inset pearls. "Why, thank you." She giggled in a way that implied that more wine than blood was currently coursing through her veins. "I'm the Comtesse de la Muzy. Ever so pleased to meet you, Princess."

Solenn fought the urge to rub her nose. She liked the scent of roses—her mother cultivated them on their estate in Malo—but these two people *reeked*. Stranger yet, no one else seemed to notice, unless others were hiding their repulsion.

"If I recall correctly, you recently returned from Albion, monsieur?" she asked. He nodded. "How long were you away?"

"Three years. A long time to be far from my homeland, but such actions are necessary for one's duty, hmm?"

Albion and Verdania had warred intermittently for five hundred years, with Albion usually the aggressor, as they claimed that a marital alliance made Verdania their dominion. It was common knowledge that they persisted in that argument now, despite a civil war a century past that had brought a new family to the throne, only because they craved the epicurean wealth of their continental rival.

Braiz, occupying the coast between the two powers, had often been caught in the middle of the conflict.

"When you were in Albion, did it take you much time to adjust to the new surroundings?" She hoped she wasn't revealing too much of her own homesickness in the question.

"Hmph! I didn't adjust, Princess. I would not lower myself to acclimating to such a lesser society. I spoke their savage language as necessary outside of my residence. I ate and drank food of Verdanian origin as much as I could. You, Princess, you are doing what is right for a person. You seek to elevate yourself by coming here, by adapting to our ways."

Oh, was that what she was doing? She grimaced and made an effort to reshape her face into a grin. "I'm here to wed Prince Rupert and become a princess of Verdania," she said, trying to tactfully correct him.

Marquis Dubray nodded, his skin still sparkling like the polished coat of a show horse. "Indeed." As if her statement had agreed with his. "By the way, expect an invitation soon after your nuptials for a river excursion upon my boat. My vessel is, I daresay, finer than anything you have in Braiz now," he said with smug pride.

He had the *audacity* to pick at Braiz's most painful scab while glorifying some ridiculous river cruiser that he probably couldn't even pilot himself?

"I assure you, Braiz still has plenty of fine boats to its credit, worthy of river *and* sea, even if many of our military vessels were lost in the tragedy of the Port of Nont." She knew that if Erwan were here, he'd motion her to let the subject change, but she was in no such mood. She had *endured* enough. "I'm sorry to find out that you were so poorly informed about the state of our affairs while you were in Albion. If you need a thorough accounting of the event, then please, regard me as your resource. I'm knowledgeable of our naval losses, but my most intimate awareness is of the significant civilian devastation the fire caused within the city. I acted as prime court liaison among our citizens, a task that has occupied much of my time since last summer."

He stared at her, blinking. "You, Princess?"

"Me," she answered with cool pride. Her education had been harsh, but she had coordinated with pentads and major merchants to ensure civilians weren't left homeless and jobless after the disaster, and then mediated between the city and her grandparents as razing and rebuilding efforts began.

"Ah," he said, his smile strained. "I see."

He undoubtedly thought she had some honorary role, or had mucked up everything. Solenn was going to say something terribly impolitic if this dragged on any longer. She looked past him, desperate for an avenue of escape.

Some ten feet away, a reedy boy caught her eye. To her surprise, he had straight silver hair drawn into a queue, and the color looked natural—strange, for someone who must have been around her own age. His companion, an older man, had to be a father or uncle, judging by their resemblance, his hair equally as striking. Even more, something sparkled about the both of them. Not like the odd sheen that smeared the Marquis de Dubray and his companion, but an aura that couldn't help but induce her curiosity.

"I'm so glad to have met you, monsieur, madamemoiselle," Solenn said with a smile as she sidestepped. "I'm sure we'll converse again later. May Hester warm you." She added the traditional Verdanian close in an effort to be more polite as she whirled to face the silver-haired man and boy. "Greetings to you both."

The two strangers looked stunned to make her acquaintance, as did the people around them. "Princess Solenn," said the elder of the two. As appropriate while in formal skirts, both fellows curtsied.

Her mind raced to find an excuse for her impropriety. She noted courtiers nearby were engaged in flurried whispers. "I beg your pardon. I've met many of court tonight but had yet to be introduced to you both."

"We're honored, Princess Solenn." The younger man spoke up. "I am Aveyron Silvacane, and I introduce you to my father, Comte Brillat Silvacane."

Theirs weren't names and faces she'd been called to memorize. They had to be provincial nobles, supposedly beneath her interests. But then, the Marquis de Dubray was among the most powerful men of the realm, and Solenn didn't think him worthy of being passed the salt at dinner.

"From where do you hail?" Their accent sounded southern but with an extra clip to certain syllables she found peculiar. Their very aura was far stranger still. It was like a glint to the air, a smell she couldn't identify.

"We come from Camarga, Princess," said Comte Silvacane.

She couldn't help but light up. "Camarga! Oh, home of the most beautiful of horses!"

Their pale complexions couldn't hide their deep blushes. "You are an equestrienne?" asked Aveyron.

"Yes! Yes." Solenn remembered herself. A Verdanian princess should be composed at all times. "I am happiest when I'm on a horse. In Braiz, I often packed a lunch and spent the day exploring the shore and woods. But coming to Verdania, I had to leave my horses behind, as they weren't included in my dowry." Because Braizian horses weren't considered good enough for her as a princess here. She had seethed over that slight all too often. "I was told that, upon my marriage, I could begin assembling my own stable of Verdanian stock."

To her relief, Aveyron's smile wasn't judgmental, but kind. "You're enthused about this prospect, mademoiselle?"

"I am." More excited about that than the wedding, for sure.

"Princess, what do you find appealing about Camarga horses?" asked the elder. A small groan escaped from Aveyron.

She raised an eyebrow as she looked between the two. Why was this question causing such embarrassment? "Most people favor Camargas because of their white coats with gray markings," she said, speaking thoughtfully, "and while they're attractive, I most appreciate their intelligence and independence. That's based on what I hear in stories, which could well be exaggerations."

Comte Silvacane smiled in delight. "What have you heard, Princess? I would love to know the reputation of our native horses in your far northern land."

Oh, how relieved she was to talk about horses. "I hear often that they won't suffer an unkind hand, Comte. If their owner is abusive, they will escape from a locked stable and, in the process, free every other horse too. I know for a fact that they're rarely bought and sold." She knew this because she had pleaded for a Camarga of her own.

"To most people, such independence would be an aggravation, Princess Solenn," said Aveyron. He studied her with blatant curiosity.

She returned the look, wishing she could find tactful words to inquire about the odd spark she felt as she stood near them. It almost reminded her of being in an intense lightning storm, though that metaphor wasn't quite right either.

"I sometimes aggravate people in a similar way, monsieur," she said, thinking of Madame Brumal. He laughed.

"Mademoiselle la Princesse." A man spoke behind her. She turned to face a palace majordomo. "Monsieur le Dauphin awaits your company."

Her breath caught. So that time had come. She turned again to the two Silvacanes. "I am glad I made your acquaintances, Comte Silvacane and son. I hope we may have the chance to speak of horses again."

"It would be our honor, Princess," said Brillat, and both curtsied, a final look of amusement shared between them.

Almost numb with escalating anxiety, she followed the major-domo across the mighty ballroom. Above, crystals glittered and lamps glowed as if the divinely blessed monarchy had snatched the very stars from the heavens to shine down on the realm's elite. People quieted as Solenn passed. She walked with a confident stride despite the pain in her pinched feet. Far off to her right, she could make out her muske-teers forming a wall against the austere white panels. She wished she could make eye contact with Erwan, but the distance was too far and humanity too thick.

A table for two had been set at the far side of the ballroom. Prince Rupert stood behind a chair in wait for her.

He came only to the level of her chest. He didn't wear a wig; his long wheat-colored hair was drawn back into a black mesh snood. He wore his country's color in a grand coat embroidered in gold, the bold buttons like rows of miniature suns. From beneath the knee-length flared skirt, scrawny legs in white tights led down to black shoes topped with gold buckles. His shoes looked far too big for his figure, reminding her of a duck's feet. Apparently men were to wear overlarge shoes and women were to have almost no feet of all. What a load of blather.

"Princess Solenn." Rupert's curtsy dipped so low his hand almost touched the floor. She reciprocated, then took a seat. Majordomos hur-ried over to push in their chairs for them.

In their few other meetings in the past week, Solenn and Rupert had only engaged in inane, very public chats regarding her journey and the weather and how she liked the palace. Now, they were to have their first private conversation, before an audience of hundreds.

"Are you having fun?" Rupert asked.

Yet more small talk with him. Sigh. "I have been breathlessly busy, monseigneur." It felt so wonderful to be off her feet.

Rupert's giggle still sounded high pitched, like that of a young child. "Such a tactful response. This isn't fun at all, is it? Ever so tedious, but necessary." He made a face of disgust. He wore cosmetics in the current fashion, his white cheeks highlighted by red paste. "You don't have to 'monseigneur' me when we're by ourselves. That gets tedious too."

"What would you rather be doing?" she asked. With her hand hidden beneath the tablecloth, she rubbed her fingers together as if to press grains of salt between her fingers, quietly beseeching Selland for aid. *Please, please let him mention horse riding.* She had pleaded to know more about Rupert's interests during the marital negotiations, only to be told that such things were trivialities. Not to her, not when she was supposed to spend the rest of her life with this boy—this man—and to carry his children, perhaps dying in the effort.

She supposed that thought should have made her blush with modesty. Instead, she felt perturbed.

Rupert brightened. "Tennis! I love tennis, and sword fighting. Sometimes we do archery too."

"We?"

"My friend Jicard. He's been by me in our other meetings this week." She nodded to indicate that she remembered him. "He's out there somewhere." He waved at the crowd. "Normally, he sits with me at meals. Otherwise—Hester burn us all!—it'd be hopelessly dull."

"I just made the acquaintance of his father."

Rupert's painted lips grimaced "He's a stuffed bag, isn't he? He didn't become more tolerable in his time away, for sure. At least he's generous to Jicard, who's generous to me in turn."

"Will Jicard be at the fete you're hosting on the morrow?"

He vigorously nodded. "*That* should be fun. We won't have to socialize with coots. There'll be trick riders too."

She counseled herself to not look too excited. "That does sound wonderful."

"Monsieur le Dauphin. Mademoiselle la Princesse." A mustached man set glasses of red wine before each of them. That was a surprise. She'd been told the wine would be poured at the table. "For you to toast to your glorious forthcoming nuptials." He backed away, curtsying.

She gripped the goblet. Forthcoming nuptials. She'd be a wife in a week. Erwan would be gone, as would the other musketeers, many of whom she'd known much of her life. She knew it was her place to initiate the toast, and yet she hesitated to celebrate a moment that wasn't glorious but was necessary, like using a chamber pot before bedtime.

"Strange, isn't it? All this talk for years and the time is finally here?" Rupert's small fingers claimed his glass.

That odd prickle started in her nose again, but the cloying taste of rose didn't meet her taste buds.

No, she tasted death.

She . . . she *felt* death.

The clench of her throat, her own blood frothing and choking her. Fire in her eyes, stomach, lungs, everywhere. Pain, as if her insides had been dropped into boiling oil, a sack contained by her skin.

But she wasn't really dead. She braced herself on the table, gasping for air. The prince stared at her. "What is it?" he asked, releasing his hold on the glass.

Solenn could only imagine the horror he had seen painted upon her features. Death still lingered in her mouth like checked vomit. "A moment of fear, that's all," she managed to get out. "My entire life has changed, and will change more."

Solenn understood three important, complicated, and terrifying things at once.

She had just perceived flavor like a Chef, like one with a peculiar empathetic ability, endowed by Gyst.

Chef skills ran in families. The royalty of Braiz had had none in five hundred years of tracked lineage.

That meant her family had somehow concealed their Chef skills—which seemed highly unlikely—or one of her parents was not truly her blood parent.

And right here, right now, someone was attempting to murder Rupert by poison. She could not warn him verbally, or he—and soon afterward, all of court—would know the truth of her family, be that the presence of hidden Chefs or Solenn's illegitimacy. The imminent marriage would fracture, and with it, the alliance that Braiz needed to stand up against Albion.

She couldn't let that happen. She had to save Rupert, and Braiz.

But *how*?

Her thoughts bounced about like hail upon cobbles. What could she do? Rupert continued to stare at her, expression placid, but his patience would not last much longer. In contrast, court had no concept of patience at all. People would already be wondering about her hesitance and what it meant, the theories growing more insidious with each passing moment.

She gripped the glass again. It felt light, delicate. A breeze could blow it from the table to the ground.

A plan took form in her mind. "Shall we toast?" Solenn sounded calm to her own ears.

"Yes, let's." He sounded relieved that they were back on script. He raised his glass again, her awareness of death threatening to overwhelm her.

Her effort to retain focus amid her horror made it easier to pull back her arm and bring it forward again with absolute violence. Their glasses met with an intense crunch, both shattering. Red wine splashed the table.

Gasps and shrieks filled the room. Solenn remained frozen in place, the remnants of her glass still uplifted. Her fingers were sticky but unhurt, and she experienced an immediate sense of relief. Her awareness of his imminent death was gone.

"I am so sorry! I have no idea how I—are you well, monseigneur?" Mamm had told her time and again that even the most egregious of situations must be handled with grace. Mamm, who may not have given birth to her or may secretly be a Chef? Solenn's deepening confusion almost made her feel dizzy.

"I'm fine." Rupert laughed shakily. Majordomos descended upon them like flies. Maids dabbed Solenn's gown from either side. Rupert stood with his arms up, subject to the same treatment. Wine had speckled them both as if they'd stood too near a butcher. The table was cleared off in an instant.

"My apologies, monseigneur, mademoiselle." The majordomo who had served them the glasses had gone as pale as the walls. "Those glasses—I don't know—"

Solenn supposed she should have been relieved that few would credit her with the strength or motivation to destroy glasses in such a way. "We're unharmed, monsieur, though our clothes suffer." She held out her stained gloves with an apologetic smile, even as she began to worry that this man might endure punishment for her ploy to save the dauphin.

He may well not be an innocent, though. Someone had poisoned Rupert's glass and not hers. This man had ready access.

"We can look at this as Lait and Gyst showering us with a blessing," added Rupert. Lait oversaw agriculture, while Gyst assisted in fermentation. Solenn appreciated that Rupert was trying to comfort the servant. Other nobles, even in Braiz, would have done no such thing.

The majordomo's smile was unsteady. "Begging your pardon, monseigneur, but I'm most concerned with Hester's warm regard upon you as you're establishing your home together."

Rupert waved a hand. "That ceremony will be tomorrow." He faced Solenn. "We have a valid excuse to make our leave for a change in wardrobe. I cannot say I mind."

"I'm relieved by that, mon—Rupert," she said. "I may see you later then."

"Maybe so, maybe not," he said airily. "Valet, find Jicard for me," he directed a nearby man, who scurried into the crowd.

"I understand." She supposed she could have been insulted by the prince's snub, but she had too many other concerns at the moment. "May Selland fill your sail and season your day."

She comprehended her mistake as soon as the words left her lips.

Rupert had started to turn away, but stopped. "Ah yes. You sea people, favoring Selland." He gave her a nod. "May Hester warm you." The Verdanian-appropriate farewell came across as a gentle rebuke. Rupert headed toward the crowd, apparently too impatient to await the valet's retrieval of Jicard.

"Mademoiselle! What happened?" Madame Brumal looked sickly pale through her powder. "What an error. I am dead, dead."

"This is *not* your fault, Madame Brumal." Erwan came up behind her, his voice brusque and soothing all at once. "Princess." He offered his arm, which she was all too glad to take. A question was clear in his eyes, and she gave him a little nod; his answers would come soon. The rest of the Braizian guard fell into line behind her as they began to walk, Madame Brumal still moaning her dismay.

The return to their apartment corridor seemed to take no time at all. Solenn remained lost in thought, her heart beating uncomfortably fast.

f"Madame." Erwan turned to her in exasperation. "We will not execute you because of this mishap. It isn't your doing. Nor will Verdania deliver punishment upon you."

"I should help the princess change for her return to the floor." Madame Brumal sounded on the verge of tears.

"No, madame," Solenn said. "The prince was quitting the event. There's no point in my return." Really, if someone insisted she go back, she might contrive to break her leg or commit some other desperate deed. "For now, please, rest in your room."

"You are too kind to me. A true princess. I am sorry." At that, Madame Brumal sniffled and hurried to her nearby room. Erwan deployed his musketeers with quick orders.

Solenn entered her room. Two musketeers checked the chambers, and they left as Erwan came in. He secured the door, and in an instant he released his checked emotions.

"What happened, Solenn?" He spoke in quick Braizian, his eyebrows pained. "The look on your face—did you break the wineglasses with intent? Why? Did he say—"

She shook her head, curled tendrils of hair lashing her cheeks. "No, no, Rupert did nothing untoward. He was kinder than expected, truly. It's just, I-I *perceived* . . ." The admission came in a breathy whisper. "His drink. It held poison. I couldn't . . . oh, Erwan." She let tears fill her eyes at last. "This feels so *wrong*. How can I be a *Chef*?"

CHAPTER FOUR

SOLENN

Wine is best within months of making, as problems arise over time and may soon turn it to vinegar. Wines with higher amounts of alcohol, such as those made in southern Verdania, are likely to last longer. A wine that has survived three years or more—with or without oversight of a Chef—is a prize that one will pay well for.

—Excerpt from *Book for Cooks to Excel as Do Chefs*

Erwan's eyes widened. "A Chef—oh." He stopped, taking in the full scope of what she had said. "I see." He pulled off his cocked hat and placed it on a hook beside the door. Even in a crisis, he would be tidy. "We dallied in marriage negotiations out of concern that this might come to be."

"We?"

"Myself, Prince Morvan, and Princess Katell."

Her parents knew? Of course. They would have to. Solenn's emotions shifted from upset to angry. "That's why it dragged on for years?"

she whispered in Braizian. "Everyone told me it was because of the detailed negotiations."

"Which wasn't a lie," Erwan said. "King Caristo is more like a child than many children. It's because of his tantrums that the alliance dissolved as it did after the last war." He released a long exhalation. "You were brilliant to spill the prince's drink. This awareness of yours—it just awoke?"

Solenn nodded. He looked to the door, lips pursed, then directed her deeper into the room. "We should sit, unless you'd like to change . . . ?" At her indignant expression, he managed a weak laugh. "Of course not."

She flung herself onto a divan for emphasis, then leaned forward to face him as he claimed a heavy wooden chair. "You suspected I might be a Chef. That means you knew that this runs in my family. My mamm, my tad, which one isn't . . . ?"

She recalled her last sight of them in the courtyard, Mamm's shoulders heaving as she sobbed into Tad's shoulder, his face stony with checked emotion.

"Solenn." Erwan clasped her hands, his fingers calloused but gentle. "Morvan and Katell have been devoted to each other, and only each other, since their teens."

"You're saying neither is related to me by blood? I'm . . . adopted?"

Again, she felt a physical sense of disorientation as she tried to understand. Why had this been kept secret? Adoption was a widely accepted practice in Braizian court. Were her parents criminals? Causes for shame or caution?

"Yes, you were adopted, but know foremost that you have and will always be Morvan and Katell's child. They love you more than Selland loves salt."

"I love them too. I've always felt blessed to be so close to them. My cousins, well—you know how things are." They had been fostered due to a political pact, and not in the best of households. "My grandparents, they don't . . . ?"

"They do not know. In Braiz, the truth is known only to Morvan, Katell, and myself."

She nodded. She didn't need to be told why the secret must be kept from her grandparents, the king and queen of Braiz, though she had faith that the truth wouldn't change their love for her. "Does that mean my other parents are dead? Or they aren't . . . aren't Braizian?" She couldn't keep the horror from her voice, and that made Erwan chuckle.

"I hope you'll take immense comfort in that your father is as Braizian as can be, pure as salt." He gripped her by both hands, his head bowed.

Solenn waited in breathless anticipation for him to continue. Why couldn't he say the name? Was he embarrassed? Did he think *she'd* be embarrassed? Erwan was usually a man of decisive action and quick wit, but now his skills seemed to have abandoned him. His wavy hair, so like hers, draped to almost obscure his face.

His hair, so like hers. His posture . . . she often sat the same way. Surely she was unconsciously mimicking him after all their hours together.

Surely.

Or perhaps the truth had been before her all this while.

Solenn gasped. "Oh. *You.* Erwan. No! You're my . . . ?"

"Yes." His head rose. Tears filled his blue eyes.

Solenn recoiled from him and stood, a hand to her mouth. She paced, one stride, two, the pain in her feet nothing compared to that in her mind, then whirled to consider him as she never had before. Captain Erwan Corre was tall and leanly fit, his height emphasized by the drape of his cassock. His skin held the copper tone of a man who often drilled in the sunlight, though he was far paler than Solenn. Silver threaded his wavy and thick black hair, which fell to his shoulders in a style most men used wigs to emulate. She and Erwan looked little alike except for their hair, eye color, and, perhaps, their rather angular noses, though many people had commented over the years that she had a nose like Prince Morvan's. It was a rather Braizian feature, she supposed.

"You're not disappointed?" Erwan asked, tone light but worry evident.

"By all the sand on the shore! No!" She sank to the divan again to clutch his hands. "You've been my daily support, even more so than my parents! You taught me to ride, to swim, to read, write, everything! You—oh, I feel so blind. You . . . you could have advanced in rank, but you stayed with me. I've heard whispers over the years, mean things—"

"I can imagine," he said wryly. "A man with my experience, staying a captain."

She nodded. She herself had assumed Erwan had stayed near out of devotion to Prince Morvan. The two were closer than most brothers. "You could have easily been a colonel by now, or possessed an estate of your own. You could have had anything you wanted."

"No, I could not have all that I wanted," he said softly, "but I had you, and have been blessed each day in that."

Her remaining restraint untwined like worn thread. Erwan held her against his shoulder as she sobbed. They separated long enough for him to fetch her water to quell her hiccups.

As she cradled the cup in her palms, Erwan leaned toward her, his expression one of concern. Solenn realized she loved him as much as she ever had, but she also felt something more.

"You lied to me. For the entirety of my life."

He flinched at her words, sharp as a razor. "Yes."

Erwan had lied to her. Her parents had lied. Solenn's very identity was a lie. She set down the cup before she was tempted to destroy more dishes this night. "How am I supposed to trust you, trust anyone?"

He uplifted his palms to her. "You have every right to be angry."

His ready agreement made her angrier. "I don't need your blessing! I just need . . . I don't even know what I need. Truth! I want truth from you. I order you to tell me the truth."

Erwan's smile was faint and sorrowful. "I will be forthright with you in all ways from here on, Princess Solenn."

She swiped away a stray tear. She wanted more, wanted him to say something that would make the world feel right again. By all logic, she knew he couldn't do that, but she couldn't help that petulant need.

"You don't have Chefs in your family," she said, her voice thick. His parents lived in a neighboring château. She had seen them all the time as she was growing up.

"I don't. Your Chef skills, along with many of your other traits, come from your mother, Adamantine Garland." He said her name with the reverence he reserved for fine horses and artwork.

"Adamantine Garland." Solenn repeated the strange name with softness, as if it might break if she spoke louder. "That's not Braizian. That's not even Verdanian."

"She is Verdanian, in fact, given an antiquated family name by her grandmother. Their line can be traced back a hundred years to one of many islands in the Southern Sea, where rule has volleyed between Verdania, Albion, Lucania, Hesperia, even an independent tyrant or two. The brief time Verdania held it, they absconded with the resident Chefs."

"Do I look like her?" Solenn blurted out. Now she understood why she didn't resemble the rest of her family.

Erwan smiled. "Yes. I see the resemblance because I know what to look for, but most would not, for which we should be grateful. Solenn, you must know that Ada loves you more than anything in this world." This, he said with surprising ferocity. "We were officers together in the Thirty-Fifth Division, a cooperative effort between Braiz and Verdania. Ada was a Chef-Lieutenant, while I was attached to govern the Braizian units and act as liaison to my superior, Prince Morvan. Ada . . . I couldn't help but fall in love with her, and we were wed. She became pregnant. Despite the dangers around us, we found happiness."

"Wait. I know that Chefs are property of the king in Verdania, but while pregnant, she was still on the field of battle?"

"Oh yes. In Verdania, only noblewomen are cosseted. Chefs are . . . of a strange status here. Property, as you say, of the Crown's Guild, yet also venerated and coveted. The Thirty-Fifth relied on her. Through her empathetic tongue, she knew if water was contaminated or if meat was spoiled but didn't smell, and she was also a competent officer and marks-swoman. If her pregnancy had caused her deep duress, she could have been temporarily assigned to a pentad, but she would have hated that. Ada was never one to idle." He stared into the distance, into the past.

Solenn considered recent history in a new light. "King Caristo severed the alliance between Verdania and Braiz right around the time I was born, didn't he? That's what forced you apart?"

Erwan's complexion darkened with anger that clearly hadn't abated after all these years. "Yes. King Caristo heard gossip that your grandparents had mocked him, which was ludicrous. You know well that they don't even speak ill of the sailors of the *Everett*."

She nodded. Several of Braiz's own sailors, while inebriated, had started the Port of Nont conflagration last year. That loss—that vulnerability—was what made her impending marriage all the more important. She replied thoughtfully, "That's when Caristo nullified all marriages between Verdanians and Braizians and forbade all Braizians from the realm." The ambassador from Braiz hadn't even been allowed in Lutecia for marriage negotiations until three years ago.

"Meaning I couldn't stay here," said Erwan. "I cannot hide my accent."

"Why couldn't she—oh, the extradition treaty."

Erwan nodded with a grim set to his mouth. "Verdania may be flippant when it comes to honor, but Braiz is not. By the treaty, as a rogue Chef, she would be arrested and returned to Verdania."

"And yet she didn't want to keep me?" Solenn couldn't help but feel wounded.

"Solenn, no. Do not judge her or yourself that way. You must understand that she was certain you would be a Chef. She wouldn't have you raised in Verdania, to be conscripted as she was. In Braiz, when your tongue awakened, you would at least have choices." Solenn knew that her home country strongly encouraged Chefs to work for the benefit of the realm, but many labored in private capacities.

"But Chef families do sometimes have mundane members. How could she be so certain of what I would be?"

Erwan sat back on his leather divan and rubbed his face with a white-gloved hand. Unlike most men here, he didn't possess facial hair; he detested the feel of it and made sure to shave twice a day. No, he never could have passed as Verdanian. "Solenn, tell me in detail what you perceived about the dauphin's wine."

She furrowed her brow. "I don't think it began with the wine, actually. When I was near Marquis Dubray and his companion, I strongly smelled roses and saw a strange shimmer on their skin."

"Aha. You perceived the use of rose fairies."

"But I've been around people who've ingested rose fairies lots of times. Mamm-gozh uses them!"

"As the old saying goes, 'The Gods can touch your tongue between the bite and the sip.'" He sighed. "Your mother began to perceive at age five."

"Five?" Solenn's jaw fell slack. "Isn't that awfully young?"

"Yes, and her skills were unusually strong as well." He leaned forward on his knees again. "Please, tell me more." He stayed quiet as she told of what had happened with Rupert. "You do take after Ada. You're Gyst-touched."

"Funny how it's described as if Gyst just touches the tongue, when it involves so much more than that. I could see and smell the glamour laid on Dubray tonight, *and* I experienced the poison like I was dying of it myself."

"You shouldn't have to endure such a thing!" Erwan pinched his fingers in a motion to Selland. "Each Chef experiences the holy differently, but everything is dependent on the tongue. As for Gyst, well, he is the God of Unknowns. His ways are more unpredictable."

"I normally associate him with things like bread, cheese, and wine."

"Which are of his domain, as he oversees the controlled decomposition of such foods."

Solenn nodded, even as she winced. She didn't want to think about how the God who touched her tongue also touched, and encouraged, decomposition, even though most every privy and chamber pot bore his signature X. "I perceived ingested and almost-ingested epicurea. That's a kind of decomposition too."

"Indeed. In contrast, Ada empathetically tastes all food and drink."

"That sounds . . . overwhelming."

"It could be, yes. However, I never knew her to fully experience impending death as you did. She would endure a few seconds of unpleasantness. You were frozen for a solid twenty seconds." He paused as Solenn's eyes widened. She had no idea that she'd been still for so long. "This will sound strange, but please tell me: Have you *seen* Gyst?"

"Seen him?" she echoed. "People don't *see* Gyst or any of the Gods. Do they?" Sensing the presence of the Gods, on the other hand, wasn't uncommon. Nor was such a thing exclusive to Chefs. "What would they even look like? I mean, people are forbidden to portray the Five except by their icons. That's true in Verdania like it is in Braiz. Isn't it?" She wasn't certain of anything anymore.

"Yes." Erwan took a deep breath. "Ada would want me to tell you this, and I must trust that you'll keep it in confidence." Solenn promptly nodded—who would she even tell such a thing? "She has been visited by Gyst more than once throughout her life. Immediately after your birth, Gyst came to her again and in very few words declared your potential."

Solenn pressed her hands to her mouth. "You can't—really? The *God*? He said that about me?" Seeing a God was extraordinary enough—but fully conversing with one?

"Yes, he said that if you lived through childhood, your tongue would be touched."

"Then why am I here, set to be married? Didn't you *believe* her?"

"I did, and do. While my opinion was considered, it didn't settle the matter." His smile was faint. "Morvan and Katell believed Ada as well, but as you grew older, they came under more pressure to make arrangements on your behalf. It became increasingly difficult for them to dismiss opportunities. I think they eventually convinced themselves that enough time had passed and that you would be fine."

Solenn was decidedly not *fine*. She swallowed dryly and stared at her lap. Her gown and gloves were still splashed in pink. "I would like to talk with her. With Adamantine. If she . . . is she . . . ?"

"I don't know, Solenn, and Five help me, I wish I did. When you were days old, she committed you to my care. I rode for Braiz. I'd promised her that you would be raised by my parents. On the way to their château, I stopped to attend Morvan and Katell and found she'd lost her baby only the day before. Mourning had submersed them like waves over the City-Eaten-by-the-Sea, their loss still kept private. You were most displeased with the goat's milk I'd been feeding you and let this be known." His smile was rueful. "Katell said she would feed you, just once, but she fell in love with you, as did Morvan. Within the day, they resolved to keep you as their own."

Solenn could say nothing to this at all.

"As for Ada, she planned to come to Lutecia and live as a rogue. A very angry rogue." He said this with fondness. "All her life, she had wanted a family of her own. We were good together, the two of us. With you on the way, we were to be even more complete."

"Oh." Solenn had wanted to hate this woman who'd given her up but, instead, found herself regarding her with more fondness than she did Erwan at the moment.

He continued. "She took the dissolution of our marriage as a personal attack committed against us by King Caristo."

Solenn had never liked the king. Now she was determined to loathe him. "So if she's alive, she's in hiding, impossible to find. Unless . . ."

"She hasn't been caught. I know that much." Erwan wore a shy smile unlike any she had seen before. "I checked the prosecutors' registry when we arrived last week."

The full weight of his loss began to sink in. To her knowledge, he'd never engaged in any romantic or casual relationships. Instead, Solenn realized, she had been the full focus of his life.

Or would be, for another week. Until her wedding.

"Erwan, what are we going to do about the prince? The poisoner is still out there."

At that, he glowered. "A well-financed poisoner, at that. They didn't settle for mundane methods but sought out fatal epicurea. That doesn't come cheap. The culprit will soon know, if they don't already, that they failed in their task. They'll try again. You could be poisoned as well, by accident or on purpose."

"I know, I know. If only we could warn Rupert about the threat we're against!" She tilted her head, frowning. "When I hesitated with the wine, he asked what was going on, but he didn't act that concerned. He wouldn't have expected me to perceive like a Chef, of course, but he didn't even ask if I'd seen anything peculiar or inquire further to make sure I was well. *I* would have, if our roles were reversed."

"You were raised to be more attentive, whereas the dauphin has been more . . ." Erwan paused.

"Coddled? Oblivious? No point in being tactful. Even worse, his staff and guards are oblivious as well. His father endured how many assassination attempts years ago? Five, ten? You'd think they would be more alert."

"There were probably far more attempts than that. To my knowledge, no assassins have pursued Caristo in twenty years. The court is complacent. Vulnerable. Nor are we in a place to educate them." Caristo had made it popular to hate Braiz after the breaking of the alliance. Popular operas in Lutecia had portrayed Braizians as country buffoons who were hilariously inept at the simplest of tasks, untrustworthy due to their bumbling and their low intelligence.

Solenn had been extensively counseled regarding the pervasive stereotypes and the harm they'd caused in diplomatic and trade circles. Her family had hoped that her position as Rupert's bride would, with years of effort, shift opinions about Braiz to be more positive.

"We can't trust them, and they believe they can't trust us," Solenn said. "That means we need to investigate without looking as though we're investigating."

"Yes, and I'll begin by reviewing the palace staff that we've already approved," said Erwan. "None of them were new hires, but sentiments and circumstances can change."

She sat up straight. "I can tour the kitchen and meet the Chefs. I'm going to be their princess. It's within my purview."

He considered this a moment before nodding. "It is. I'll arrange it. Solenn, I know I probably don't need to say this, but I will all the same—please be discreet about your newfound abilities, especially if we're with the palace Chefs."

"Erwan, you trained me to take care with my tongue. Now that my tongue has been touched by Gyst . . . well, I'll take even more care."

"I have faith that you will," he said.

She now understood that his worry for her wasn't simply because she was his royal charge, but for her as his daughter. Tears again filled her eyes. She flung her arms wide and hugged him even as he sat on his divan.

"I'm glad you're my father," she mumbled against his shoulder. "But I'm still mad at you."

He said nothing, but she needed no grace from the Gods to perceive how he shuddered and quietly cried.

CHAPTER FIVE

ADA

Being a Chef means channeling not only the blessing of the Gods but also their compassion. Remember well the tale "How Kindness Quelled Hester's Rage." On one occasion, Hester fumed as she is wont to do. Her furious stomps created new indentations in the earth. The next day, she found her footprints now held briny water, along with fish and other marine creatures; they were pretty and pleasing, and she smiled. Selland had arranged this surprise during the night. Later that day, after finding honeyed pears alongside fresh-made cheese curds, she understood Melissa and Lait had likewise approached her with compassion. Hester's anger faded—for the time being. In this way, think of those around you and what food may offer them succor.

—Excerpt from *Manual for Tour Chefs*

The attendant who came to Maman's gate regarded them with disdain until Ada stated that she had urgent news for Monsieur Ragnar. That inspired the fellow to deploy a runner to the manse.

"Thank the Five that Ragnar is still with the comtesse," she whispered to her grandmother, who only shivered in reply.

Ada wrapped an arm around Grand-mère, willing more warmth into the old woman's body.

The sight of Ragnar had never been a welcome one in the past. If he came around, it meant that her mother wanted something from her. But this time, the approach of his tall, broad form was enough to evoke relieved tears.

"Let them in, monsieur, let them in!" Ragnar impatiently beckoned to the gate attendant. A valet beside Ragnar held up a lamp. "It has been a long time, mademoiselle, madame. Have you been well?" He asked the question as if this were a chance encounter in a boulangerie, not a prolonged estrangement, and she noticed he still referred to her as "mademoiselle" despite her age.

Most anyone looking at Ragnar would think that since he was the size and thickness of a brick wall, he was as dense as one too. Ada knew better. Ragnar had been raised in the Confederated Duchies and spoke cultured, flawless Lutecian, one of his many languages and patois. The only error in the man's intelligence was his decades-long loyalty to her mother.

"We've been better, monsieur." The gate opened, soundless. By the time it was wide enough to admit them, Ragnar had removed his own greatcoat. He draped it over Grand-mère's shoulders. With him so massive and her so shrunken, the hem dragged past her knees. "Is Comtesse Alarie in residence?" Ada asked.

"Indeed she is. Monsieur," Ragnar said to his companion, "I will take the lamp. You go ahead. Have a guest room prepared, second floor." The man left with a bow, leaving the trio alone to walk up the level gravel drive. "I can take your bag, mademoiselle."

Ada pursed her lips, considering his offer and how strange it would look for her to enter the household burdened while he carried only a lantern. She grudgingly relinquished the satchel, which he hefted as if it were as light as a meringue.

"Well, aren't you nice, monsieur," said Grand-mère. She'd met him before when Ada was a teenager but clearly didn't recognize him now. "And so handsome."

Ragnar smiled. He was probably ten years older than Ada, his hair turning a bolder white than her silver threads. He still had an oddly handsome visage, even with a scarred, crooked nose that looked as if pugilists had once used it for practice. Which may well have been true.

"I am honored by your words, madame. I take it that you have been together all this while?" he asked. Such a polite way of inquiring if they had been companions in desertion. Ada nodded. He continued, "You are safe here. I will handle the palace prosecutors. I've been in regular meetings with them for years now, lest you come to their attention. By morning—"

"Wait. You've been associating with the prosecutors for years? In case they caught me?" Ada gawked at him.

Ragnar looked surprised. "But of course. Do you think the comtesse would permit them to prosecute you and remove your tongue?"

"Permit?" Ada felt the need to repeat everything Ragnar said to grasp the full meaning. "How powerful has she become? I mean, I'm aware of this . . ." She gestured to the glamorous château they neared, the palace quartier entire. "But beyond her standing in society, has her business granted her . . . a different sort of access?"

"It is crude to speak of such things." His tone was gently chiding.

"It's crude for a woman of her status to be an entrepreneur at all, much less one in an illegal trade." Ada said this in an especially low voice.

Maman had been comfortably bourgeois by birth and married a comte. The bourgeoisie and nobility detested the very idea of work, especially for a woman. Highborn women were to look beautiful and produce heirs. Working-class women could manage businesses, own property, and perhaps most importantly, serve as soldiers. As often as Verdania warred, the country needed as many weapon-bearing bodies as it could get.

Maman would never have been satisfied with a life of idleness alone. Around the time that Ada had been conscripted by the army, as a Chef expedited into the officer program, her mother had chosen her own unique, rebellious line of work: to become a distributor of black-market epicurea within Verdania.

A shame that Maman's drive for success had never extended to her role as a mother.

Ada's bitterness dragged her thoughts to a darker place—to her own inability to fully mother her own daughter. She didn't even know her child's name; she had respected Erwan's Braizian tradition that infants remain unnamed until their half year. She didn't even know whether their babe had lived that long.

All this time, and that loss could never heal. But then, the rare sight of Braizian musketeers still pained her heart too.

She couldn't dwell on such things. She needed her wits so she could focus on their current dilemma. "To return to what you said before, we aren't fleeing prosecutors tonight but dealing with other concerns."

He stopped beneath a chestnut tree. The rustle of horses and low, distant voices carried from the nearby stable. "As I'm aware of your . . . tenuous relationship with Comtesse Alarie, these other concerns must be serious indeed to drive you here. Your last parley was not a positive one."

Ada guffawed. "She demanded that I assist in her nascent business. It's dangerous enough that she peddles in what's supposed to be the property of King Caristo, but *I'm* supposed to be his property as well. The penalties for me having—shall we say—divided interests would have been more severe for me than for her. Not that I could change her mind, of course."

"Madame can be rather stubborn," Ragnar acknowledged in a neutral tone. He looked between Ada and Grand-mère. "In front of the staff, I will refer to you as Mademoiselle and Madame Gray."

"Madame Gray," murmured Grand-mère. "A good color, one often unappreciated due to its associations with mourning."

Such subterfuge was nothing new when visiting Maman. Ada had been aware, from an early age, that she was Maman's dirty secret. Their relationship had perplexed her through much of her childhood, but like a wound changing to an ever-itchy scar, it had resolved into resentment as she'd aged. Some foolish part of her never stopped craving a mother who loved her for who she was, not what she could do. Even when she was as young as seven, a discreet summons to Maman's meant she was to cook a grand meal for prestigious guests, with her reward being five minutes of small talk with her mother afterward.

Ragnar strode ahead and opened the door. The kitchen's heat and light welcomed them inside. Two cooks looked up in surprise. One worked on yeast dough while the other wiped down a table.

"These mesdemoiselles are guests in need of food and warmth," he said brusquely.

The cook who cleaned left her rag and, nodding, began to move a chair close to the room's original hearth. "What can we get you two?"

"There's the day-old bread, and that chicken," suggested the second woman, wiping floury hands on her hips.

"With wine to warm their spirits as well." Ragnar faced Ada and her grandmother. "I will leave you here. Anything else you need, please ask. I'll return shortly." He gave Ada's satchel an extra heft. "I will take this to your room—"

"Please, no. Leave it here in case we need anything," Ada said. Glad as she was to see her grandmother take a seat near the fire, her unease had only increased.

Maman had worked with prosecutors for years so that she could "save" Ada. This was not done out of love or even devotion. She had never given up on her plot to utilize Ada in her business venture. Raw epicurea was worth a great deal, but a Chef could create imperishable magicked goods of incredibly high value.

When Ada had last argued with Maman, she had been able to say that her foremost loyalty was to King Caristo and, through him, the Gods. Ada had no such defense now. Instead, Maman could threaten to deliver Ada—and her grandmother—to Guild prosecutors if they didn't do as she bade.

Ada had deluded herself into thinking they might find refuge here for even a single night. They had to flee as soon as possible, and leave the entire city. Someone still sought her death.

Ragnar, Five bless him, left the leather bag leaning beside the hearth. "I will confer with the comtesse now, as she needs to depart soon. If you will excuse me." He exited with a bow.

"Here you go." The younger cook brought over cold pieces of chicken, a bread boule, and a carafe of red wine, then retreated.

Ada's mind gnawed on thoughts as tough as the chicken. Maman wouldn't simply let them leave, and if they did manage to escape, they would need to afford shelter or horses.

Her ruminations remained muddled until the cat strolled in. The lithe orange tabby, his strides confident, came straight up to Grand-mère, who greeted him with kissy noises and dropped her chicken bone to the floor. He accepted the offering with a purr.

Ada motioned a grateful X to Gyst. She and Grand-mère would leave here using the same magical means that she'd once used to spy upon Mallory Valmont to uncover the sordid source of his rupic powder.

"I need to prepare oatcakes for my grandmother to eat later," she announced, standing. "They help her digestion like nothing else." Grand-mère cast her a curious look as she continued to eat.

"By all means," said the elder cook, genuflecting. Ragnar had granted the guests full access, after all. "If we may be of help . . . ?"

"I must make them in a particular way," Ada said, motioning to the smock she still wore. That seemed to give her adequate credibility, and the cooks continued their own duties.

She began to rummage in cupboards, an activity she might have enjoyed under other circumstances. She found butter and salt on a nearby table, and hulled oats to spare their own supply. She didn't go too near the locked cabinet that held an array of ready epicurea—empress bee honey, unicorn tisane, the sort of ingredients any well-to-do household would keep for immediate culinary and medicinal needs. Ada found it curious, really, how basic the assortment was, considering Maman's business. The good stuff was being kept elsewhere.

She stoked the hearth fire and set a skillet to heat. Among pentads, it was a subject of some contention as to whether Hester favored hearths or modern coal stoves, or whether she held a preference at all. In this case, Ada simply chose the heating source most convenient and private for her needs.

"Hester, help us," she whispered, placing more awareness in her tongue and in the presence of her gathered ingredients.

Grand-mère watched. "I don't need more food right now."

"This is for later."

She gave the oats a light chop, adding a sprinkle of salt with a pinch-finger appeal to Selland. As she worked in the honey, fragrant of clover from the Lynette Valley, she appealed to Melissa. The soft butter was the stuff of Lait, made the day before from city cows still fed on hay. To that she added water from a nearby pitcher, its purity noteworthy in a city frequented by dysentery. With the added heat of the fire, four of the Gods were represented in these oatcakes.

Then there was the contribution connected to Gyst, the epicurean element that Ada had discovered by accident in her twenties.

She reached for the cat, now purring in Grand-mère's lap, and gave him a quick stroke up the spine. A palmful of hair was chopped into the oat mixture.

"Gyst," she whispered. "Please help me utilize the mysterious ways of the cat again."

Her tongue prickled as if she'd eaten an excess of ground pepper. By the grace of Gyst, the hidden potential of cat hair had awakened—though she still found the inclusion repulsive. The chewiness of the oats would mask the texture. Mostly.

"Aha! You're making your blessed oatcakes." Grand-mère huddled closer. "I can't sense anything." Every generation of Ada's paternal line, as far back as records existed, had been a Chef blessed with an empathetic tongue.

"You will soon. Please, keep your whisper lower."

"My whisper was just fine," Grand-mère grumbled, still a bit too loud for Ada's liking.

Ada used the weight of her palms to mash the oats into an even layer on the table. With a critical eye, she cut the cakes into thin rounds of equal size. They sizzled as they met the hot skillet. Turning to the scraps, she added a touch more water to bring them together, and she cut more cakes. The warm, nutty pleasantness of cooked oats filled the air.

"Ah yes. There's the magic." Grand-mère took in a deep breath. "Amazing."

"Don't act like they're anything unusual," Ada muttered.

"I know," Grand-mère grumbled.

The first batch finished, and she heated the next. Grand-mère fanned the finished cakes with a hand to cool them faster as Ada set about cleaning up the mess she'd made.

"You needn't do that," called one of the cooks.

"I do. Where do you keep clean rags?"

The wise cook didn't argue further. "The cupboard behind you with the blue knobs. Thank you."

Ada removed one rag for cleaning and used a second one to wrap up the oatcakes. She tucked the warm bundle into one of the many pockets of her green coat.

"Mesdemoiselles?" Ragnar emerged through an interior doorway. "Comtesse Alarie will see you now."

Ada paused. "Grand-mère, it may be best if you—"

"I should stay here, monsieur." Thank the Five, but Grand-mère sounded more like her coherent old self for the time being. "Hester's fire is kind to these old bones, though I should return your coat to you."

"Oh, I have a blanket you can use, Madame Gray," said the older cook. "If that's acceptable, monsieur?"

"Quite so, mademoiselle." Ragnar's tone was warm.

Ada lifted the heavy coat from her grandmother's shoulders as the cook approached with what looked to be a well-patched blue wool blanket fringed by yellowed Braizian lace. "Stay here," Ada murmured to Grand-mère, meaning that in more than a physical sense. "I'm leaving my bag with you."

"I'll be fine." Grand-mère snuggled deeper into her new blanket, smiling up at Ada. "Go."

Ada hated leaving her here with strangers. Grand-mère would probably say things she ought not—but it would be far worse if she voiced such things before Maman.

Ada turned to Ragnar. "Kindly lead the way to the comtesse, monsieur," she said, her tone confident to mask the dread that chilled her more than her distance from the hearth.

CHAPTER SIX

ADA

While a Chef relies upon the conduit of the tongue to know all, the humble rôtisseur knows when to rotate meat by their eye alone and can read doneness by the sizzle of fat upon the coals. Is this not also a divine skill?

—Excerpt from *Book for Cooks to Excel as Do Chefs*

"Madame is overjoyed at the prospect of your reunion," Ragnar said, voice low.

"I'm sure."

He gave her a sidelong glance as they continued along a chandeliered hallway. "In consideration of your grandmother's sensitivity to cold, she'll be more comfortable if she remains in the kitchen until your bedchamber is warmer. You will have heated irons and extra blankets ready for you there as well."

"I can't say that I'm glad to be here, but your kindness is much appreciated," Ada said.

His smile for her held genuine fondness.

Really, Ragnar had to be the most kind and stalwart man her mother had ever had in her life. Ada's Chef father had been scarcely more than a stud. He had been attached to the army and deployed more often than not, but unlike Ada, he practiced alcoholism with contemplative rigor. He'd met Gyst after a violent encounter with a carriage when Ada was ten. Maman's husband the comte had chosen a different vice, the company of various women, with his resultant death of slow disease. Ada doubted that he'd known that his wife had borne a child at seventeen, not long before their marriage. During Ada's early childhood, she had rarely been in Maman's presence, even when they resided in the same house.

Ragnar guided Ada to the servants' narrow passage upward. Her coat brushed the walls to either side. Up another flight, they entered a hallway with pristine wainscoted walls. Another turn, and he escorted her through double doors and into a lush bedchamber. What was not pure white glistened in gold.

"Don't step on my rug," came a commanding voice. "Ragnar, you should have—"

"I beg your pardon." He bowed. "Don't step on madame's unicorn rug," repeated Ragnar, contrite.

Ada looked down. The poor unicorn. To be harvested for select ingredients, then to end up on the floor in a place like this. "I would not dream of causing such offense." As a point of respect to the deceased magical equine, Ada walked around the rug to her mother, who sat on a plush stool before a triptych mirror.

"I should've had the grooms wash you down first, as they do the horses after they roll in muck." Maman frowned up at Ada in the middle mirror. "You're looking old."

"Thank you, Maman." To Ada's chagrin, they actually looked about the same age. Ada's life had been one of exposure to the elements and harsh kitchens, in contrast to Maman's more cosseted existence and generous applications of facial powder.

"Let's not dither. My business kept me late, and I've likely already missed the presentation of the princess." Maman sighed. "Tell me what's brought you here."

"I'm sorry. Next time, I'll consult your social calendar before I flee for my life."

Maman spun on her seat to face her. "Ragnar said this doesn't involve Guild prosecutors."

She wanted to know all the details. Ada wouldn't oblige. "I returned home to find that my grandmother had killed a man in self-defense. He'd asked for me by my true name. I don't know who sent him or why, but it was clear we had to leave."

The role of rupic and stony owl epicurea continued to confound Ada. Not even Maman would peddle such ingredients—not because of morality but because of outright rarity.

"Your grandmother. How is she?" The question was clipped.

"Old."

Maman's eyes narrowed. "You don't trust me."

"I'm here, aren't I? When we last spoke, you told me I could return to you if I ever needed aid."

"That was over seventeen years ago! Seventeen!" Maman stood and stalked around her. Ada pivoted to watch, noting how Ragnar stood within the chamber, his back to the door, a more formidable barricade than the actual walls. "A year after we last spoke, I heard through my channels that you had deserted. I thought then that perhaps you were hiding like Lait in the winter and that you'd come to me in time." To Maman's credit, she didn't feign maternal devotion. "No one, not even your grandmother, possesses your level of empathetic skill. The Chefs I've employed have been decent, yes, but they aren't *you*."

"I suppose I should be flattered." Ada didn't mask her weariness. "By your societal rise, I can't help but wonder if you now dominate the epicurea market in Verdania."

Supposedly, after the palace had called first dibs on epicurea, priority then went to the military, with the occasional excess available for public sale. Of course, nothing was ever that tidy. Black markets existed in every village and back alley.

"Yes." Maman didn't bother with modesty. "And beyond."

Ada shook her head in disgust. "What, do you sell to the Duchies? Braiz? Please tell me you're not selling to Albion."

"We supply those willing to pay," Maman said without shame.

"You *are* peddling to them. Hester's fire, Maman! Well, they would certainly pay well for our ingredients. Last I heard, they had overharvested their native epicurea in their efforts to kill Verdanians and anyone else who stood against them. Me included." And Erwan and Emone and Petry and Didina, and so many others she knew and cared about.

"The war is over. Verdania is now engaged in formal trade with them again. I'm no different."

"Except that what you're doing is *wrong*." The illegality of selling epicurea to Albion was not what perturbed Ada—it was selling to Albion, period. They were the enemy. They had killed hundreds of people she'd known well and had come terribly close to killing her and her fondest comrades too. The entire island of Albion could sink into the sea, as far as she cared, and the only loss would be the fine cheeses they produced.

Maman blew a rather undignified raspberry. "Stop with the moral posturing and accept that, because of my largesse, I can accommodate you and your grandmother in resplendent comfort as my employees."

Not full comfort. Someone was still seeking to kill Ada, someone with unusual resources. Ada wouldn't be an effective Chef if kept locked away; she'd need to oversee procurement of groceries and goods. Whoever pursued her may find her again, and the protective might of Ragnar would mean little against someone in the full sway of rupic.

Ada said with slow care, "Does that mean that if we refuse to work for you, you'll force us out?"

Maman's grin was toothy and victorious, her teeth mottled brown. "If you're here, you won't be able to resist my employ. Tell me, Ragnar, has she already cooked this evening?"

"She has, madame." Ragnar bowed.

Realization bloomed in Ada's mind like yeast in warm liquid. "You didn't bring us into the kitchen for subterfuge alone," Ada said to Ragnar. "You *tempted* me."

Maman chuckled softly. "You haven't even been here an hour and yet you had to cook. If you're denied access to the kitchen, how will you subsist on meals by my cooks? How will you react, I wonder, to the presence of my current Chef-prepared epicurean delights? Oh, the food is good enough to sell right now, but will it meet your standards of quality? I think not."

Maman knew her well, for all their limited time together. Ada was vexed by the very thought of perceiving such imperfection, and she knew the low-quality food would perturb Grand-mère as well. She would be even more vulnerable to manipulation.

Oh, Grand-mère. Once Maman knew of Grand-mère's condition, she would provide awake oak flour. A single bread roll made with a combination of that and regular flour could keep Grand-mère grounded in the present for a full day, though her overall mental decline would continue. Not even unicorn marrow could reverse that. The flour would simply make her a better laborer, at least for a while.

Her throat dry, Ada couldn't help but ask, "Would our duties involve cooking epicurea for immediate consumption, or for preservation?"

"Most often for preservation," said Maman. That meant communing with the Gods while grinding roots, drying and salting meat, and washing cheeses. This was drudgery to some, but Ada found such tasks to be soothing. "Though there would be commissions for fresh meals as well."

The freedom to cook for people, using her full range of senses and skills. Tears stung her eyes. She could never even cook freely for

Grand-mère in recent years; they were too poor to enjoy diverse options, and if their meals smelled too delicious, the neighbors would be dangerously curious. Most anyone could develop some modest cooking skill with effort, but they could never equal what even an apprentice Chef could do.

Yet not even an apprentice Chef knew the freedom that Ada and her grandmother had experienced. For the first time in their lives, they hadn't been *owned*.

"I need to discuss this with Grand-mère." She turned away.

"Of course. Tell me, why did you become a rogue?"

Ada stopped, her temper flaring as hot as Hester's rage in the old tales. If Maman really knew her, she wouldn't need to ask. She would already know that Ada had been married and pregnant, and that King Caristo's idiocy had cost her the family she had cherished more than anything.

Ada glanced over her shoulder. "I tired of being told what to do," she said simply.

"That's ridiculous. You're a Chef. You were born to serve the Gods through King Caristo."

Ada almost heard "and serve me too" as well. "If I had been allowed to work in pentads or tour with apprentices, I might have better tolerated being property," she replied. Her own tour days were some of the fondest of her life: years spent traveling Verdania with mentors and a small group of peers, learning to identify variances in terroir and to cook with whatever food and implements were available. "With my skill level, though, I could only ever work within the palace or the military. I wasn't going to do that anymore."

Maman huffed. "No, instead, you squandered your talents for years by likely cooking mediocre meals for *peasants*."

"I don't expect you to understand." Ada stalked toward the door, her body rigid, aching with a hollowness that could never be filled. "Enjoy what remains of your evening, Maman."

"What, I don't even get a kiss good night after all this time?"

Ragnar still barricaded the door. He shifted his eyes to coax her to turn around.

"You won't move until I do as she asks, will you?" Ada muttered. He answered by remaining stationary.

She stalked back to Maman to lay quick kisses upon each cheek.

"There. Was that so terrible? I'll see you tomorrow, my dear." The cheery words were as much a threat as a brandished knife. "Ragnar, is my sedan ready?"

"I will make certain of it this instant, madame." Ragnar opened the door to the hallway and to Ada said, "If you will return to the kitchen, mademoiselle . . . ?"

"I can find my way, thank you, Ragnar." She appreciated that he trusted her to get there on her own.

Ada had hoped that she might find Grand-mère alone in the kitchen, but the two cooks were still present, the younger woman engaged in more food preparation, the other in Ada's former seat beside Grand-mère.

"And that was when the extraordinaire collapsed!" Grand-mère was saying, one arm raised dramatically.

Ada's heart sank. That was a tale from Grand-mère's decades working in the palace.

The cook gasped. "Oh, but all the hours spent on that sugar structure. I can't even imagine the horror of seeing it come down, and all because an ambassador's dog stole one of the columns?"

"Grand-mère," Ada interrupted. The cook caught her tone and retreated, leaving the two alone. "How are you feeling?"

"Fine. We've been having a wonderful talk."

The time for talking was done. Ada looked toward the cooks. "If you could please direct us toward the cellar, I would like to choose a wine for us to enjoy before bed."

As Ragnar had already granted them such liberties, the elder cook didn't even blink. "But of course. The stairs are this way." She headed toward a far doorway.

Grand-mère didn't budge. "I could stay here." She snuggled deeper into her blanket.

Ada quietly appealed to the Gods to carry her intent to her grandmother. "You're more knowledgeable about wine than I am. You may not like what I would choose."

The appeal to pride may have been more effective than divine intervention. "Well, that's true. I *should* help."

With her grandmother beside her, Ada hefted up her bag and followed the cook to the stone steps downward. There, the cook proffered a lit candlestick before saying farewell.

Ada's tongue prickled as her footsteps resounded in the stone-bound darkness of the cellar. Such places were among Gyst's most favored domains. Her hand glanced storage racks, her proximity strengthening her perception of the casks and bottles. These were fine reds from Lynette. Farther along, she appreciated sparkling wines from the hills near Rance. Melissa and Gyst had combined their efforts to sweet, delicious results.

"Mmm, a lovely selection," said Grand-mère, taking in the array with a blissful sigh. Faint creaks from above signaled footsteps in the house. "For bedtime, we need one aged in—"

"Grand-mère, we're not really here for wine." Ada kept her voice low, even though she knew no one was nearby. "We need to leave the house."

"Well, you're going about *that* all wrong, then. We're as good as trapped in the cellar."

"Not if we move fast. Can you hold this, please?" Ada passed Grand-mère the candle in its metal cradle. Setting down her bag, she reached into her coat for the oatcakes. "We're going to eat some of these and then go back upstairs to find an egress."

Grand-mère brought the candle dangerously close to Ada's face. "What is—oh, oatcakes? There's epicurea in there. Are these—"

"Yes, like the ones I told you about years ago." Grand-mère had already forgotten what Ada had done not a half hour before. "Hold this." Ada pressed an oatcake into Grand-mère's hand as she reclaimed the candlestick. "We'll eat at the same time."

As she brought her oatcake toward her mouth, Ada heard especially heavy steps above. That could only be one person.

"Eat now," she hissed, scanning the area around them to memorize the layout. She bit into the thin wafer, the flavor of freshly toasted oats with butter meeting her tongue alongside the tingle of enchantment.

Gyst, awaken the hidden magic of cats in us both, please, Ada prayed as Grand-mère chewed with open-mouthed smacks. The prickles upon her tongue intensified as Gyst heeded her plea.

They were both turning invisible.

Color was fading from Grand-mère's candle-brightened form, granting her the appearance of thin watercolor over a background of etched ink. Ada glanced at her own hand to find the same eerie phenomenon in effect. She forced herself to swallow another bite of oatcake. This magic never ceased to disturb her.

Late in her apprenticeship touring days as a teen, Ada had recognized the telltale tingle of epicurea one day when cat hair became mixed with her food. This had baffled her. Cats weren't documented as epicurea; they didn't fit the most rudimentary definition, as eating particular morsels of their bodies didn't imbue people with magic. She'd never sought to experiment with *that* concept, however. Such an idea had thoroughly repulsed her; cats had unique personalities, like people, and were much more suitable as company.

She had spent months secretly experimenting with cat hair as she sought ways to mask its appalling texture and, most importantly, figure out its magical effects.

Despite her efforts, some aspects remained a mystery, like an explanation for the gauzy things and beings that became visible while using cat-magic.

As Ada finished chewing, she spied something as tall and gangly as a tree walking through the cellar walls, its body made of dark-gray mist. She refused to stare at the strange thing; she couldn't risk Grand-mère seeing it and screaming. Ada had told her about this side effect of the epicurea, but Grand-mère likely wouldn't remember.

The door to the cellar opened with a soft clang.

Ada dashed away from her grandmother. She had her destination mapped out, an empty place upon a flat shelf about seven feet distant. That was where she would set the candle.

She had planned out that much, but she hadn't anticipated that Grand-mère would follow her, her footsteps scuffing the floor in Ada's wake.

"Grand-mère!" Ada hissed, pointing her back toward the other wall. Her sleeve was a faint green blur.

"If we're leaving, I can't steal that cook's blanket!" Ada could barely make out the glint of tears in Grand-mère's eyes.

There was no time to argue. Ada whipped the blanket from Grand-mère's shoulder as she motioned her away. This time, Grand-mère heeded. As Ada continued along her planned route, her heartbeat pounded almost as loudly as Ragnar's heavy footfall along the stairs. She set the candleholder upon the shelf and, having no place to set the blanket, had to drop it on the ground. Grand-mère let out a small cry of dismay as Ada blew out the candle.

In the profound and sudden darkness, Ada relied on her tongue to guide her back to the oats and other familiar supplies in her bag. She couldn't see her grandmother at all.

"You can't leave the blanket on the floor like that," Grand-mère cried. "That blanket is loved, it should be—"

Ada used her grandmother's voice to locate her exact whereabouts. She gripped Grand-mère's upper arm with gentle firmness, pushing her farther back into the nook. "You're invisible now. So am I." Ada's whisper shook with anxiety and frustration. "You *must stay as quiet* as rising bread so he passes us by. Can you do that? Be even quieter than me?"

"Of course!" Grand-mère accepted the challenge in an imperious tone.

"Mademoiselle? Madame?" Ragnar called. He had reached the floor level but remained on a different aisle. A distant, indirect glow shone from a lamp. "I see no light down here," he called up the stairs.

Ada gave Grand-mère's arm a soft squeeze in reminder.

"The cook said they just came down. The candle kept up top is gone." Maman's voice jolted Ada, as she'd hoped her mother would have left by now. The distinct echo in her words indicated she was along the stairwell. "They can't have vanished."

Ada's smile was thin.

"I do smell fresh smoke," said Ragnar, tone hopeful. He came their way, audibly inhaling. Shadows rendered his craggy face into a ghastly mask. "Mademoiselle Ada?" he called, angling the lamp every which way. He abruptly stopped and stooped down. When he rose, he held the blanket. His focus then went to the snuffed candle. He was utterly still for a moment.

"Mademoiselle Ada," he repeated, this time with softness. "If you hear me, know that I understand that you don't wish to work for your mother, but she will take care of you . . . the both of you. You cannot hide here in the dark forever. She has already deployed people in search of you throughout the house."

Of course Maman had. By the Five, if only they'd had fifteen minutes' grace to escape. Was this whole effort doomed to futility?

Ragnar threw the blanket over his shoulder and advanced toward them, lamp held high.

Light fell over them. Ada glanced down. Her body truly was invisible, as was Grand-mère's. The cat-magic had worked.

Ragnar strode past them, his motion stirring their clothes like a breeze. "Let us help you, mademoiselle, please," he murmured.

"Well?" Maman said the single word, shrill and impatient.

"I found the candle down here, madame. Snuffed. With it, the blanket being used by Madame Eglantine." His voice boomed in the enclosed space. "I cannot see them here. They must have promptly ascended again."

Footsteps tapped downward. "Has anyone gone through the cellar passage?" The nature of the echo had changed. Maman must have been standing at the base of the stairwell.

Cellar passage? Ada felt as if her ears perked like those of a cat. Appropriate, considering the epicurea in effect.

"Not since you returned an hour ago. I shut the door myself." He walked to the far side of the cellar, his voice echoing. "It's still closed."

"Come back upstairs, then. I absolutely must depart. You'll find them." Maman's tone left no question as to that.

"Of course, Comtesse." Ragnar passed by them again, his expression troubled. He climbed the stairs, taking with him the light. The door closed.

Ada waited another long minute before daring to speak. "Come along," she hissed. "These first oatcakes won't last much longer."

"He truly couldn't see us," marveled Grand-mère. "*I* couldn't even see us."

"For now, yes. Let's find this passage they mentioned."

Thank the Five that Ragnar had shown them which way to go. Ada walked through the darkness, a hand to the shelves, her bag thumping against Grand-mère more than once.

"Wait," Grand-mère hissed. "There's very good cheese stored back there."

"Grand-mère, now's not—" Ada paused. "The Arinth?"

"Yes."

They backtracked. Relying on perception alone, she explored with her fingertips until she found a rind reminiscent of pebbles. A full wheel of Arinth was eighty pounds; this was a smaller piece, recently cut, preserved here in the cellar. Its sublime flavor of candied hazelnuts caused her mouth to salivate.

"I know where I can sell this." Ada fumbled open her bag to stuff the cheese inside. "The fellow won't mind the late-night awakening, not for something this fine and rare." This cheese would enable them to afford horses and flee to Petry like the rogue Chefs they were.

"Perhaps," said Grand-mère, tone hopeful, "we can spare a slice first?"

She gave Grand-mère's arm a fond squeeze as she shouldered her bag again. "We'll see."

They continued to the far corner of the cellar. Ada caught a whiff of new wood. No sounds carried from above; they were below the garden or drive. She frowned and touched the flagstones. The grit had been swept in an arc.

"The door is on this wall." Ada groped at the wooden panels.

"Why would a tunnel even exist here?" asked Grand-mère.

"We'll know more once we see what's on the far side." Her hand found a wooden handle, and she jerked it downward.

The door released toward her with a sigh of air. She pulled it wider. To her relief, the door made only a soft grinding noise upon the ground. Maman would never tolerate a squeaky door. By sound and feel, Ada recognized this to be a small tunnel, some seven feet in height—made large enough to fit Ragnar, she had no doubt. She could make out that the walls had been whitewashed, as they were a visible deep gray amid greater darkness. By that, she also knew the tunnel lay fairly straight.

Misty shapes shifted around them, vaguely human.

"Ada!" Grand-mère clutched at her. "What—"

"Remember what I told you ages ago? When using cat hair, I saw things." She waved to a figure that passed before them and through the wall. "If we had full light, you'd see the shapes of buildings and trees too." She shut the door behind them.

"But do they see us?" She sounded more curious than scared.

"Not that I can tell." Ada shook her head. "I can only guess that when cats vanish in our world, they're slipping to some other place where these things also exist. When I access their magic, through Gyst, we straddle both realms and can be seen by beings in neither."

"Incredible. We owe Gyst many secrets—"

"Not now." Ada tried to maintain patience as she hurried her grandmother along.

Some two hundred feet later, they found another door. Before opening the way, both Chefs knew what lay on the other side.

"Epicurea," breathed Grand-mère.

This next cellar was dark and quiet. Just within the chamber, Ada spied a thick candle within a sconce and lit it so that they could visually take in the wonders around them.

"I haven't seen this much assembled epicurea since my army days," Ada said, carrying the candle as they walked forward. Only by dint of extensive training was she able to form coherent thought, as the quantity and density of ingredients screamed and shouted within her brain. She paused, frowning, as she took in the signs above each shelf of goods. "They are using our same organizational system too. Whoever did this was a veteran." Not necessarily a Chef, either, but one of the vast system of storekeepers who kept the military alive.

That meant she would be able to find awake oak flour, if it was stocked here.

As she opened her lips to speak, voices carried from far across the room. Ada hurried Grand-mère behind stacked barrels of salt-packed kraken steaks, her awareness of the brine causing her mouth to pucker in reaction. She dug into her coat pocket.

"Here." She held out an oatcake. "Eat fast." In the low light, she could see her own hand, her coloration dimmed.

Grand-mère instead rubbed above the ligature marks hidden by her high coat collar. "I have a whisker you need to pluck."

"Later, Grand-mère. Please. We must stay hidden."

"Oh, fine," she huffed, taking the oatcake.

The deep voices remained faint, from some distant vestibule, so she let the candle remain lit as they ate. She knew the dank presence of Gyst as she called upon him again, the God making himself known through the cacophony. As Grand-mère faded from sight, Ada gripped her by the hand. Behind the cover of barrels and boxes, she risked returning the candle to its original berth, where she then snuffed it.

"Good. Maybe they won't know we were here," whispered Grand-mère.

"That's the idea, Five willing," Ada said. "Do you remember the lessons on sneaking back in our pentad days?"

"Of course!"

"Good. We're going to practice them again now."

Ada was agonized to pass by such a wealth of ingredients. All of them were prepared, too, ready to sell. There had to be another storage location for ingredients that were raw and aging. No wonder Maman lived in such opulence. She had become a black-market queen.

A queen who knew her subjects too well. To Ada's chagrin, she had to admit that these preparations were decent, but not to her standards. Maman would have succeeded in tormenting Ada into compliance.

Clutching Grand-mère's hand, Ada crept across the shelf-lined room. As usual, Grand-mère readily remembered a skill from her youth; she moved with only a soft swish of fabric. They passed through a broad doorway to a separate chamber illuminated by several candles on a table: this was a kitchen, the hearth fire low as if to risk Hester's displeasure. Two deep-voiced figures sat hunched over the table.

"We'll need to call in all of our packers. There's no other way. This is our biggest order of the season, and the men can't tarry at the rendezvous."

"Understood." A pause. "How's he doing tonight?"

"Better." He yawned so widely his jaw popped. "This new ingredient seems to be helping." Ada and Grand-mère padded behind his chair.

"Thank the Five for that!"

"Yes," said the man, deep emotion in the single word.

Thank the Five indeed. Ada gestured to the Gods as they reached the doorway.

The next room held a crooked path through an area of staged crates and packing rags, the residual odor of epicurea heavy. The trail ended at a massive door latched from within.

They made it outside.

Ada paused long enough to take in a deep breath of night air as she glanced back.

The building from which they had emerged was a fine manor house worthy of the palace quartier. The bulk of the home loomed above, the kitchen and cellar belowground. Lights glowed from upstairs windows. People lived here—employees of Maman, she guessed.

The two continued onward through a potager, a kitchen garden, the rows tidy with early-spring growth. No one was about at this late hour.

A pedestrian gate to the street was locked. Using a skill from her army days, learned from her good friend Didina, Ada picked the mechanism. The second round of oatcakes was beginning to fade.

They continued down the block to an alley of vine-shrouded stone walls. There they found a nook of deeper shadow, a place for clandestine meetings. If there were better light, Ada knew she would see Gyst's X carved into the wall.

"How are you feeling? Not too cold?" Ada asked, patting Grand-mère's black cap.

"Ada, where are we going?" The fear in her small voice struck Ada like a blow.

"I'm going to sell that cheese; then we're going to a livery stable to get horses. We'll ride for Petry's."

"Ah, I haven't been on a horse in years." Grand-mère's hazel eyes lit up with childlike glee. "I'm a wonderful rider."

"Yes, you are." She began to tug Grand-mère away, but the old woman remained anchored.

"We need to thank Gyst right now."

Ada looked on her with exasperation. "He'll understand our need to hurry."

"He'll know our gratitude *now*." There'd be no arguing with her. "I'll go first."

Ada stepped about five feet away, keeping an eye on the street as Grand-mère thanked Gyst by whispering secrets for his ears alone. People connected with the Five through transactions, giving in order to receive. If the Five were scorned, their blessings could be withdrawn, but only to a point. Snub Gyst and one's bread might be reluctant to rise, but Gyst wouldn't stop it from rising entirely. Bread had risen before the Gods walked the land, after all. Gyst only made it rise better.

"Your turn," Grand-mère said, shuffling back. She was fully visible now—they both were. Ada took her place in the dank niche. The darkness seemed denser now, as if the God were casting his shadow over her.

"Gyst," she whispered. "Thank you for again using me to channel your greatness . . . and the greatness of cats." She smiled briefly as her tongue tingled with warmth, but then she grew somber. "Here is my great secret for you. I'm terrified, and I can't let Grand-mère know. What if I've erred? In my mother's home, she could have known warmth and more coherence through epicurea, but she would have been enslaved again. Comfortable slavery, perhaps, but slavery nonetheless." She blinked back tears. "You've endowed us with your blessings today. Please continue to do so, but I beg you, let me keep Grand-mère alive and safe. Let her know you through her tongue, not eye-to-eye. Not yet."

With that, she motioned an X and joined Grand-mère. Though they walked in the open, the particular dankness of the alcove lingered with Ada.

She couldn't repress a shiver.

CHAPTER SEVEN

SOLENN

Young tour Chefs often ask: Is there magic in the world yet to be found? I assure you, the answer is no, as we have explored the full bounty offered to us by the Five. Why, think on the uses for a common chicken. Breast meat for paillards; the legs, thighs, and wings stewed in red wine as coq au vin; the bones for soup; livers saved for terrine; the heart and other organs boiled in stock but then also saved for salads; the feet for gelatin; feathers, for pillows and mattresses. Our knowledge of magical flora and fauna is likewise comprehensive. Some creatures, such as unicorns and dragons, are imbued with magic throughout their bodies and can be used much as chickens are; others, such as gruff goats and Farrowby cows, are normal but for their milk. Stony owl stomachs are the only magical parts of their bodies, but oh, what a potent part that is.

—Excerpt from *Manual for Tour Chefs*

At her parents' estate, Solenn could drop by the kitchen any time of day to nick some fresh bread or a chunk of cheese, listening to the cooks gab as she petted the resident cats with her foot. As she entered the massive kitchen of the Lutecian palace, in contrast, the bustling workers immediately froze. Solenn inwardly sighed. Such formalities would never cease here, no matter how many years passed by.

"Princess Solenn, welcome," they said in an off-kilter chorus, bowing.

She acknowledged them with a smile and bow of her own, her hands clasped at the front of her woolen pantsuit. "Thank you for your welcome. Please, continue your labors. Whatever you're working on smells blessed by the Five." The day's bread baking was underway, the air redolent with a wonderful yeasty aroma, while several spits of still-raw beef were rotated by a little dog in a wheel set within a wall niche. She had heard of small dogs bred for this very purpose but had never seen one before.

She had never seen a kitchen so large, either, easily the size of her parents' great hall, though with a much lower ceiling. Some thirty cooks and scullions resumed their duties. To think, this was the slowest time of day for them, being midmorning. She could only imagine the frenzy later, when the platers and porters joined in on the work. She saw only the main kitchen, too, not the additional pastry and confectionary rooms, which were kept separate and much colder to preserve delicate works in progress.

"Princess Solenn." A breathless woman hustled over. She wore a white tabard over a uniform of dark blue and burgundy with gold braid. "I'm Chef-Lieutenant Pedroza, master cook on duty. I'm honored that you've taken the time to visit our lowly abode." She bowed.

"Rise, please. I hope my presence isn't too much of a distraction."

"How considerate of you, mademoiselle. We are busy here, but we always are. Just now, I was overseeing an inventory check on our wine cellar, as we anticipate going through some volume this next week. It's taking longer than anticipated, but it will be done today." She flushed, likely realizing too late that such excuses were beneath her visitor's concern.

"Yes, that's always how it goes, isn't it?" Solenn hoped her smile provided the Chef some ease. "I hope to gain more understanding of your kitchen operations. This is more complex than anything I knew in Braiz. How many Chefs are attached to the palace?"

"There are three of us, mademoiselle, two assigned each day." Chef Pedroza began a slow walk of the kitchen. Solenn, accompanied by Erwan and two additional musketeers, followed.

Several massive raised iron stoves of contemporary design lined the walls, but they hadn't replaced the traditional stone-set hearth that was being used as a soup station. That fire was where Hester would be sent her due as well.

"Forgive me if this is rude, but do you and your Chef peers have particular endowments from the Gods?" Solenn asked. She paused to admire a broad basket piled with fresh-baked bread rolls. Their glorious scent awakened her hunger. Her stomach had remained unsettled by the previous night's events, and she hadn't broken her fast yet.

When Erwan had asked her how she felt upon awakening, she hadn't even known how to answer him. Sick with terror? Angry? Betrayed? And yet, also determined. Today, she would do her utmost to uncover more information about the threat against Rupert. Ignorance was vulnerability. She must be armored, for his sake and her own.

"It is perfectly fine for you to ask about our blessings, Princess. Hester has granted me a higher tolerance for heat. I can reach into a fire to retrieve a fallen roll, for instance, but if I linger too long, my skin will blister and burn, same as anyone else. Chef-Lieutenant Raoul Amaza has been blessed by Lait. He oversees our cheese making, and I have never seen his equal in affinage." Solenn arched an eyebrow, impressed. Little as she knew of Chefs, she understood that aging cheese was considered a high art form. "He also oversees our pastries, as butter behaves for him even on our hottest days. Chef-Sous-Lieutenant Louella Robida is straightforwardly blessed by the Five." That meant she was a talented

Chef without a specialty. "Please, follow me this way." Overhead, drying herbs draped in fragrant bundles.

Maybe Solenn could learn more about her own newfound blessing while investigating the near poisoning. "Chef Amaza's skills as an affineur would arise from Lait but also Gyst, would they not?"

"No, no, put that over here, and add more salt—yes," the Chef hissed to a cook, then faced Solenn again. "I beg your pardon, mademoiselle. Yes, there's often overlap among the Gods and their roles. Gyst's touch is heavy when food and drink are aged, raised, or brewed. He understands and fosters these processes in ways we cannot fully perceive."

"I've heard that endowments from Gyst are the most rare." Out of the corner of her eye, Solenn saw one of her musketeers whispering to Erwan. The third idled some distance away, fascinatedly staring at a pile of onions as staff scurried around him.

"They are. 'His mysteries are myriad,' as the saying goes." Chef Pedroza frowned. "I hesitate to mention this, Princess, but I cannot ignore the matter either. Last night, there was a problem with the wineglasses brought to you and Prince Rupert—"

Solenn raised a hand. "Please. I was perhaps too . . . aggressive in my toast."

"For the glasses to break like that hints of some flaw, Princess Solenn. I am horrified that the glasses passed through so many hands and no one noticed. I want to assure you that we're inspecting all of our dishes in advance of tonight's dinner and the feasts of the forthcoming week."

"I trust in your judgment, Chef Pedroza." Behind her back, she pinched her fingers in thanks to Selland for the flow of their palaver. She knew Erwan had already made inquiries on this matter, but now she'd find the answers first. That pleased her. "You say the glasses passed through many hands. How many people were involved?"

The Chef's silvery brows pinched together. "The cups were fetched from storage and then cleaned and dried. Master cooks inspect all ware before it is used. Then came the sommeliers . . . we had five on staff last night, supervised by myself. When we use bottles rather than casks, we usually pour at the table, but I am embarrassed to admit this—"

"Please feel at liberty," Solenn said softly. The steps of Erwan and the other musketeers tapped the flagstones behind her. Her three guards were together again.

"We unsealed a special wine for this occasion, Princess, one made in the prince's birth year. One of a set reserved for this occasion. The others weren't of quality . . . Gyst and glass are finicky alone, even more finicky together. This bottle, being the last, unfortunately had a cork fragment."

"Ah, the wine then had to be strained."

"I'm relieved you know of the practice, Princess." Really, she sounded scared, and with good reason. Solenn dreaded to think of how King Caristo would react to anything less than perfection. "We could have poured the wine back into the bottle after filtering it, but you had already been seated for several minutes. In the interest of time, we . . . I judged it best to present it as we did."

Several cooks bustled by with a laden tureen. "I respect that you take responsibility," said Solenn. "It's a shame that we weren't able to drink it."

"Indeed. Sometimes I wish I could empathetically taste as some Chefs do."

Solenn picked up on the hint. "Have you known Chefs touched in this way?" Could any of them taste death as Solenn had?

"Oh yes. Chefs so blessed are committed to either the army or the palace, but at this time we have none within the Guild." Solenn couldn't contain her gasp of surprise. Pedroza continued: "Empathetic Chefs are the rarest of the rare. When I first came here, my superior was an empathetic Chef named Eglantine Garland. Never was there a Chef more kind and patient with a student fresh from her tour days." Chef Pedroza smiled warmly at the memory. "Her sugar-work remains legendary."

Garland? Solenn tried not to visibly perk up in recognition of her birth mother's surname, but she must not have done an adequate job, as Erwan provided a subtle touch to her back that Solenn took as a warning. "What has become of her now?" She retained a tone of idle curiosity, but she was unnerved. She had no idea empathetic abilities were *that* rare.

"She has since gone to the wind." The polite way to reference a Chef gone rogue.

"Oh, I see." How long ago had that happened? she wondered. Had Eglantine and Adamantine deserted together? Solenn was relieved when a nervous cook approached and drew Pedroza's attention.

"Pardon me, Chef. The calf's head, we are unsure . . ."

Chef Pedroza sucked in a sharp breath. "I'm sorry, Princess. If I may have a minute . . . ?"

Solenn smiled and gestured her to attend the necessary work. Chef Pedroza bustled off. Solenn turned to Erwan.

"Did you know there were so few empathetic Chefs in Verdania?" She spoke Braizian in a low whisper.

He replied in kind. "No. There were a few dozen during the war. Some died in combat. Others were older and would've met a natural end by now. I wouldn't be surprised if a couple more had also 'gone to the wind.'"

"No one else could have perceived the contamination of the wine, not even Chef Pedroza," she said close to his ear. "Now tell me, did our ploy work?"

"Yes. We are looking for suspects, but there are many here who do indeed regard *you* with suspicion and contempt."

Her two other musketeers had been advised to act ignorant of the Verdanian language as they walked the kitchen, playing the part of dull-witted Braizians. The hope was that this would encourage the staff to freely gossip and gripe, highlighting those with the motivation and access to poison Prince Rupert's wine.

"What did they say?" She braced herself for the unpleasantness.

Erwan's expression stayed stoic. "'We must wash whatever she touches in here.' 'She'll kill the dauphin within five years, mark my word.' 'What horrid things must we cook for her soon? I hear they eat raw meat in Braiz because they don't know how to properly heat it.' That's a sampling. More were committed to our memory."

He would tell her the worst comments later. Solenn had actually requested that of him; she didn't want her anger to leak through when so many people watched their every move. "You've marked who spoke?"

"Of course. We'll investigate further and involve the Chef-Lieutenant when we have evidence to act upon."

Solenn had thought that she would feel at ease when her musketeers uncovered suspects. Instead, she felt all the more anxious. "How soon until—" She couldn't finish the sentence as Chef Pedroza returned.

"There! I am sorry for the interruption, mademoiselle."

"That's fine, Chef," Solenn said, switching her speech back to Verdanian. Her mind raced. She had to find out more information. Her life depended on it. "I'm curious about your use of epicurea. I've heard that everything harvested in Verdania is first offered to the palace. Is that true?"

"Yes. Due to the size of our country and our array of climates, we have at our disposal the best larder in the world." Chef Pedroza said this with pride. "Would you like to see?"

"Please, Chef." Solenn inwardly bounced in profound relief but was somewhat annoyed when Erwan again gave her a cautionary tap. She was doing a fine job. She didn't need his warning.

Chef Pedroza guided them through a far doorway. "We store most of our epicurea locked within ready access of the kitchen. The cellar hosts another vault. Among many other delights, we have brandy aged in awake oak barrels, Princess. We are using it for ortolan for your wedding feast."

Solenn kept a carefully neutral expression. Mundane ortolan wasn't even served in Braiz because her bird-loving grandmother abhorred the whole process: cheery songbirds were blinded, force-fed to plumpness, drowned in brandy, and served whole to diners. Everything was eaten except for the beaks. The magicked barrels used to marinate the birds would imbue diners with boosted vitality and physical regeneration. Solenn would need to delicately get this dish off the menu.

Chef Pedroza continued, "We receive seasonal milk from kept herds of gruffs and wildling sheep. Chef Raoul uses that for cheese. He sometimes applies blessed alcohol to mundane cheeses as well. We're aging cheeses rubbed in unicorn tisane for when the royal family becomes ill or is otherwise in need of balms." She cast Solenn a sidelong glance. "The result has stronger curative powers than the typical tea, though of course, we have that too."

Such a polite way to imply that at some point, Solenn would be pregnant and in need of comfort. She swallowed dryly. She dreaded to think of how the pressure to produce an heir would increase in the coming years, though she understood the importance, especially after last night. If that poisoner had succeeded, the dauphin's death would mean civil war as his relations squabbled for the throne.

They passed through a long corridor flanked by high cabinets, each door and drawer labeled in calligraphy. "Is all palace epicurea reserved for the royal family?" Solenn asked.

"Oh yes, and anyone else so directed to receive it." Chef Pedroza pulled up on a chain at her neck to reveal a large skeleton key. "I—and my comrades—would be happy to serve you whatever you desire and boost its inherent effects."

As the Chef opened the passageway, Solenn caught a heady whiff of warm spices. Was that unicorn tisane? She knew the smell well, that blend of clover, marigold, rose petals, lavender, chervil, and whatever other edible flora grew in a meadow planted over unicorn bones. She drank the brewed tisane whenever her monthly grieved her. The dried herbs seemed terribly strong, and—did she smell roses too? It was as if Marquis Dubray loomed over her again, as if—

"Focus, Solenn," Erwan hissed.

She blinked, comprehending more of the here and now. Her legs had gone slack. Erwan held her upright, a discreet hand at her waist. The other musketeers had drawn protectively close.

". . . sixty epicurea in our current catalog, and . . ." Chef Pedroza stood within the larder, head tilted back to take in the tiers of shelves that surrounded her like a horseshoe. She didn't seem to have noticed that Solenn had swooned.

Solenn pushed herself off Erwan and did as he advised. Even as she concentrated on the present, she perceived the epicurea like an illustrated tome with fast-fluttering pages. The ingredients she knew from experience leaped out at her, evoking visceral flashes from memory. But for far more items she could only guess at their sources and the powers they could grant. They were scripts she couldn't read, smells she couldn't identify or describe. If the poison used in the wine was present, she couldn't isolate it amid the chaos.

Chef Pedroza stopped talking. Solenn, blinking, realized she must have been asked a question, but she hadn't a clue what it might have been.

Erwan, however, was looking out for her. "Chef, dare I ask, what epicurea is the most popular?"

Chef Pedroza laughed. "Captain, you would get me in trouble."

"I've heard rose fairies are popular at court," Solenn suggested. "But I'm not even sure how they are used." Mamm-gozh tried to hide that she used the fairies at all.

"I can answer that." Chef Pedroza hoisted a clear glass jar from the shelf. A nauseatingly strong waft of roses threatened to suffocate Solenn, and the sudden roil of her gut wasn't helped by what she saw in the jar: humanlike bodies the size of her fingers, aswim in yellow brine. "More often than not, rose fairies are pickled. Unlike most of the epicurea here, these are ready to eat now without adverse effects, though they taste best accompanied by cheese, sausage, and bread."

"They are pickled . . . whole? Like how ortolan are immersed in brandy?" As a credit to her training, none of her inner horror seeped into her voice. How could her grandmother rail against the murder of ortolan yet eat things like *this*?

"Yes. They are like an especially crunchy cucumber. As young and pretty as you are, Princess, you have no immediate need of their enchantment to enhance your appearance, but if you ever wish to eat one, we'd be happy to oblige you."

Chef Pedroza held the glass upward. The naked fairies bobbed in their broth, obviously dead, their faces strangely passive with shut eyes and mouths, the bright colors of their butterfly wings muted.

Solenn's empty gut threatened to find matter to eject. "I appreciate the offer, though I won't take advantage at this time," she managed.

Erwan cleared his throat. "I regret to say that the princess has an appointment on the hour. We must make our farewells."

"Thank you for your time, Chef." Solenn added, relieved as the jar was set out of sight. She and her musketeers backed up to give the Chef space to secure the larder. "Before we go I must ask, does the sight of the fairies . . . disturb anyone? They do look vaguely human."

"Certainly, their appearance does bother some people, but there are those who refuse to eat beef or birds as well. I prepare the fairies as a pâté sometimes to make them more palatable." Chef Pedroza shrugged. "Personally, I find nothing about these creatures to be the slightest bit human. They have eyes and a nose and mouth, yes, but so do cows, sheep, and goats. These fairies fly around flowers with all the vacant awareness of bugs. They can't *think*. But even more, through the perceptions given to us by the Five, we know that rose fairies are food and there for us to eat. Who are we to deny the judgment of the Gods?"

Who, indeed? Her stomach still roiling, Solenn didn't feel particularly blessed at the moment. Chef Pedroza set off for the kitchen with the fast clip of a person with many things to do and little time to do them.

Erwan leaned close to Solenn. "Are you better now?"

"Yes, much, now that the door is closed."

"The epicurea overwhelmed you." His features darkened. "I've seen the like before."

Adamantine must have dealt with similar situations, but Verdania's Guild also trained their Chefs to handle such circumstances. Solenn needed to be careful if she was going to successfully hide Gyst's touch upon her.

"Erwan," she whispered, "you came to the palace during the alliance, didn't you? Do you know of the Eglantine Garland that Chef Pedroza spoke of?" They neared the kitchen, their opportunity to talk dwindling.

"Yes." His face softened in a smile. "I met her on several occasions. I'll tell you all that I know of her once we reach your apartment." The bustle of the kitchen surrounded them again.

"Thank you," Solenn whispered, voice hoarse with yearning. This woman must be an aunt, a grandmother, someone in close relation to her, someone who was likewise touched by Gyst. Solenn didn't even know whether this Eglantine was still alive, but she nevertheless experienced a small sense of relief. Her birth mother was out there somewhere, as was this other relative. She was a little less alone.

CHAPTER EIGHT

ADA

*Choucroute is a simple food that keeps well, thanks to
the grace of Selland and Gyst. Thinly sliced cabbage
is stored in barrels that once held white wine, then
is layered there with copious amounts of coarse salt,
juniper berries, and peppercorns, where it ferments.
Such cabbage is a delicious bed for salted fish as well
as sausages and many cuts of pork.*

—Excerpt from *Book for Cooks to Excel as Do Chefs*

The sun shone bright and cheery over the green, rolling hills north of
Lutecia. Birds flirted amid the grasses and trees. It was the kind of day
that could convince a person that spring truly approached and that this
year was one full of hope.

A shame that people were trying to kill Ada and now the wilderness
might do the job for them.

In the late afternoon, they reached the vaguely familiar road toward
the hermitage. Grand-mère awoke from a doze and took in their new
surroundings with a spinal stretch that included an audible pop.

"Those are fairly fresh hoofprints," she said, pointing to the mud at Ada's feet.

"Yes. Looks like two horses, perhaps a day old. They rode toward Petry's and back."

"Does he get guests often?"

"Yes." Something rustled in the brush to their right. Ada motioned for quiet, suddenly glad that she hadn't reminded her grandmother about the rogue Chefs they had sent to Petry. "Someone's watching us. I can feel it."

Forest lay as thick around them as wool packed into bags. It'd be hard to see a deer in this brush, much less a person waiting in ambush. Lingering here wouldn't make them less vulnerable, though.

"Let's hurry on to the hermitage." She walked fast, leading the horse. Grand-mère sat wary, watching, ready to duck low.

The trail opened up to reveal vine- and moss-draped worn stone walls. Only the Gods knew the age of this place. The main structure of the kitchen-temple, with some walls still twenty feet in height, had the adjoined pentagonal layout of a pentad with several crumbled out-buildings around it.

Ada brought the horses within the old central nave. Hooves clopped against the moss-furred stone floor.

Grand-mère dismounted with a small moan. "Now what?"

"If we were going to get shot, it should have happened by now." Ada looked around.

"Tsk. We are *always* good targets for gunfire," said Grand-mère in a chipper tone.

"Petry!" Ada called out. Birds fluttered from the greenery-adorned walls. Again, she heard rustling nearby.

"What if he's not here?" Grand-mère's voice was small.

"Then we'll stay the night and go someplace else."

"Where?" Her insistent tone reminded Ada of a small child's.

"I don't know yet," Ada said in exasperation. "Petry!" she yelled again.

"Yes?" His head poked out from the end of a wall.

Ada clutched a fist to her chest. "Ah! Don't do that!" Grand-mère, surprisingly undaunted, cackled.

Petry doffed his hat to Grand-mère as he walked over. "Madame Eglantine Garland. Good to see you."

"What is his name again?" Grand-mère asked in a stage whisper. Petry's eyes widened; Ada cringed. She'd written to Petry of Grand-mère's mental decline, but witnessing it was something more.

"This is Petry, Grand-mère. You met him a few times at the palace, and you've exchanged letters over the years, remember?"

"Oh, of course," she said, nodding.

"Something bad has happened?" Petry asked; then he whistled long and low. Two dogs bounded over, both shaggy, one of chestnut coat and the other with black and white spots. They circled Ada and Grand-mère, sniffing, but seeing these strangers had their master's approval, they ran off again. "They watch the road and let me know if anyone approaches," he added.

"What makes you so certain we're not here for a social call?" Ada clapped him on the shoulder. He had become more ursine since she had last seen him some dozen years ago. White hairs frizzled through the brown of his beard, his pate now as smooth as a baby's bum.

"Do you now send advance parties?"

That sent cold dread through her anew. "We saw day-old tracks on the road."

"Two horsemen came yesterday, armed with muskets and pistols. They were irate when they couldn't find me, though they didn't look that carefully. They never found my cottage. Luts, eh?" He shook his head in disgust of Lutecian city folk. "As they left, they grumbled that they needed to grab me within the week."

"Grab you?" Ada echoed.

"Apparently, they intend to kidnap me within the next four days, not kill me. At least, not immediately." His grin was grim.

"Hester's fire. We had similar visitors, with similar designs on me. One of them barged into our flat, asking for me by the name Corre. He was about to kill Grand-mère, but she got him first. He had a pouch with rupic residue on his person." She raised a hand to silence Petry's exclamation. "His comrade confronted me in the street. The drunken fool had ingested stony owl and was set to meet Gyst, but I sped along the encounter."

Petry's thick brow furrowed. "Not normal brigands."

"No. Here I had thought I was special, but you seem to be as blessed." That meant the other living officers from the Thirty-Fifth were under threat too. Didina. Emone. Erwan. Another dozen were already dead. "Can we get Grand-mère settled before we talk more?"

"Of course, of course!" Petry flushed, flustered. "Sorry! Follow me." Ada brought the horse. Grand-mère stayed on foot, her strides pained.

"Tell me about this place!" Grand-mère asked brightly. "Have you been here long?"

Petry told her of his years there, Grand-mère his eager listener. After a few minutes, his cottage came into view. Built from stones scavenged from the pentad, it was roofed by heavy thatch. No smoke rose from the chimney.

Ada situated Grand-mère onto Petry's cot for much-needed sleep, then went outside. Petry listened as Ada detailed select events from the past day as she untacked the horse.

"There are only two reasons people would come after the two of us—either it's because of our efforts to funnel rogue Chefs away, or because of our time in the Thirty-Fifth. Right?" asked Petry.

"If it was because of the rogues, we'd have the might of Verdania's prosecutors upon us, not the dregs of a quayside tavern."

"That's a good description of the two louts I saw as well. But why now, all these years later? And how did your two callers get rupic and stony owl? Those ingredients make me think of—"

"Mallory Valmont." They shared a somber look as they stepped outside the corral.

Petry closed the gate behind them. "Valmont *must* be with Gyst by now. No one survives Mont Annod for a year, much less seventeen."

"Most people don't survive the sheer amounts of rupic he ingested either. He ate entire people, Petry, spoonful by spoonful, battle after battle. In the other cases I witnessed in my younger years, people became so addicted within days that they soon descended into mania and suicide when they couldn't continue their regular indulgence."

"Mallory was always regimented and efficient. The best supply officer I knew."

"He was intelligent, helpful, even kind . . . if you stayed in his good graces," Ada said.

Petry gave her a level look. "You would be his foremost target if he survived. He was angry with the rest of us when he was arrested, but he maintained a special . . . respect for you, and felt all the more betrayed."

"By 'a special respect,' you mean that he was obsessed with gaining my approval, like an overeager schoolchild fawning over a favorite teacher."

"Not that it makes it less perturbing, but he treated all Chefs in such a way. I saw his clinging, cloying fascination play out more than once. We trained as officers together, remember? Our superiors had to order him to leave the other Chefs in our class alone."

"Any other officer would've lost their commission at that early juncture. Sometimes it's nice to be a distant cousin of the king." Ada grimaced. "But then, that's why he was given a sentence at Mont Annod."

"Execution would've been kinder than that place," Petry murmured. "Worse to torment a person with vain hope."

Ada paced along a stacked-stone wall. "But he still doesn't fit into our current dilemma. Stony owl is practically extinct. Rupic powder is even rarer because even *if* you acquire stony owl, sneaking it into someone's food is no easy task. The Mallory Valmont we knew would not share such resources."

"We were officers over thousands of unwilling conscripts who could want revenge for one thing or another. Someone from Albion could even hold a grudge, eh?"

"Or Braiz," she added absently.

"Or Braiz." His heavy body deflated in a sigh. "If someone's after us, Erwan's at risk, too, you know?"

"He should be safer in Braiz. He must still be near Morvan, likely with a cadre of musketeers around him." She tried not to show how speaking of Erwan pained her, but by the sympathetic look Petry gave her, she had failed.

"Ada. I've exchanged letters with Erwan," Petry said softly. She froze. "A few a year, enough to keep up with him."

"How's he doing? Has he mentioned—"

"Your daughter loves horses and spends all her days riding wild through the countryside. He's only referenced her in the vaguest ways, but I know who he's talking about."

Ada pressed a fist to her lips.

Her daughter *lived*.

She loved horses.

Petry continued, "Erwan always, always ends his epistles with a note that if I were ever to see you, that I should extend to you his fond regard."

"You've never told him how we've—"

"Of course I've never mentioned what we're doing for rogues. No one with sense would commit those words to paper, right?" Petry sounded offended at the suggestion. "He does know we write sporadically. No more than that."

"That's good." She nodded, facing away. "That's good."

She had been tempted to write Erwan more than once, but what she wanted most was his reply, and that would make it too easy for investigators to track her whereabouts. She knew for a fact that the Guild monitored the post and had snared other Chefs that way.

Ada couldn't help but smile, though. Her daughter loved horses. Erwan still asked after her.

"Show me your garden," she said. "You know I need to cook for you tonight."

"Oh, Five grant us enough respite so that you can make supper." He motioned to the Gods. "No Chefs are your equal."

"Flatterer." They walked to the far side of the house. She checked on his nascent garden as he listed his available stores of aged cheese, preserves, and salt-packed meats, most of which had been prepared by previous rogues. That pleased her, as if she had found means to take care of him from afar. At the same time, she was left saddened.

"This place is so homey," she said with a wistful sigh.

"Why are you sounding guilty? *You* didn't bring this threat."

"Maybe I did, maybe I didn't. We don't know enough yet."

"Ah. I know that tone."

"I need to find out who's behind this plot, Petry. It's bad enough that men came after me and almost killed my grandmother, but the rest of you . . . I need to go back to the city, and yet—"

"You're worried about your grandmother. Stop. I'll take care of her."

"That's asking a lot, she's—"

He held up a hand. "I've been thinking about this. I'll go to Rance with Madame Eglantine. I have a trusted friend there who I can let rooms from. I'll stay with your grandmother however long is necessary. It'll be easier to safeguard her there. Here, with the woods, even with the dogs to help, I worry that she might wander off and be difficult to find."

Ada shifted in place, ill at ease. "She needs routine, her mind—"

"Ada." His tone was gentle, chiding. "My father was much the same at the end, remember?"

Ada nodded. She hadn't thought of that in years. Petry's father had sustained a crushing head injury when he was thrown from a horse, yet he'd lived for a year after that, his coherence shifting more often than the wind.

"I appreciate this, more than you'll ever know." Her voice was gravelly with emotion.

"Cook me a fine meal and we'll call it even, eh? Oh, I have a fine barrel of choucroute! Traded goods with a neighbor for it last fall, and I've enjoyed it all winter. It'd be a shame to not partake from it one more time," Petry said, tone light. "We can depart tomorrow, us for Rance, you for Lutecia."

"Where can I find you in Rance?"

"Through Luida's Hotel. Write or ask after me there. You would be welcome to join us too. You could hide from these would-be killers. Maybe you'd even decide to stay on in Rance." He laughed as she made a face.

"Their sparkling wine is fine and their cheeses exquisite, but I never felt at home in my past visits there." She shrugged. Grand-mère's soft snores carried through the open-shuttered window. "I could stay for a few weeks, maybe, but not for the long term. If you weren't going to take care of Grand-mère, would you come back to Lutecia with me? Work with me to hunt down whoever is behind this?"

"No. I'm tired, Ada." At that instant, he suddenly looked more haggard. "My gout is worse. My back and knee"—he patted his left side—"are wretched, especially in the cold. I need to stay put as much as possible. You're incapable of that."

"I need to warn Emone and Didina, if I'm not too late." Her voice cracked.

"By Hester's hearthstones, Ada, you had no idea that someone was targeting all of us. You can't expect to know all unknowns, even as a Chef."

She conceded his point with a small grunt. "As if being a Chef is packed with blessings galore. Sometimes I've wondered if it would be best if the prosecutors *did* remove my tongue, but then I think, What would I be if I wasn't a Chef? It's been hard to hide my outward skills all these years, but I've never lost that truth within myself."

Tears softened his eyes. "You never had a chance to be anything else, did you? You were like a melon, grown and shaped in a wooden box, designed to be easily stacked for market day. You know no other shape."

Ada burst out laughing, her bleak mood shattered. "That's not a simile I would have considered, but it's apt. Thank you for that, Petry. I should start cooking now. I need to do *something*, or I'll only stare at the road and wait for the attack. I'm joining you in prayer that we get a night of respite. Grand-mère needs some peace."

"So do you." Petry clapped her shoulder.

Ada nodded absently. She knew better than to ask for such a thing for herself. She hadn't known full peace in nearly two decades, and she wasn't about to expect it now.

CHAPTER NINE

ADA

The shelf must be cool and dark, the air moist. The cheese must have space around it and be turned once each day upon its mat. If the conditions are right, Gyst's presence will soon be known. A smell of yeast and fruit should be present within three to four days. Then, over the next five, the surface of the cheese will dry and be kissed by white mold. If it grows especially thick, turn the cheese twice or thrice daily. Show thanks to Gyst by whispering to him your choicest secrets.

—Excerpt from a recipe for abree cheese

The quiet night that followed was not a restful one, not for Ada. Unaccustomed as she was to the sounds of the wilderness and wary of an attack, every creak and chirp caused her to bolt up from her blanket on the floor. Petry's gargling snores didn't help, but she couldn't resent him for the nocturnal orchestra. The most important thing was that Grand-mère was continuing to sleep as she contributed flutelike snores of her own.

Breakfast consisted of cheese and gooseberry preserves. Grand-mère was picking at her last morsels when Ada heard fast footsteps and heavy breaths. The happy jostling of the dogs outside informed her that this was Petry, returning from his patrol along the road. She met him at the doorway.

"Those same men are back." He leaned on his thighs and gasped for air. The dogs whirled behind him, feeding off his anxiety. "Recognized the red feather in a hat."

The timeline for farewells changed as a new plan took form. "I'll talk to them. You both need to go."

"Talk?" echoed Petry.

Ada pulled on her pack, lighter now without Grand-mère's gear, then reached for the additional accessories that Petry had gifted her with the previous night: a turn-off pistol and kit. The pistol fit in her coat pocket, the powder horn and bullet bag strapping crosswise to rest beneath her breasts.

"Talk," she repeated, patting the powder horn.

"Ah, *talk*." Petry's smile was tight beneath the broad brim of his leather hat. "Madame Eglantine? We need to—"

"I'm still eating." Her mouth was full of cheese.

"Grand-mère, I'm sorry, but you need to go with Petry now." Ada did her utmost to keep her voice level and patient, even as she wanted to scream at her grandmother to hurry.

Grand-mère looked at Petry, her eyes widening with fear. "But I don't know him! I'm not going with him! I want to finish this good cheese," she added, taking another bite.

Ada muffled a moan against her hand. Normally Grand-mère was coherent at this time of day, but their recent travails must have increased her instability. "You'll get to ride a horse again," she said encouragingly. Behind her, Petry bustled to get his gear on.

"I rode a horse yesterday." She had remembered that much, all the good it did.

"Madame Eglantine." Petry loomed over her. "We're going to go to Rance together. My friend there makes a lovely sparkling wine. Would you like to try it?"

A sudden brightness lit Grand-mère's eyes. "Is it especially sweet?" Ada shot a glance out the open door. This was taking too long, and they had to go! She didn't want to haul Grand-mère out screaming and flailing. Not only would that alert the encroachers, but it wasn't how she wanted to say farewell.

"Their newest was described as being sweeter than a hive of honey," Petry said, smiling as Grand-mère stood. He handed her the canteen on a strap, which she automatically pulled over her head.

"That's how I like it," Grand-mère said. "I know sweetness like few people do." This, spoken with considerable pride.

Petry hooked her arm as if they were about to go strolling down a promenade. "So I've heard." Out the door they went.

Ada released a long exhalation. Thank the Five for Petry's gentle ways. She looked around, making sure she had everything. A length of rope on the wall caught her eye. That just might come in useful in her forthcoming conversation. She looped it over her shoulder.

Grand-mère had saddled up. Petry was guiding her mount from the corral, the dogs quiet yet excited underfoot. The horse, fortunately, was unbothered.

"Ada, I'm going to Rance!" Grand-mère declared.

"You'll have to tell me what you think of the wines." Ada managed a tepid smile. She wanted to grasp her grandmother in a big hug but dared not. She couldn't risk getting her upset again. "Petry . . ."

"I'll take care of her. Go. You take care of yourself." His gaze was tender and understanding as he jerked his head, motioning her away.

Ada made her legs keep moving on the path toward the old pentad.

At the top of the slope, the highest walls of the ruins visible through the trees, Ada turned around. She had a final sight of Grand-mère in the saddle, and then the greenery and shadows stole her from view.

Ada faced forward, a grim set to her mouth.

She took a narrow track parallel to the road. The rattling of her pack prevented her from moving too fast with any subterfuge. When the faint sounds of horses met her ears, she crouched.

She pulled the pistol from her pocket and unscrewed the cannon-shaped barrel from the chamber. Ada favored turn-off pistols, named for the manner in which the barrel twisted on and off. Such pistols were small, handy, and fairly reliable, and oftentimes pretty as well. This one had an engraved barrel.

With frequent glances at the road, she loaded black powder into the breech left by the missing barrel, then set a bullet ball on top. Two riders became visible through the brambles—a man with a broad tan hat capped by a red feather and a man in a smaller black hat. Both looked a bit younger than her, their clothes grubby, horses shaggy from winter. She hastened to screw the barrel back into place.

"Who lives out here, anyway? How's a person even get a drink?"

"From a cask, same's anywhere," said Red Feather.

"I'd be needing a lot of casks, then." The duo spoke with an accent associated with Lutecian quays. Despite their subject matter, both sounded sober.

"We'll buy plenty when we get this job done." The riders drew parallel to her, their horses at a casual walk. Ada crept to keep up with them.

"What if we can't find 'im again?" asked Black Hat.

"Then we gotta return the advance and the food, and we'll be out the coin for these livery horses."

Food? That had to mean something prepared with epicurea. She needed to get closer.

"Return the advance?" Black Hat's voice rose high in incredulity. His comrade shushed him. He added quietly, "Better to avoid that tavern, get our drinks elsewhere."

Ada aimed her pistol. Both men were some ten feet away.

"No." Red Feather reined up. "These people'd find us. They got money and resources."

And Ada had questions that needed answers.

She fired.

The flintlock flashed, bullet exploding outward. The shot impacted in Red Feather's right shoulder with a spray of crimson. Both horses reared. Red Feather slumped to one side, his horse spinning. Ada worked at her own spinning, twisting off the warm barrel to reload.

"Dodo! Dodo!" Black Hat cried, pulling a pistol from his pocket. He brought his horse in a circle, gaze flitting to the bushes all around. He fumbled for his powder horn but kept missing it in his terror.

Ada grinned. His gun wasn't loaded. Hers was.

Dodo slid off his horse to land in the trail with an agonized moan. His horse, the whites of its eyes showing, partially reared, then bounded off the trail on the far side, vanishing with a crackle of branches.

"Dominique—Dodo!" Black Hat wailed again, distraught enough to use his companion's full name as he looked between his gun and the ground.

Ada fired again. The bullet grazed the flank of Black Hat's horse. With a scream, the horse bolted back up the trail whence they'd come, Black Hat clinging on for dear life. He held on to everything but his pistol. That struck the ground feet away from Dodo.

Ada cursed beneath her breath as she shoved her way through the bushes that acted as a living wall between the parallel paths. She hated striking horses by accident. With a gesture to the Five, she hoped that the creature wouldn't come to further harm in its pained frenzy.

Dodo lay facedown on the moist dirt, moaning. Ada first went to the dropped pistol. At a glance, it looked as grimy as its owner. She pocketed it as she approached Dodo. She perceived the epicurea on his person and fought a rise of nausea.

Without gentleness, she used his good shoulder to roll him faceup. He blinked dust from his eyes. "Who're you?"

"A madame with some inquiries, Dodo, and you'd do best to oblige me."

She liberated him of the pistol at his waist as well as his powder horn and bullets. His knife joined other acquisitions in her pack.

Those urgent needs addressed, she then pulled out what she'd sensed as she approached: a small lamb pie, mixed with stony owl stomach. The pie's crust was flaky and buttery, the mixture of herbs sublime, and the magical potency of the pocket-size meal adequate to transition an adult into stone within the course of five hours.

The fact that she and Petry had been the intended victims of kidnapping, not murder, now held a dreadful intended fate.

"What's this? Lunch?" she asked.

"You can't have that." He looked paler now, and not from blood loss. "That's an important thing, it is."

"Who's supposed to eat it?" she asked.

He made a slow swipe at her arm. With a sigh, she lodged her boot in his kidney. She pocketed the pie. Moving fast, she cut a length of rope and bound his hands over his head. One of his own handkerchiefs muffled his screams as she dragged him off the path.

After a minute, she found a good, stout tree not too surrounded by undergrowth. She kept him gagged as she used the rest of the rope to secure him against the trunk.

"I'm going to pull out the cloth so we can chat. Don't try to scream for your friend or you'll know regret."

Of course, the idiot began to bellow the instant she pulled out the gag. She kicked him again.

She stood back, impatient, as he almost retched from pain. "Let's begin again. Keep your voice at a moderate level. Who was supposed to eat the pie?"

He glared at her through a mop of hair. "Petry Montrell. But not yet."

"What were you supposed to do? Answer me." Her voice was as sharp as any knife, and he flinched as if she'd drawn more blood.

"Drag him back to Lutecia. Once we're there, we force him to eat, and then guard him till the boss comes."

Curious that the boss didn't want to attend the dirty work. "You know what that pie could do, then?" His bowed head and silence answered that. "Who's your boss?"

"Don't know his name." He sat, knees loosely curled to one side. "You letting me bleed to death?"

"You're not going to *bleed* to death from that." Ada waved in dismissal. "Infection is what's more likely to kill you. Take up your concern with Gyst. Where were you supposed to take Petry Montrell?"

"Why would I tell you that when you're leaving me to die?" he retorted.

Ada wasn't keen on torture. She understood well the unreliable answers it could produce, but she was also impatient and irate. She stepped on one of his feet, forcing it downward at an unnatural angle. With an intent not to break, but to hurt. By his agonized gasp, she'd succeeded.

"Again. Your boss, monsieur."

He hesitated, not from petulance this time but to gather his wits. "Same place where we got the job. Hester's Grace Inn, on the south quay by Old Bridge."

Ada released the pressure on his foot. She knew that area of Lutecia well enough to avoid it. It held too many people, and their morals were looser than bowels after food poisoning. "Describe this nameless boss of yours."

He sneered. "Or what, you—"

This time, she kicked him behind his right knee.

Ada was not feeling kindly toward the man involved in the plot to have her and her dearest old friends *eaten*. That could be the only intent—to curse them into statues, then grind them down for consumption.

This plan couldn't involve Mallory Valmont, but it must be *about* him. This was an effort at revenge delivered at the point when he should have been freed, but who was behind it all? Mallory had family. He also had scads of admirers; the man was adored for his feats, and not everyone was disillusioned by the revelation that he was a murderer. During his trial, the Guild's prosecutors had been quite busy arresting people who were peddling both real and fake stony owl, as Mallory's sordid use of the ingredient had made its popularity boom in the black market.

Which made her again ponder the two fools who had come after her.

Stony owl stomach was potent enough that it didn't require a Chef to activate the magic. Whoever was behind this plot had the epicurea and had provided it to the contract killers. Ada's two goons had become drunk and sampled both the stony owl and the rupic. If Dodo and his companion had also been provided with some rupic powder, it had long since worked out of their systems. They had also taken the time to have the owl ingredient cooked into a hand pie, an incredible show of competence that, unfortunately for them, hadn't carried into their other actions.

"Come on now," she said in exasperation as Dodo moaned. "I have much better things to do today. More detail about who hired you and the circumstances, monsieur."

"No. You can't make me." His jaw had a stubborn set.

Ada sighed and pulled out the pie. His pasty skin took on the color of fresh snow.

"I'm sure you're hungry." She rotated the pie on her fingertips. It looked disturbingly delicious, even as she perceived its terrible potential. "As your hands are bound, I could help you eat. It would be the kind thing to do."

"A man hired me. Wealthy, he was," he blurted out. "He had two blokes with him. Big 'uns. Otherwise, that man would've been bait the second he entered the quartier. The three of them, they were hiring a bunch of us. I said I'd take Petry Montrell. All the other jobs're in Lutecia."

She leaned closer, waggling the pie in front of his face. "Describe them." She needed confirmation.

"What, you expect me to remember . . ." His whining died as she bonked his nose with the pie. Crumbs fell on his shirt. He wiggled against his bindings as if ants had dropped on him. "There was Montrell, Rochamp, uh, Jourdain." Didina Rochamp. Emone Jourdain. By the Five, Ada prayed they were still alive. "Oh, a man and a woman named Corre. That's it." He looked between her and the pie, tears streaming down his cheeks. "Please don't make me eat it."

She ignored his concern as she asked the first question that came to mind. "Why didn't you choose the man named Corre?"

"Boss already knew he'd be a harder target. He's a chevalier from Braiz, in the palace with that newcome princess. I didn't want to wait around for him to poke his head out."

Erwan, guarding Morvan's daughter instead of their own? Ada felt a flare of anger, followed by despair. He had promised to stay with their child . . . Had something happened to her since he'd last written Petry?

No, no. Her daughter could be a lady-in-waiting to the princess. They had probably grown up together, much as Erwan and Morvan had. The logic of that thought comforted her.

She needed to get back to Lutecia.

She stuffed the handkerchief in Dodo's mouth again. "I'm not wasting any more time with you. You had best pray you're found soon." She dropped the pie to the ground and mashed it under her heel, grinding the food into the hard mud until her tongue no longer recognized it as food. He sagged against his bindings as he sobbed in relief.

Ada left. On foot, it'd take her three days to reach Lutecia, but the trade highway wasn't far and relay stations were spaced out along its length. With a few hours' labor, she might earn a handhold on a wagon going toward the city. If the Gods favored her, she could make it there by late tonight.

She gestured her five fingers in appeal. The thought of Emone, Didina, and Erwan enduring such terrible deaths left her ill with horror. She had perceived how such a thing would feel, if only for mere seconds. The reality meant hours of agony, to become an obscene harvest. No one deserved such a fate, no one.

Emone would be the easiest to find, but therefore easiest for the brigands to track down as well. Ada would go to her first. If Emone was well—Gods help them all!—she would know where Didina now lived, and maybe how one might access Erwan.

Erwan, in Lutecia. What would it be like to see him again, after so long? How had he aged? How had *she* aged? She was graying and saggier, but not quite a decrepit hag.

Erwan, becoming rupic . . . no, no, she wouldn't envision such a repugnant thing. He would be hard to capture, fighter that he was.

Please, Gyst, don't have met him yet; let him be well.

Something heavy thrashed through the woods.

Ada dropped to a knee, hand reaching for her pistol again. This could be Dodo's pal upon his injured horse. She cringed again and motioned to the Five on the steed's behalf.

A chestnut horse jostled in the bushes, no rider in sight. Branches had snared the reins. Ada crept closer. The horse danced in a half circle, eye whites showing.

Ada heard a loud buzzing noise and stopped. A cloud of bees hovered near the horse's flanks. The poor thing! It must have encountered a hive in its mad dash through the woods.

The bees hovered a second more, and then they zoomed away. Ada stared after them a moment, confused, then slowly approached the horse.

"Shh, shh. You've had a wretched day, haven't you?" she soothed. The horse—an older stallion, by the look of him—stayed still, foreleg stomping, ears back. In the dappled light, she couldn't see how badly he had been stung, but she did notice the lack of a bullet's path across the rump. "You're Dodo's mount, huh?"

The horse squealed alarm as she extended a hand. Ada paused in thought, then dug into her pack. She reached outward again, this time with a white carrot in her grip. Ada continued to murmur, inching forward as the horse began to take bites. The horse was still chewing as she gripped the bridle's cheekpiece.

A moment later, she had the reins untangled. She guided the horse from the thicket into a more open, sunny spot.

The horse calmed more as she ran her hands along his crest and legs and hindquarters. Not a beesting to be found. The saddlebag contained water bags, coarse bread, wedges of firm mountain cheese, and to her delight, a tolerable white wine in glass of such crude manufacture that the Gods had surely interceded to enable its survival thus far. It was stoppered, with not a new-fashioned cork but an oil-soaked rag.

"You're fine now. The Five were looking out for you," she said, stroking his neck. "Melissa in particular."

Her motions were slow with thoughtfulness as she fixed the saddle and adjusted the stirrups. Certainly, she had gestured to the Five for help, but she hadn't anticipated such a blatant intervention. It reminded her of the sporadic visits that Gyst had made over the years. Those occasions had been blessings, yes, but also causes for abject terror. The Gods did nothing for free.

Ada wasn't fool enough to spurn this gift of a horse, though. And besides, Melissa may have directed the stallion this way, but Ada had been the one to earn his trust.

"I'll offer livre to sponsor a pentad beekeeper as soon as I can to show my gratitude, Melissa," she spoke aloud. There was no acknowledging the tingle upon Ada's tongue, but she still had the uneasy sense that she was being watched.

"Why this attention, why now?' she muttered, asking the question of mysterious assailants and of the Five. The horse accepted her astride with a slight side step. She brought him around to face south.

If the weather held, she would see the spires of Lutecia by nightfall.

CHAPTER TEN

SOLENN

Enjoy these prepared Fairies as You would corni-chons in accompaniment with Your afternoon sliced sausage, bread & fruit. Eat but One before an evening fete, and only Once each week, as You are already beautiful, and an indulgence of too many Fairies will add a gleam of falseness to one's Appearance.

—Instructions pasted upon the crock kept in
Mamm-gozh's boudoir

In Braiz, Solenn had known how to sneak around. Even more, she realized now that she had been *allowed* to sneak around. As the grand-daughter of the king and the cousin of the heir, she was permitted her wildness. After her morning studies were concluded, she could jump on her horse and explore shore and hill until sunset.

In Lutecia, Solenn wasn't just a princess, but *the* princess.

Therefore, there was no sneaking into the garden fete hosted by Prince Rupert, no playing wallflower among the just-budding trellises of roses that bounded the close-cropped meadow. As she entered, everyone stopped what they were doing to cheer and applaud.

She smiled graciously and nodded, even as she muttered to Erwan at her side, "I feel like I should have done something extraordinary, like catch an infant dropped from a loft window."

"You could still do a handstand. That'd be sure to elicit reactions." The applause faded. Young courtiers resumed conversations within their clusters. "I shouldn't give you ideas, though. Leave the handstands to the acrobats today."

She let out an exaggerated sigh. "Very well." Solenn spotted Prince Rupert with his friend Jicard. It eased her spirit to see her fiancé well.

"Try to have fun, Princess Solenn. Without going for the horses first thing," said Erwan, tipping his hat toward the far side of the lawn. Several men in leotards were tacking up five all-white horses.

"I'll wait ten minutes, then."

Erwan bowed along with his two companion musketeers. They retreated toward the fringe of the fete, where adults supervised at a distance.

She hadn't proceeded more than five strides—tender ones, courtesy of her healing blisters—when two girls near her age practically pounced upon her.

"Princess Solenn!" they chirped in a chorus, then erupted in giggles. "Your suit!"

"Yes, your suit! Was it made here? Or was it made in Braiz?" She pronounced the z in a drawn-out way, like a drunkard's slur. Both girls giggled again.

Braiz was famous for its lace production, and indeed, the white pantsuit did incorporate tiers of lace amid the satin, like stacked layers of elegant meringues.

Solenn positioned a smile on her face as if balancing a fulcrum on its point. "I had it made here in Lutecia, by the House of Chandis." Their false smiles faltered at the name of the famous maker. They didn't need to know that the incorporated lace was all of Braizian make.

"My summer suits are currently on order there. I'm Prim de la Horace, Your Highness." The blonde bowed.

"As are mine. I'm Madeleine Morraine, Princess. You must tell us what you think of the city. I imagine it's a great deal for you to take in."

"Oh yes! And tell us about Braiz."

Their motives were as obvious as the sparkle of salt. They wanted to gain her favor so that she might choose them as her ladies-in-waiting once she was wed. Madame Brumal would remain with her only a few weeks more to ease her transition into her new role.

Prim and Madeleine, in a constant series of exclamations, began to discuss everything they knew about Braiz and how *wonderful* it was. If Solenn hadn't been able to perceive otherwise, she might have pondered if they had ingested gabby jay epicurea to induce them to babble so.

She gazed past them to where the acrobats had mounted their horses and begun to exercise. She couldn't identify the breed of horse, but they weren't Camargas. They were too large and lacked the gray points.

"Do you have pentads there?"

The chirpy question caused Solenn to face Madeleine as she fought to keep her jaw from going slack in shock. "What? In Braiz? Of course we do. Pentads are all over the world."

"But are pentads like they are here?" Madeleine was sincere.

"Braiz is so wild compared to Verdania," added Prim, nodding.

By "wild," she had to mean more primitive, its citizens *lesser*. Tad— Prince Morvan—had told her that during the war, he'd encountered people here who were amazed Braizians were literate, as if they were half-feral beings who wallowed in the City-Eaten-by-the-Sea described in old stories.

Solenn decided she'd had about enough of these two dandelion-puff brains. "In some ways," she conceded with a conspiratorial whisper. "I often spent whole days out riding. *Astride.* I'll start riding parties here once the weather warms." The idea had just occurred to Solenn, and she delighted in their thinly veiled horror. "I hope you might join me. Depending on the route, jumping may be involved." She smiled as she stepped away. "Talk to you later, Prim, Madeleine."

"Princess, I'm glad to meet you at last," said a boy with two girls flanking him. Introductions were made, small talk ensued. Solenn soon extricated herself and spoke with more young courtiers as she gradually made her way across the lawn. She nibbled on some food and drank sparkling wine. Rupert and his same small group remained where they were, a mountain peak to reach through sheer endurance.

When she made it to them at last, she promptly perceived the presence of epicurea. Who held it within the cluster, she wasn't sure, but it embodied a musty waft reminiscent of a barnyard.

"Solenn!" Rupert greeted her with a bright smile. "Are you having fun?"

"Yes, I am!" She meant it. Her first conversation had certainly been the worst. While she wouldn't say she had made friends yet, the other guests had been intelligent and polite. A shame that Aveyron Silvacane from her debut wasn't here, as they could have talked about horses again, but his provincial origins must not have ranked an invitation.

"This here's Jicard." Rupert nodded to the lanky boy beside him, who wore a black cocked hat atop his blond hair. "With us are Blanche Fontaine and Pierre Laurent."

Greetings were exchanged. Solenn recognized Fontaine as the surname of the finance minister and knew Madame Laurent was one of Queen Roswita's ladies-in-waiting.

"You're just in time, Solenn." Jicard showed off a bucktoothed grin. "I brought something special to share." He delved into a jacket pocket.

"What is it, what is it?" squealed Pierre.

"This." Jicard opened his fist to reveal one-inch buttons of white soft-rind cheese.

Solenn's mouth watered against her will as her perception strengthened in the open presence of the epicurea. "It's goat cheese," she murmured, earning a nod of respect from Jicard.

"But what do they *do*?" asked Rupert, obviously impatient with the theatrics.

"This is a crottin of gruff," said Jicard. "Gruffs are found in the southern mountains. They can walk up vertical cliffs—"

"Oh! This is the stuff that thieves like to use," Pierre said, rubbing his hands together with glee. "It makes their fingers and toes especially good, see, and their reflexes are incredible. They can climb up the side of a house, fast as Hester's flames."

"As I was saying." Jicard scowled. "Because of how goats can climb, they are hard to capture alive, and of course, you need a female one to milk. The army uses this cheese for special missions. Elite thieves and assassins use this epicurea, too, if they want to break into a château." Solenn couldn't help a nervous glance at Rupert. He looked entertained. None of this came across as a potential personal threat.

"How else are gruffs harvested?" asked Rupert.

"People eat the meat, which is valuable, too, but it doesn't *do* anything. Only the milk carries magic, and of course, the whole cheese-making process needs to be done by a Chef."

"That means they must call on Lait and Gyst," said Blanche.

"That's right. Blanche here is like our resident acolyte; she knows lots of religious stuff," Jicard said to Solenn. Acolytes were pentad workers who were neither cooks nor Chefs—unblessed, ungifted, but there to shovel manure or handle other drudgery. Blanche flushed at the insult and ducked her head.

Discomfited, Solenn looked toward the acrobats. The prince's party had the closest view of the act. As a band played, an acrobat vaulted from one cantering horse to another. Few of the young courtiers watched. Most seemed immersed in their own conversations.

Rupert bent closer to the crottin, sniffing. "Is it safe to eat on its own?" White mold covered the nuggets, the coating not unlike the thin fuzz on a ripe peach.

"Yes. That's part of their high value. Tuck them into a pouch, and they're ready to go. No need for a Chef after the affinage stage is done."

"Nice." Rupert plucked up one. Solenn was glad she didn't have an empathetic ability to taste as her mother—Adamantine—did. How had Adamantine even tolerated working in an army camp? Solenn shuddered at the memory of how the palace larder had overwhelmed her, and she hadn't even stepped inside.

She needed to understand more about Chefs and epicurea without looking suspicious. Maybe Jicard could be of help.

"How do you know so much about epicurea?" Solenn asked him.

"It's my father's passion. He has an incredible larder."

"Are you going to try one now, Rupert?" Blanche asked the dauphin.

"No, we'll be stuck here for hours yet. Maybe we can try it in a few days." He nodded to Jicard, making it clear who the real "we" was in this group.

"Come on, you can all take one. Use it whenever." Jicard nodded encouragement to Blanche and Pierre. "You too, Solenn."

She hesitated. "Your father won't know they're missing?"

Jicard laughed. "He gave them to me. Come on. Who knows, you might need to climb up a wall soon."

If only he knew how she yearned to escape the palace, fling herself onto a horse, and ride for Braiz. As she picked up the small cylinder of cheese, power drifted over her in a languid wave. The cheese hadn't even gone to her stomach yet, but she already perceived its potential: the flexibility, the strength, the defiance of gravity. The awareness left her feeling wistful. If only she could trust that her future exposure to epicurea would be as pleasant.

"Thank you," she said, tucking the cheese into the small drawstring bag affixed to her waist.

"I'm going to use this for my next sword-fighting lesson," said Pierre. "I won't tell a soul, and I'll amaze them all. Ha!" He lunged, arm extended.

"It won't make you *good*, Pierre, just fast and sure-footed." Jicard rolled his eyes.

"Meaning it'll be easier for you to hurt yourself. Again," Blanche added. Pierre scowled at that.

The sound of nearby hoofbeats pulled Solenn's attention to the riders. A pale young man had reined up about twenty feet away from them, his expression a dark thundercloud as he dismounted. He jerked on the reins as he faced his mount.

"You stupid thing. How often did we practice this, eh? But you're stupid. Stupid."

With that, he hauled back his crop and began beating the horse.

Solenn gaped for a moment, unwilling to believe her eyes. Rupert's group was oblivious. Actually, no—the prince glanced up at the noise, then faced Jicard again. Other courtiers were equally dismissive.

Solenn couldn't wait for someone else to act. Such abuse was intolerable.

"Stop that!" she yelled, stalking closer, fists balled at her hips. "I order you to stop!"

Her regal tone caused the acrobat to pause, crop upraised. With his other hand he gripped the reins close to the horse's chin, a position of tight control. The mare's nostrils flared, the whites of her eyes showing. Blood had yet to be drawn, but this horse knew pain and fear.

"Mademoiselle?" He sounded perplexed. He didn't know who she was.

"What do you think you're doing, beating a horse like that?"

She could almost see his hackles rise. "This horse is young and stupid. This is her first event, and she shouldn't have been brought. She's not ready."

Behind the man, an older acrobat approached, his expression one of blatant worry. Farther back, through the wall formed of rosebushes, she caught a glimpse of moving color. People watched from the neighboring section of the garden.

"If this mare was debuted too soon, was that her fault? Did she choose to be here?"

He flushed, expression petulant. "She needs a firm hand if she is to learn."

"You're teaching her to fear. That's what you're doing."

He looked her up and down. "Mademoiselle, you should return to your party. I will tend to my horse."

"You are not fit to own a horse, much less ride one." Solenn advanced on him. "Give her to me."

Confusion flickered in his eyes. "Mademoiselle?"

"I am confiscating this horse. You'll be reimbursed for her honest value, which is now considerably less because of the medical attention and compassionate retraining she'll require." She lowered her voice as she drew closer. "Hello there, shh." She tugged the reins from the man's hand. He didn't resist her, instead looking at his approaching comrade for counsel. The other man shook his head with the intensity of a dog shedding water.

"This horse is not for someone like . . . She is dangerous!" stammered the young man.

Not for whom? A woman? A Braizian? A person of different complexion than his own? Solenn, irked, thought to swing herself astride the mare and demonstrate how she could ride—but in the process, she would only inflict a different measure of cruelty on this poor horse. No, this mare needed time to heal, body and soul.

"If she is dangerous, it's because you trained her to be so." Solenn stroked the length of the mare's muzzle. The horse's ears perked, her movements less agitated. "Come on, you sweet thing. Life will be better now."

Solenn turned around to find that the entirety of the fete had stopped to stare in stunned silence. A flush crept up her neck to her cheeks, but she kept her chin up and strides even. What was done was done.

Erwan emerged from the pack, his musketeers a step behind. His expression was neutral, but she could well imagine the scolding she would get later.

"Princess Solenn, here I thought we were going to visit stables soon to acquire horses," he said.

"Princess?" the acrobat squawked, blatantly bewildered.

"Yes, you fool," hissed the other performer. "The *princess*."

Solenn looked past Erwan. "Lieutenant Talia, could you please take this horse to the royal stable?"

"Of course, mademoiselle." Lieutenant Talia nodded, an amused gleam in her eye. "I'll tend to her myself and arrange for her future care."

"Thank you." Solenn handed over the reins. "Do inform the grooms that I'll be by to check on her myself later."

"I'll inform them." Her tone implied this would be more of a warning. Talia turned and saluted Erwan. "Monsieur le Capitaine."

He nodded crisply. "Have a new third sent here immediately."

"I will, monsieur." With another salute, she departed with the horse.

"Captain Corre, I—" Solenn began.

"Later." A single word, overflowing with threat.

"Solenn!" Rupert approached. Five Verdanian musketeers traveled in his wake.

Solenn's musketeers had come to support her during the confrontation with the acrobats, but why had Rupert summoned five chevaliers to accompany him? The Verdanian musketeers, all men, wore their pistols and rapiers; the Braizians were not allowed their gear. The imbalance of power was blatant and perturbing.

She bowed. "Rupert, I didn't intend to interrupt the party. I'm sorry."

He raised an eyebrow. "Sorry for interrupting the party, or doing what you did?"

She met his gaze levelly, for all that she towered over him. "I don't regret interceding on the horse's behalf, monseigneur. Someone needed to. I didn't expect the entire gathering to stop and watch, though." But she should have. She already knew that everyone studied her, waiting for a misstep, a careless word, anything.

"You like horses a lot, don't you?" Rupert asked.

"I do."

"Hmm." He considered this fact for a moment, glanced at the crowd, then back at Solenn. With a casual air, he moved past her, toward the acrobats. "Give me your name, monsieur."

Solenn recognized that Rupert was replicating the mannerisms of the king. A sinking sensation filled her gut.

"Hauteforte. Emanuel Hauteforte, monseigneur." The young man dropped to his knees on the grass, his comrade doing likewise.

"Monsieur Hauteforte, you disrespected my fiancée. What do you have to say for yourself?"

"I did not know who she was, Monsieur le Prince. I'm sorry."

Before the prince could speak again, Solenn backtracked to face him. "Monseigneur, his greatest offense is how he treated the horse, not me."

"I see." He paused a moment, then grinned. "Monsieur Hauteforte, for abusing your horse, you will be treated in kind. Grab him." He beckoned to his musketeers. They wore cassocks, calf-high boots, and plumed hats much as the Braizian musketeers did, but in a different shade of blue and with considerably less lace. Two of them advanced to haul up the stunned acrobat. "You will be beaten in the same manner in which you beat your horse."

"Monsieur le Prince?" Hauteforte sputtered. The musketeers began to drag him away. "I didn't—I mean—"

Solenn swallowed dryly. She caught Erwan's eye, the slight shake of his head.

"Monseigneur," mumbled the other acrobat, his face still in the grass.

Rupert ignored him. "There!" He looked pleased with himself. "How was that?" he asked Solenn.

"Regal," she managed to get out.

"It was, wasn't it?" He waved to the whole of the party. "Come on! This part of the show is done. Have fun again. That's an order!" he said, loud as he could. People laughed and resumed their chatter. A moment later, the band struck up anew. The remaining acrobat remained face-down in the grass.

Rupert walked back toward Jicard. Solenn jogged to catch up with him. "If it's all right with you, Rupert, I'm going to retire for the time being."

"That's fine. Hey, Jicard!" He didn't even look at Solenn again as he hurried away.

"Indeed, a choice moment to make an exit, Princess," murmured Erwan. With Erwan and his subordinate in close accompaniment, they left, with no one making an effort to stop Solenn for more chitchat. The gazes upon her showed bewilderment, the voices around her in hissed whispers.

She released a deep exhale as they entered another, quieter, segment of the garden. Palace walls towered above them.

Erwan's gaze stayed forward. "Do you have any idea how proud I am of you?" he said in a low voice.

"What?" She had expected him to be cross with her—she almost wanted him to be. It'd make it easier for her to stay angry at him.

"You threw incendiaries upon court gossip, but you handled yourself, and the acrobat and dauphin, with considerable grace."

She couldn't accept the compliment. "That acrobat is being beaten right now. I was able to speak up on behalf of the horse, but not the man." She couldn't hold back her bitterness.

"I will be forthright, Solenn, as you have ordered of me." She jerked up her head, surprised at his acknowledgment of her recent demand. "You succeeded in interceding for the horse because you surprised the dauphin and everyone else. The dauphin's actions, however, were a demonstration of power. A present for you, in a way, but also an act of domination." He said this with sober softness.

"I embarrassed him, by speaking up when he did not," she murmured.

"Yes. How would he have reacted, then, had you argued with him more?"

"Not well." Solenn felt vaguely ill at the possibilities.

"The acrobat will be hurt, but only to the extent he hurt that mare. In which case, it's a good thing you stepped in when you did, is it not?"

"That's one way of looking at it." She released a long breath.

"In more pleasant news, we'll likely be bombarded with offers for more horses. You may have your own stable sooner than you anticipated." At that, the musketeer behind Erwan couldn't withhold a soft snort of amusement.

Not for the first time, she thought wistfully of the horses she'd loved and had to leave behind in Braiz. "Well, my new mare is a nice one. Good lines, beautiful gait." Solenn needed to focus on the horse she had saved, not the acrobat.

Another Braizian musketeer hurried toward them—Talia's replacement, as expected. But what they had not anticipated was the chevalier's furrowed brow and letter in hand.

"Monsieur. Princess." He saluted them both. "A missive from home."

Erwan opened the envelope and frowned at the contents. "This is curious." He handed it to Solenn. She skimmed the page, then looked up, confused.

"A messenger from Albion arrived, broaching another marriage arrangement for me? Surely they received the formal notice of my forthcoming nuptials?"

"They did. We had a letter of congratulations from Albion before we departed." Erwan accepted the letter and returned it to the envelope. "I don't like this."

"Albion is always up to something, Captain," said the messenger, earning a grunt of agreement from his peer.

"Indeed. This inconsistency on their part—their Lord Whitney must have erred. A pleasant rarity, that."

Solenn nodded, thoughtful. Lord Whitney was one of the most powerful figures in Albion—some muttered he was more king than the king. He had come to her parents' château years ago to speak on matters of trade and of a potential alliance between Albion and Braiz through Solenn's marriage. The man had been average of face, his clothes and wig extravagant, mannerisms brash, but something else about him stood bold in her memory now.

"Lord Whitney was obsessed with epicurea, was he not? He asked for great stores of Braiz's ingredients as part of my dowry, had that betrothal gone forward." He'd spoken with passion on the subject of the Albionish royal pantry and his own quest to try the breadth of the world's magical offerings. Was that why he'd continued to push for the union?

Erwan's gaze on her was sharp. "Indeed. That was among many reasons why such a deal was not entertained for long. The man is a rare noble-born Chef. He is certain of the divinity of his position and was not amenable to negotiations."

Solenn nodded to show she understood the lesson—and the warning—in his words. Chefs held powerful positions around the world, but few could claim titles outside of militaries. People tended to be jealous and wary of superiors who seemed *too* superior. Yet another concern for Solenn in her increasingly tenuous position.

Erwan motioned to his musketeers. "We must confer. Verdania will be receiving this news from their own informants. I'm curious as to how they will react."

They hastened the return to their apartments.

Erwan summoned his available musketeers. Solenn often liked to sit in on such discussions, but today she declined.

Instead, she paced her quarters, alone. Madame Brumal was attending a practice for the ball tonight, where she would be in direct service to Solenn.

Why would Albion send another marriage offer? Did it come from a party unaware of her acceptance to Verdania? Or was this social faux pas of a more ominous nature, a hint of some dread ploy by Lord Whitney?

As unpleasant as it was to be in Lutecia, she would much rather be here than anywhere in Albion, where people said that it rained even more than it did in Braiz. Besides, the prime candidate to be her fiancé in Albion was all of ten years of age. He was a *child*.

Thoughts troubled, she crossed the room to where a blue-painted traveler's chest sat on the floor. The lid swung upward, exposing more boxes nestled within, each labeled with the names of places across Braiz. She unclasped the one marked "Malo" and brought it to her face to breathe in the scent of her favorite beach.

The small container was half-full, the gray sand coarse and flecked with shells, pebbles, dry seaweed, and whatever else had been brought up by the shovel. She set it down to run her fingers through the wonderful grittiness, touching home, touching a past when things made far more sense. The roughness created a quiver that traveled up her arm, causing a small convulsion when it reached her torso. There, the sensation rested near her heart, like a candle's glow.

"Selland," she whispered, closing her eyes, taking solace in her connection to him. Overwhelmed as she was, she didn't have a specific query for the God. She just needed to know that he was as present for her in Lutecia as he had always been in Braiz. Pentad canon assured her this was the case—the Five were everywhere—but how could she trust in old certainties now?

She'd known few people who felt Selland as she did, as Erwan also did. When she was small and craved exposure to the oncoming energy of storms, he had been the one who would stand with her on the balcony as rain droplets stung her face and wind pressed exhalations back into her throat. She knew such comforting exhilaration in those moments as thunder reverberated through her bones, the onslaught of ocean air savory to her tongue. Beside her, Erwan stood with eyes half-shut, likewise basking. She had thought, then, that she was blessed that her captain understood her so. Oh, how little she had known.

She put away the precious box, then took a moment to open each of the others. They carried sand from other beaches, flasks of water both briny and pure, dirt from apple groves and verdant meadows, crushed granite from notable passes and hillocks. Gifts from her people, pieces of Braiz to bring with her to Verdania. She acknowledged each with tears in her eyes, then shut the larger chest.

The sharpness of Selland's presence faded, but she knew innately he was still with her, sure as she could feel salt crust her drying clothes after being lashed by a surprise wave.

A knock at the door caused her to lurch to stand, smoothing her clothes. "Yes?" She opened the door's view slot.

"Princess." Jean, her musketeer on duty, stared back. Consternation furrowed his thick brow. "There's a young man calling upon you, an Aveyron Silvacane, son of Comte Brillat Silvacane de Camarga. Were you expecting him?"

CHAPTER ELEVEN

SOLENN

A nugget of goat cheese, sometimes unflatteringly called a crottin (the name also given to certain like-size animal manure; such comparisons are inappropriate), is best eaten when it is not too fresh and white, or harder and brown. One touched with beige or even speckled with blue mold is fine. Serve with fresh or preserved fruit, crusted bread, and a white or red wine that is fruity and light.

—Excerpt from *Book for Cooks to Excel as Do Chefs*

Solenn blinked. Aveyron Silvacane was here? "No, I was not expecting him—or anyone else—but we can talk now. What would be the most appropriate way to do so?"

This was an awkward time for a courtier to come calling, as she wasn't yet a bride; Madame Brumal had warned Solenn that the weeks after her marriage would bring an inundation of visitors. For Aveyron to break with propriety made her curious. He may have been provincial, but that didn't equate with ignorant.

"He brought a gift for you, mademoiselle, which he wants to offer you personally. One of us can supervise in your parlor."

Gifts should wait until after the wedding too. All the more curious. "Thank you, Jean. Please accompany him in."

She claimed her favorite seat in the parlor. Setting her hands on her lap, she rediscovered the gruff cheese. She'd become accustomed to the continued tingle upon her tongue and forgotten the cheese was there, or she would have put the pouch aside. A quick probe with her fingers assured her that the morsel was still intact.

A moment later, Jean entered with young Monsieur Silvacane. His attire was immaculate, as it had been the previous day—a pantsuit of red velvet, tailored to his thin form. The white lace lining the lapel didn't look to be Braizian but was fine nevertheless. Tucked beneath his arm, he held a bundle wrapped in blue satin.

He maintained that odd aura about him. She could only guess he utilized some form of epicurea, but one unfamiliar to her experience.

She rose. "Monsieur Silvacane. Your visit is unexpected but welcome."

He bowed, a slight flush upon his pale skin. "Thank you for seeing me, mademoiselle. I'm aware that my visit and gift may seem premature, but in light of recent events, I felt the timing was appropriate."

"Recent events?" She gestured him to sit on the divan as she claimed her seat. Jean assumed an attentive stance nearby.

"Yes, your actions at the garden fete. I wasn't at your party, but the one adjacent," he said, answering the next question poised upon her lips. "Those of lesser nobility were invited to a separate engagement that occurred on the other side of the hedgerow."

"Oh." This took her aback. "How large was this separate party?"

"Thirty attendees near our own age, and more adults besides."

"Are there often parallel functions like this?"

"My understanding is that this is common for daytime fetes. Court comes together for important events such as the ball tonight."

Solenn looked to Jean. "Is this your understanding as well?"

Jean regarded her from beneath his black hat, the magnificent silver feather in the crown matching the embroidery upon his blue cassock. He had no flintlock musket with him—none of the Braizian musketeers did, in their common duties. Within their apartment corridor, however, he and his comrades were allowed rapiers. She noticed his hand hovered near the hilt.

"Yes, Princess." Of course, the musketeers would be aware of the adjacent fete as a matter of her security.

Monsieur Silvacane bowed, his expression apologetic. "My intent was not to complain. My gathering was pleasant. If I may shift the topic, I'd like to explain why I'm visiting now." He paused. Solenn nodded that he could continue. "A number of us watched the other fete for idle entertainment. I witnessed how you advocated on behalf of the abused horse." He paused again, but this time to control his emotions. Tears glistened in his eyes. "I am . . . something of an equestrian myself. The way you interceded . . . you were tenacious, Princess. No one else would have stepped forward as you did."

Her fists balled. "I did what I must. I don't understand how they could stand there, sip their wine, and regard the beating of a horse as a mere distraction."

"Your passion for horses and their well-being was clear. My father and I have been unsure of what to offer you as a wedding gift, Princess. You answered that question for us. For me, anyway. My father is out today and doesn't know what I'm doing. I suppose he won't be pleased with my lack of propriety." He shyly grinned, shifting the bundle on his lap. "One of our companions at court could be termed a master craftsperson. I asked her to make this for you." He looked back at Jean. "I beg your pardon, monsieur. There are no maids or valets to assist us. How should we . . . ?"

"You may unwrap it on the table, Monsieur Silvacane," Jean advised with a small smile. Solenn appreciated the kind regard in which her guest regarded her musketeer.

Silvacane set the parcel upon the low table and tugged the lace bow. The lush cloth rippled as it draped open like a fast-blossoming flower, revealing the most beautiful statue of a horse she'd ever seen in her life.

Smoothed pale wood revealed the elegance of whorls and knots across the ten-inch figure. The legs, with the exception of one upraised foreleg, melded to a ground that was coarse in texture, carved to resemble waves of grass. The tail and mane were flared out, adding to the drama.

Tears stung her eyes. "I've never seen artistry on such a fine scale. With the warm-toned wood it's . . . it's almost like it's *alive*. You said that your friend just made this, Monsieur Silvacane? *How?* Something like this, it should take weeks and weeks!"

"Should it?" His smile was tense. "She's . . . she's very good, Princess."

"I'll say. The bottom here, was driftwood used?"

He relaxed again, grinning. "Yes. I'll tell her you noticed. She only uses salvaged wood in her pieces. *Never* fresh cut." He said that with emphasis.

"Thank you, monsieur. I'll need to find an appropriate place to showcase this when I move to my new apartment next week." Such a strange idea, that she would soon be decorating her own domicile as a married woman.

Silvacane stood. "Thank you. I'll relay your compliments to the artiste."

"I don't think you gave me the gift too early," Solenn said. "It does have extra meaning today. Now I'll remember this gift as the first and the best."

His gaze shifted downward, near her hands. "I beg your pardon, mademoiselle, but I've noticed . . . some at court use such pouches to carry epicurea. Do you do the same?"

She couldn't recall courtiers using pouches for that specific reason, but perhaps she hadn't been paying adequate attention. "The pouch is for general use, but I was indeed given epicurea at the fete." As Jicard hadn't been secretive about the epicurea—quite the opposite—she saw no reason to conceal it now. She set the cheese on her palm. The prickles in her nose and throat increased, feeling an awful lot like a repressed sneeze. "It's gruff cheese. In case I need to climb up a building." She laughed, but Monsieur Silvacane looked oddly somber.

"Gruffs are held in terrible conditions in order for this cheese to be made. They are hauled far from their mountain home, closer to Lutecia." He spoke in a soft, even tone, as if reciting literature read to memorization. "They are excellent jumpers and climbers, so they cannot be contained by any field or corral. Instead, they're constrained by slatted boxes little bigger than their own bodies. They have room to bow their heads to eat, no more. People reach through the slats to milk them and clean the floor. Gruffs won't breed in captivity. Males are slaughtered outright for the value of their meat. Females won't provide milk beyond the warm season. If they live as long as the fall—and many don't—they're then killed for their meat as well. Their milk is their only magical aspect. Everything else is considered to be valuable derivatives."

Solenn gaped at him. "Selland preserve us. Have you heard the same?" She looked at Jean.

"I confess, I know little of gruffs, Princess," said Jean. "Our mountains do not host them."

"They used to," Silvacane said, "but as I understand it, they were killed off in Braiz centuries ago."

She gazed at the cheese with revulsion, then back at him. "I don't want to believe you, yet it sounds plausible. It's one thing to slaughter an animal for meat, another to torment them for months beforehand."

"Indeed." Monsieur Silvacane dipped his head in agreement.

"Jicard mentioned this cheese is used by elite military units but that thieves use it as well. Do they break into the army's larders to obtain it, I wonder?"

Silvacane looked at Jean as if for help, and the musketeer obliged with a slight smile. "Not quite, Princess. Officially, all Verdanian epicurea is property of King Caristo and distributed where he wills it. In reality, only a small portion is in his possession. Most goes on the black market."

"You're saying a cheese like this would be sold to assassins and thieves," she said hollowly, thinking again of the danger to Rupert.

"Princess, you cited the name Jicard?" asked Monsieur Silvacane.

"Jicard Dubray. His father, the Marquis de Dubray, apparently considers epicurea as his passion. He provided these cheeses to Jicard to share with his friends."

Monsieur Silvacane's dark eyes widened. "These cheeses are rare and expensive. That's an indulgent gift for mere play."

"Certainly not worth everything the gruffs endured, but what *could* make that sacrifice worthwhile? I don't even know what to do with this thing now." She didn't want to stash it in her rooms. The very scent of it, knowing what she knew, made her feel vaguely ill.

"This may seem forward of me, for which I apologize, but I could handle its disposal," he said. "I have . . . rather strong views about epicurea and its use, Princess. I wouldn't eat it myself or give it to anyone else for that purpose, this I vow."

"How would you get rid of it, then?" she asked.

"I would discuss those specifics with my father." He bowed his head. "Again, I apologize. The value of this cheese considered, this is akin to me asking for jewels."

Solenn caught Jean's expression, which was skeptical, to say the least. "You would think me a fool for handing this to him, wouldn't you?" she asked Jean.

The musketeer looked aghast. "I would never think such a thing of you, mademoiselle!"

"Yet you doubt him."

Jean looked between her and Monsieur Silvacane. "I don't know monsieur. This cheese isn't simply expensive. You must also consider that it's a weapon."

"Monsieur le Mousquetaire is right in that," said Silvacane.

Solenn considered this for a moment, then extended her hand. "I choose to believe you, Monsieur Silvacane. Here."

He accepted the cheese with the gravity of being trusted with the king's own crown. "Thank you, mademoiselle. Your compassion is without parallel."

"Maybe so." Her laugh was weak. "A shame that my compassion won't make me more popular or welcome here in court. The dauphin supported me today, but I don't know if that will happen next time." And there'd almost certainly be a next time.

Monsieur Silvacane tilted his head, his straight silver hair swaying to brush his shoulders. "You'll soon be a princess of Verdania as well as Braiz. You'll come into more power and respect. As my father says, some people are burned at the stake, others do the burning, and far more watch." He pocketed the cheese.

He'd said it matter-of-factly, but the words sent a chill through her nevertheless. As an untrained Chef—a rogue, by the law—she understood that if the truth of her ability were revealed, she would more likely lose her tongue than be burned, as were common criminals.

"You're right. Maybe I can use my new position to do some good." She sighed.

"Think of the good you already did for that horse today, Princess." He stepped back and offered a rigid bow. "I'll take my leave. Thank you for admitting me, against propriety."

"Thank you again for the lovely gift, monsieur. I suppose we really did something of a trade today, didn't we? A horse statue for cheese."

He paused by the door. "A trade with inequity, Princess Solenn. I will remember my debt to you." He tapped his pocket with the cheese and, bowing again, departed.

"A strange young man, but a sincere one," said Jean.

Solenn took in a deep breath. She felt much better away from the epicurea. The odd aura around both Silvacanes wasn't bothersome in that way, just unusual.

"Jean, how long until I must begin my toilette for the ball?" she asked.

"Not until after sunset, Princess. As the captain is indisposed, I should remind you that Madame Brumal advised you to nap this afternoon."

"Ah yes. I will be up much of the night. I should do that, but first, I would like to walk to the stable."

His grin widened the deep lines in his clean-shaven face. "Of course you would. I must inform Captain Corre. We'll need to increase our company."

"Please do so."

She stared at the door after Jean's departure, her thoughts drifting back to what Aveyron Silvacane had said: that some people are burned, others do the burning, and far more watch. As princess, she had the power to burn others—or have them beaten, as Prince Rupert had ordered of the acrobat. Truly, though, none of the options settled well with her.

"Verdania. Here, everything comes back to Hester and fire," she murmured, a glance toward her own hearth. The staff had let the fire dwindle. To some people here, that would be akin to blasphemy. She'd even overheard some maids speaking, near tears, about an old pentad devoted to Hester that was being torn apart before it fell down.

Her thoughts again turned to Braiz with longing. Her beloved home. Her beloved people. The fact that she wasn't a princess by blood changed none of that.

She had to somehow keep them safe—and herself as well.

CHAPTER TWELVE

ADA

Braiz boasts of its cider, but often its apple brandy is not given adequate appreciation, likely because the vast majority of it is exported to the Confederated Duchies. Brandy has its uses both medicinal and social, but small amounts of the Gyst-blessed liquid can also be used to prevent wine from spoiling and can even keep stored water from going sour. The beverage is due more respect.

—Excerpt from *Book for Cooks to Excel as Do Chefs*

Lutecia welcomed Ada with rain that resembled stone shrapnel more than water. After stabling her horse, she braced her shoulders against the onslaught as she sloshed to the fine tavern known as the Golden Horse.

At this time of night, lamps illuminated the span of multipaned glass windows across the front of the establishment. She could hear laughter, voices, and a flute melody over the churn of hooves and wheels and the cries of vendors. The avenue wasn't as busy as it could be, and for that she was grateful.

She wasn't attired as one should be for the Golden Horse. The establishment was staunchly bourgeois. She was confident and cranky, however, and she knew the magic phrase to gain access.

"I'm one of Emone's, monsieur, and I need help," she said to the thickset man who stood suited and noble beneath the shelter of the eaves.

As she'd approached, his expression had been of tired disdain, but his glower vanished in an instant. "Your pardon, madame," he said before ducking inside, only to return seconds later. "Wait over here." He gestured to the deeper shadows on the far side of him. "Someone will come in a moment to escort you inside."

Ada was relieved to find her designated spot would save her from the stinging rain. "My thanks, monsieur."

She detected the tilt of his head as he glanced over. "Will you be needing a physician?"

"No, I don't, but please tell me: Is Emone well?"

He stiffened. "Is there a reason she shouldn't be?"

Ada appreciated the man's devotion to Emone. Five knew, she wished she had even a pinch of Emone's natural charisma. "There's word that someone with a grudge seeks to do her harm. I was afraid . . . I was afraid that I might have already been too late to bring a warning."

His quiet made her worry that he might regard her as the more immediate threat, but then he spoke. "Building's been set ablaze twice this week. Both fires were discovered quickly. Last one had a witness, a bloke who saw it done on purpose."

"Fire?" Her brow furrowed. That didn't fit the pattern, though it'd work well for outright murder—if one didn't care about other lives lost in the attack. "I'm not sure if that is connected to this other threat, but in any case, I'm grateful you're on the alert."

He nodded, his hat outlined by distant light. "But of course. This place—and Emone—mean much to many people."

A woman with her hair crowned in lace leaned out the double doors. "Simon? Where is . . . ? Ah, there you are. Come with me, madame." Her smile was friendly.

As Ada hurried to the door, the guard's hand glanced her arm. "I'll let other people know. We'll be vigilant. Thank you."

She paused to nod. "And thank you for watching over Emone."

"It's the least I can do," he said with warm sincerity.

Ada followed the woman in scullion's garb. They took a hard left turn, away from the kitchen and the dining hall. Stairs creaked as they climbed a narrow servants' passage upward, continuing past the second floor and to the topmost level. Ada's laden pack jostled the walls with each stiff, sluggish stride.

"Do you need a physician? Or food and drink?" her guide asked, glancing back.

Ada almost laughed. She must look wretched if everyone thought she needed healing. "Any food and drink would taste like the Feast of the Five about now, thank you."

"But of course," said the woman. "We look after each other here."

Ada's tongue might have been God-touched, but she had a hunch that Emone had been divinely touched in her own way. Emone Jourdain had the knack of recognizing people in need, whether it be from poverty or abuse or a reliance on drink, and then doing everything in her power to better them. In the Thirty-Fifth, she'd been regarded with adoration by the soldiers: *You have a problem with a peer or an abusive commander or are distracted by worry for kin back home, you go to Emone; your friend has a problem, you go to Emone.* Her people skills sometimes seemed magical, mundane though she was. She could intuit what job best suited a person, know what accommodations they required to thrive, and rouse someone from the darkest of moods by listening and asking the right questions. Upon the disbardment of the division, she'd gone about establishing her dream tavern, a place of fine food and company and comfortable beds. The Golden Horse had gained increasing renown in Lutecia—Ada couldn't help but follow news of it—and likely every employee had been saved by Emone in one way or another.

They trod down the third-floor corridor. A head topped with a magnificent bundle of blonde curls leaned into the hallway. Crimson-painted lips fell slack.

"Ada!" Emone gasped. "You must be in desperate straits to come here. My thanks, Maria."

Emone hustled Ada into an apartment packed with heavy furniture. Luxurious clothes were flung over every chair, leaving no space to sit. The combined scents of rosewater perfume filled the air. Emone gripped her by both arms and craned back to take in the sight of her. "I'd hug you, but I need to be downstairs on the half hour, and my look is perfect."

And it was. Emone wore a satin dress the vivid pink of a cloudy sunset, her boots the sleek black of a polished show horse. Her rouge was a matching pink, applied across her high cheekbones in the soft swirls that were so popular among the bourgeoisie right now.

"You've had me worried for ages, you know," Emone continued. "I believe your last words to me were, 'See you soon.'"

"The definition of 'soon' is relative," Ada said, letting her pack drop to the floor. "I heard your building has been set afire twice in recent days."

Emone arched a brow darkened by lampblack or coal. "Most people would begin a reunion with, 'How've you been?' but you always were down to business, weren't you?" Her expression sobered. "What's going on, Ada?"

Taking in a deep breath, she told her the basics. Emone listened, slender body leaned against a shut wardrobe, brow furrowed.

"Arson fits in with the Mallory Valmont theory better than you know," Emone said. "He saved me from a fire once. Embers blew onto a tent where I met with soldiers, and the canopy went up in an instant. Burning cloth came down on me. I knew a moment of blackness and suffocation; then he was there, dragging me to safety. I wasn't even singed."

"By the Five, Emone! I don't remember that."

"You and Erwan were on another mission at the time, enduring your own near-fatal escapades. We all had so many in those days. Back then, I'd almost forgotten about it, too, until Mallory's arrest. He saw me once and said, accusingly, 'But I saved you from that fire! How can you let them do this to me?' As if that one incident in the tent redeemed him of the murders and cannibalizations he committed." Emone rolled her eyes.

Ada frowned. "He could have told people about that fire. He may have distributed a list of grievances to hundreds of people, as far as we know."

"Or he could be as tenacious as a cockroach and still be alive, overseeing his revenge. The Crown likes to boast that Mont Annod is an impregnable prison labor camp that no one escapes alive, but what is the truth? You of all people know to question that. *You're* supposed to be deliriously happy in your commitment to the Gods-ordained royals who oversee our Gods-blessed realm."

Ada snorted. "That puts me in mind of a tract I found in my tour days as I rummaged around, bored, in an old pentad. The ink had faded such that it was hard to read, but it spoke of Hester and the reason for her anger."

"Isn't everything supposed to make her angry?" Emone asked, eyebrow prettily arched. "Some of her devotees in the city are certain that she's furious because King Caristo is razing the oldest pentad in the city."

"That old building was falling apart back when I was a child. For once, I can't fault Caristo for a choice." How strange, to say such words. "To return to the subject of Hester's rage—"

"Yes, sorry. Do tell."

"This ancient tract said something I'd never heard before, that Hester was cursed into being a God and forever angry about her fate."

Emone's jaw dropped. "Well, well, that sounds blasphemous by current canon."

"Oh yes. At that time, I was already chafing at the idea that I'd be forced into the army, and I found I could relate to this cursed Hester more than the angry home guardian I was supposed to send my best bread to."

"What other juicy bits of blasphemy did this paper include?"

"Most of it was damaged and illegible. When I asked my mentor-Chefs about it, I was told to forget I'd read such a terrible thing. I couldn't find the booklet again later. I assume it was destroyed, probably burned. And speaking of things burning . . ." Ada looked around the clothes-strewn room. "This would be a terrible place to be in a fire."

"Undoubtedly, but I have no intention of dying anytime soon. Claudette would be *furious*. I'd be unhappy too—I almost have these projects done." Emone stroked a drape of blue silk. "We're getting flooded with guests who've come into the city to enjoy the royal wedding revelry. My fingers have been worked to nubs this week, sewing suits in Braizian blue for our musicians."

Those fingers had made Emone the fastest sharpshooter among the Thirty-Fifth's officers too. Her accuracy had been rivaled only by Erwan's.

A soft knock echoed through the door. Maria had returned, carrying a platter of fresh lamb, mashed turnips, and crusty bread. Ada could have cried in joy. Instead, she wedged the plate onto a sliver of space left empty on a table and stuffed food in her face.

Emone used the lull in conversation to pull a small, ornate pistol from a drawer, along with other gun paraphernalia.

"Where *is* Claudette?" Ada asked, pausing to drink the accompanying warm cider. The cozy heat and spices seemed to soak right into her weary bones. Thank Hester for the blessing of a hot drink on a cold, wet night.

"On a trip to the south coast for a spring fabric market. As fiercely as I miss her, I'm now glad that she's away from the danger here." Emone hummed absently as she polished the pistol.

Emone and Claudette had met during the campaign against Albion. Claudette, who at that time managed her late husband's textile-shipping firm, had been trapped with goods in a town during an Albionish siege. Emone, as one of the Thirty-Fifth's two supplies sous-lieutenants, had reason to inspect goods within the town. She'd discovered something of greater interest than fine textiles.

"Do you know where I can find Didina?" Ada asked. "I'd rather not knock on all doors in the Ricardian quartier. Most wouldn't be kindly inclined."

"Of course I know where you can find Didina. Unlike *some* people, I try to keep up with my friends." Ada cringed beneath her glower. "She lives on the south side of the river near Pont-du-Bois. The Thierry Hotel, ground floor, room one thirteen. She's married, a few children, very hap—oh, Five shut my fool mouth. I'm sorry, Ada."

She shrugged. "You did no wrong in stating facts, Emone. And I'm glad she's happy. No one needs their bliss dimmed on my behalf. Except King Caristo."

"Mm-hmm. You're still burning that grudge like a pentad hearth fire. Don't suppose I should mention the old 'a thousand recipes for revenge' line for you."

Ada gave Emone a look. "During my tour days, I had it stomped into my memory with all the weight of a draft horse's hoof. So, no." She drank the last of her cider and wiped her mouth with a napkin. "I need to go. I'll be at her door at a woefully late hour as it is."

"Very well. I won't preach at you. I will, however, invite you to come back here after you see Didina. And yes, I will say that with optimism. She's a tough old bird, our Didina, and I'm going to believe in the best for now. So warn her, then return here. I'll be awake until almost dawn. You can sleep on the divan." She motioned to the furniture, currently buried by satin breeches and buckets of buttons.

"I'll take you up on that," Ada said. "I trust your staff to be vigilant, but you could use a personal guard while Claudette is away."

That woman was among the best civilian rapier duelists she had ever encountered.

"Oh, I almost forgot!" Emone clapped her hands together and scurried into the next room. A moment later, she returned, a small paper envelope in hand.

Ada's tongue and nose tingled. "Unicorn tisane. From Braiz?"

"You'd know more than me. A friend gave it to me when I fought a cold over the winter."

"I can't accept this, Emone. This is too—"

"Don't you dare insist it's too expensive. Say 'thank you,' then shut up and take it. Didina may need it, not you."

"Such insubordination," Ada muttered, stuffing the packet in her coat. "Thank you. Five willing, I'll see you again in a few hours."

"I'd better. Don't make me deploy my people in search."

Ada shook her head, grinning. "Good thing the prosecutors never hired you to hunt me down. They would have found me a decade ago."

Sadness suddenly draped over Emone's painted features. "You have no idea how tempted I was to seek you out, Ada. I've never ceased worrying and wondering about you. I was afraid that by searching, though, I would only drag attention onto you again."

"You don't need to apologize or justify, Emone." Ada shouldered her pack, resisting the urge to groan. She might need to use the tisane for her stiff, aching body. "You were always here in plain sight and easy for me to visit. I just . . . didn't. I'm glad to finally get a look at what you've done. Your cook is excellent too."

"I wish I could tell them that a Chef said that." Emone's expression was tender. "You could leave that bag here, you know."

Ada glanced at it over her shoulder. "With the way my days have gone, I wouldn't trust the sea to stay salty. I need to keep my supplies at hand. Or somewhere not at risk of arson."

Emone shook her head, smiling. "Be careful out there."

Outside, Ada found the rain still falling, painful and relentless.

An elaborate coach rolled by, glossy black horses in the shafts. Ada glanced in the direction of the palace. She couldn't see it through the close press of buildings, but she could well imagine the pomp and circumstance underway at the royal ball. Erwan was there, and maybe her daughter, too, if she was indeed in attendance to the princess.

Ada took in a deep, resolute breath. She needed to channel Emone's relentless optimism. Her daughter was alive. Erwan was alive. Didina was alive. Somewhere in the wilderness, Petry and Grand-mère were alive too.

And, Five be praised, she was still alive too. With determined strides, she sloshed her way back to the stable. The night wasn't yet done.

CHAPTER THIRTEEN

SOLENN

Sea air and sea salt season the grasses upon which the lambs feed, thus imbuing them with the flavor of salt before the addition of a single grain. Hence, this is a meat closely associated with Selland, especially in Braiz, where flocks are reared among the meadows and marshes. A Chef should listen to the inherent saltiness of the lamb and adjust seasonings as necessary.

—Excerpt from *Manual for Tour Chefs*

"You cannot be clumsy tonight, Princess Solenn." Madame Brumal fussed over Solenn's hair. "This ball is more important than your debut. More symbolic. Everything must be perfect."

So Madame Brumal had repeated some two dozen times in the past hour. Solenn sighed. "I know." She sat rigid at her vanity, facing a mirror. Her visage looked fine, she thought, though like a stranger. Like an *adult*. Solenn wore red tonight, Hester's color, the robe volante revealing the broad V shape of a stomacher heavily embroidered with gold-threaded flames.

"You must be vigilant as you attend to the dauphin." Madame Brumal seemed to be determined to place every single hair on Solenn's head in its appropriate position. "He will be looking at your actions as confirmation that you will be a dutiful wife."

What about Rupert proving to her that he could be a dutiful husband? She kept the thought to herself. The last thing she needed was to worsen Madame Brumal's pother. Besides, ultimately her gripe was with not Madame Brumal but the antiquated notions of Verdanian society. Common women could be soldiers or merchants or fishers, but if a woman was noble born, she was to be pretty and produce babies.

Braiz enjoyed prettiness and babies, certainly, but the winds were relentless, the sea benevolent yet merciless, and everyone contributed toward survival. Men tended to work the boats, but no one regarded women's lots to be easier because they stayed ashore. The craggy, worn appearance of elders' faces, so like eroded cliffs against the water, testified to that.

Oh, Braiz. Would she ever see it again?

She blinked back tears that would muss her cosmetics if they fell, and she almost gasped aloud in relief at a knock at the door. "That must be Captain Corre. It's time."

Madame Brumal humphed and didn't budge. "You'll be ready when—"

Solenn slipped from beneath her grip and stood. The structure of her pannier gave her hips the shape of a bell, with perfect pleats draping to just above the ground. "I'm ready, Madame Brumal," she said in a brusque tone.

Madame Brumal's jaw opened and closed like that of a fish exposed to air, but she nodded. "I suppose you must do. I will be behind you much of the time, should any questions arise."

"I know."

"Tonight, the deed will be done," Madame Brumal murmured as she swished across the room to admit Erwan. Solenn nodded to herself.

The deed would be done, for certain. The ritual during the ball tonight effectively bound her to Verdania—and to Hester, by proxy. Being wed to Rupert next week would be the culmination of that larger union.

Erwan bowed to them both. "Madame Brumal. Princess Solenn. You are both lovely." His eyes revealed a hint of moisture. "They are ready for you, Princess. Shall we?"

Jumbled emotions lodged in her throat. She nodded and took his arm. The rest of the musketeers awaited in the hallway. Solenn took a moment to meet their gazes and smile. A few of them gave her little winks and nods of assurance. Madame Brumal joined their ranks. Together, they exited their apartment corridor.

"You look so grown up," Erwan murmured.

"I *am* getting married next week."

Low as her voice was, something of her true mood carried through. "Tempting though it may be, don't climb down a trellis and flee for the wilderness."

Her smile felt brittle. "I don't need any reminders about my duty to Braiz. Besides, the trellises around here probably wouldn't hold my weight. A twenty-foot fall sounds unpleasant."

"I suppose it's for the best that you gave away that magicked cheese," he teased. Solenn had told him about the curious visit from Aveyron Silvacane.

"No epicurea sounds appetizing about now." She said that in an especially low voice.

"There may be some of a more innocuous nature included with dinner tonight."

She took his meaning. "Like rose fairies. Their use isn't innocuous to *the fairies*." She shivered at the memory of those horrid pickled bodies.

"Even so, try to eat a few bites of each course, if given the opportunity. The night will be long and there will be many toasts, before and after the dancing."

"I *know*." Her head felt ready to explode from all the things she'd been told to remember. "At least the kitchen-staff matter was addressed."

Three cooks and two scullions had been dismissed as a result of the Braizian investigation. Her musketeers also currently oversaw the frenzied work in the kitchen, alert for any suspicious behaviors. Verdanian musketeers were also present.

"Five of theirs, accompanying two of ours," Erwan had said of the arrangement immediately prior to her evening preparations. "A pointed effort to outnumber our chevaliers yet again. Supposedly they're there to watch the cooks."

She sighed. "No. They'll be watching our people instead."

"Indeed. I doubt the palace musketeers' opinions of us are much better than those of the fired staff, but they'll save their griping for later, when they're in their cups."

Solenn took immense comfort in that her musketeers were on duty to guard her and Rupert against further attack. In them, she placed her full faith.

"Have you heard anything else regarding Albion?" she murmured.

"That's a deft change of topic, if ever there was one. Word of their proposal has spread around court. It's created a new layer of gossip as the provincials come into the city for the week's events. Most people seem to be laughing off the proposal as Albion's usual foolish tactics." His tone made it clear he was not so dismissive.

"People here want to disregard Braiz as being stupid and quaint too."

"Yes. To underestimate your enemies is perilous indeed."

Solenn took in the extra meaning of his words as they made another turn, the grand ballroom ahead. Beyond Erwan and her trusted musketeers, everyone here was a sort of enemy. They all wanted something from her, be it a smile or a show of favor or a male heir. She couldn't forget that, or the hundred other things she must remember tonight.

Wine flowed along with superfluous words as the meal began. Solenn sat at the royal table along with about twenty other people, the queen and king at opposite ends with their favorites around them. In keeping with this theme, Jicard sat across from Rupert. The two friends volleyed dialogue and laughter, punctuated by mouthfuls of food.

Solenn sat to Rupert's left, a smile frozen upon her face as if she had eaten stony owl, mostly ignored as she engaged in her vital duty: she cut his food.

This apparently was a proud tradition among Lutecian court brides, and it made no sense to her. If Rupert had an injured hand and couldn't utilize a knife and fork, she would have gladly helped him, but his hands were fine. She was here to be subservient, no more. It was a wonder that this stupid tradition didn't have her shoving food into his mouth too.

She felt her stomach moan piteously. She'd managed only a few bites of food. Madame Brumal could serve Solenn a plate only after Rupert had eaten his, and he was so busy conversing with Jicard that he'd scarcely eaten. At this point, she had lost count of how many saucers and bowls had passed by—seven? Twelve?

The partridge breasts before her smelled so very, very good. Swallowing her resentment and salivation, she sliced the meat so that each morsel retained some crisped skin. The curved green beans she cut into diagonal slivers the size of fingernails. Leaning forward, she used a small spoon to lift salt from a gold- and pearl-encrusted saltcellar in the shape of a galleon, a nef, symbolic of Verdania's supposed might at sea. Back in Braiz, she would have pinched out salt with her fingertips, but such an action was regarded as crude here. She blinked fast to hold back sudden tears as she craved the texture of Malo's gritty sand and brisk, salty air more than she ever had in her life.

With a murmur of warning, she slid the partridge before Rupert. He reared back, giggling over something Jicard had said, then leaned forward to gesticulate.

Solenn pressed her fists against her embroidered stomacher, as if the pressure would somehow fill her gut.

Rupert cast her a rare sidelong glance. "What do you think, Solenn?"

Aroused from her stupor, she tried to recall what they had been discussing. "I know the basics of tennis, Prince Rupert, but I'm unfamiliar with these athletes." Despite his past assurance that she could refer to him in a casual manner, she couldn't do so tonight, not with her role so carefully defined.

"You'll get more familiar. We watch lots of bouts." He stabbed his fork through three pieces of meat and stuffed them into his mouth at once.

Jicard waved his fork to catch her eye. "I noticed that you haven't gotten to eat much, Solenn. My father says that's a good thing about feasts like this." His face was flushed almost the same shade as Solenn's dress. "The bride eats less, and it helps her retain her figure as she bears children later on."

Solenn took a delicate sip of white wine and resisted the urge to snap the glass in her fist. "Childbearing won't be a concern for years yet. We're too young."

"But people are already talking about it. They're even placing bets on if you'll have a boy or girl or survive the labor." He said this matter-of-factly as he poured back the rest of his glass. The valet behind him refilled it. Solenn had never seen wine poured so freely to diners of every age.

"Jicard, you're speaking of her as if she's a broodmare, and at our ball of all places." Rupert sounded exasperated. "Solenn's right. We don't need to discuss this for years yet." He didn't seem embarrassed, but irked. In any case, she was grateful.

"My apologies." Jicard shrugged. His servant whisked away his empty plate. Solenn glanced at Rupert's saucer. It remained half-eaten.

"Anyway," said Rupert. "About tennis. You need to get more of that gruff cheese after all this wedding fuss is done, Jicard. I'd like to eat that when we have a full afternoon to play. It'd be the best game ever."

A soft bell intoned behind them. Rupert's valet took his saucer. Another course was done. Solenn's stomach griped.

"I'm not sure if I can. It's a seasonal cheese. There will be more good stuff, though," said Jicard.

Solenn felt the need to say something. "It must have been difficult for you when your father was away in Albion."

Jicard grimaced. "Not like I see him that much now, but when I do, he usually has something for me."

Solenn sat up straighter as she caught a whiff of her favorite food—lamb. She turned to intercept the dish as Madame Brumal passed it over her shoulder. The madame's thumb slipped, causing an ornate knife to drop to the floor, soundless amid the loud chatter.

"Wait a moment, Princess," murmured Madame Brumal. She hurried away.

Solenn took a moment to breathe in the glory of the dish before her. This was Braizian salt meadow lamb, in clear tribute to her. It would just be coming into season—why, it must have been rushed by wagon to make it here fresh for this dinner. Sprigs of rosemary hugged each side of the cut; she had to think for a moment to identify the southern-grown herb, as she'd had it only a few times in Braiz, always at her grandparents' court. Salt, pepper, and a mélange of spices crusted the leg, the meat braised in the apple cider her country was famous for. It smelled like a fine Laitsday feast; with the exception of the piney note of rosemary, it smelled like *home*.

"Princess." Madame Brumal passed her a knife. Solenn promptly brought it down to the meat.

As she sliced into the lamb, noxious fumes seemed to billow and fill her nose even as high-pitched, undulated singing roared in her ears.

She perceived how toxins would unfurl from her stomach. Fever would come first, then sweat. A rash, flashing over the entirety of her skin as if she'd been dipped in boiling water—that, as her organs began to sour and boil. Pain would follow, quick and unrelenting, as the lining of the lungs and throat became viscous. That's when the coughing would start, pressure in her chest worsening with every breath. Blood would sputter out with her exhalations, the flow worsening as she breathed harder, needier, as her internal organs failed in a fast cascade.

Solenn calmly set down the knife. That lessened the epicurea's grip on her mind, but the presence of potential death lingered like gangrene after a bullet's removal.

This dish couldn't be served to Rupert. To anyone.

She jerked her arm, skidding the platter to her far side, away from him. Just as it seemed ready to tip, a shadow loomed behind her.

"Princess," murmured Madame Brumal. "You must take care." She scooted it back to a centered place before Solenn.

Solenn had almost dumped it . . . almost. She didn't care if people had thought she was drunk and clumsy. This dish had to go. "Madame Brumal," she said, thinking fast. "This lamb isn't appropriate. It must go back."

"What?" Madame Brumal squeaked out.

"What?" echoed Rupert. He and Jicard had ceased their palaver and now stared at Solenn. "What're you going on about?"

What *was* she going on about? She thought fast. "This lamb dish. It's wrong. Northern salt marsh lamb shouldn't include herbs from the southern coast." She set the knife on the plate's edge and tucked her hands on her lap before anyone could see how they trembled. "It must go back."

Rupert frowned. "Looks fine to me."

"It's not, I—"

A fork pierced a slice of meat, and before she could exclaim, Jicard was stuffing it into his mouth. "It's fine."

Death slid down his throat.

"Jicard, no!" Solenn cried.

Then Rupert moved, fast as a quick-hare, and snagged a piece for himself. "Solenn, our cooks and Chefs are the best in the world.

Whatever they do will be *far better* than what you've had in Braiz." He moved the plate over and began to cut the rest himself, even as he still chewed. "This is really quite good. You should try some."

She shook her head. Her intimate awareness of the poison told her that there was no cure. Not even unicorn bone broth could compete with the damage it would render. Maybe that potency was why the assassin had chosen such a means of death, well aware that the palace larder could counteract most mundane poisons.

This attack had somehow evaded her vigilant musketeers. She couldn't call for help. There was no help. Appealing to Erwan would not only make her appear childish in her reliance upon him but would also serve little purpose; he couldn't save them.

"Selland." His name was a breath, her fingers pinched together beneath the cover of the table. "Mercy. Please."

A strange cold chill traveled the length of her spine. Had he heard, his presence attuned to her? Or was the quiver from her own fear?

Or could both be true?

Her one certainty: Jicard and Prince Rupert were going to die this very night, even though, at the moment, they were smiling and laughing and having a grand old time.

If she warned them, they wouldn't believe her.

Or they would—later, if not now—and she would be blamed. But that was the entire intent of this exercise, wasn't it? Solenn was being set up for murder.

Through her cursed tongue, she perceived not only their doom, but her own.

CHAPTER FOURTEEN

ADA

In Ricardy, a land that has often been traded between Verdania and various bordering duchies, beer is a frequent influence upon the cuisine. This is apparent in a Ricard cheese, formed into a small cone, then bathed in beer weekly for two months. Seasonings vary by the village and maker, as does the cheese's name. No matter the variations, this cheese is a pungent one. Enter a room that holds this cheese, and you'll know that Gyst was a recent visitor as well!

—Excerpt from *Book for Cooks to Excel as Do Chefs*

In the dark of the hallway, Ada found Didina's door, but she had no need to knock. Black cloth had been nailed above the frame, symbolic of passing through the veil with Gyst. She might've concluded that some other person had died here, but to one side of the doorframe was pinned a pennant of the Thirty-Fifth Division.

Ada leaned on the wall, head against her forearm. She was too late. Her remaining energy evaporated like flavor from a forgotten glass of wine, and yet she maintained a peculiar kind of relief. If Didina had died here as indicated, then she hadn't been kidnapped, nor had she been cursed by rupic.

But she was still dead.

Ada had befriended Didina Rochamp on her first day in the Thirty-Fifth. They'd shared a similar taste in horses and boots, but not in men. Didina had encouraged Ada's relationship with Erwan but had vowed to never wed a soldier. "Give me a simple man who knows a trade well enough to keep bread on the table. I need no more'n that," she'd said more than once in her Ricardy-accented drawl.

The weathered floorboards creaked, warning Ada that someone approached. She slid a hand to her knife as she turned to face the door across the way. It opened. An old man peered through the gap, his bald pate cast shiny by the candle aglow in his hand.

"What you doin'?" he asked.

"I came to see Didina," Ada said with a slight bow. "But by the cloth . . ."

"Aye. She be huggin' Gyst about now." He eyed her up and down. "Who you be?"

"An old friend. Do you know what happened?" He withdrew slightly, suspicion in his gaze. She cursed herself for her ineptitude—residents of Ricardy tenements in Lutecia kept to themselves, with reason, as other city folk regarded them as foolish provincials, easy to scam. This man would be offended if she pulled out coins too. Instead, she dug into her knapsack for the bottle she'd liberated from Dodo's horse. "Perhaps we could talk over our cups? 'To Selland's breath over our green fields!'" she said, evoking the old Ricardy blessing.

The door opened wide, as if she'd used a key, the man's toothless smile broad. "Be comin' in now."

Ada discovered her new friend was Tomrick, a widowed man from Ricardy who made his coins as a neighborhood timekeeper. With the nearest pentad too distant for most people to hear Melissa's bells toll the hours, Tomrick knocked on doors to awaken people for work and appointments. "I be knowing everyone and everything," he said as he downed his white wine.

Therefore he knew the gab regarding Didina's demise.

He'd heard the scuffle for himself, the walls thin as they were. The door had slammed, someone running away. Then the caterwauling began.

"Them chil'un see it all, and they told us every bit a what happened," he said, rubbing his whiskery chin. "The missus next door took them in until Didina's man got home. Didina, she fought like a dragon, she did. Claw 'n tooth. The men, they tried to drag her out, but she weren't goin'. One of the men, she stabbed, good in the gut." He said this with pride, motioning beneath his own ribs. "But she took a knife, too, and bled fast. The other bloke, he ran faster than a winter wind, he did."

Neighbors thought they had tracked that man down, but only after beating him did they heed a witness who attested to his innocence. Now they had no survivor to blame or abuse, and the gendarmes cared nothing about a dead woman from Ricardy.

Ada drank from an earthenware chalice. "The children were unharmed?"

"Beyond seeing what they saw? Aye. They be with Gregoire's people now. He still works the mill each day, y'know."

Ada hadn't known. She hadn't spoken to Didina since the dissolution of the Thirty-Fifth, days before she gave birth. Didina had been a great help through Ada's pregnancy, often remarking that what she learned would help her when her own time came.

Ada blinked back tears as she finished her drink.

"Thank you for your hospitality." She stood, pulling up her knapsack again. "Enjoy the rest of the wine, in her memory." The half bottle that remained would warm him more than these thin walls.

"In Didina's memory, aye." Tears filled his eyes. "You're a good sort, even if you're a born Lut. If'n you need a room, her old place'll be let next week." He regarded her with hope.

She managed a small smile. "I'll keep that in mind, Tomrick. Selland keep your meat."

Ada returned to the street, tiredness spattering her like rain. She was too old to be awake this late after two days of hard travel.

She mounted her horse and splashed back toward the Golden Horse. Fewer people were out now. The usual music of the late hour was subdued, as if to suit her mood.

Didina, dead. Petry, on the run. Emone, threatened. Erwan, safe as he could be in that viper's nest of a court.

The boss behind these brigands would know his plot had failed thus far. He'd need new hires. She knew where that would likely happen too: Hester's Grace Inn.

Ada needed to go there and make some inquiries, but by the Five, she also needed to rest her old bones. She thought back on her younger years, when she could get by for days on vapors of sleep, and gave a wry shake of her head. Her body was going the way of Hester's old pentad, ready to sink into the earth.

With the city rendered dank after a day of deluge, Ada was a block away from the Golden Horse when she smelled the smoke. She pushed aside her melancholy and put her heels to her horse. Mud kicked onto her coat and face as they cantered toward the sight of Emone's home and business, fully engulfed by flames.

CHAPTER FIFTEEN

ADA

Young tour Chefs often wonder why Hester, God of Hearth and Home, is also associated with anger. This is not as contradictory as it appears. What greater reason for rage is there than the violation of home? Just as a firebreak can defend a town against a wildfire, Hester's fire can be wielded in defense of what we love most—but beware, as flames will indiscriminately consume anything in their way.

—Excerpt from *Manual for Tour Chefs*

A crowd was beginning to gather in the intersection, but fortunately for Ada, the numbers were still few and most people had the good sense to stand farther back. She studied the illuminated faces in a desperate search for Emone. Instead, as she neared the conflagration, she recognized Simon. He'd lost the fine coat he had worn as sentry, his white blouse now blotched in gray.

Ada dismounted and gripped Simon's shoulder to get his attention. She yelled to be heard over the crackling din: "What happened?"

He stared at her for a moment; then recognition dawned on his face. "We were being vigilant. We were. Whoever did this . . . two people were stabbed at the front door, and many of us went there to attend matters, and that's when the blaze began around back." Agony lit his eyes, as bright as the flames. Simon blamed himself for falling for a clever distraction. He bent over with a sudden, fierce cough.

"Where's Emone?" She squeezed his shoulder.

Still bent over, he pointed into the flames.

Ada's horse danced in place. She tried to still him with a hand on the bridle. "How many people remain inside?" How many more innocents had died in this wretched scheme?

"Emone is trying to get everyone out; she—" He coughed again. Tears cleansed paths in the gray of his face. "She won't give up until she checks every room."

That was such an Emone thing to do; it made Ada want to scream in frustration.

Two figures in silhouette emerged from the charred double doors and staggered into the street—Emone, her arm around a man's shoulders. Several men and women surged forward to drag the man away. Emone turned as if to go back in.

"Emone! No!" Ada yelled, her words lost against the din. She lunged forward, but her horse balked. A thick-fingered hand overlaid hers to take the reins. She nodded a quick thanks to Simon and rushed to stop Emone. Sparks rained around them.

"You can't," Ada yelled.

Emone tried to shrug her off. "There might be—"

The Five must have known Ada needed reinforcement, as Emone was interrupted by a resonant cracking sound and collapse deep within the building. Cinders showered down. Another thud rang out with a retort like a firing cannon. Ada flung herself over Emone as people cried and screamed behind them.

A wave of heat washed over Ada. She braced herself for falling debris, but only a few chunks bounced off her back. As she rose up, she dragged Emone with her. Despite their closeness to the conflagration, Emone began to shiver.

"I need to go back in." Ada could barely make out Emone's hoarse voice.

"There's nothing to go into," she said, gently as she could while making herself heard. The doors Emone had just exited were no more. The entire building was engulfed.

Emone butted her head against Ada's shoulder, a cough racking her body. Simon hovered over them both. "Need to get you to a doctor, Madame Emone," he said.

"That can't be our first priority. The arsonist may be watching us even now," said Ada, cringing at Emone's pain-filled cough.

Simon was wise enough to not study the crowd with suspicion. "How can I help, madame?"

Ada bowed closer to him. "I'm getting her away. That may lure the arsonist too."

"Should I follow them?" Simon asked, then averted his head to cough. His lungs must have been almost as damaged as Emone's.

"You can't do so with any subtlety." She had to be blunt, lest he be tempted into heroics. Simon didn't need to meet a valiant, stupid end like the protagonist of a Peppeti opera. "Take care of people here. It's what Emone would want. Then have tea with honey. That'll be the best thing for your throat."

She hated that she must hoard the unicorn tisane, but half the people here hacked and coughed. She had to play favorites.

Simon nodded, bending close to Emone. "We'll take care of them. You come to me when you can," he rasped at her.

"Don't let word get to Claudette that I've died." Emone gripped his blouse with a fist.

"A messenger will be deployed tonight," he vowed. "Don't make a liar out of them." He gave Ada a crisp nod, which she returned.

Together, they helped Emone onto the horse. Others tried to assist, too, questions and concern ringing all around, asking how Emone fared, where they were going. Ada ignored them, trusting the rest to Simon. She led Emone away from the mayhem, coldness and renewed awareness of the rain increasing step by step.

"I'm bait?" Emone managed to croak out.

"Yes, with the hope that Gyst is watching and will help us resolve one of his mysteries. Here, there's water." Ada pulled a canteen from her pack. Emone guzzled it down, pausing to cough before drinking more.

Ada glanced back. Few people walked their same direction. By the Five, she hoped a group of arsonists hadn't been assigned this duty. "How many times did you go back inside, Emone?" she asked in a murmur. "Were you *trying* to help the arsonist succeed?"

"You know me," Emone croaked. "Always helpful."

Ada shook her head. "Next time, try to ingest fire salamander first. That will grant you some physical resistance to fire."

"Next time," Emone wheezed.

A lamp in a window shone onto the street, and Ada used the brief light to check Emone. "Your dress is burned through all over, and you've lost some hair too. Where are you hurting the worst?"

"Here." Emone pressed a hand to her heart. "How many others have died tonight because of this old vendetta? The Golden Horse wasn't simply my home and business, Ada. It was a sanctuary for those who are shunned and lost, as I was as a youth." Grief clouded her eyes. She had defied her father's demands that she marry, opting to risk her life in the army instead. For that, she had been disowned, forbidden to use her own name or to inherit title or fortune. She'd made her own way ever since. "Where will they go? What will they—"

"Shh." Ada hated shushing her friend, but Emone's voice had grown too loud in emotion. "All is not lost. You've already saved many people, and they're looking after each other, even now."

A fast-walking figure a block back seemed to be following them.

Emone hunched over the pommel. "Did you find Didina?"

"She's dead. Two men tried to nab her. She fought back." Ada blinked fast to hold back tears.

Emone's head jerked up. "Her children—"

"They saw but weren't physically harmed."

"Not physically harmed." Bitterness crept into her tone. "But for the nightmares they'll know the rest of their lives."

"I can't cope with crowds and bustle now," Ada murmured. "My imagination returns to the Battle of the Tents. I can't stop it. I've learned Lutecia's backstreets. I've only worked in small kitchens. Thing was, that particular fight happened—what, a year before the war's end? Before I was pregnant, certainly. I didn't have these problems at all until after I'd deserted. I can't make sense of why my anxieties continue to worsen."

"War does that," Emone rasped. "You think you make it through intact, but the things you see and do are a slow poison. I've choked Claudette in the night a few times, mistaking her for an Albionish soldier. Once, she had to punch me in the face to get me to truly awaken."

Ada motioned Gyst's X. "Five save us."

"They're doing a prime job so far. We're still alive, right . . ." Emone bent over, coughing.

Ada thought of how Melissa had herded the horse her way. "We need to get you to a refuge. Didina's place could work, but I hate that we might drag trouble there." That, and the neighbor would be a wee bit too nosy.

Emone shook her head. "No. Five blocks ahead, by the river. Friend's place. Empty."

In the distance rang the bells of a fire wagon.

Ada glanced back. That lone figure continued to follow them with brisk strides, the muted glows of lamps and window candles revealing them to be some 150 feet distant. No one else traversed the thoroughfare. "Do you happen to recognize the person following us?" Ada didn't want to set up a snare, only to entrap one of Emone's people, who pursued them with a dogged need to help.

Emone twisted to one side to cough, making a subtle check behind them. "Don't think so."

"Will you be able to quell your coughs?"

Emone started to answer, only to cough again. Well, this wouldn't do.

"Where's this refuge?" asked Ada.

"Tringa Hotel, ground floor, seven."

"Get there," Ada said, applying a soft slap to the horse's hindquarters. Emone rode off, still coughing. Ada hurried in her wake on foot, turning at the next block as Emone did, but not following any farther. Instead, she ducked down an alley across the way, pulling out her pistol.

She was unsurprised to hear footsteps smacking through puddles in their pursuit.

Ada spun the barrel back into place and raised her gun.

Their pursuer came into clearer view, dark as it was: a stout figure, face obscured by a hood that was pushed back as their steps slowed. Above their rounded cheeks, a monocle glinted from over their left eye. They stopped moving, seeming to realize that their mark had cantered away and out of sight.

Ada remained frozen, willing her target to come ten feet closer, into range.

Instead, they backtracked with fast, sloshing steps. Ada started forward, then stopped. She couldn't pursue this person through the wet city streets, not with Emone in such terrible condition. Ada had already lost one dear friend. She wouldn't lose another.

She waited in stillness for a minute more, then, with wariness, followed Emone's directions toward the refuge.

In the stable beside the Tringa building, she found a sleepy-eyed stable boy rubbing down her horse. Entering flat seven, she tripped over Emone huddled just within the room. Her coughs were muffled by her mouth against the floor.

"I'll get water, Emone. Hold on," Ada said, shrugging off her pack.

Ada grabbed a pitcher and hurried to the pump outside. She perceived no major contamination in the water. Returning, she found Emone in the same state, her shoulders heaving with repressed coughs. Ada poured water into a tin cup and helped Emone drink. "The water's as good as it can get in the city," Ada assured her, not that Emone would've been particular.

The drink eased Emone's immediate need to cough, but Ada knew that wouldn't last long.

Ada set half the remaining water to heat, then used her flint to light nubby candles around the flat. The place consisted of a single room with a cot and rudimentary furniture.

"Can we expect anyone else to come by?" Ada asked. "Shake your head if you can't speak."

"Friend out of town," Emone said in a hoarse whisper. "Our pursuer, did you . . . ?"

"No. They retreated after realizing they couldn't match your horse's speed. I didn't follow. I can't bless the tea until the water's hot. Let's address your burns."

A cabinet contained shabby yet clean clothes. Emone, wincing, stripped off, gasping at the tug of melded skin and cloth. That triggered more coughs, and after a pause for water, Ada helped her fully undress.

"About three really bad spots, and a dozen more smaller burns," Ada said. By dim candlelight, she used a wet rag to clean the injuries as best she could. That would help the tisane do its work. "A shame you lost such a chunk of hair." She tried to be gentle as she dabbed at the blood-matted mess.

"I like wigs," Emone whispered. "I have . . . I *had* quite a few." Her flinching wasn't solely from physical pain.

The water was ready. As Ada brewed the tisane, she closed her eyes to focus. The heat immediately drew out the dormant flavors of the floral mixture and the healing potential already therein. A Chef had prepared the tisane so that it could mend anyone, but Ada could draw out far more power. Power Emone desperately needed as she erupted in more agonized coughs.

Heal Emone, Ada beseeched the Gods, especially Lait, the deity most intimately connected with new growth. *Dull her pain, enable her to breathe, flush out the unknowns that could make her sicker yet.* In Ada's mind, she felt the concealed power of the tisane open like budding flowers, the fragrance growing bolder as her tongue tingled.

Satisfied, Ada opened her eyes. As the tea continued to steep, she pulled bread and cheese from her bag.

"Eat," Ada said to Emone as she sat on the room's sole cot.

"You can't order me around anymore." Even so, she bit into the bread round with a violent crunch.

"I'm ordering you as a friend, not as your superior."

"Oh, that's different," Emone said, wincing as she swallowed. "Then you're just being bossy."

"That's right. And drink this too." She withdrew the spent tisane and handed the mug to Emone. "Slow sips, now. It's going to hurt."

"As if everything didn't already hurt," Emone muttered. The first sip induced a new coughing fit. Ada just saved the cup from spilling. Emone resumed drinking and interspaced her sips with more bread and cheese. Ada indulged as well. The bofor was especially good, originating from cows in the southeastern high mountains. The toothsome texture felt good as she chewed.

"Thank you." Emone's voice still rasped but was stronger.

"It's your tisane."

"I wish I'd gifted you with so much more." Emone rubbed her face. "Everything's gone."

"You're alive. Claudette wasn't there. Everyone probably escaped."

"I know." Her voice held a different sort of pain. "Why are we worth this effort, Ada?"

"I don't know, but I'm going to find out." She stood, stretching. Emone took her meaning. "You're going out again."

"Yes. I need to go to Hester's Grace, where our would-be killers are acquiring employment. I might need to visit more than once to meet this boss of theirs."

"Don't you need to sleep?" Emone frowned.

"If I sat still for a minute more, I'd fall asleep for certain. That's another reason I need to keep moving." Ada began to rummage through the dresser. "I also need to try to get a job tonight. What do you think of this?" She held a cotton tunic up against her body.

"A job? Oho! What, you think you'll get hired to finish me off?" Emone winced as she probed at her scalp wound. "I'd be an easy target now."

"No. I intend to change my look," Ada said, brandishing a limp lace bonnet. "I plan to see if I can be hired to kidnap and kill myself."

CHAPTER SIXTEEN

SOLENN

*One may assume that a Chef or cook specializing in
butchery must be strong to lift meat and hew bone, but
consider also the experts in patisserie who whisk egg
whites for prolonged periods to develop the stiff peaks
required for light cakes or refreshing syllabubs. These
artists boast of upper arms like those of a pugilist!*

—Excerpt from *Book for Cooks to Excel as Do Chefs*

The next courses passed in a nightmarish blur. Jicard's flush deepened, ruddiness that others would dismiss as signs of an excess of alcohol. Small veins visibly began to burst along his cheeks and neck. Rupert cleared his throat often as he jabbered and laughed. As the epicurea was digested, deploying its poison, Solenn's perception of the intimate ways in which it worked also diminished. That was one mercy—at least she wouldn't experience their deaths as she watched them succumb.

Both poisonings against Rupert had been timed so that she would be in his immediate proximity. If someone simply wanted Rupert dead, that could have been carried out in numerous ways, as his lax guards regarded the Braizian contingent as their most immediate threat. At the fete earlier, a potent poison could've eliminated most of the elite youth of court. Whoever did this wanted Solenn present. They wanted the foreign princess to be blamed.

As the clock neared midnight the endless feast proved it could indeed end. Solenn joined Rupert before a white marble hearth at the head of the ballroom.

The August Chef from the Grand Pentad, a rotund woman swathed in Verdanian blue embroidered with the icons of the Five, greeted them with somber nods.

"Today we celebrate the union of not only Prince Rupert and Princess Solenn, and Verdania and Braiz, but also the kindling of a new hearth fire, one that will warm soup and cold bodies and children to come."

The August Chef waved a bell-sleeved arm. King Caristo wobbled over. Red faced from drink, he grinned broadly beneath his mustache. He stood to the left of the Chef. A majordomo handed him a stout piece of wood. The king brandished it to great cheering and applause.

To the other side stepped Erwan.

The greeting for him was polite rather than enthusiastic. Solenn sought to meet his eye, desperate to provide some hint of the disaster already underway, but he maintained his focus on the ritual. He gripped a stick equal in size to what the king held, cut from an oak on her home château's lands.

"Oh, August Hester!" The August Chef rolled her eyes as she extended her hands upward. "Warm this union with your fire! Prove to the world how Verdania glows by your blessed flame!" She gestured behind her. Erwan moved forward first, then Caristo. At the same time, they thrust their sticks into the low-burning hearth fire.

Solenn knew from preparations for this event that the sticks had been treated so that they would erupt as soon as they joined the fire, but they didn't.

She glanced sidelong at Rupert. He swayed on his feet and didn't look entirely aware of what was happening.

A laugh rang out from among the seated courtiers. Another person heavily coughed. The August Chef made a slight motion. An acolyte ran over. They briefly conferred, the Chef's face hidden as much as possible, but Solenn caught her worried scowl.

Was Hester expressing disfavor in this union? Or was this happening because Hester also knew Rupert's death was imminent?

King Caristo leaned toward the hearth, his hands clasped at the small of his back, then made an elegant twirl about on his heel. "How wonderful. Hester smiles upon us, as ever!" he cried, his shrill voice booming in the quiet. The fire remained at a low glow. The August Chef and acolyte looked at each other, perplexed.

Solenn, though, understood that the king was not a drunk buffoon but incredibly clever.

King Caristo knew the fire was low, but he also understood the weight of his power. If he said Hester had shown favor upon Verdania and the marriage, people would nod in agreement.

The monarch's gaze raked over her. A small smile curved his face when he likely realized she had seen through his ploy, but he frowned when he faced his son.

"Have you imbibed to excess? What is the matter with you?" King Caristo whispered.

"I'm fine," Rupert was quick to say.

Caristo compressed his lips. "Make it through the dances, and then we'll find reason for you to retreat." He returned to his seat.

Rupert coughed against the back of his fist, the noise lost against the racket of people chatting as they moved toward the dance floor.

Erwan had slipped back to his post.

The August Chef waved over more Grand Pentad staff. They took up positions with their backs to the hearth. The near-nonexistent fire was obscured from view.

"Monseigneur?" whispered Solenn. "Rupert?" He slowly turned toward her. "It's time to dance." She managed a small smile.

"The dance. Yes." His brow furrowed. They grabbed each other's hands, his touch hot, sticky. Blinking back tears, she walked with him toward the royal dance floor.

This moment had made her anxious for the past year, and now all her concerns of public embarrassment and of making a good impression on Rupert meant nothing at all. She stood on the Verdanian seal inlaid in the marble floor, and as the strings began to play "Hester's Waltz," she and Rupert danced.

His feet were a touch sluggish, and he tripped more than once, but he still knew the moves. She wasn't at her most graceful, either, distracted as she was. As the first song ended, other elites of court joined them.

"You should smile," Rupert whispered as the music picked up again, his words full of phlegm. He released her with one hand to twirl her around.

His advice had merit. She should smile and act as normal as possible. Even so, she fought a sob. She scarcely knew Rupert, but she already understood that while he could be oblivious to the point of cruelty, he wasn't a terrible person overall. Perhaps she could have come to love him.

"It's been a very long night," she said in a hoarse whisper.

"Yes. Very long." He coughed against his free hand and absently dried it on his jacket, leaving a dark smear. "I'm relieved we're nearing the end of this ritual. There will be cake soon, light as clouds. I do love cake." His voice faded, focus lost even as he continued to move like a puppet governed by strings. "Did you spend weeks practicing these dances too?"

"Yes." She'd even practiced with a maid who was about Rupert's own height. Those many hours of repetition, for this.

"I'm not—excuse me," he said with a cough, "a fan of dancing. At least it's made me faster at tennis." He turned to burp against his shoulder. "You'll like tennis."

A tear slipped down her cheek. Perhaps she would have.

The song finished. The entirety of the room applauded as Rupert and Solenn curtsied together. The next tune began. On the far side of the ballroom, the lower nobility began to dance. The Silvacanes must have been there, but they were even farther away than Erwan if so. She'd never felt so surrounded, so very alone.

Slippery as Rupert's hand had become, she almost lost her grip as they turned. Beads of sweat dappled his brow, shadows hugging his eyes. He gasped for air.

Solenn caught a glimpse of Jicard. He was dripping sweat, his pale face fully red. His dance partner, Blanche from the fete, looked tense with worry. Solenn took that as a sign that she, too, was now allowed to show concern.

"Are you feeling well?" she asked, her murmur loud enough to be overheard.

"I think . . . I think I had too much wine. I usually don't drink that much. Or eat over such a long time." Phlegm rattled in his throat as he coughed again, a hand pressed to his chest. Several people stared as they swirled around. His cough had sounded as though it tore flesh.

"Perhaps you should sit down," she said. "A physician—"

"No. We're supposed to dance now. We dance." His small hand squeezed hers, almost painfully, but she knew he was simply trying to hold on through sweat and weakness.

She couldn't cry. She wouldn't. "Prince Rupert, you're ill. Come, rest." Physicians needed to give him unicorn broth, dull the worst of the pain, help him sleep.

"I'm—" The cough caught him off guard, like a dagger slipped between the ribs. He bent over, hacking, the nearest dancers recoiling in alarm.

"Rupert!" Solenn cried. He started to wave her silent, but another cough dropped him to his knees. She whirled around, desperate for help. A single look toward Erwan was all she needed to send him charging forward at long last.

"Monseigneur?" asked an elderly courtier, crouching to help.

"I'm fine." Rupert's words were strangled. The music continued, but the closest dancers had stopped to gawk. Farther out, dancers continued, oblivious, the tune a merry one.

"Captain Corre." Solenn greeted Erwan with crisp formality. "The dauphin requires a physician."

A slight widening of his eyes told her that he understood the dread implication of her words. "Understood, Princess Solenn." Half the Braizian contingent had followed him. With a wordless gesture, he deployed several from the room.

Rupert wobbled as he stood again. "Solenn." His bloodshot, glassy eyes revealed fear as another cough shuddered through him. He covered his mouth, but the violence of the eruption sent blood spraying between his fingers, all over her red dress. She recoiled in horror. A nearby woman emitted a small shriek.

"Rupert!" Solenn grabbed him with both arms to hold him upright as he collapsed.

"What's happening?" Queen Roswita rushed over, skirts clenched in a fist. Her broad panniers struck men to either side, toppling them to the ground. She paid no heed, her focus completely upon her son.

"Mère, I—" Rupert choked. Solenn felt the intense convulsion jolt through him, as if he'd been struck by lightning. His eyes rolled back, blood pouring from his mouth. As he fell slack, Solenn guided him to the floor right atop the emblem of Verdania fringed by Hester's flames.

The music wavered to a tentative conclusion as Solenn cried out, "Help! Fetch a physician, quickly! Please!" She already knew the plea to be in vain, but she needed to speak the words to court, to the very Gods, as at last she was able to sob.

"I'm so sorry," she whispered low enough to be heard only by Rupert and Gyst.

CHAPTER SEVENTEEN

ADA

In the most remote of villages, residents sometimes cook all their bread for a year in a span of days. The bread soon is stale, and must be soaked in water or other liquids for a prolonged time to be edible. They rely on this bread for many months. Their other food offerings are also scarce. Imagine the joy in such a place, then, when tour Chefs arrive. We bring not only our own supplies but knowledge and a willingness to learn more. To these peasants with such stony bread, we are direct representatives of the Five, come to offer them new life and sustenance. Be humble, and do good work that will meet with the approval of those we serve—both people and the Gods.

—Excerpt from *Manual for Tour Chefs*

The rain washed most everything foul and disgusting toward the river, making its stench more pronounced than usual as Ada walked along a rickety boardwalk over mud.

She found Hester's Grace to be a tiny establishment, a stone building surprisingly ancient for a city often razed by fire. The crooked doorway stood so narrow that her shoulders brushed either side as she entered. To her relief, she found few people within and the noise level tolerable.

She stood at the counter, close enough to the alcohol to ascertain that no drinks were poisonous, but neither were they of quality. Here, forgotten wine barrels came to die and then haunted drinkers afterward. She ordered wine and knew before taking a sip that it was nigh close to vinegar. Even so, she grimaced as the liquid glossed her tongue. The acrid odor alone would act like smelling salts to keep her awake.

"I need work," Ada said to the barman.

"What you do?" He spoke with the even tone of a person of Dordone. He resembled a stick figure in a saggy, stained smock. Much of his body weight had to be in his luxurious black hair and matching beard.

"Whatever needs doing." She spoke with a thick accent of south river Lutecia to match the linen and wool clothes she'd borrowed from the flat. "I was a soldier, once." She let the implications of that settle as obvious as the sediment in her cup.

"Never seen you about before."

Ada shrugged. "Never had need to come by until now, but I heard of this place, kept it in mind."

"You need to shoot to get the jobs on offer here."

She slid a few coins across the counter. "I can shoot. And use a blade."

"Man over there with the red cravat, he's looking to hire," the barman said, then shuffled to another patron.

Ada sat across from the aforementioned man, hoping she exuded cocky confidence rather than sheer exhaustion. "I was told you're hiring." She had another sip of her wine, her tongue now numbed to its shocking awfulness. She couldn't decide if its aggressive potency would be good or bad.

"I am." He tucked the booklet he'd been reading inside his jacket. "I need sure shots to escort freight to Arden. Got five wagons. Two-day trip to the city, if the Five smile upon us."

They wouldn't. That road was more of a muddy river in this season. "No pay for the return?"

He shook his head. "You get paid in Arden. Make your own way from there."

"I need to stay in the city. I've obligations here."

"Two days isn't that long. Leave the children some food; they can manage."

That left sourness in her mouth that was not from the wine. "No thanks. G'night to you." Ada moved back to the bar.

A fellow soon sidled up beside her and made a different sort of job offer, which she declined with a hand on her knife. The man wisely moved along. After a few more minutes, the barman brought her more wine, then nodded toward the door as it opened again. "They been hiring here these past few weeks," he said to her, then called out, "Same for you lot?"

"Aye," said one of the three, giving her adequate excuse for an open appraisal.

The men were dressed not unlike her—careworn clothes, spattered by mud and rain. The two in the lead possessed the confident strolls of men who knew these streets with dark intimacy. The young man who followed them was shorter, his handsome face too artfully smudged, his prim walk the sort associated with nervous clerks trying to rush home late at night with a day's earnings. Anyone quayside would know him for an easy mark, were it not for the two brutes in accompaniment.

These men fit the description provided by Dodo. Even more, the mustached guard carried on his person several pouches containing stony owl stomach. By the Five, how had they been able to acquire this much?

She studied the trio as they collected their drinks and went to a table at the back of the room. These were the men who sought to have her murdered and cannibalized—and tried to do the same to her oldest, dearest friends. Who had murdered Didina before her children. Who had tried to burn Emone alive, without care as to who else died or lost everything in the process.

Ada tempered her quivering rage with another sip of wine, then ventured to their shadowed alcove.

"The barman told us that you're looking for work," said the clerkish man. He had to be around twenty in age.

She owed the barman some extra livre. "I am. Been a soldier. I can do what needs doin', if the pay's good and proper."

"You fine with sending people to Gyst, through unconventional means?" he asked, his gaze on her open and curious. He and his companions showed no hint of recognizing one of their very targets. Her disguise—and her audacity in being there—seemed to have done the trick.

"What you mean by 'unconventional'? I can do more 'an cut and shoot."

"Epicurea. Can you utilize it?"

"I'm no Chef, 'course, but I can get by." She hesitated a moment, deciding to add some pressure. "If you can get good stuff, what're you doin' having the likes of me cook up ingredients? Can't you get a Chef of your own?"

The two guards studied her levelly, and their employer's smile was taut. "Some things, not even a rogue Chef is willing to cook," he murmured.

"Well, well." Ada reared back in her rickety chair as if impressed. "Sounds like I wouldn't get to try any of this quality stuff for myself, though. A shame."

"Some incentives would help you move past this shame, yes?" asked the young man. At her nod, he continued, "There's a woman in the city.

A former soldier, like yourself. She needs to be brought to a let room here to eat something."

The ceiling ominously creaked with footsteps above. "Only brought here?"

"We check with our people here each night," added the second of the guards.

The young man drank his wine with clear distaste. He was clearly accustomed to finer things.

"Sending someone direct to Gyst—now, that's easy—but hauling some unwilling person here, making them eat . . ." Ada gestured, palms up.

"We're aware of the . . . complicated nature of the task." His face formed a pretty pout. "You're fortunate that others have failed, really. We've increased the promised pay as of today. Ten livre in advance, plus your choice of a catalog of epicurea to aid in your quest. Fifty livre upon completion."

Ada almost choked on her wine but, after a cough, kept the acidic sludge down. Sixty livre to see herself dead? That was more than the majority of the city saw in a year! Fortunately, her reaction was nothing unusual—such a figure would make many people sputter in shock.

"That much, *and* epicurea?" she rasped.

"We have resources," he said with some pride.

Resources, indeed. Ada thought of Maman. Were these men filching from her organization, or working with rivals? In any case, Ada now understood why her original brigands had possessed rupic powder.

Which brought her back to one of the lingering mysteries: How was Mallory Valmont involved?

"Barman said you'd been hiring often of late," Ada said, speaking slowly to think through her words. "If I do this job, might there be more up for offer?"

The young man glanced at his mustached guard. "Perhaps. Our other agents are taking longer than I'd like. The timeline is perhaps not so urgent now, but I still want these jobs completed soon." His fists opened and closed, anxious. "Do you have access to the palace, perhaps?"

The palace. *Erwan.* "No, not for lack of wishing." She gestured to the Five. The mustached guard chuckled. "Why's there less urgency now?" she added. "Not that I intend to dally, not with such money on offer."

"Sending these souls to Gyst will be . . . a gift for my father. Old wrongs, righted."

This was Mallory Valmont's *son.*

She could now see the resemblance in his eyes, though he took more after his pale, blonde mother, especially in his slight build. Ada had seen him a time or two as a young child but hadn't paid him much attention.

"My father has been ill," he continued. "Days ago, we were certain he'd know the resolutions to his mysteries at any moment, but he's better now."

Ada kept her face composed as she made an appropriate gesture. "Blessed be the Five."

Mallory Valmont had indeed survived Mont Annod, and his son wished to gift Mallory with his old favorite epicurea, the cursed-stone remains of his enemies.

"Monsieur." The mustached guard nudged his boss as he looked past Ada. "Perhaps we have more news."

Ada glanced over her shoulder. A buxom figure stood beside the bar, hood pushed back to reveal a soot-smeared face with a monocle over one eye. The newcomer's gaze met Ada's, and both eyes widened.

The arsonist had undoubtedly gotten a good look at Ada at the scene of the crime, and the fact that Ada had cleaned her face and changed clothes apparently hadn't fooled her.

"You!" the arsonist cried, looking between Ada and the men beside her in bewilderment.

Ada shoved the heavy wooden table, hard, pinning the three men against the wall. For good measure, she flung her goblet, enjoying the brief sight of it arcing through the air to strike young Valmont in the face.

She jumped to her feet, ready to confront the arsonist next, whereupon she was promptly struck with vertigo, courtesy of the heady wine sloshing in her gut.

She grimaced. An amateur mistake. She clung to the back of a nearby chair, and as dapples faded from her vision, she swung it toward the arsonist. She had brandished a knife, which did nothing to fend off the weight of the chair against her chest. Ada shoved her backward into a card game in progress. Men and women screeched as they stood, their spilled alcohol creating a foul perfume. With the entirety of the room in turmoil, Ada bounded into the rainy night.

Yells of outrage followed her, tables and chairs scraping on the floorboards.

She ran for all of ten feet, then found mud slicked on the boardwalk. One instant she was upright; the next she was down, landing hard on her left shoulder. Air expelled from her lungs with a shocked gasp. Dank odors of mud and manure filled her senses. She propelled herself upright and staggered forward. The yells behind her grew louder again.

Her pursuers were outside.

Ada willed her exhausted, battered body to run.

The quay was dark, the flooded street looking little different from the neighboring river. Many people moved about, most on foot, some by horse and wagon, their numbers high enough that they would have perturbed her during the day, but in the dark, everyone and everything was blurred by the absence of light and her sheer panic.

Past a large, rowdy group, she made herself slow down, even as her heart threatened to outpace her. And her gut . . . that wine hadn't been undrinkable, but oh, it was still bad after such rapid movement. Feet pattered after her, but she didn't spur herself to sprint again.

Instead, she blended in with her peers on the quay by leaning against a building to retch.

Footsteps and voices hurried past her.

She remained still a moment more, still unsteady. Her shoulder throbbed like a glowing coal, but it wasn't broken or out of socket. Bruised, most likely.

Slowly, she began to move again, the rainfall heavy and steady.

She ducked down one alley, then another, snaking her way deeper into the city. No feet smacked the rainy streets in her pursuit, but she still took extra care, pausing every so often to listen and let any stubborn sloshes of wine settle again before she continued to her apartment of refuge.

Ada slipped inside the flat, quiet so as to not disturb Emone, only to find the cot was empty. The blankets had been folded, the pillow fluffed.

"Oh, Emone. Don't you know how to rest?" Ada muttered, though she was as guilty. At least she knew the arsonist wasn't still lurking around the Golden Horse, which had to be where Emone had gone.

Annoyed as she was at Emone's departure, there was a considerable positive: the sole bed was now hers.

She cleaned her face, shed her shoes, and changed into her own clothes again. She set a pistol and knife within easy reach, then allowed her weary body to meet the straw mattress.

"Gyst, guard us from unknowns," she said to the darkness, then let slumber claim her.

CHAPTER EIGHTEEN

SOLENN

For a Chef to shun their obligation to king and country and the Five is an abomination, but for a Gyst-touched Chef to do so is egregious. For them to lose their tongue is too gentle a punishment. Take from them not only their connection to the holy, but all the senses by which they know the world. I say, leave them alive and bereft, as they left their king and Gods bereft.

—The fifth August Chef of Lutecia, often quoted
across Guild canon

Solenn awakened to sunlight and the deep, resonant tolling of bells.

She pushed herself onto her forearms, groggy, then collapsed again. What time was it? By the angle of light, it had to be late morning, but she never slept this late, so why—

The events of the previous night overwhelmed her like an avalanche. Rupert. Jicard. The dinner, the dance, the poison. With a moan, she pushed her face into her pillow.

The door burst open. "Solenn, are you—?" Erwan stood there, changed from his formal attire into the standard blue cassock of Braiz.

"I *remembered*." She held out her arms as she sat up. He rushed over and crouched to meet her embrace. "The bells, oh no, the bells," she said through sobs, her head against his shoulder. Her fingers found the tiered lace upon his sleeve and gripped it tightly, as she had as a small child.

"I hear them too," he murmured. The largest, most resonant of the pentad bells rang only for the worst of tragedies.

"He's dead." Her words were muffled; everything was muffled. Still, Melissa's grand bells tolled.

"He must be, yes. We'll receive official confirmation soon."

Sudden fear caused her to push back. "I need to be ready."

"As do we all," said Erwan, his tone grim. As he stood, she noted that he had donned his rapier—as he most always did—but now carried turn-off pistols as well. Palace musketeers would undoubtedly interpret his arsenal as demonstrating an offensive lack of faith in their abilities. She took immense comfort in that he looked prepared to defend her against physical threats.

If only their enemies would be so blatant.

She thought of Rupert as she had last seen him. His wide, bloodshot eyes had stared straight at her, blankness in his gaze. Blood streamed from his gaped lips as he convulsed slightly, as if he had hiccups. Across the dance floor, Jicard lay in a similar state. A woman's screams rang out over the chaos.

Solenn didn't remember the return to her room, but once there, she'd told everything to Erwan.

"I want to go home more than anything," she'd said, voice rattling like a bare tree in a winter storm. "But I can't. If I run, I'll only look more guilty. I don't think they'll kill me. I'm more useful alive. But the rest of you . . . the rest of Braiz. Whoever did this wanted to cause a war between us and Verdania."

"And King Caristo is fool enough to take the bait." Erwan's lips had pulled back in contempt. "Or this could simply leave us all separated and strained, and the more vulnerable to Albion."

"Hasn't King Caristo kept one of his old rivals locked up in a castle for twenty years?"

"Yes. The cousin who rivaled him for the throne, back when they were both teenagers. One Merle Archambeau, who's been stripped of his titles. He's not kept in a grimy, rat-infested dungeon but in a palace with a devoted staff, apparently playing tennis every day when the weather is fair."

"But he's not allowed to leave," she'd added softly.

"Nor to have guests, unless expressly approved by the king, and it takes months for a yea or nay." Erwan sighed. "I won't lie to you, not about this. You wouldn't be treated so favorably, not with this blot on your escutcheon. Not that you would get the dungeon, but . . ."

"They wouldn't let me ride."

Erwan's smile was sad. "No. They would seek to make you miserable, while still declaring you to be an honored guest."

Solenn swallowed down a further urge to sob. She couldn't let emotion overwhelm her right now. She had to *think*. "Such captivity wouldn't be done out of sheer cruelty, though. They would also be preventing me from making another marriage alliance with a country such as Albion." That thought caused her to gasp. "That news—the proposal—"

"The timing is rather curious, isn't it?" Erwan said, lips pursed. "As if Albion expected Rupert to already be dead for days or weeks, leaving them free to make an overture anew. Someone—or several someones—erred in the handling of their intrigue."

"That should be evident to King Caristo as well, right?"

"Solenn." Erwan clenched her hands, grief in his blue eyes. "That would be a logical conclusion, yes, but do not rely on logic, not in Caristo and Roswita's court. *You* are the target before them. They will take aim."

At that, her grief and fear hardened to anger. "Then we must make me a more difficult target."

Late as the hour had been, she'd taken the time to walk her rooms in case any poisonous epicurea had been hidden to further incriminate her, but she'd perceived nothing. Erwan noted that her visceral experience of the poison, especially the strange screaming she'd heard, put him in mind of singing mushrooms, a rare epicurea that grew nearer to the northern coast.

"People would think we were stupid enough to use an ingredient almost exclusive to Braiz?" As soon as she'd said it, though, she sighed. "They *do* think we're that stupid."

As Solenn had readied herself for an attempt at sleep, another pressing concern emerged.

"Madame Brumal cannot be found," Erwan had said upon receiving a report from his musketeers. "She was last seen as the dancing began. Most of her belongings are also gone."

Now, the morning light cast beams upon Solenn's rumpled sheets. She touched one, as if she could absorb hope along with its warmth. "Has Madame Brumal been found yet?" she asked, remembering Erwan's declaration from the night before.

"No, and our efforts are constrained, as the palace is currently sealed to the outside."

"How convenient for her to make an escape," she muttered, then closed her hand in a fist. "Could you please have Talia sent in again?" The grandmotherly musketeer had aided her in disrobing after the ball. "And—oh no. I have nothing in mourning gray." Her new wardrobe fully focused on cheery outfits suitable for a Verdanian spring.

Erwan stood. "I should have thought of that. A palace tailor will be contacted forthwith. What else can I do?"

"Just . . . be near," she whispered.

He planted a kiss atop her head, such a rare fatherly gesture from him that now meant even more than it had before. "I'll let you know if need arises for me to be more than a room away."

A tiny smile crept onto her face. "You can use the privy."

Erwan smiled in turn. "Thanks for granting me permission, Princess Solenn." He stepped back to bow with a flourish.

As soon as he left, she rag-bathed herself and changed her small-clothes. Talia then arrived, and together they studied her wardrobe before settling on a pantsuit in Verdanian blue and crimson.

"That's almost as good as gray to show proper support for the court in mourning," Talia said.

"I fear that nothing I do will be proper right now." She blinked fast to hold back more tears.

Wearing the pantsuit made her feel more empowered, though. Breeches would make it easier for her to ride, and oh, how she yearned to escape.

Talia's deft hands, having practiced on her own daughters and granddaughters, made quick work of weaving her hair into a sequence of braided buns. Solenn glanced to the window, expecting a gloomy day to suit her mood, but instead witnessed a sunny morning.

Talia admitted Erwan to the room.

"Your presence is required for a public address on the balcony at noon," he said. About an hour away, she noted. "A mourning pantsuit is being rushed here, with more garb to follow."

"Good," Solenn said with relief. "This attire would've worked within court, but the balcony . . ."

"Yes." The balcony meant thousands of commoners in the street and square, people as judgmental and cruel as those of court, but more likely to wield weapons rather than words. In that regard, she was safer in the palace.

"I want to walk through Madame Brumal's room to see if there's anything to perceive. Have you learned anything more about her whereabouts?"

"We now know she exited the palace and entered a diligence as the dance began. We still cannot trace her from there. However, I must show you something in her quarters." Erwan motioned her to follow.

Madame Brumal had resided a few doors away. Solenn encountered many of her musketeers in the corridor, each of whom greeted her with salutes of support. There was a grim determination about them that brought tears to her eyes anew.

Erwan alone stayed with Solenn as she investigated Madame Brumal's apartment. Like her own temporary domicile, it was high ceilinged and well appointed, though small, as was suitable for a lady-in-waiting for a visiting royal guest. Dresses and pantsuits still filled half the wardrobe, while written paraphernalia was scattered atop the table and dresser. Solenn made her circuit slowly, breathing in deeply to give her senses time to react, but in the end she shook her head.

"Even if we had found epicurea, the evidence alone wouldn't have convinced Caristo. He and his ilk would argue that she had acted on your behalf," said Erwan with a sigh. "We did discover something else of use in our investigation. Look here." He motioned to a tablet left on the dresser, a singular sheet beside it. The paper had what looked to be charcoal rubbed across the surface, revealing white letters on the page.

"That's her handwriting," Solenn observed. Madame Brumal had written plentiful instructions for her in recent days. She looked between the sheets. "Her nib left an impression on the papers beneath? You taught me to be wary of that sort of thing before I'd even lost all of my baby teeth."

Erwan shared a small smile of pride. "Apparently Madame Brumal's instructors were more lax, or she was careless. We used a partially burned stick to make these words legible. From the impressions of a single page, the context is clear. She wrote to an agent of Albion, apologizing for her previous failure and saying she would succeed in her next effort and be at the rendezvous as scheduled."

"Albion," she murmured, thinking of Lord Whitney. "I wonder how long Madame Brumal worked on their behalf. She'd been with Queen Roswita's staff for, what, five years?"

"Yes. Her references were exemplary. Having freshly reviewed them, I don't believe them to be lies either. I suspect she's been a spy for some time and hid her activities well up until now." He motioned to the charcoal-rubbed paper.

"I suppose none of this information would convince King Caristo of my innocence."

"He could declare you were a co-conspirator or that this was a forgery. King Caristo believes what he wishes to believe and cares not who's harmed by his incompetence," said Erwan with uncharacteristic bitterness. Solenn thought of her Chef-mother with a pang. Did she still mourn and rage over the dissolution of her marriage as much as Erwan did? Solenn knew she shouldn't blame the woman if she had moved on to other relationships, but she hurt to think of how that might devastate Erwan anew if they could reunite.

"Well, we need to be the competent ones if we're to endure this," Solenn said crisply. She felt better acting like a princess in command. "What strategy do you have underway?"

"My foremost concern is your security. You must be accompanied by our own at all times."

Erwan was terrified, she realized. He might have been able to hide that fact from everyone else, but not her.

"That may not be possible for long," she added softly.

"As I well know. But even if you are sent someplace such as the tower, we can keep that under watch from afar." The tower. That was where rogue Chefs were sent upon capture. Not a dungeon, certainly, but far from freedom. "Keep in mind your martial training. You may have cause to use it at last." His expression was grim.

Solenn nodded. In the past year, as it had become more apparent that she would be moving from the security of Braiz, Erwan had arranged it so that Talia and other women musketeers drilled Solenn on matters of self-defense—how to slip from a hold, what to do if pinned on the ground, where to most effectively strike a person, et cetera.

"We are using all possible means to track Madame Brumal," he continued. "I won't say more, in case they impose gabby jay upon you."

The mention of epicurea took her aback. "Surely they wouldn't compel me to speak! That's the kind of tactic they use in *Albion*."

"Don't underestimate what they may do. Verdania is our enemy."

"Telling them how our musketeers managed to penetrate the closure of the palace seems minor compared to what else they could learn from me."

"It's not minor to those who aid us, who could well face execution if their roles were known," he said softly. "We *will* find Madame Brumal. We know that she was to rendezvous at a tavern, and with that—"

"Oh, Erwan, in a city of seven hundred thousand, that must be, what, a few thousand places to check?" A wail crept into her voice.

"Keep faith, Solenn. We will find this woman. She will know justice in Braiz if not in Verdania." Erwan's dark scowl declared this with certainty.

A knock came at the door, and Talia entered with bows to them both. "Captain, Princess, the tailor's come."

Solenn returned to her quarters. In the company of Talia, she donned the gray pantsuit. The tailor adjusted the justaucorps to highlight her waist. Not far beneath the hem of her coat, her breeches ended right below the knee. Black boots completed a look both elegant and somber.

The tailor departed. Solenn stared at herself in the mirror, tugging at the black satin cravat to make its loops fall just so over the frills of her blouse. Were the attire in a different color, it would make for a nice riding outfit.

She studied her face as she blinked back tears.

"Princess?" Talia said gently. "Noon approaches. If you're ready, we should inform the captain."

Solenn nodded, not trusting herself to speak. She gave her justau-corps a final tug, then turned away. This was not riding attire—not today, perhaps not ever. For her, it must be armor, as a battle awaited. This was among the first conflicts in what might become a dreadful war.

CHAPTER NINETEEN

ADA

Bakers in Lutecia have traditionally used three to four leavens, with the starter taking twelve to fifteen hours to activate. Barm, or brewer's yeast, has become popular in recent years as it hastens fermentation and creates a lighter loaf. Some elements in society, however, argue that barm should not be used because it is not a technique of Verdanian origin. Bakers often acquire the leavener through an increasing number of city beer brewers who emigrated from the Confederated Duchies. Detractors also note that Albionish bread bakers often use barm from ale, making it all the more offensive.

—Excerpt from the *Times of Lutecia* newspaper

"Will someone please stop that unholy noise?" Ada moaned, pressing the thin pillow to her ears.

"That may be rather difficult as the bells are holy in origin, and likely to ring for a while yet due to the dire news they announce."

The surprise of Emone's voice caused Ada to bolt upright in the cot. The shutters had been opened to release slats of vivid yellow light, along with a whiff of brisk air. Emone sat leaning against the opposite wall some seven feet away, a blanket puddled around her bare feet.

"You slept *there?*" Ada said, feeling stupid as soon as the words emerged.

"It's a perfectly fine floor." She gave it a pat-pat as if to reassure its feelings. "Besides, I recall what happened a previous time when an unwelcome person crawled into your bed. That man ended up with, what, three broken ribs?"

"And a shattered hand," Ada said absently, swinging her feet to the floor. The entirety of her backside ached, and her shoulder—ouch. She pulled her collar over to confirm her shoulder had developed a large bruise the deep purple of an aubergine. Sniffing the air, she faced the room's sole table. "Food?"

"Yes, yesterday's stock, as the bakers were working their dough for the morning, but—"

"I don't care." Her mouth felt fetid from that poor wine, her stomach still burbling in mild dismay; bread with butter would settle that nicely. She went to the table to find rounds that were light brown, made of coarse grain. The bread tasted nigh divine before she had even taken a bite.

"Do you want the bad news," Emone asked as Ada tore a round into pieces and slathered on butter, "or the presumed worst news, as far as the fate of the realm goes?"

Ada arched an eyebrow as she began to chew. "What, did King Caristo fall into a pile of manure and decide to outlaw horses in a fit of pique?" Saying his name seemed to make her mouth taste worse.

Emone joined her. Her long tunic dangled to her bare, burn-flecked thighs. "No, but this does involve him. As much as you hate the man, you wouldn't wish this upon him and Roswita." She paused as she, behaving in a far more civilized manner, used her knife to split open a bread round. Crumbs shattered across the table. "Prince Rupert is dead."

Ada choked. Emone delivered several blows to her back that cleared the block and spiked pain through her aching shoulder. "What?" she squawked out as soon as she swallowed.

Emone explained that as she was returning shortly before dawn, the early bustle on the street had slowed to share the news that the prince had swooned at his formal betrothal ball.

"And not because of drink?" Ada asked.

"Alcohol normally doesn't cause a person to spew bloody bubbles and convulse on the floor." She applied a layer of butter as thick as her pinkie finger.

"Ideally, no. You're right. As much as I loathe Caristo for the loss of my family, I would never wish *this* kind of grief on him. Unyielding rashes upon his nether regions, yes.' Oh, if she had known a recipe for revenge that caused that kind of petty assault, she would have utilized it years earlier. She wiped crumbs from her lip. "Exactly how old was the boy? I know he was born in my early years as a rogue." There had been bells then, too, but the sweetest of Melissa's peals, meant to be as joyous as the God's honey.

"Fourteen."

Fourteen. Not much younger than her own daughter. "Now look at what you've done, Emone. You're making me feel sad for Caristo."

Ada's old friend gave her a wry look. "Feel for Morvan, too, and for his daughter most of all. She's in a right political sty. She's a foreign princess who'd be sneered at for her origins alone, but she also *looks* different from the rest of court. You know that her appearance was only tolerated because of the perceived benefits of the alliance."

"You know I know." Ada felt angry and tired, and tired of being angry. The composition of the Chef's Guild wasn't much different from that of the court, with any variety arising from territorial acquisitions.

She'd often been regarded as more *useful* than welcome, though her family had been classified as Verdanian for a century.

"Princess Solenn couldn't have done this crime. *Wouldn't* have," continued Emone. "It's too blatantly foolish."

Ada found the baker's stamp upon her bread and absently stroked the raised ridges with her thumb. "Which is why Caristo will believe it. He'd blame Braiz for clouds over a picnic. Princess Solenn *is* in a terrible spot as the perfect scapegoat, and Erwan is right there with her. He'll be harder for me to reach and warn."

"Harder for his personal brigand to reach as well, though—and safer from city mobs. I already heard a person outright eager to lay guilt upon Braiz because he thought they would actually prefer an alliance with Albion. The third-born prince there is a bit younger than Rupert was."

"Morvan would rather chop off his hand than force his daughter to wed into Albion." Morvan had spent intermittent weeks with the Thirty-Fifth, back in the day. He was a good sort, jovial, unafraid to muck in with everyone else. *Nice.* Quite contrary to her expectations of royalty.

"If it comes down to a wedding or a full invasion from Albion . . ." Emone shrugged as she leaned back. "They lost almost all their fleet, Ada. They've never been this vulnerable. Verdania's navy has never been the best, but even they could likely win Braiz's ports right now. Albion—you know what their navy is like." Yes, annoyingly good. "Lord Whitney heads their entire forces now."

Ada sucked in a sharp breath. "Ah. *Him.*"

They had met a few times during peace negotiations. Lord Whitney had the bearing of an intelligent predator. He didn't simply look at people or places. He studied them, and as an empathetic Chef, he did so with more than his eyes. He was disturbingly devout in his adoration of king and country, a true believer that his Chef talents were endowed upon him by the Gods. Therefore, in his view, his every action was right and righteous.

"I remember how you described him once," Emone mused. "You said something like, 'Lord Whitney would fart and declare it to be a divine wind.'"

Ada laughed in surprise. "I'd forgotten about that. That statement is probably truer now that he has consolidated more power." She drew thoughtful. "The success of this attack on Prince Rupert makes greater sense now. Lord Whitney would have arranged this with care."

"He favored complicated strategy, though. Pieces in rapid sequence—which also made his ploys fail at times. An attack on Prince Rupert would not be an isolated act. There will be more to come."

"Yes, but Albion may not even need to make a direct move. With the dauphin dead, Verdania has no direct heir. Caristo's cousin and maybe his other kin who *aren't* already imprisoned must be eyeing each other like hungry dogs around a bone. If Albion is patient, Verdania may soon tear itself apart in civil war, and they can then waltz in and plant their flag. How are you feeling, by the way?" Shiny red patches on Emone's forearms proved that the tisane had worked its magic.

"Surprisingly well, I daresay. I woke up while you were out and felt downright spry, so I went for a glance around the city." Emone ate more bread.

"Did you check on the Golden Horse?"

The bells stopped at last. The morning noise from the street seemed subdued in the aftermath.

"Yes. No bodies have been found in the ruins yet. The rain helped speed that search, at least." Emone made a reflexive gesture to the Gods. "That done, I happened by an establishment named for Hester."

"*What?* You followed me? You needed to rest!"

"As if you didn't need rest too. Someone had to watch your back and make sure no knives sank into it."

"I didn't see you there."

"I lingered outside, enjoying the rain and the few proposals that came my way. I'll laugh about those with Claudette later. Your fall on the walkway was quite spectacular, by the way. If you'd stayed down, your pursuers might have passed on by."

"Or I would've been trampled by them."

"You, always with the downside." Emone made a tsking noise. "I followed them as they pursued you and then happened to hitch a ride on the back of their diligence as they went home."

Ada guffawed. "I'm not the only one still attempting the antics of my youth, then."

"You may be determined to be old and decrepit, my dear, but I remain in full flower." Emone patted her head, then cringed as she found a tender spot.

"Oh, stop with the dramatic pauses." Ada leaned forward in eagerness. "Where did the carriage go?"

Emone serenely smiled. "To a house. I can show you."

Ada stood. "Let's go. I'm curious about where the son of Mallory Valmont now lives."

Emone's face flickered through various emotions in the span of seconds, settling on a feral, toothy grin. "The son! He's behind this?"

"Not the son alone. Mallory Valmont apparently is alive as well, barely." Ada appreciated her own manufactured drama as Emone's jaw dropped. "I'll tell you more of what *I* learned as we prepare to go out."

⌒⦾

Though they avoided the major thoroughfares in Lutecia, the strange tension of the city remained palpable—that terrible sense that something bad had happened, and worse would follow. Street gossip was flurried but hushed.

This same mood of distraction and anxiety carried into the palace quartier. With the sun shining high after a day of drenching rain, a number of the well-to-do had stepped out for a stroll or ride, though many hadn't made it far. Several wagons sat parallel on both sides of the broad avenue as occupants jabbered through coach windows.

Ada had returned to the outfit she'd worn to Hester's Grace, which could readily be excused as servant's attire, while Emone left their refuge for a brief while and returned with a maid's outfit in light blue. That Emone knew people nearby, ready to hand out clothes willy-nilly, didn't surprise Ada in the slightest.

What did make her mood turn grim was that they were almost to Maman's residence.

"There's a house coming up that I dare not get close to," Ada said. The fact that Comtesse Esme Alarie was her mother was known only to her grandmother, Erwan, Ragnar, and Gyst, and it needed to stay that way.

Emone cast her a sidelong look and nodded. "Can you describe the house?"

"It has the vine-covered stone wall, three chestnut trees visible beyond." They stopped walking as Ada feigned digging in her boot as if for a stone. The chestnuts were just visible from where they stood.

"We needn't go farther, then. Our former peer's spawn entered the gate of the home beside it, the one closer to us."

"Let's turn around," Ada murmured.

Mallory Valmont's son—and presumably, the deathly ill Mallory Valmont—lived next door to Maman, in the house Ada and her grandmother had utilized in their escape. Maman and the Valmonts, business partners. Maman wouldn't be involved in the plot against Ada and her compatriots, though . . . no, that had arisen from the Valmonts alone.

"What are you thinking?" murmured Emone. They crossed the grand square before the palace, normally a place of bustle to be avoided, but today the vendors and passersby were sparse.

"That the mysteries being solved are still snarled, even by Gyst's standards."

Bells tolled again, this time not from the pentad but from the palace ahead to their right.

"Summoning bells?" said Emone, her brow furrowing. "They must be making the official declaration—oh no."

Ada heard the roar behind her, like an oncoming flood, as people emerged from homes and businesses to fill the streets. Wagons, riders, and pedestrians began to converge around them.

"Emone!" Panic warbled in her voice. "I need out of here."

Awareness flashed in Emone's eyes. "This way."

They faced an alley, but it, too, began to fill with humanity. People, people, everywhere. Ada and Emone briefly fought the flow, trying in vain to reach the doorway of a haberdasher, but the twenty feet may as well have been a deep chasm. Heat flashed over Ada's skin, her breaths quickening, sweat sopping her like an instantaneous, personal rainstorm. Usually, her hot drenches came only during the night a few times a month, but her panic had dragged her body's reaction into the daytime to make everything even more nightmarish.

Around them, faces were eager with anticipation, voices jabbering, the sweat and stink and press of people filling her nostrils, her mind. A wagon clattered with a cannon-like boom, horses screaming. Her sweat worsened, memory draping her like a heavy veil.

The cantonment, overrun. Gunfire smoke fogged the lanes of tents, thicker than the billows from campfires. Albion's colors were bold against the dark of night. She was surrounded, jostled, slashed, and all she could think was, *I must find Erwan, I must*—yelling, talking, the report of a gun, a scream, clashes of rapiers—

"Ada!" Emone screamed in her ear. "Stay with me. We're in Lutecia." Her small hand gripped Ada's in a painful, welcome vise, anchoring her to the present.

She nodded to acknowledge that she heard, but the past still overlaid the present, her breaths still rapid, her heart at a gallop.

"I'm in Lutecia." She couldn't even hear herself say the words against the loudness of the crowd, but comfort came in the very act of speaking. She made her eyes go wide as if she struggled to stay awake, making herself take in the current scene. A tall stone wall tipped by spear points towered twenty feet ahead of them the intervening space packed with humanity. Above that, the nearest wing of the palace loomed, the balcony high and set back enough that someone using epicurea would have trouble striking the royals by bullet or bolt.

"Nod if you're a little better," Emone asked.

Ada nodded.

"We're stuck here for now," Emone said. "At least we have a spectacular view of the balcony. However, if there's a riot, we'll be trampled to death." She said this in a chipper tone.

Ada leaned close to Emone's ear and burst out in a surprised, giddy laugh. "Is that supposed to help me?"

"My sunny disposition is always here to brighten your day. I'm here with you. We survived the Tents. We'll survive this."

Ada made herself breathe in, deep and slow, expanding her lungs as if the extra air would push thoughts from her mind. The most vivid images had faded, but anxiety lingered like a bloodstain in white silk. From past experience, she knew she needed to find something to focus on.

She let her consciousness linger on her prickling tongue. A person just steps away had tucked an apple into their pocket, a sweet-tart variety found around Rem, one that made for especially good cider. This particular apple had a bruise that had just started to turn the fruit mealy. If it wasn't eaten within the day, Gyst's unknowns would claim it with swiftness.

To her other side, a cluster of people had brought produce already thoroughly touched by Gyst. If they thought they could lob rotten vegetables at anyone on the balcony, they were about to be quite disappointed. Food in that state of decomposition would make for poor missiles.

A rousing cheer jolted her as if she'd awakened from a doze. King Caristo and Queen Roswita had emerged at the railing.

Anger and bitterness surged within Ada as the crowd erupted in a mix of applause, cheers, and boos. The royals wore mourning gray, the finery of the cloth apparent even at this distance. Both wore crowns, something Ada had never seen in practice before. Behind them came a slender girl, her skin markedly darker than that of the Verdanians around her.

This had to be the Princess of Braiz.

At a glance, Ada wouldn't have known the girl to be Morvan's daughter. Now Katell, his wife, did have a darker, more olive complexion than many Braizians because of a marriage alliance a few generations back, but this girl's skin was more brown, like Ada's. Beautiful.

Her body type also reminded Ada of her own at that awkward age—a buxom stick, with a head still a bit large for her developing body. Ada couldn't make out distinct facial features at this distance, but black hair was visible beneath a very Braizian lace cap that lacked a mourning veil.

How strange that the princess looked so like her.

Ada blinked. Could that be . . . her own?

No, if her daughter was here, she would be a lady-in-waiting. She wouldn't be on the balcony behind the king and queen. That was the place for the Braizian princess.

Wasn't it?

"Oh, Erwan. What happened?" she said beneath her breath. "Is that really . . . ?" She couldn't finish the sentence aloud, even amid the crescendo of the crowd.

Could that truly be her daughter, standing there for all to see?

CHAPTER TWENTY

SOLENN

In Verdania people often break their fast with what is called "Braizian toast": a chicken egg beaten with a touch of fresh milk, the mixture then used to fully coat a bread slice. It is then toasted on both sides upon a hot skillet. To add epicurea, substitute eggs from golden chickens. Be attuned to Bait as the egg is cracked so that you may know her might and create delicious food that will embody a person's voice with strength and endurance. Only by mastering such minor recipes will a Chef ascend to utilize more potent eggs such as those of roc and gabby jay.

—Excerpt from *Manual for Tour Chefs*

Solenn had known many Lutecians would be summoned by the palace bells, but oh mercy, there were so many people down below, a dumped-out saltcellar's worth. They packed the avenue as far as she could see, a sea of heads, bonnets, and hats, with a few horses sprinkled in for variety. The crowd's babble quieted as Caristo and Roswita took their places at the balcony's lip.

Solenn hadn't even spoken to them yet. She had awaited them for minutes, a condolence speech prepared in her head, and then they'd arrived and walked to the balcony without even looking at her. She'd promptly taken her position behind them.

In her training, Solenn had been told that whenever she stood on the palace balcony, she should smile broadly so that the mob below could see. No one could have anticipated that she would first be displayed there for such a terrible reason. Now, smiling wasn't an option, but if she looked too grieved, she would seem unbelievable or weak. In Braiz, this wouldn't be a dilemma at all; she'd have a lace veil over her face.

A shame that Madame Brumal couldn't advise her, as this was all her fault.

A servant in kitchen livery approached King Caristo with a cup in hand. Solenn caught a whiff of magic as the king tilted back the contents. She didn't need to ponder the ingredient: this had to be his favorite nonalcoholic drink, white fluff, infused with magicked egg whites from golden chickens. The beverage involved cream, eggs, and flour beaten frothy and then strained, with rosewater added to sweeten it.

"People of Lutecia." King Caristo possessed a shrill, tremulous voice, but thanks to the near-instantaneous magic of his drink, his words boomed—though still shrill and tremulous. "With the deepest of regret, I inform you that my son and heir, Prince Rupert Caristo Xavier Archambeau, found resolution to all mysteries as the sun rose at dawn."

A wave of dismay arose from the crowd, several high voices screaming in grief. These same people would have torn Rupert limb from limb if he had tried to wander freely among them. Why, his teeth would've even been yanked out, based on an old superstition that the royal family ate epicurea so often that their teeth absorbed the magic. Such a thing had actually happened to a relation of Rupert's decades earlier.

As the outcry dimmed, Caristo continued, "Our mourning period begins today and continues until Laitsday under the next full moon. Mourn Rupert, and what may have been if he hadn't met with Gyst so soon." He turned around, controlling the projection abilities of the magic to mutter to Queen Roswita, "Are you going to speak now or go straight to your performance at the Grand Pentad?"

He labeled the queen's oversight of the official mourning rituals as a mere performance? Solenn schooled her expression to remain stoic.

Roswita cast him a cool glance as she stepped forward. "I'll speak here first. Why don't you go have some wine? It'd be a shame if this event disrupted your regular consumption." She faced the crowd, her actions as smooth as her silken attire. "My people!" she began, her voice projecting almost as well as her husband's, though without the aid of epicurea.

Solenn turned slightly as several Verdanian musketeers entered the foyer behind her. Erwan moved from his place at the cusp of the balcony to intercept them.

This couldn't be good.

Roswita continued to speak regarding charity to be provided at city pentads, in Rupert's name. Solenn dithered for a moment, then began to take small steps backward. When no one motioned her to stop, she fully retreated to the foyer.

"I protest most vehemently—" Erwan was saying.

"Messieurs," she murmured. She bowed in greeting to the Verdanian musketeers, outwardly collected even as she was on the verge of becoming ill. "I am Princess Solenn. Whatever is the matter?"

"Princess, I should formally introduce myself." By his insignia and hat, he was captain of like rank to Erwan. She had often seen him as a vigilant shadow of the king. "I am Captain Fredero. These men, under my direction"—he nodded to the four men in his company—"searched your quarters for the epicurea that led to the dauphin's demise."

"An effort in vain, I'm sure." She tried to keep her voice calm, but her pitch rose nevertheless. Erwan had warned her that a search would come, but she'd wandered the rooms and perceived nothing. Had evidence been planted in her absence?

"What is this?" King Caristo approached. The musketeers, Erwan included, snapped to attention and saluted. Solenn bowed. The king's scowl scraped over the men, taking in the context of the altercation, then settled on Solenn. "Did you kill my son, Braizian ninnyhammer?"

Her blood felt as if it had been rendered to icy sludge in her veins. "Of course not, sire. I was honored to be—"

"My men found singing mushroom hidden in her rooms," Captain Fredero continued, his attention on his liege. "It's a Braizian epicurea so potent that even unicorn derivatives cannot counter it."

"Where was this found, monsieur?" asked Erwan with deadly levelness.

"Secured to a chandelier."

A chandelier! The ceilings in her rooms were so high that the chandelier must have been out of range of her perception. Erwan looked ready to retort, but Solenn restrained him with an upraised hand. "I'm well aware of how Verdanians regard the intelligence of my people, Captain Fredero, but do you truly think I—and my subjects—are so stupid that we would use Braizian epicurea and leave it in my chambers to be found?"

Captain Fredero stiffened. "The ingredient was well hidden."

"Apparently so, monsieur," she said, thinking fast. "The chandeliers are far too high for anyone to reach by standing on furniture. I was told—and knew by smell—that my quarters were painted right before my arrival. Your musketeers are attentive, so please, tell me, have any ladders been brought to my rooms during the week when we Braizians have been in residence?" Solenn was pleased by her argument.

Captain Fredero frowned. "Mademoiselle, I would need to confer with our records before I could speak on that matter."

"I should also like to know why you thought to inspect the chandelier at all," Erwan added. "Captain Fredero, you did receive the notice I sent you regarding the absence of the princess's lady-in-waiting assigned by Queen Roswita, did you not? One Madame Brumal? We have reason to believe—"

"What is clear," King Caristo broke in, the magic projecting his voice to drown out Erwan, "is that the epicurea used to murder my son was found in Princess Solenn's chamber."

Solenn spoke up before Captain Fredero could. "So it seems, sire, and evidently planted to incriminate me. I'm glad that with Captain Fredero's help, we were able to determine that right away." She affected a tone of relief.

Captain Fredero blinked fast. "Mademoiselle, I did not—"

King Caristo's face distorted in a sneer. "A typical Braizian play at wit that, in substance, is as empty as air. The epicurea was found in her room. We needn't feign ignorance about their plot anymore, Captain Fredero."

"Plot?" echoed Solenn, any remaining wit evaporated by increasing terror.

"Oh yes. We know that Braiz decided on a union with Albion after they sweetened their trade offers." King Caristo sounded smug.

"Then why am I here, sire?" asked Solenn. "Why make this long journey, begin the—"

"I know about the boat!" King Caristo went shrill, facing Erwan. "I learned of it this morning."

"What boat, King Caristo?" Erwan's tone was mild, but Solenn detected his battle-ready poise.

"The boat you have ready to spirit her away to Albion! My agents have secured it, even now."

"I know nothing of any boat, sire, and if you suggest that we would take a boat from Lutecia to Albion, that journey would be incredibly long and inefficient."

Not to mention stupid. The river meandered and was constantly bogged by other vessels. Floods at this time of year made it especially precarious. The trip could easily be two weeks, if not more, more than twice as long as by saddle—and that was just to reach the coast. Albion would be at least a day away over the Sleeve Sea, likely more, depending on the tides and the destination.

Captain Fredero shifted in place, the picture of awkwardness. "Sire, I advise that we—"

"My son is dead. This marital arrangement is dissolved. Thank the Five that this . . . this crude girl's blood will not mingle with ours!" He shuddered, and Solenn's fury swelled. *Crude girl!* She uptilted her chin in defiance. Her blood wasn't less than his. Her skin wasn't less than his. Her tongue detected a tang of salt, her heart suddenly warmed by Selland's presence. His endorsement moored her feet and soul against continued gusts of anxiety. "I want her locked in the tower. She will not escape to Albion or anywhere else."

"Yes, sire." Fredero saluted, any doubt gone in an instant. With a dramatic flip of his capelet, Caristo exited the room.

The injustice of everything overwhelmed Solenn for a smattering of seconds, then increased her rage and frustration. "If I'm a threat to the royal family, why am I here right now?" She gestured around them. "I stood right beside the king and queen!"

"Surrounded by musketeers," Captain Fredero said stiffly. "We keep them safe."

Like they kept Rupert safe? The charge came to her lips, but Erwan must have guessed at her incendiary thoughts and spoke up first. "My brother-in-arms, I appeal to you. You have an investigative mind. You know this entire scheme was arranged to incriminate Princess Solenn. It's done up too neatly, a book plot with a convenient resolution."

With the king gone, Captain Fredero's posture and expression softened. "I worked with you and Prince Morvan during the war, Captain Corre. My respect for you is immense, and your ward is likewise bright and charming." He dipped his head to acknowledge her.

Erwan sighed. "But."

"But," continued Fredero with a sigh of his own, "my liege has ordered the princess to be imprisoned, and it must be so."

"I will keep my contingent with me," said Solenn, trying to mask her terror with royal arrogance.

"We permit no attendants in the tower unless they're also imprisoned."

"That is easily solved," said Erwan. "King Caristo already accused me of conspiracy. Lock me in her company." He held his arms wide in invitation. He'd had to leave behind his armaments before accompanying her to the balcony, not that they would have served him in this circumstance.

"No, Captain Corre. She will be kept isolated in the tower as our investigation continues. We will look into this matter of the missing Madame Brumal as well." He granted Solenn a small smile, as if to comfort her. It failed.

"During my initial tour of the grounds," said Solenn, "I was told, with some pride, that no one has escaped the tower in its century of use."

"That is true, Princess Solenn," said Captain Fredero with grave sincerity, "but if anyone could carry out such an effort with success, it would be Captain Corre. You will be kept separate out of necessity."

Though she appreciated his respect for Erwan, she was irritated that he had no such consideration for *her* abilities.

"Princess Solenn," said Erwan, "your parents and grandparents will know of this injustice within the week, and we'll—"

A roar from the crowd interrupted him. Their attention went to the balcony. Queen Roswita tried to speak again, but the people's noise didn't dim. She turned and met Solenn's eye. "You."

"Me, madame?" Solenn asked, her sense of dread impossibly worsening. "I did not kill your son or Jicard Dubray. Nor did any of my contingent."

Queen Roswita shook her head, sighing. "That doesn't matter."

"How can you say it doesn't matter, madame?" asked Solenn.

Queen Roswita looked past Solenn. "Captain Fredero, proof of her guilt was found?"

"Madame, singing mushroom was found in her quarters, and she's been ordered to the tower."

Queen Roswita looked among Solenn, Erwan, and the other musketeers. "And the Braizians are protesting this, are they? That's unwise. She's safest in the tower."

"Queen Roswita?" A tremble crept into Solenn's voice.

"Word spreads faster than fire, which says much in this city. The palace may be secured, but I imagine this gossip has been fanned to spread. Come." Queen Roswita gestured Solenn closer. "Come close so that you may hear."

Solenn stopped at the arched doorway. Everyone below, it seemed, had engaged in a discordant chant.

"If you are considering an escape, keep what they say in mind," said Queen Roswita. She stood behind Solenn, her manicured hands set on her shoulders. The gesture might have been supportive, but her nails dug in like talons.

"Listen to me as well," the queen whispered. "My husband is a highly intelligent man. Give him numbers, give him soldiers, and his brilliance shines. But mention some plot involving Albion, and he becomes as fixated as a cat before a bird feeder."

"He thinks . . . he thinks I killed Rupert and was set to flee on a boat to Albion."

"Yes." Queen Roswita sounded tired.

"What would you advise? What can I do?" The queen's sympathy had broken through the wall of restraint Solenn had taken such care to maintain. "I want to go home."

"Oh, Solenn." Pity steeped each word. "That's all I've wanted for eighteen years, yet here I am."

Queen Roswita released her, leaving Solenn standing alone, the words of the crowd increasing in clarity.

"Kill the princess!" they shouted. "Kill the princess!"

CHAPTER
TWENTY-ONE

ADA

The "tower" in the Butecran palace is a place not of punishment but of contemplation. It is a place where nobles and rogue Chefs are to consider their errors of judgment before coming to trial before the king and the Gods. Those who are imprisoned know their stay will not be long. Justice in Butecia is efficient and swift, and always right, as the royal family exists at the blessing of the Gods, and can do nothing but right.

—Excerpt from *Manual for Tour Chefs*

The crowd began to still their shuffling and quiet their voices, with the exception of one persistent baby somewhere nearby.

Ada had needed something to focus on to seal her flood of panic behind a dike, and now she'd managed instead to trade anxieties. How could her daughter possibly be standing in the place of the Braizian princess? What had happened to Morvan and Katell's child? If her daughter had been raised as theirs . . . that switch must have occurred early on. But why? *How?*

If that was what had happened, it now made more sense for Erwan to be in Lutecia. He had promised to keep their child safe, but if she was the princess, he'd also exposed her to new dangers hundredfold!

She pressed her palm to her mouth and groaned. Her daughter would be a Chef. Gyst had told her as much the last time he'd revealed himself to Ada: his presence as fragrant as hot whey, a shadowed hand over her newborn, the words *Blessed, if she survives her younger years* emerging like fermentation bubbles. His appearance—his warning— was why she'd made certain to send her newborn to Braiz.

Yet here the girl was.

Ada didn't even know her name.

Erwan must have been on the balcony behind the princess. Ada wanted to see him, shake him, pour questions on him like salt into a stew.

King Caristo waved to the crowd. Ada's old rage flared as hot as ever, and she felt almost let down at the brevity of his speech. She would have welcomed a chance to dwell on her hatred for a while.

Queen Roswita took his place. Ada regarded her with disgust. Nor was she alone in that—many Verdanians disliked her because she'd been born a princess of Grand Diot. Never mind that she'd now lived in Verdania for more than half her life—she was forever a foreigner.

The Braizian princess would be regarded with even fresher contempt. The princess, her daughter? Ada grappled with the concept as if trying to catch a fish with greasy hands.

Queen Roswita made a pretty speech about charity, and had begun to speak on the subject of nightly curfews—a necessity, as Lutecia was breaking out in riots the way a baby's bum breaks out in rashes—when the people nearer the palace wall let out howls.

"What's it?" yelled a man behind them.

"D'you hear?" called a woman.

"The princess!" Those words were echoed.

"The Braizian princess! She did it!" Those clear, shrill words shook the crowd like a nearby cannon blast. People physically recoiled, then broke out in yells and cries anew.

Ada clung to Emone with sweat-slick fingers, her stomach a deep pit of nausea and despair.

"To the tower!" someone shouted. That was echoed, but some boos accompanied it.

"Take her head!"

"Kill the princess!" boomed a voice. This rhythmic phrase at last succeeded in snaring the mob's enthusiasm, and the chant began. "Kill the princess! Kill the princess!" Steady, heavy, each word resonating through Ada's bones.

These people didn't care a whit about Rupert's death. What they cared about was the turmoil that it would cause—that if their stomachs weren't empty now, they would be soon because of chaos, civil war, and the general horrid ways in which people treat each other. Besides, the only people Lutecians hated more than their own royalty were royals of other realms.

Queen Roswita withdrew from the balcony. Musketeers remained poised there, expressions unreadable beneath the shadows of their broad hats. The chant continued a moment more and then faded with people's interest. People began to move, but not Emone and Ada. They were too near the front. She gritted her teeth and maintained a steadfast grip upon Emone as people finally shuffled from around them.

Ada shivered as she and Emone began to walk, the flow of air making her aware of how sweat drenched her clothes were. Too many people were close for them to dare talk. Emone maintained an iron grip upon her hand as they returned to their refuge, as if Ada were a toddler prone to running into the street.

"When you said that you reacted to the presence of large crowds, you didn't jest." Emone poured water from a ready pitcher and shoved the brimming mug into Ada's hands. "Drink."

Ada apparently needed guidance on the most basic of functions. She'd remained standing just inside the room, her feet braced wide and her breaths ragged in the enclosed space. She stared into the water as if trying to find her own reflection, then took a drink.

"Emone, I need to turn myself into the Guild prosecutors."

Her friend considered her with an artfully arched eyebrow. "You drank a sip of water, not a steady stream of cider brandy. Why are you saying such nonsense?"

"The princess, Emone." Ada kept her voice low by necessity. "Did you really look at her?"

"I saw her. Resembles Katell more than Morvan, I sup—"

"But does she look more like someone else you knew at almost that young of an age? Someone who looks more ragged now, I admit." They had first met at around age twenty, both newly commissioned in the army.

Emone blinked. ". . . No?"

Ada gestured to herself.

Emone's eyes widened. "Now that you mention it, yes, I can see the resemblance, but how can this be? Erwan, he was taking the babe to his parents—"

"The same questions are swirling through my head. You pay more attention to politics than I, Emone. Does Morvan have only the one child?"

Emone chastised her with a glare. "I pay attention to news of Morvan because he's an old friend, not because of an interest in politics. Yes, he has the one child."

"Morvan and Katell's child must have died early on, Hester grant them comfort and warmth." Ada stared into her cup, overwhelmed by belated melancholy. Throughout the Thirty-Fifth's last campaign, Morvan had seen his beloved wife little, and so had often peppered Ada with queries as he sought to understand what Katell was enduring afar. "He and Erwan were thrilled about becoming fathers at the same time."

"He still got to be a father," Emone said quietly.

"Apparently." She released a long exhalation. "Morvan and Katell are genuinely good people to be foster parents. If only they weren't *royalty*." Ada rubbed her head, as if last night's wine lingered still. "Emone, do you . . . do you know her name?"

Emone blinked fast. "You didn't—oh, right. Braizians wait a half year. Oh, Ada. Her name is Solenn."

"Solenn." The name was a pleasant breath. Ada smiled. "It's beautiful. Very Braizian. I would have chosen that myself."

"Knowing Morvan, he *did* let Erwan choose. I wonder if Solenn knows her own parentage."

"If she doesn't know by now, she will soon. Every generation in my family has had a Chef." That was a generalization, a necessary one; only Erwan and Grand-mère knew how Gyst had directly interceded in her life. "If she develops my empathetic skills . . . oh, Erwan, how could you put her in such a predicament?"

"Ada, Erwan is no fool. I understand your anger, but—"

"You understand it? How?" She paced. "I wanted her raised in Braiz so that she could live freely as a Chef. Instead, she's more of a prisoner than any Chef in Verdania! And she is now literally a prisoner!" It took all her control not to yell.

Emone regarded her coolly. "Hence your daft idea to turn yourself in and be imprisoned in the tower, as if you'd be kept on the same floor."

"I'd be closer than I am now." Ada yearned for closeness, any closeness.

"And do what, exactly? You wouldn't even be within yelling range, and you couldn't yell what you wanted to, anyway. And how would you launch your big dramatic escape from a tower no one has escaped from, hmm?"

"The palace claims no one has escaped. They also claim that only a couple of Chefs become rogues each year." She'd helped ten escape

Verdania this past year, and she was only one of many avenues for desertion.

Emone waved the comment away. "Spare a moment for logic, Ada. Even if the princess was found standing over Rupert with a bloody knife, Caristo wouldn't have her executed."

"No, he'll keep Solenn imprisoned as long as possible to deny Braiz any marriage alliance with Albion. That will eventually lead to war, and if Braiz and Verdania go to war, Albion will sweep in from behind. Five, what a mess."

"Someone's still lurking in wait to petrify Erwan too," added Emone. "If you don't off him first."

"He's going to be even more difficult to reach now, even by message. The palace will intercept everything with suspicion."

"You need to think of ways to gain access through the back door, then," said Emone. "On the subject of doors, or the lack of them, I need to check on my people at the Golden Horse. Yes, yes, I'll be careful. Yes, I know my arsonist might make another attempt, or someone else may get the job." She rolled her eyes. "Normally, I'm all in favor of helping people find work, but my murder shouldn't be up for offer."

"Ways to gain access through the back door," echoed Ada, her thoughts returning to how she and Grand-mère had sneaked out of Maman's house.

"You have an idea?" asked Emone.

Her enchanted oatcakes wouldn't be an effective means to access the palace. She would need so many, and the palace was packed with moving people. She'd be certain to be tripped over and caught. "Erwan may be out of reach, but perhaps I can do something about these attacks made against us."

"What, are you thinking to kill Mallory Valmont? Eradicate the need for this gift of revenge? If so, I should go—"

"I can't say that I'd mourn the man, but right now, I'd foremost like to understand how he's still alive at all. You have other priorities, though. Go check on your people. You'll need to intercept Claudette soon enough."

Emone nodded but still looked uncertain. "But she couldn't arrive for days yet. If you need my help in the meanwhile—"

"I know where to find you."

"How do you even think you'll gain access to the Valmont house?" Emone asked.

"I have ways," Ada said.

CHAPTER TWENTY-TWO

SOLENN

Many denizens of court break their fast with toast in the Lutecian style, wherein pieces of bread are topped with softened fresh butter, grated bofor cheese, a spoonful of cream, and a sprinkle of salt and pepper. On top of this add a thin slice of sausage and a sliver of bofor thin enough to read through. Toast to melt the cheese throughout. If you are serving a new mother, try to acquire cream from Farrowby cows to increase the mother's milk. As all know, bofor cheese carries no magic and needs none, as it is divine even in its mundane state.

—Excerpt from *Manual for Tour Chefs*

"This is my room?" Solenn asked. The main living space of her prison cell was maybe half the size of the guest quarters she had just left, but at a glance, it had everything a person could need. A large canopy bed with lush layers of pillows and blankets dominated the area, a vanity with mirror alongside it.

"Yes. Not what you expected, eh, Princess?" The Verdanian musketeer in her escort of six had chatted good-naturedly the entire walk across the palace. She couldn't be sure whether he was genuinely friendly or cozying up to try to make her "confess." The truth was likely somewhere in the middle. "A maid'll come to clean once a day, and when that happens, you'll be guarded in another room instead. Food comes out thrice daily. Garderobe through that door." He motioned to the other door in the room.

"There's a privy?" Few estates in Braiz had indoor plumbing.

"Certainly, but don't you be thinking to clog the pipes to cause mischief. That'll only gift you with the stench of Gyst and a few days' reliance on a chamber pot instead." He even scolded in a pleasant way. She might've liked the man under other circumstances.

"I will confer with Captain Erwan Corre this evening," she said.

The musketeer held his feathered hat to his chest as he backed away. "Approval for such a thing must come from King Caristo, mademoiselle. *Anyone* coming to see you must be approved. Don't try chatting up the maids to be your confederates either. You'll get 'em tossed out of a job, sure as an offering onto a fire." He gave her a gap-toothed grin. "Goodbye for now, Princess."

The heavy wooden door shut, followed by the loud click of a key in the lock. Footsteps echoed away.

Solenn walked into the luxurious prison, feeling incredibly alone.

A nearby table held a basket loaded with small rounds of bread, two jars of preserves, and a stone crock of what must have been butter. A wedge of hard bofor cheese sat to one side. Behind that loomed two packed bookshelves, both taller than her. A check on the attached room confirmed the existence of the garderobe.

"I heard that rogue Chefs were treated well here, to remind them of the benevolence that they had scorned in their desertion," she said aloud, as if Erwan stood over her shoulder. "But I suppose that even this luxury isn't much comfort when you know you're about to lose your tongue."

The lushness of her accommodations verified, Solenn next set about finding means to escape.

The room had three small, high-set windows, the stained glass depicting the Five's icons. If the glass were broken, she'd fit through the spans only if she were the size of a cat, and all the good that would do—the sheer drop had to be fifty feet. Even a cat likely couldn't manage that.

The entry door was thick and heavy. The doorknob didn't so much as wiggle, even with her full weight pulling on it. The walls were solid stone.

Solenn unpinned her lace cap and tossed it upon a table before flinging herself back on the bed, arms spread wide, tears in her eyes. It seemed that the only way she'd escape was by reading books and imagining herself elsewhere—but as much as she enjoyed a good book, this was not the time. Erwan and her musketeers were working for her freedom. She couldn't stay idle in wait of a rescue.

Sounds echoed from the hallway. Solenn sat up. This couldn't be a maid with food, as her room was already stocked. Had Erwan already managed a way to see her? She reached the door as footsteps came to a stop on the other side.

The lock undid with a loud clang. Solenn saw the pleasant musketeer first, his expression more sober than before. None of his prior company were with him. Instead, two unfamiliar women in armored palace livery stood there, faces colder than the stone floor.

"Mademoiselle," said the musketeer.

She acknowledged him with a nod. This was no place for full niceties. As Erwan had observed, she was now among the enemy. She made eye contact with the women behind him. "Who may you be, mesdemoiselles?"

"You are to be questioned." One of the women held up a thick cloak with both hands. "You will come with us. You will not try to run or scream or communicate with anyone we may meet. If you do, there will be immediate consequences."

Suddenly, the tower had become the safest place to be. "Why can't I be questioned here?"

"You are coming with us," said the second of the women in a tone that brooked no dissent.

Solenn looked to the musketeer, but he gazed away. Whatever was afoot, this man was discomfited, and that terrified her.

"I am a princess of Braiz and I want—"

The blow to her gut crumpled her over. She gasped, pain dappling her eyesight.

"What you want is irrelevant," said the first woman. "Cooperate, or we'll deliver more pain without ever leaving a mark."

Solenn straightened, both hands to her sore torso. "Can you at least tell me where we're going? Who I may speak to there?"

In response, the cloak was shoved at her. She accepted it. At least she would be out of her impossible-to-escape room.

The cloak's hood was so deep that with her head angled down, she saw only her feet and those of her companions. She was effectively blind, and no one could identify her.

With her new guards flanking her, Solenn walked down the hallway. The door to her prison cell thudded shut behind her, but she felt far less free than she had been minutes before.

The labyrinthine palace had confused Solenn from her arrival, and a week on the grounds had done little to acclimate her. Now, within the confines of the hood, she found herself utterly lost, but she tried to take in what details she could from the floor. They traveled from the smooth gray stones of the tower to the tighter hallways and coarser stones of the servants' passages. Up, down, and around they went; Solenn eventually wondered whether her guards were purposefully trying to disorient her. The people they encountered offered no greetings.

The mindless rush of their movement gave Solenn a chance to think: Where might she be going?

This couldn't be a straightforward verbal interrogation. That could have happened in the tower. The assault by her "guard" suggested that more treatment in kind might be forthcoming as well.

They crossed a courtyard, sunlight warming her shoulders. Solenn ached to raise her head. As if sensing the temptation, the guard on her right pressed against her, but she needed no reminders of their proclivity for aggression. Her kidney still ached.

Along another back passage they went. A laugh and the soft voices of women carried from another room. Then outside again, into a hallway with inlaid marble floors and a resonant echo to their steps. They traveled up three flights of stairs to another ornate hallway, whereupon a door was unlocked to admit them.

Her hood was yanked back, forcing her head up to meet the eye of the Marquis de Dubray. Jicard's father. The pompous jerk she'd first met at her court debut.

She wasn't totally surprised to see him, but she was taken aback by his pleased smile.

"Marquis Dubray," Solenn said in a cool tone, "I would like to know why I've been brought to your private rooms to speak with you." One of the guards pulled the cloak away. Solenn stood straighter without the burdensome weight.

"I had you delivered here because I'm hardly in the mood to go sneaking about," he said with contempt. He wore what must have been casual attire for him—no wig, his black-gray hair tugged into a queue, no coat over his gray blouse and skirt. Black leggings led to matching shoes that shone like mirrors.

"King Caristo ordered me to remain confined in the tower. He will be angry when—"

"Oh, you know King Caristo well enough to predict his moods, do you? He happens to know where you are now. He advised that I not muss your appearance in any visible way. Cosmetics can only do so much." Healing epicurea was not a consideration for her now, then. "You'll return to the safety of your tower soon enough." He jerked his head toward the guards. "Bring her along, then station yourselves outside to intercept anyone bearing condolences."

"Yes, monsieur," they said in unison.

As they traversed a hallway, the first prickles traveled up her tongue. A step later, and her nostrils and mouth felt seared by tastes and imagery and *everything*. Dizzied, she followed the marquis into a room easily twenty feet high, the tall shelves custom made to fit labeled boxes and bags of epicurea.

Perception and panic were scattering her focus like dandelion seeds to the breeze. Gritting her teeth, she willed herself to concentrate, to remember how she'd coped when exposed to the palace larder. She breathed in deep and low, and within her clasped hands, she dug one of her fingernails into the tender flesh of her palm. That pain grounded her against the onslaught of visceral scenes, smells, and the surges of power that made her calves throb with the need to jump and a second later overwhelmed her with a sense of wellness and a second after *that* caused her lungs to feel oddly heavy.

This was worse than the royal larder, not simply because of her proximity to the ingredients but because of the sheer quantity. There had to be twice as many varieties here.

The door shut behind her with a quiet, ominous click.

"Welcome to my personal larder," Marquis Dubray said. He gestured in obvious pride.

"It's highly inappropriate for me to be alone with you, Marquis." She was relieved that her tongue could still form words.

"Hmm." Dubray paused for dramatic effect. "Do you know what else is inappropriate, Princess Solenn? *Murder.*"

She pivoted to keep an eye on him as he circled her, his hands clasped at his back. Shelves lined three sides of the room, while the fourth consisted of a broad span of crystal-clear windows. Bushes trimmed to squares lined the other side of the glass. Through the propped-open door, she spied the white marble of a balcony rail and, beyond that, scraggly treetops. The apartment overlooked the gardens. Good; that gave her a rough idea of where she was.

"I agree that murder was committed, Marquis Dubray, but not by me."

"Let's dismiss the honorifics for now, hmm, Solenn? I wish to speak frankly with you."

As if they could speak with any equality, especially here in the privacy of his larder. "I am a princess of Braiz. You will do well to not forget that."

"What do you know about my son's death?"

"Death," not "murder" this time. Was he testing her reactions to the different terms? In any case, this was a question she could *mostly* answer. "First of all, I am very sorry for Jicard's death. I enjoyed the time I spent with him in recent days," she lied. Dubray could have been rupic with his lack of reaction. "He sat beside my fiancé last night. They joked and spoke through dinner. As the time of the dance came, Jicard was flushed and sweating, as was Rupert. They had enjoyed an excess of wine."

"And as the dancing began?" Dubray continued to circle her.

"I was with Rupert. I didn't see Jicard up close again."

Marquis Dubray stopped, the windows at his back. "I watched you. All of us did, from our end of the table. You were nervous at times. Your hands shook."

She stopped herself from addressing him with an honorific. He deserved none. "I'm homesick. Scared. My family prepared me for Lutecia as best they could, but it has still been *so much*. I know my every action is being watched and judged, reflecting not simply upon myself, but my people." She spared a fleeting thought for her scandalous actions to save the acrobat's horse. What a minor thing that seemed, a day later.

"You're a princess. You should be accustomed to such attention." Dubray waved away her words as if they were a fly. Solenn's fury boiled. "You were set to marry the dauphin," he continued. "You had every reason to be ecstatic. You were the envy of every young lady in the *world*."

This man was certain he understood her feelings better than she did. "Why are you questioning me as if I'm culpable in the deaths of Rupert and Jicard? Why would I do such a thing?"

"That's what I am trying to understand." He continued to pace around her. "Albion made another offer for your hand this week. I know they are well aware of your arrangement with Verdania—I delivered the news in person to my peer Lord Whitney!" So the two epicurea collectors did know each other. By his tone, he respected Lord Whitney more than anything else about Albion. "By the way, I've met young Prince Cambo, the child they wish you to wed. He is a pale, sickly thing, with none of the vitality that Rupert had. But maybe that weakness would be advantageous to a motivated young woman such as yourself."

She would rather he assumed she was stupid. She needed more advantages over *him*. "An alliance with Verdania was the most beneficial for Braiz. Of course we considered other offers. Verdania did the same on Rupert's behalf. That's no indicator of guilt."

"That much is true, but there is other evidence. A boat with a manifest for the coast, berths registered in your captain's name—"

She couldn't contain herself anymore. "Do you all truly think we Braizians are that stupid?"

"No." He surprised her. "I find that suspect as well, but King Caristo . . ." He shrugged. "My friend and liege has no patience for nuance. He appreciates clarity. He sees the boat as proof, whereas I look at you. Your behavior. Your peculiarities."

Dubray pulled a box from the shelf. As he opened the lid, she heard jabbering voices in a language she couldn't understand, their tone friendly and fast.

"My collection includes some rare epicurea—things difficult to find and cultivate not simply in Verdania, but around the world," Dubray said.

He tilted the hand-size white box toward her. Within, a small speckled gray-white egg nestled upon a velvet cushion. Her perception of chatter increased.

"Is that a gabby jay's egg?" she asked, hoarse in horror.

"Oh yes. It's fresh, delivered to me this morning. A Chef has already blessed it, raw though it is. Eating this will make you babble for hours and hours without the slightest control. I can ask you whatever I want, and you will answer."

Selland preserve her. She took a small step back. "Albion used it on Braizian prisoners during the war. My father spoke with survivors. They . . . they said they had the compulsion to talk until their voices were gone and their mouths bled. They couldn't even pause to eat or drink. Based on their testimony, he had the use of the eggs banned within the Braizian military."

"Well, you're not in Braiz now, and neither of us is involved in the military. Convenient, hmm?" Dubray's glowing smile faded as he looked Solenn in the eye. They were near the same height, though he had to outweigh her by some fifty pounds. "Jicard was my only child. My son, my heir, my darling. He is being . . . forgotten amid the grief over Rupert's death, but in this household, we remember him. We treasure him." His voice dropped to a rattling whisper. "I must know about my son's murder, Princess Solenn."

Behind Dubray, movement amid the bushes on the balcony caught her eye. For a second, she thought it was a bird; then a head with slicked-back silver hair emerged.

Aveyron Silvacane.

He pressed a finger to his lips, then withdrew again. How had he gotten to the third-floor balcony? How long had he been listening by the open door?

Solenn focused on the Marquis de Dubray again. She dare not let him know that someone was behind him. "I've told you the truth."

"Have you?" He regarded the little egg with fondness. "Unlike many ingredients in this room, this egg is fine to eat fresh, shell and all. It's quite thin. The shell, that is." Solenn glanced back at the door into the apartment. Dubray chuckled. "You can try to leave, and you know who is awaiting you out there, while this balcony behind me"—he pointed without looking—"offers a nasty drop to the ground."

"Forcing *anyone* to eat gabby jay is wrong. Cruel." She listened harder to her perceptions. Maybe she could identify something around her that she could safely eat that might empower her to escape, but the very thought of ingesting any epicurea made her stomach clench in a knot. *Everything* in this room was wrong, not just the gabby jay egg.

She couldn't see whether Monsieur Silvacane was still on the balcony. Maybe he had gone for help. Even if he had, she couldn't wait for rescue. Dubray was savoring her terror for now, but soon enough, he would move on her, and if she ate that egg, she'd end up losing her tongue and her life.

"Life is cruel." Dubray shrugged as he advanced. She retreated the broad width of his desk to her immediate right. Atop it sat a small stone statue of Gyst's X, the divine icon most strongly associated with Chefs and epicurea. Beside it were quills, ink, and papers. Nothing so handy as a letter opener.

"You've already concluded I'm guilty. Why bother with the egg at all?" More than anything, she wanted to hear pounding knocks on the apartment door, to recognize the clash of rapiers and the cry of Erwan's voice.

"I need *answers*. You're hiding something. I know you are. I need to understand why my son is dead." Dubray cupped the egg in his hand, letting the fancy box fall to the floor, then lunged at her.

Solenn screamed. Panic gripped her as Dubray's fingers likewise snared her arm, but her drills with Talia flared in her mind.

Stay still. Feign helplessness. Move in ways your opponent doesn't expect.
Dubray would anticipate that she would pull back, enabling him
to get a stronger hold on her wrist. Therefore, she did the opposite. She
careened forward, smashing her forehead into his face. He screeched.
Warm blood spattered her brows and cheeks. She'd crushed his nose,
but she'd rather shatter that egg!

Dubray hadn't relinquished his hold on her. She let her body go
slack. With a grunt of surprise, he released her as she smacked the floor.
She immediately rolled to one side, but a heavy blow caught her in the
ribs, pain dazzling her sight as the air was shoved from her lungs. He'd
kicked her.

Even so, she was free. She kept her momentum, rolling to the far
side of his desk. As she sprang to her feet, he grabbed her again, this
time by the coiled braids pinned atop her head. They provided him
with a perfect grip.

"Your fight only proves your guilt." Dubray panted heavily as he
bent her backward over the desk. Papers scattered as she flailed like a
turtle caught on its back.

"Anything that I did would prove my guilt in your mind," Solenn
said, gasping, then clenched her lips tight as she remembered the threat
of the egg.

She looked around, desperate, and saw the stone X upon the desk.
She twisted to one side, gripping the statue by its ornately carved top,
then blindly swung it behind her head. She struck true, hitting him and
herself. The blow was enough to get him to let go. She pivoted on her
hips, still sitting on the desk, her head aching. Dubray stood with his
feet braced wide, a hand to his bleeding temple.

She screamed as she swung again with the force of both arms,
smashing the statue into the side of his head with a horrific crunch and
gush of blood. She swung again. He toppled, and she slid off the desk
in pursuit, landing on her knees to hit him again. Again, again. Sobs
shuddered through her as she raised her arms once more.

"Princess! Solenn. Solenn, stop."

Monsieur Silvacane's soft voice caused her next blow to arc above Dubray, striking only air. Blood streamed down the man's face. Wide, blank eyes stared up at her, his final expression of soft wonderment.

"I killed him?" she whispered.

"You defended yourself against an assault."

She looked up. Silvacane stood some five feet away, half the distance between her and the glass door. He gripped a knife, but both hands were held aloft in a position of surrender.

"That will mean nothing to King Caristo and the court." Her entire body began to shake. The heavy X struck the carpet and bounced to rest in the curl of Dubray's limp arm. "They'll determine me to be guilty of everything. I'll never get to go home, and even if I did, war would come soon." A war that was her fault. Oh, she knew taking the full blame was illogical, but despair fit her like bespoke clothes.

"*They,*" he said with contempt, "are fools."

"Fools with power." Solenn looked at the door to the outer apartment. "I need to get out of here, somehow, but he has two guards stationed in the hallway. How did you get onto the balcony?" Terror caused words to flow from her as if she'd eaten the egg after all. A glance down confirmed that albumen oozed from Dubray's fist.

"I'll help you escape." Her stunned gaze jerked back to him. "You will not be treated justly by the Lutecian court, though your actions are just. It's only right to assist you."

She shook her head. Loosened tendrils of hair whipped her cheeks. "I'm sorry, I can't ask that of you. If we're caught together, you'll be incriminated as well."

"Foremost, you're not asking. I'm giving. Second, I don't plan on being caught, and thanks to you, the purpose of my visit to court has reached a conclusion." Monsieur Silvacane sheathed his knife and gestured to the shelves around them. "We came here to trace the epicurea market through Lutecia. Here we have a vast stockpile of ingredients and documentation besides." He toed papers on the floor. "You have no idea the service you've rendered to us. By my honor, I must help."

"You *came to court* because of epicurea?" She could scarcely believe his nod. "Why were you on the balcony? Did you follow me here?"

"I won't feign chivalry. I had no idea you would be here. I thought to investigate ways to break into the apartment later, after dark, due to our recent talk about Jicard Dubray's access to epicurea. I heard your voice, though, and climbed to the balcony to better hear." How could he have heard her before she screamed? "Can you stand on one leg?"

"What?"

"The blow to your head. Has it left you unsteady?"

"The turns of our talk have left me more addled than my head wound." She steadily stood on one leg and then the other.

"I'm sorry. Even if I had leave to reveal more personal details, we haven't time for explanations. Do you trust me with your safety?"

She hesitated only a second. "I mean no disrespect when I say that I have few options available, none of them safe."

"I cannot promise absolute safety, either, but I will help you to my fullest abilities." He motioned her toward the balcony. "Take off your shoes. We're climbing up."

CHAPTER TWENTY-THREE

ADA

Beast Tongue Prepared in the Manner of Neat's Tongue enables tour Chefs to practice calling upon multiple Gods in sequence over an extended period. The beast, shaggy lupine and leonine creature that it is, falls in the domain of Lait and her wild woods, so heed her throughout your work. To the sliced slab of tongue, rub equal measures of bay salt and saltpeter, and then cover completely to dry. Thank Selland often as his elements do their work over time. The tongue must become hard and stiff. Roll in bran to scrub off all salt, then dry again prior to boiling with the aid of Hester. Leave it in that water overnight, then bring to a boil again.

—Excerpt from *Manual for Tour Chefs*

Accessing the Valmont château required patience. Ada waited more than an hour for a wagon to near the gate. She hurriedly ingested an oatcake as the attendant and driver conversed. Ada then hopped onto the tail of the wagon as it rode onto the estate, as unseen as a black cat in the night. The vessel stopped just outside the packaging rooms for epicurea, the door conveniently propped wide to welcome her.

The presence of epicurea had dazzled her on her previous visit, but now her perception was all the stronger, as young women labored at tables with open bins before them. Cloth masks covered their noses and mouths as they packed ingredients into smaller parcels for travel. The workers wore layers of clothing, and with reason—the basement room felt colder than outside. Ada eyed the proceedings with curiosity as she edged around the room, trying to ignore the frost-like images of trees that were overlaying her vision.

"We need more dahu—get the dahu," growled a male overseer, motioning a young boy back toward the storage room.

Dahu—rare mountain goats, the dried meat endowing eaters with incredible endurance. Already on the table was another dried meat, from wildling sheep, which increased muscle mass and strength for prolonged periods. Nearer the door, ready to go, were massive quantities of unicorn bones, ideal to make large batches of broth to bolster healing for a multitude of people, and treated tongues from forest beasts, which endowed a general sense of wellness that defied logic. A soldier could be bleeding out but, under the gustatory effects of that portion of beast, continue fighting with only a distant awareness of pain.

Nothing here was for the usual nobility and bourgeoisie who indulged in black-market ingredients. These were supplies for soldiers.

Ada thought of Maman's flippant admission of selling epicurea to Albion, and her lip curled in disgust.

Tempting as it was to sabotage these efforts, she couldn't linger. There were too many people and things that would likely impede her own quest. She had to practically bend backward over freight to avoid the boy hauling in the dahu.

In the other world that veiled her sight, a thing the size of a draft horse but thorny and *wrong* ambled through the room to pass through a far wall.

The kitchen was empty, but beyond that room were more voices. People worked among the prepared epicurea. Ada didn't go that way, but down a hallway she had seen at a distance before. There, she found a narrow staircase upward. She trod the stone steps slowly to avoid an echo, praying all the while that no other person came downward. She gestured gratitude to the Five as she reached the top.

Her thoughts clearer away from the bounty, she let her perception seek out what she truly sought within the main household: rupic powder.

Killing Mallory Valmont, as Emone had speculated about, would be easy if he was as near death as his son had described, but that was not her intent. No, Ada sought to deprive him of the vile epicurea that had perhaps kept him alive all these years. The man had suffered in that time, undoubtedly, but he hadn't learned any lessons about right or wrong.

Valmont had sought to turn her into stone and eat her. Ada wasn't going to be *nice* in her tutelage.

For a house of such size, few domestics were present. Two women gabbed as they attended a pot over a hearth. As the main kitchen facilities were devoted to the business effort, this room was being used for primitive means of general food preparation. A pot held a simmering, poorly salted chicken, while other victuals covered a nearby table.

"I think he's about to rouse. I could hear him, tossing about in his sheets. That's the sign, y'know."

"Did you tell the young master? He's been brooding about in wait."

"No, I haven't seen him since I came down. I should slice some of that bread—"

Ada moved past them and into a formal dining room in disuse. Sheets smothered a table, chairs, and most all the furniture, reminding her of the overlaid world that was now fainter in her vision. Time for another oatcake; she had four left. She found a shadowed recess by an armoire and crouched to eat. Her heartbeat stayed anxious. She needed to move with care and deliberation. Her horse was stabled a quarter mile distant. If she had to make a mad dash there, she could, but traversing the streets while invisible would be even more perilous than the household.

Ada followed the guidance of her tongue and tread up the grand staircase.

Her perception warned her of something . . . strange. It lured her in, like fragrant soup to a starving person, though her perception was not couched in positivity: this thing embodied the foulness of a house fire, of charred wood and stone. Her tongue felt defiled, as if it had come into contact with charcoal, the residue chalky and chunky.

That was disturbing unto itself, but she was most bothered that she didn't know what it could be. For all Ada's complaints about the Guild and the obligations that came with being a Chef, her training had been thorough. She knew the specific ingredients offered by the continent and surrounding world—and more, counting her discovery of cat hair.

What had the Valmonts found?

She crept down the white-walled hallway to double doors that stood partially open. Deep voices carried from within. Ada let herself inside.

There, on the edge of a high-canopied bed, sat Mallory Valmont, no longer the vital figure she once knew. His sharp cheekbones now looked sunken, cadaverous, a darkness in his eyes that had nothing to do with the late-afternoon light. He appeared thin to the point of frailty, though thick layers of clothing bulked up his form, and by necessity—the room was icy. A valet crouched before the nearby fireplace, trying to coax greater flames from embers.

The mysterious epicurea—and rupic—were in a grand desk across the room, set within the niche of a bay window.

"You needn't play my nursemaid," Mallory griped to his son, who stood at the bedside. "I needed more sleep, that's all. I'm as fine as I was yesterday, but your face—what happened to you?"

Ada had no choice but to stride across the room. With a gesture to Gyst, she did, angling her head to understand what Mallory had observed. His son, now attired as a proper dandy with silk waistcoat and curled hair to his shoulders, had a beauteous black eye.

A smile bloomed on her face. She remembered throwing her cup at his head but hadn't confirmed that it made contact.

"My injury is cosmetic," said the son.

"Segal."

"Père, I'm fine, really. I've simply been . . . busy. I've been trying to arrange a surprise for you, but I fear it's not going well."

Ada reached the desk. She didn't dare open the drawers, as they faced the bed. She took shelter on the far side, between the furniture and the curtained windows. The stench at her back made her feel nauseous.

"Tell me, my boy. Five know I saw little of you as you grew up, but I can tell you're hiding something." Ada bit her lip. The fact that they had seen each other at all said a great deal about the truth of Mont Annod. It wasn't the death sentence the public was led to believe, or at least not for a privileged man of Mallory's ilk. His life there had obviously not been easy or shortened in sentence, but it still had its perks. "We both know I'll meet Gyst soon. Gift me with what the gift would have been. You, girl. Leave the fire be. Have more irons warmed for my bed."

"Monsieur Valjay," said the servant, then exited.

Valjay. Of course, the Valmonts lived under a new name, just as Ada had.

Ada motioned gratitude to Gyst. The timely revelation of secrets had his signature odor all over it. This seemed like as direct an intervention as Melissa's bees delivering her a horse.

Segal took in a deep breath. Ada couldn't see him, but she could imagine how he'd gird himself for his big revelation. "I sought to have your betrayers made rupic. That way, you would know they were dead, and their forms would grant you sustenance to live a little longer."

"Oh, Segal." Mallory's voice broke with emotion.

"I know, having rupic isn't as important now since your new powder works so much better, but to know it was from *them*—I thought it would embody more meaning than the other powders we sent you."

Ada pressed a hand to her mouth to cover her quiet gasp. His family *had* kept supplying him with rupic—every statue likely a homicide—all throughout his imprisonment. That's how he had endured, even as the labor physically broke down his body. She didn't know of anyone who had survived rupic reliance for more than a few months. He had ingested for nearly *twenty years*.

"The thought alone is a compassionate gift," said Mallory. "I wish your plan could still come to fruition, but you needn't inconvenience yourself. Our supply of stony owls is limited, after all."

"That's a major reason why I *can't* continue." Segal sounded sheepish "The people I've hired . . . I fear I've squandered much of what we had."

"Come here." She heard the rustle of clothes and could imagine how they embraced.

Ada was stupefied by how casually they spoke of cannibalization. The son had clearly been raised to think this was all quite normal. Their emotional relationship made everything even more disturbing. These were no opera villains, cackling over their dark machinations, but a father and son with a loving bond.

This, even though Mallory had spent the majority of Segal's life incarcerated. Ada had learned her own daughter's name only today.

Her bitterness over that was as profound as the horrid presence of the epicurea.

"Segal, sit here." Mallory sounded as if he were crying. "You and your mother—may her memory keep like honey—did much for me. You don't need to endanger yourself in these efforts. I note that you haven't mentioned exactly how that black eye came about," he added, his tone dry. "I won't press you further on that detail, but I will ask that you put greater focus on our business enterprise. This is our legacy. This is how we'll make King Caristo and his lot suffer as well."

"I know." Segal's voice was small, childish. "I haven't scorned our work. Our people are packing the order for Albion even as we speak."

Albion! So it was confirmed.

"Good, good. I'm sorry I haven't been able to assist with that more."

"Père! You've done plenty. Your maps, your planning—if you're up to it, I can show you the storerooms. You haven't been down there in weeks, and our hunters have been incredibly busy as Lait brings us out of winter."

"I'd like that," Mallory said, voice warm.

By the Five. The Valmonts were purposefully trying to undermine Verdania and spite King Caristo. Mallory had been furious, back in the day, that his distant cousin hadn't promptly pardoned him.

Maman couldn't know the true motivations of her associates. She was born bourgeoisie. She craved those higher echelons. If she held a grudge against Caristo, it was as brief as a rose's bloom.

In the bright window light, Ada was beginning to see the vague form of her knees and arms. It was time for another oatcake.

"Would you like to break your fast in your room or downstairs?" Segal asked his father.

"I'd like to go down and enjoy the garden view. Besides, I'll then be that much closer to the basement."

"Here, I'll help you."

There was a prolonged groan as Mallory stood. His steps were slow and dragging, his effort audible, for which Ada was grateful, as it covered the soft sound of her chewing

As soon as the door closed, she rounded the desk to pull open the third drawer down. There she found a tin of rupic powder, by its strength, freshly ground. She recognized the distinct stony flavor; the man whom her grandmother had killed had carried a pouch of this same epicurea. Segal must have raided his father's stash.

Beside that tin rested the mysterious epicurea she had perceived from downstairs.

The finely ground dust within the leather bag was in some ways like regular rupic powder, yet not. She perceived how the soft gray grit would coat her tongue with the taste of mineral and char, how eating it would consume her body with fiery energy and an incredible sense of well-being—a feeling of security, of home. She had known that sensation in brief flares as she had evoked Hester over the years, but this powder could induce such states that could last from minutes to hours, dependent on the dose.

This bag seemed to contain Hester's very might in concentrated form. As if it *were* Hester.

The God was supposed to be like the granite used in the hearths that cradled her fire. But Hester, actually made of stone? Like rupic?

Ada shook her head. Theological ruminations could wait until later. She tucked both epicurea inside her coat, shuddering at her close contact with such foulness. They would make it hard to perceive most anything else.

She was about to close the drawer when a velvet bag caught her eye. Inside: jewels set within gold and silver, rings mostly. She took those as well. They just might buy her means and access to get Solenn free from the tower.

Her gaze raked over full shelves of ledgers nearby. A wall hosted a four-foot colorfully inked map of Verdania covered with annotations, likely of sources of epicurea. Mallory had always had a brilliant mind for strategy and supply sourcing. He had applied those same talents to Maman's venture, to great success.

As she exited the room, she thought again of the sheer quantities of epicurea in the basement. If Maman's company continued these vigorous harvest methods, Verdania would soon be as devoid of magical flora and fauna as Albion was, but maybe that was part of the Valmonts' strategy as well.

Maman, comfortable in her privilege, had never been one to give much thought to the finite nature of anything. What she wanted, she acquired.

Ada hurried downstairs, grateful for the breadth of the stairwell, as it was easy to avoid several domestics going upward. The distant, deep voices of the Valmonts carried from some room unseen. Ada needed an open door to outside, or an unoccupied room that would enable her to let herself out.

She turned a corner, walking straight into Ragnar.

Her face bounced off the broadness of his buttoned chest as she staggered back. Ragnar, large man that he was, hesitated only a second before he swiped at the invisible form he had collided with. A gasp escaped Ada as she bent back, narrowly missing the blow. She collided with the wall. Ragnar's eyes narrowed, both fists balling. His next strikes wouldn't miss.

"Ragnar!" Ada hissed. "Stop! It's me, Adamantine!"

He froze. "Mademoiselle Adamantine?" His whisper was a quiet rumble.

"I'm using epicurea that hides me from sight." Oh, how she hated revealing this secret, but he had her trapped, and she wouldn't physically attack him.

"How can I be certain you are who you say?"

"I'll lay my hand on your arm. You can feel my coat sleeve, the same coat I wore the other day." She laid her hand on his wrist, and he hesitantly touched the sleeve. "Please, keep my presence here a secret. These are dangerous people."

Ragnar considered her words with an inclined head. "Most people are dangerous, in one way or another." The voices of the Valmonts grew louder, closer. "I begin to understand how you recently vanished from the comtesse's household, but I have many questions yet."

"You can't question me here!" she hissed.

"No," he murmured, his hand gripping her arm with gentle firmness. "You will return with me to the residence. We will speak there."

CHAPTER
TWENTY-FOUR

SOLENN

*If called upon to cook in the palace, a Chef must recon-
sider what food is. The royal family does not eat as do
other people, and not simply because of their bounty
of epicurea. Contemplate birds. The wilder and the
more exotic the bird, the more appropriate the meal
for our ordained betters. Practice cooking pheasant,
partridge, quail, and songbirds such as the lark. Such
sweet-singing birds, such sweet and tender meat.*

—Excerpt from *Manual for Tour Chefs*

"You were on the *roof* when you heard me, Monsieur Silvacane?" Solenn
asked. She sat on the cool flagstones of the balcony while he dumped
epicurea from a sack that would soon fit her stockings and shoes within.
She marveled at her increased clarity of thought by being mere feet
outside the larder. "Don't you need to take off your shoes too?"

"Please, dispense with formalities. Call me Aveyron. Yes, I was on the roof. I have good ears and am sure-footed as well," he said, joining her in a crouch. He tied the bag to his waist.

"What if we're seen from the garden as we climb upward, Aveyron?"

"That *is* a risk, but I see no one at this moment. Solenn, if I may also be familiar?" His grave tone pulled her attention, and she granted him a nod of permission. "Watch where I place my hands and feet so that you may do the same. The roof is right above us. You are an athlete. You can do this."

"This is a bit different from riding a horse," she said, willing her still-shaky limbs to become steadier. "But I'll try. I must. I can't stay here." From where she sat, she could see Marquis Dubray's soles.

"Let's go, then." Aveyron stood, and she followed.

He used a stone planter to step onto the balcony rail—that pose alone made her balk! From there, he reached a decorative ledge, then lifted his right foot to a sconce. He stood taller than the doorway now, the roof feet above his head. So close, yet so far.

He grabbed another ledge and heaved his lithe body higher, now standing atop the fluted decor of the doorway. From there he reached the tiered edge of the roof. He paused, evaluating for a moment, then gripped the top lip. His legs bounced once, twice, and he heaved himself over the top.

Solenn swallowed dryly. He almost made it look easy.

"I'll help you once you're in reach." Aveyron scanned the garden. "I still spy no one. Now's the time."

Thank Selland that the tailor had readied a pantsuit for her today rather than a formal skirt. Taking a deep breath, she made the first step upward. The marble rail was smooth and cold beneath her bare feet, inducing a small shiver. She knew not to look down but couldn't help but notice the bare-branched bushes far below.

"Reach above you, to the right, about six inches—yes. You want to angle yourself to go over the doorway."

"You speak with such collected calm. Have you scaled a lot of palaces?" she asked. Her heart almost galloped into her throat as she stepped atop the doorway. A breeze rustled her clothes. She had the definite, eerie sense that she was high up.

"This was my first. In all truth, I don't believe I'll practice it with frequency."

"I feel much the same." The ledge she gripped was only an inch in width, gritty beneath her clammy fingertips.

"One more step up and you can reach the top. I'll help you from there."

One more step. That made it sound doable. She stretched out a hand, finding a hold, then propelled herself up.

"Grab the top."

She did. His hand encompassed hers, the squeeze painful, but she didn't mind.

"I'm going to count down. Bound up at the end. Three, two, one—"

Solenn heaved herself upward. Aveyron had her by both hands and dragged her over. The stone edge scraped across her torso, almost catching on the broad buttons of her justaucorps, but then she was on the flat of the roof, sprawled beside Aveyron. She panted for air, heart aflutter, and finally let out a giggle. "I did it!"

"You did." Aveyron regarded her with pride.

According to the stories she'd read and heard, her heart should have been fluttering because of Aveyron about now too. He'd shown himself noble and helpful, the model of a hero. But as grateful as she was, as much as she respected him, there was no such flutter, no desire for something more between them. No desire for such an experience at all.

She was fine with this.

"I didn't even need gruff cheese to make that climb. Ha!" She grinned.

He regarded her with a tilted head as he handed over her stockings and shoes. "I had half expected you to consider ingesting some of that epicurea."

"Trust me, I was well aware it was there, but it didn't appeal to me in the slightest." She garbed herself again. With the larder beyond her range of perception, she was aware anew of Aveyron's odd aura.

At a crouch, they crossed the broad width of the whitewashed roof. "As a princess, you've certainly had epicurea many times." She could tell he was making an effort not to sound judgmental.

"I have, but in Braiz, we don't . . . relish in it as they do in Verdania. We have less available to harvest. It's often reserved for emergencies or high holy days, even in my grandparents' household." They started down a flight of stairs into the building. She gripped his arm as they came to a door. "I need a cloak to hide beneath if we're to make it across the grounds."

"The apartments for provincial nobility are a building away. We can grab supplies there."

A building away. She had wanted to think that climbing to the roof would be the worst of this adventure, but it seemed as if she must keep climbing in other forms. "I'll trust in your attuned ears, then."

They crept down a quiet hallway less opulent than the one above. Aveyron motioned her to the left. They hunkered behind a broad plant as two men passed by, engaged in deep conversation. Continuing, they made it around the corner, where they hid again, this time in a recessed doorway. A gaggle of maids hurried along, enthusiastically arranging bets as to how long the Braizian ninnyhammer would stay locked up in the tower.

The gossip left Solenn feeling irate for a moment; then she grinned. The maids had already lost and didn't know it.

Sunlight seemed strange and delightful as they stepped outside, crossing a small courtyard to the next building. They hid again, impatient as several men argued over a horse racing bet gone awry, then reached the Silvacanes' room. Aveyron almost pushed her inside as he closed the door behind them.

She released a deep breath of relief, and then Brillat Silvacane was upon them.

The man swooped past Solenn to grip Aveyron by the front of his cravat, the peculiar aura about him even stronger than that of his son. "What. Have. You. Done," he said through gritted teeth, scarcely sparing her a glance.

"Père! I had thought to do reconnaissance around the Dubray apartment but—"

"*We are not here to meddle in royal affairs.* You've put—"

"Excuse me, monsieur." Solenn evoked her regal tone. "Marquis Dubray had me escorted to his private residence to brutally interrogate me with a gabby jay egg. I resisted and killed him in self-defense." She'd slain Dubray. Watched the light dim in his eyes as Gyst guided away his soul. She took in a deep, rattling inhalation, tears stinging her eyes as she yearned to see Erwan and talk through what had happened. "Aveyron helped me to escape the apartment via the roof."

Brillat released his son to stare at her. His nostrils flared. "What? That marquis with the larder is dead?"

"And his larder is the largest and most diverse I have ever seen, Père, and it's accessible from a balcony! His guards are in the interior corridor, clearly under orders not to interfere even if they hear screams."

"I see." Brillat relaxed into a grin.

"There's paperwork too. He cataloged everything. You should be able to trace his supplier," added Solenn, but she realized her error when Brillat turned on his son with a fresh scowl. "I assure you, monsieur, he told me frustratingly little, but I do know your purpose at court in regards to epicurea. I support you in this effort."

"Our effort. Yes." Brillat drew quiet in thought, then headed across the room. "We must move quickly to obtain the contents of the larder. If we can find the supplier this very day . . ."

"Is the rest of the team here?" Aveyron said, to which Brillat nodded. "Good. I'll join you after I help Princess Solenn from the city."

She gaped in surprise. "You'll help me beyond the palace?"

To her greater shock, Brillat nodded as well, his straight silver hair swaying. "We owe you much for the service you've done for us. I must rally our kin." He continued to the next room.

Aveyron lightly touched Solenn on the arm. "Use the garderobe. Drink some water. I'll gather supplies."

She did as he advised, then found him packing a knapsack with food and flasks. "Is your monthly anytime near?" he asked.

His casual question made her eyes go wide. Nothing about these Silvacane men was normal. "No, fortunately." She had been irked by bleeding and cramping during her trip to Lutecia.

"I'll still pack rags. One never knows when bandages will be needed." He never even looked up to register her surprise. "My room is to the left. Could you please grab us both cloaks from the wardrobe?"

"Of course," she said. She donned a deep-green one herself and brought him one in brown. "I think these best for hiding in the woods."

"Wise choice," he said. "Are you sure you haven't done this before?"

"I have fled into the forest many times, but never under such circumstances. The way things are now, I wish I could never emerge."

"Be careful what you wish for. The Gods listen."

Brillat returned. "We will depart within minutes. Are you both ready to make your own escape?"

"Ready as we can be," said Solenn. "However, I do want to be assured of your intentions in the Dubray larder. You truly intend to dispose of the items? They won't be resold for favor or profit?"

"I vow to you, no epicurea in our possession will be utilized or sold." Brillat considered her, and she wondered whether he perceived something odd about her as well. He leaned close to Aveyron. Rather than embrace the boy, they pressed together, cheek to cheek. "To many returns home."

"To many returns home," Aveyron echoed.

That must be a farewell oath among their people, she thought, shouldering her pack as they exited. With their hoods up and heads down, she and Aveyron would look like young nobles making a bold escape of the palace despite the king's mourning edict.

"You should talk if guards stop us," she whispered. "My accent will give me away."

He nodded. "As will mine, but they'll only know me for a southerner."

Through a hallway window, she could see her own residential building far across the garden. "If we could get word to my captain," she murmured.

"We dare not try. The Braizian delegation will be closely monitored."

"We are going to procure mounts right now, correct?"

"Yes, if not from the palace stables, then I'll get you to a livery stable in the city. There's money in your bag." He hesitated. "Though I confess, I'm not entirely certain about how to go about letting a horse."

"Neither am I." She swallowed a nervous giggle. "I'll be better at surviving in the woods than in Lutecia."

Bells began to ring. Aveyron glanced over at her. "Those aren't the deep bells of this morning."

"No, they're not." These were higher pitched, their clanging more urgent. "This can't be good." They walked faster.

Other people emerged from their rooms, eager to discover the source of the clamor. "I say!" called a servant. "Do you know what that's about, monsieur, mademoiselle?"

"We were wondering ourselves," answered Aveyron.

"Most peculiar. Those are the summon bells for palace guards and chevaliers, but surely they wouldn't drill today, not with mourning underway." He withdrew again.

Aveyron and Solenn shared a look, then rushed outside along an arcade. Not only were the bells louder, clamoring from several towers, but yells and fast footsteps rang out from above and all around.

"We're not going to make it," she said. Even if they could reach the stables, that would be the first place to be secured in the guards' search for her, as these alarm bells could indicate nothing else. Did that mean that Marquis Dubray had been found as well? She hoped not. Brillat Silvacane needed time to do his work.

"You're right. The stable isn't an option. You'll only escape now if you can do so with speed." Aveyron nudged her toward a small garden, a pocket surrounded by walls on three sides. At this late hour of the afternoon, it was heavily shaded and cool, fragrant of musty moss. In such a perfect alcove to Gyst, she was unsurprised to see his X etched into the bricks.

Aveyron went to a dark corner and unclasped his cloak, letting it fall to the flagstones.

"I beg your pardon," Solenn asked, "but what are you doing?"

"My father readily forgave me for helping you, as that also helps us. But for this action, I fear, he may well want to kill me." Still, he didn't hesitate to pull off his shirt.

Solenn looked away. "He may not be the only one!" Even so, she didn't feel threatened by his behavior, only baffled.

"Look at me long enough so that I can hand you my clothes, please," he said. "I hope they will fit in your bag."

She resolved to play along with whatever he was doing. "I think they will if folded, and I can wear your cloak atop mine." She packed away his clothes and shoes, accepting his breeches and smallclothes, with a blind grab his way. His cloak fell heavily over her shoulders.

"I won't be able to speak your tongue, but I'll understand you. I can nod and shake my head to communicate. You are trusting in me, and I will trust in you."

"Whatever do you m—" Her tongue prickled as if set upon by ants. She gasped, her head jerking up in time to see Aveyron's naked form on all fours inexplicably *expand*. His milky-white arms and legs stretched, becoming impossibly paler where they met his body, darkening near the ground. The bow of his spine grew, his torso thickening. Most disturbingly, his neck bulged, in an instant arcing forward as his head likewise lengthened, his nose and mouth drooping outward like a tube and then gaining sinuous dips and curves as it darkened at the distal end. His silver hair flared, its volume increasing, and at the base of his spine, the same thing occurred, as out of nowhere hair grew and lashed outward like a sudden gray silk banner.

There was no flash of light, no sound, no drama. Everything happened within a span of seconds.

Where Aveyron had crouched a moment before stood a beautiful, juvenile Camarga horse.

CHAPTER
TWENTY-FIVE
SOLENN

As the Author of this volume, I will make a statement sometimes controversial among our ranks: despite the resemblances they bear to each other, unicorns are not horses. Gods-touched creatures are set apart, much as Chefs are set apart from common people. In truth, Unicorns and Chefs are in close relation, for both are divine, both created to serve their betters: the Crown and the Five.

—Excerpt from *Manual for Tour Chefs*

Aveyron had turned into a Camarga, right before her eyes.

By the look of him, as a horse, he was just of age to be ridden. Camargas were born dark brown and black and changed to a gray-white around their fourth year; Aveyron's coat retained a soft gray.

But what was she doing, appraising him as if he were up for auction? They needed to *go*. Seemingly of the same mind, he jerked his head in impatience. Solenn surged out of her stupor and threw herself astride.

The instant she found her seat, Aveyron began to move. She ducked low against his neck—his mane so like his silver hair as a young man—as they passed through the archway into the arcade. She felt him coil in eagerness, and she pressed in with her heels to acknowledge. He sprang forward, his hooves clattering upon the old stones.

She had ridden many horses, but never one like this. Aveyron moved like liquid bound in equine form as he galloped across the courtyard. Oddly enough, though, the peculiar ambience around him was now gone. To her perception, he was a normal—though extraordinary—horse.

Their raucous hoofbeats drew curious onlookers. A hood couldn't cover her head, not at Aveyron's speed. Guards began to pursue them along a parallel arcade, but they were on foot. Aveyron left them behind almost instantly.

Mamm and Tad used to chastise Solenn for her frequent bareback rides along the beach, but now more than ever, Solenn was grateful for her practice of defiance. She held her seat as Aveyron dodged people, carts, trees. He leaped over a low wall. The tall gray of the palace walls loomed ahead, the lower bailey stretching before them. The palace must have ended its closure at some point during the afternoon, as the gate was open and commoners had formed their usual queues for audiences and other affairs. The still-clanging bells had created disarray, but most people doggedly kept their places.

A higher-toned bell began to ring. If a bell at that pitch meant the same thing here as in Braiz, it signaled an imminent closure of the gates.

The palace was an odd mismatch of ancient and modern, still retaining many defensive elements from the era prior to gunpowder. Along the high parapets, Solenn could see musketeers in distinct Verdanian blue running as if to catch them—but that was hardly necessary. All they needed to do was drop the gate, which seemed to be their very intent.

Aveyron moved impossibly faster. The curtain wall's deep shadow fell over them as she heard the grinding noise of the portcullis as it began to lower. A guard with a pike veered close to them, but for some reason he didn't strike. Maybe he had orders to retain her unharmed or maybe he loved horses too much to risk harming one, but in any case, they galloped so near him that she could see a hair growing from a mole on his forehead.

Aveyron rushed through the brief darkness of the tunnel. Sunlight lay ahead. His hooves struck different music on the wooden bridge, and they entered the city. Curious throngs had gathered as the palace bells tolled. The dense pack of humanity screamed and scattered away from the charging horse. Aveyron cleared a woman huddled protectively over a fallen man, while feet away, a barefoot child grinned in delight, oblivious to danger.

Aveyron's pace slowed to a canter as they entered the narrow lanes of Lutecia, his breath fast with strain. She offered his neck a reassuring pat-pat. He didn't need to be told that they must still hurry; they had to make it beyond the city gates before they, too, closed, but they also had to navigate the wagons and horses and humanity of Lutecia. Solenn had no idea which way to go, but Five be blessed, Aveyron did.

Her thoughts raced almost as fast as him. No wonder she had sensed something strange about Aveyron and Brillat! She had never heard of Camargas being an ingredient, though; unicorns were the only equine kindred with such potential. Magic, by its definition, was something derived from living flora or fauna that could be eaten or could otherwise alter food to empower humans, wasn't it?

Magic though he may have been, Aveyron labored for breath as they reached the city walls. The gate was still open, carts clogging the way. Aveyron hesitated only long enough for people to dodge. Again came those terrible yells—"Close the gate!" A musket fired, and Solenn's heart threatened to pulse out of her chest, but no blow arrived and Aveyron didn't skip a stride.

They made it through! They were out of the city!

Aveyron decreased his speed to a smooth canter but lost none of his urgency. The crowds awaiting entry to Lutecia gawked as they passed by, horses in the shafts staring with perked ears. Vendors watched gape mouthed, as did the dusty men grouped before a tavern. They passed one farm, then another, the press of people soon left behind. The stacked-stone fence along the road ended. Aveyron left the highway, crossing the choppy mud of a field. When they chanced upon a shallow stream, he slowed more, staying in the fetlock-deep water as they continued toward forested hills.

Solenn glanced back and found no one in immediate pursuit. "Good. We'll be harder to track if we can stay in the water awhile." He agreed with a brief toss of his head.

Aveyron continued up the stream for a good half mile or so, until the bed became rocky underfoot. He picked his way up the leaf-strewn embankment and into the woods. He walked, head hanging.

"I'll dismount so that you can cool down," she said. He granted her a weak nod as she slid off. Salty sweat frothed his neck. Horses couldn't run fast and simply come to a stop. If not cooled down properly, they could die. Whatever powers Aveyron possessed, he still seemed to carry the vulnerabilities of any mortal horse.

"Is it healthier for you to stay a horse right now?" she asked, already suspecting the answer. He nodded.

"The palace is bound to send dogs after us. If you change form again soon, I wonder if that would confuse them? You don't smell horsey as a human, you know." He blew out a weak raspberry, which she interpreted as a laugh. "I wonder what Erwan will think when he hears of my escape. He'll probably be jealous I got to ride a Camarga." She hesitated. "Are . . . are all Camargas like you?"

After a thoughtful wait, he nodded. Shadows deepened as they walked, birdsong falling over them.

Solenn let that revelation set in her mind for a few minutes before she spoke again. "Are there many other beings out there with magic that people don't know about?"

Another nod.

"By Selland's rake," she murmured, pinching her fingers. All her life, she'd been told that Chefs knew everything about magic, that such power was the Gods' ultimate blessing upon humankind. Chefs made it sound so straightforward. A matter of graciously accepting a divine gift.

The truth was anything but simple.

"It's good that humans don't know," she said, speaking slowly. "People would slaughter you and everything else if they thought there was so much as a drip of power to be had. Oh. *Oh*. Now I understand why you are so vehemently against epicurea and want to take the contents of the larder away. Those are . . . remains. Like soldiers who die far afield, their bodies being—oh, Five, no." She stopped, horror dousing her like a bucket of ice water. "Aveyron, are all sources of epicurea as . . . awake as you are? Conscious, thinking, feeling creatures?"

He had cooled down enough that he could pause without injury. He regarded her, ears flicking, and nodded.

Her hands went to her mouth. "Oh no. But I've eaten—I've *eaten* things like you. I—the singing mushroom that poisoned Rupert and Jicard. It *screamed*. It knew pain." Erwan had told her that the mushrooms were said to emit an audible sound when they were harvested, hence their name. The mushrooms cried out as they were being *murdered*. Aveyron's head pressed close to hers, his breath a huff at her ear. "I'm sorry. We need to keep moving, but . . ."

She realized the entirety of what she'd said and groaned. "You revealed your major secret to me. I just revealed mine." She had always felt free to speak her mind with horses, and now she'd done so as if she'd eaten the gabby jay egg after all.

His ears were perked, attentive, showing no immediate negative reaction. Therefore, she continued.

"At my debut, right at that time I first met you, my tongue awoke. Gyst has . . . endowed me in a strange way. I can perceive nearby epicurea. It overwhelms me, especially in a larder. I even knew there was something strange about you and your father, though I didn't know what to make of it." Aveyron released a surprised huff. "Most disturbing of all, though, is that when epicurea will provoke death, in my mind, I experience what will happen if the food is ingested. Someone tried to poison Rupert during my debut. I purposefully spilled his wine. When I realized his food at the ball was also poisoned, I tried to stop him from eating the dish. Braizian salt marsh lamb," she added, with bitterness. "But Jicard grabbed a bite, then Rupert. I perceived the entirety of how they would die in slow agony."

She couldn't hold back her sobs. Aveyron rested his head on her shoulder, simply there.

She calmed herself after a moment, and they kept walking.

They soon reached a small, burbling stream. Aveyron bowed to drink. Solenn wiped tears from her cheeks. "I can't even sense anything from the water. Normal food and drink are the same as ever. My tongue has an empathetic taste for death, it seems."

Aveyron nuzzled at her knapsack strap. She took the hint and pulled out his clothes. As she faced away, magic swelled in her perception, to dissipate seconds later.

"I had wondered at your attitude to epicurea." Aveyron's voice was soft, tired. Cloth rustled as he garbed himself.

She asked, "Can all ingredients . . . no, I can't bear that word, 'ingredients.' It's too degrading. Can all things of magic take human form as well? Even awake oaks?" And mushrooms?

"May my kind forgive me for sharing this word with you, but call us 'Coterie.' That's the appropriate term for our collective here on the continent."

"By 'continent,' you mean Vercania, Braiz—"

"Lucania, Grand Diot, Belja, and so on. The continent entire, yes. Human borders change often. Ours are more set in place. As to your question—all of us lead dual lives, but few of us change form in ways that let us speak and live with humans. We the Camarga are in an oddly privileged position. We can pass as humans, and our equine forms exude no magic when eaten, so we are safe from being used for epicurea. That enables us to have a better relationship with humans than many others do. I'm clothed now, Solenn."

She faced him. Aveyron looked wan with exhaustion. She returned to him his cloak. "Now I see why you were so grateful when I defended the acrobat's horse. You would be vulnerable to abuse in horse form, too, but . . . Camargas are known for being independent. I've heard they choose their people. Is that true?"

He chuckled as he fastened on his cloak. "Yes. We only ally ourselves with decent people. If we encounter otherwise, well . . . we know how to work keys and latches."

"You're fine with being . . . ridden?" The question felt both awkward and belated.

"That's a personal choice, but most of us enjoy it. The bond of a horse and rider—well, you know what it's like from your side. It's a special kind of athletic partnership that can develop into friendship." He waved her to follow him. They trekked parallel to the stream. "Camargas are indeed difficult to track with dogs, for the reason you noted."

She released a deep exhalation. "That's one less thing to worry about." She glanced up through the mostly bare canopy. "Some clouds are moving in, though."

"Yes. I smell distant rain. I'll change again soon, but for now, we really must talk."

She picked her way up a rocky, brush-clogged rise. "You said before that you were only going to get me outside the city. As much as I appreciate your company, I know your father needs your help too."

Really, the idea of being alone out here was terrifying, but even more appalling was that she might impose upon him.

His laugh was strangled. "My father's going to kill me. I would like to live awhile longer yet."

"You mean—oh. I suppose changing into a horse in front of a human is likely forbidden?"

"Likely? I'm not jesting about this, as humans do. Among the Coterie, secrecy means life. What I did *is* punishable by death."

Solenn soberly considered this. "The entire city will be speaking of my escape."

"Yes, and so I'd best not return." He walked with his head down, stomping.

"Oh, Aveyron. I'm so sorry."

His head jerked up, hair falling away from his face like a slick veil. "Don't feel guilty, please. I don't regret my actions. You had to escape the palace. There was only one way to succeed in that."

"Surely, if you explained the circumstances, your father and others would see reason?"

"I don't know," he said softly. "I don't even know what our goal should be now. Where might you be safe?"

Where indeed? "I want to return to Braiz, but for a single horse to make the journey, it could take over a week. I don't want to ask you to go so far. And I would be returning there a failure."

Aveyron regarded her with a furrowed brow. "Your family. How will they assess these accusations against you?"

"My family will go to war with Verdania in my defense, which I don't want. That would play into the hands of our greater enemy. Albion had Rupert killed and arranged for me to take the blame. My marriage was supposed to bring Verdania and Braiz together and prevent war, at best, or be a united defense, at worst. And now . . ."

"This was the principal reason for your marriage?"

"Yes. Certainly not for fondness of Rupert. I neither hated him nor loved him. Gyst, keep quiet the unkind words I spoke of the dead." She motioned his X.

"Your words weren't unkind, but honest. I beg your pardon if I'm prying. I've studied human ways all my life, but concepts like monogamy and marriage are still strange to me."

His statement came as a relief. She'd been starting to worry that he had a romantic interest in her. "They're strange to plenty of humans too," Solenn said, to which he laughed. "I sometimes wish I could reside in a quiet cottage in the woods, away from all people."

"If you were going to do so, now would be the time."

She blinked at the sunlight that pierced the leaves. He was right. She could vanish into the wilderness and live the life she wanted.

Beneath an anvil's weight of guilt.

"I can't," she whispered. "My cousins, the direct heirs, are younger than me. If they marry out of the country, the line of succession will be at risk. I need to make this union."

"Pardon me for my bluntness, but it sounds to me as if you're the one that Braiz can afford to sacrifice." He shook his head, hair tousling. "For beings so short lived, I'm amazed at how you all manage to make things so *complicated*."

"Surely there are squabbles within the Coterie?"

"Yes, but we have the benefit of stable leadership." Solenn snorted out a laugh and was joined by Aveyron as he realized his pun. "Our queen has ruled for thousands of years."

Solenn perked up. "You're ruled by a queen?"

"Yes." He hesitated. "I'm not supposed to tell humans about her."

"We've been sharing many things we aren't supposed to." He still looked reluctant. "We've already earned death sentences, haven't we?"

"True enough." He released a long exhalation.

She decided to take a different tack. "The Coterie lives in many different environments, don't they? Woods, cities, sea, mountains? Can one entity rule over all of these domains?"

"Queen Abonde does, with the help of governors selected by each kind. My mother has represented Camarga for several seasons in the past." His note of pride withered as he seemed to realize how much he'd said. "You're sly about getting information," he added with chagrin.

"I learned from the best." Solenn panted as she followed him up a slope, the exertion giving her a chance to think. Women, allowed to rule on multiple levels? And to do so with respect? In the human realm, militaries and pentads allowed women to lead, but among the nobility, such a thing could only be temporary, like a widow holding a hereditary council position until a son came of age.

The idea of absolute power didn't appeal to Solenn, but she very much liked the idea of having a voice. As terrible as the Port of Nont tragedy had been, she had relished in having such a major responsibility and actively helping others. She hadn't even been allowed that kind of influence during her marriage negotiations.

"I can see why you and your father were sent to Lutecia. You're probably among the few who don't have outright cause to loathe humans."

"Yes, though we care very much about the plights of our kin. You see, we're aware of how Albion has harvested our cousins there to extinction or to the very brink. That's why we were compelled to go to Lutecia in an effort to dismantle the trade network however we could."

"I've heard many stories from the war about how Albion utilizes epicurea even more aggressively than Verdania."

Aveyron's expression was grim. "Yes. A war with Albion would be disastrous for us. Our kin will only be more ruthlessly harvested, and our lands laid to waste too."

"Albion is as much, if not more, your enemy as ours," she murmured, her eyes going wide as an idea gripped her mind. "Does the Coterie ever engage in war against humans? I mean, I hear about beast attacks in the deep woods or krakens eating ships, but is that—"

"If my kin feel threatened, yes, they strike out, but most always in self-defense. Truly, we wish to be left alone to live our lives in peace."

She nodded, trying not to appear too eager as a giddy sense of hope dissipated the mental muddle she'd been working through for the past while. The Coterie and Braiz had a great deal in common. As her father would observe in his diplomatic endeavors, there was room here for negotiation and cooperation. "Could the Coterie come together to act in a more aggressive manner?"

Aveyron's steps slowed. "Solenn, what are you broaching?"

"I need to make an alliance to protect Braiz. Albion is our mutual enemy. If Braiz and the Coterie could ally, it would be to our mutual benefits."

He stayed quiet a moment. "I . . . don't know. Many of my kin would be pleased to see humans destroyed."

"Wouldn't it be better if we could learn to work together, rather than against each other? Braiz is caught between Albion and Verdania, the two major culprits of harvesting! Not that Braiz is innocent, of course, but no other people comprehend what epicurea really *is*." Select portions of murdered intelligent beings. She shivered again.

"You cannot suggest that humans be told of our nature." His paleness told her of the gravity of what she proposed.

"That cannot be for me to decide. That would be up to Queen Abonde." Solenn took a deep breath. "Aveyron, can you escort me to her?"

He tripped and staggered to regain his footing. "I'd rather you asked me to take you to the court in Albion," he rasped. "That may be safer and wiser for us both."

"Oh, Gyst condemn Albion to rot! Surely other humans have been to the Coterie's court? Haven't we coexisted for ages?"

"Things are more abstruse than you know, Solenn, and Gyst and the other Gods play roles in that as well. But you're right. If we could find a way to work together, maybe positive change could begin. I just don't know if this is the time."

"When would be a good time, then? You and your father went to Lutecia because you knew the danger posed against your kin and you had to act. We *still* need to act, Aveyron."

"Right now, we need to act by hurrying for shelter before rain arrives." Aveyron's hand went to his shirt. She took the hint and stepped away, gaze averted.

"We can't talk if you're a horse." She paused. "Is that the intent? Is this discussion over?"

Clothing rustled as he stripped down. "Solenn. Many, many of my kind want you dead. You're human. You've eaten epicurea. Out of ignorance, yes, but nevertheless this is an immoral, evil act to us. They would want you dead before even knowing that your tongue was Gyst-touched. Even so, I'm considering your words, because you're right. The relationship between humans and the Coterie needs to change if we're all to survive. An alliance with Braiz may be the way to begin this process. Our lives . . . are already in imminent danger. You, from all sides. Me, from humans, from kin, my father." He sighed. "My homeland is far to the south and not in imminent danger of being a battlefield, but our unmagicked equine brethren always suffer terribly in war."

They were both quiet for a moment.

"We'll keep going north," he continued. "By nightfall, we can decide our course."

"Braiz is that way," she said with soft yearning.

"It is. That remains an option. My clothes are on the ground right behind you."

"That's what we need right now. Options, and hope." She fastened on his cloak again and packed everything else away.

Magic flared in her awareness, twigs and leaves crunching under Aveyron's new weight. She faced him with a smile. When it came to looks, his horse form was far more appealing to her than his human form, which wouldn't have surprised Erwan one bit.

Oh, Erwan. She hoped the tale of her exodus hadn't made him too frantic . . . though maybe he should be anxious for a while. She'd been raised on lies, and this was where they'd taken her.

"I have a lot to think about. We both do," she said as she mounted up. He nodded, then set off at a smooth trot.

She had to figure out how best to negotiate with Queen Abonde. After all, Solenn was not simply arbitrating on behalf of herself and the people of Braiz, but for Aveyron. He had risked everything to help her. She wouldn't see him suffer for it.

CHAPTER
TWENTY-SIX

ADA

Oatcakes are among the simplest of recipes to learn. A handful of hulled oats, chopped. A sprinkle of salt, pat of butter, drizzle of honey. Just enough water to bind everything together. Form the cake into a patty within the palm and cook upon a skillet until golden and set on each side. These hearty cakes will fill a body with energy and vigor without even the aid of magic.

—Excerpt from *Book for Cooks to Excel as Do Chefs*

When Ragnar walked through a place, people moved as if from the path of a stampeding draft horse. Ada followed a step behind as he headed downstairs to utilize the passage between houses, her tongue prodding at a piece of oat stuck in her teeth. She had asked him to wait a moment while she ate another cake. One was left.

The cellar passage was not hidden now. Doors were open at either end, with lamps lit along the corridor. She was pleased to find that her estimate of the tunnel's length had been correct; it had seemed like a long way in the dark, and indeed it was.

She felt the urge to tell Grand-mère what she'd learned and, with a surge of longing and worry, motioned to the Five.

If most anyone else had kept Ada bound in place by promise alone, she would not have been so cooperative, but this was Ragnar. He trusted her to follow in his wake, and she trusted him more than her own mother.

And Maman, oh, *she* was the difficulty. If she told Ragnar to do something, he would. And yet, Ada had a rare opportunity now to speak with him first. She could use that advantage.

She could also use a stiff drink after the day she'd had.

Ada had to exercise extreme focus to perceive the qualities of Maman's wine cellar as they passed through. "Wait," she called softly, causing Ragnar to pause. "I'm thirsty."

He tilted his head for a moment, listening, and spoke only when he was certain they were alone. "Can you even carry a bottle?"

"Once it's in my grasp, it'll disappear."

Concern clouded his craggy face. "Such a power would be disturbingly beneficial for burglars and assassins."

"Which is why it's a secret I've kept as close as fire to wood. It's not chronicled by the Guild. To my knowledge, I'm the only Chef who's done this."

"Ah," he said, his eyes widening as Ada pulled a sparkling wine from Maman's small collection of bottles.

"We can go on," she said, tapping him on the shoulder.

On the second floor, on the far side from Maman's room, he took her within an unused bedchamber. Not unlike the formal setting in the Valmont house, the furniture was protected by sheets. Ada threw back the covering on a chair and sat, setting the wine on the table beside her. Ragnar shook his head in awe as the bottle became visible again.

"Do you require food to accompany that wine, mademoiselle?" he asked, standing before the shut door.

The oatcakes had been little better than nothing, but even so, she shook her head, then remembered he couldn't see her. "Ragnar, I cannot stay here long, and my mother cannot know I'm here, or how that came to be."

"Mademoiselle, I cannot keep—"

"If she knew I was here, she would order you to restrain me, and I can't stay. *I can't.*" Her voice broke.

Solenn needed her. And Erwan—his assigned brigand was still out there somewhere.

Ragnar was quiet a moment. "Where is Madame Eglantine?"

"Outside the city. I had to get her away from the people that are trying to kill me . . . and from being used by the comtesse."

He stiffened. "Your grandmother's treatment would have been—"

"Good in many ways, yes, but she still would have been enslaved alongside me. I won't see her bound again."

Ragnar seemed to accept that this particular line of discussion was best concluded. "Am I correct in my guess that this epicurea you're employing will soon reach conclusion?"

"You'll start to see me within a matter of minutes." She relaxed into the high-backed chair. Her aching shoulder actually had support. If she closed her eyes, she had no doubt that she would be asleep faster than Lait could cause a flower to bloom.

"Since you escorted your grandmother away, you cannot have lingered within these connected households in recent days. You took the risk of returning—and to the shop, not here. Why?"

"First of all, the wine?" Ada asked, rubbing her face. Ragnar promptly obliged, fetching a glass from the far side of the room. He poured for her, and when he was done, she went and got a glass for him as well. When he opened his mouth to protest, she said, "I insist. I'm not going to drink alone, and it would be a travesty to waste this wine.

Please, sit." The city of Rance made wines that were incredibly bubbly and sweet—too sweet for most Verdanian tastes, in truth; her grandmother was a major exception to that. Most of their wine was exported to far-distant Ruthenia.

"Very well, mademoiselle," he conceded, folding back a sheet to sit across from her as she poured.

Ada took a drink and sighed in bliss. Perfect temperature. Perfect effervescence. She required something with such a bold, clean flavor to be enjoyable through the nastiness of the stolen epicurea on her person. "Maman's business associates. You know them only by the name Valjay?"

"Messieurs Valjay, yes."

Ada drank again. "Their true name is Valmont."

"Valmont." The name struck like a dart. "As in Mallory Valmont, the 'Hero of the Thirty-Fifth'? I saw him in the city more than once during his glory years, and I've worked often with the elder Valjay in the half year he has been here. I struggle to believe that he is the infamous Valmont. Surely they are decades different in age?"

Ada didn't take offense at his disbelief. "Mont Annod and years of rupic powder will likely do that to a person."

"Rupic," he murmured, his heavy brow furrowed. "We don't sell that . . . or stony owl gut, for that matter."

"From what I overheard, the family continued to supply him with rupic throughout his incarceration. This seems to be how he survived Mont Annod. They apparently are keeping owls somewhere."

"You speak with many uncertainties, mademoiselle."

"I can only perceive immediate effects of epicurea, not the damage and benefits of accumulated years. Most people on rupic are dead within *weeks*."

"I didn't recognize him. None of us did." Ragnar sounded apologetic.

"He could have passed me on the street and I wouldn't have recognized him, and we bled together for years," she said simply. Ragnar surely understood such bonds, and he soberly nodded. She added, "You asked why I was in the Valmont household. I've been investigating the attack that forced me to come here for refuge. That took me to 'the shop.'" She drank more, as did Ragnar, his sip dainty.

"*They* sent men to assault you? I fail to understand why," he said, then added: "Your form is becoming visible, mademoiselle."

Ada studied the outline of her hand on the cup as she set it down. "During the war, I was ordered to tolerate Mallory Valmont's rupic use. I did, until I discovered he didn't source his powder from long-cursed people but from his own fresh homicides. I'm the one who revealed the truth, and he and his kin haven't forgotten that. I understand that Mallory was close to death recently?" Ragnar nodded. "The son decided to make my own death a gift to him." She didn't include her old friends in this telling.

Ragnar looked vexed. "Mademoiselle, I must assure you, the comtesse didn't know her associates were—"

"I know she's not involved. The Valmonts are oblivious to my intimate connection with her." As Ada drank again, the pleasantness of inebriation kicking in, she could see the green of her sleeve.

"Monsieur Valmont *has* been in better health in recent days, though he's still fragile, as you undoubtedly saw. His mood has also been improved." He shook his head. "I feel like a fool now. He would enter these terrible rages over the slightest of matters . . . throw objects across the room, scream, even fling himself on the ground like a small child in tantrum. These are symptoms of rupic ingestion, are they not?"

"Yes. You're fortunate that he didn't kill anyone while in those moods. That rage is considered an asset of rupic. He used to go into frenetic rampages on the battlefield that even we found frightening to behold, especially in melee combat. He could bludgeon and slash his way through Albion lines, severing arms as if snapping strands of sugar candy, with his own skin impervious to damage all the while."

Ada paused in consideration of the mystery powder she carried, so fragrant of fire and stone. The potential for rage was there, too, but a brooding, quiet anger, not necessarily the brief explosiveness of rupic. She could sense how, if she ingested it, every slight would be amplified, every grudge made lifelong. That was reinforced, not by stone skin, but by physical power—Godlike power, all the weight of boulders behind it.

Hester's power. Hester's flavor, on her tongue.

But again, she wondered, how could that be possible? How could the God let Mallory defile her in such a way . . . or were they working together? She frowned at the vacant fireplace beside her. As cold as it was in this room, the shop was far worse.

The Valmonts had offended Hester. She'd withdrawn the blessing of her heat.

Those maps in Mallory's bedchamber. He had hunters exploring Verdania in a systematic grid to find magical beings to harvest. Somewhere, they had found Hester. Who was made of stone, like rupic. That old fragment of forbidden lore Ada had found years ago said Hester was cursed. Becoming rupic was the most notorious of epicurean curses.

"Mademoiselle." Ragnar's gentle, gruff tone roused her.

"I'm sorry." She straightened. "This has been a hard week, and with the wine . . ." Thank the Five that, of all men, she was with Ragnar while in such a condition.

"I should have fetched you food straightaway to absorb some of its effects."

"It's a bit late for that now." Ada ruefully considered the empty bottle. She didn't remember pouring more. "Tell me, Ragnar, now that you know about the Valmonts, what can you do? Maman can't know that I was the one to uncover this."

"No," he said slowly. "However, you have provided me adequate information to investigate further. I will substantiate your claims and present them as my own, with your permission."

Ragnar, ever the considerate gentleman. "Under these circumstances, I don't mind."

"The use of perverse rupic would be adequate reason to justify madame dissolving their business arrangement, but I would like to tell her of his attack on you. That would provide the strongest argument of all."

At that, Ada didn't withhold a bitter laugh. "Because he sought to kill me—and eat me—while she wanted to simply hold me captive and utilize my skills."

"Eat . . ." Ragnar took in the full subtext. "That was his goal, then. Of course." His face twisted in revulsion.

"Yes." She hadn't intended to reveal that detail.

"I don't think I will tell *that* to madame. Such a revelation may make her too upset." When Ada guffawed, he tilted his head to regard her under sobriety. As big as he was, he probably needed to down four bottles to feel the liquor. "Your mother does love you. I will admit, she's not certain of how to show that love, but her fondness and respect for you is real."

"I can believe that she respects what I can do. Few other people would demand that their young child, on a rare visit, prepare a five-course holy day feast for a relation of the king." For her full day of labor, Ada had been given a small porcelain horse. She'd treasured it for years and mourned when it was irreparably broken during her tour days.

Ragnar gave her a small smile. "Her effort to keep you here, while undeniably in her self-interest, is also out of a desire to protect you. She was upset and confused when you deserted the army and

Guild, but eventually came to realize that you must have had strong reasons to take such action. She would take care of you, since they cannot."

Ada shook her head in disgust. "That's the logic used by nobles who keep marriageable young daughters locked in tight confines 'for their own good.' I don't even understand why you've stayed with her as long as you have, monsieur." The thought, often mulled since her teenage years, finally was voiced aloud.

He was quiet for a long moment. "I cannot say that I have no regrets, but I have found more solace here than I have anywhere else."

She wondered at that. The Duchies enforced universal conscription for lesser tiers of society. Ragnar had probably been a soldier of one sort or another since he was a child.

"I'm glad for that," Ada said, and meant it. "Though I wish you had no need for regret at all."

"Life will always have regrets." He smiled as Ada yawned so widely that her jaw popped. "Mademoiselle, our talk should cease so that you may get some sleep."

She glanced at the window, where the light was turning gray. "No, I should go. I have one more oatcake. If you can open doors for me, I can—"

"You are exhausted. From how you sit, I can see that you favor your shoulder. You're under myriad threats. Don't make yourself more vulnerable. I'll bring you necessities, and you can sleep here." He held up a hand to squelch her protest as he continued, "If you should decide to exit on your own after some rest, so be it. You're not really here, after all. No one saw you arrive."

"Thank you, Ragnar," she murmured.

"And I thank you. What you have told me will enable me to better protect the comtesse, my utmost of duties." He saluted her, five fingers splayed over his heart, as he stood.

Ada's mind drifted as she dozed in wait of Ragnar's return, the room descending into full darkness. A short rest here would be good. She could creep out in the wee hours, check on Emone, fence the jewels she'd stolen from the Valmonts. She could then see about gaining access to the palace . . . to Erwan, and Solenn.

That plan felt dreamily possible in the embrace of wine.

CHAPTER TWENTY-SEVEN

SOLENN

Veal bones, sawed into rounds and baked by Hester's fire, develop a softened marrow that can then be spooned onto Gyst-touched toast and sprinkled with the finest salt of Selland. Such a delicacy melds well the contributions of four Gods and can satisfy the stomach in modest quantities.

—Excerpt from *Book for Cooks to Excel as Do Chefs*

Rain began to fall as Solenn and Aveyron reached the dolmen.

In the early-evening gloom, the deep gray of the lichen-flecked old stones stood in contrast to the likewise gray clouds. Large upright rocks acted as walls, forming three distinct rooms set in a semicircle, only two of which still had broad, flat stone roofs. Solenn studied the ancient site with curiosity as they approached, as it was simpler than many she had seen. Dolmen were common across Braiz. No one knew who'd erected the ancient buildings, though some said they were as old as the

City-Eaten-by-the-Sea. Moving stones of such size and weight would be a challenge, even in these days of gunpowder and scientific innovation.

Aveyron stopped just outside the sturdiest looking of the structures, its horizontal stone about level with his head. Grasses and moss furred the very top of the rock. Solenn dismounted, shaking collected water from her cloak. A moment later, Aveyron changed form. She had a glimpse of his lean backside as he scampered for shelter. She followed him inside. The dirt-floored room was some seven feet high by twenty feet in diameter. She set down his cloak and promptly pulled out his other clothes.

"Is it safe to make a fire?" she asked, nodding toward an oft-used firepit feet away. This would make a perfect shelter for hunters or scavengers in the wilderness.

"We may not be here long. Could you please pull out the food, though? I'm beyond famished."

Food did sound like a brilliant idea. A loose, flat stone by the ashes acted as a table for the dishes she set out. "You never did eat as a horse. I only saw you have water." She'd spoken little over the hours. Relying on equine nods and headshakes was awkward when her questions were complex.

"There's a reason for that." Aveyron sighed as he sank to his haunches to tug on his shoes. "I've been trying to decide how best to broach this topic, as there are things you must know if we attempt an audience with Queen Abonde. Do be aware that knowledge of any of these details is worth your life."

"I continue to accumulate deaths, then. I don't suppose the magic of the Coterie can kill me and resurrect me, with the intent of killing me again?" She said it in jest but with a chill, suddenly wondering whether it could be true.

"I'm sure some of my kin wish they could do so, but no. Our powers are limited these days."

She picked up the hint. "They were not so limited in the past?" Brushing her hands on the flared skirt of her justaucorps, she began to eat a sizable piece of straw-colored, firm cheese that contained a slight streak of blue. A Verdanian cantala cheese, she believed. Aveyron reached for a small boule. It crunched as he bit in.

"The Coterie once ruled the land, and openly so." His voice was quiet, and he paused only to chew. "But then the Gods awakened. They were human mortals before they came into their power, and they favored people. Hester especially loved humans. The Coterie attacked people and drove them from their homes, the place Hester regarded as most sacred. She was furious."

"Woe to anyone against the rage of Hester," Solenn said, quoting the common idiom.

"Yes. Her rage isn't always instantaneous either. On this occasion, she nursed her grudge as she accumulated power. Any prayers or thanks offered her way, she hoarded them, for years and years. When she was near ready to burst, she directed her full ire at the Coterie and our like kind around the world. Our city of Ys, a place of grandeur and magic, stood along the coast of your Braiz. She sank much of it into the ocean, but the force she used scattered debris across the world."

Solenn, wide eyed, looked around her. "Ys is the City-Eaten-by-the-Sea? I've never heard of it having an actual name before. This building was part of it?" He nodded. "But this seems . . . basic to have originated from a magical capital city."

"Different kin have different needs. Some live in homes built into trees; others build narrow stone towers ten stories in height; others use more humanlike accommodations. Sometimes the simplest of buildings lasts the longest."

"How did this even get here, intact? Sorry. It seems like a silly detail, but I'm trying to understand."

He was the picture of strained patience. "From what I understand, some aspects of the city flew through the sky to impact the land and create craters, while other things were spontaneously moved great distances by Hester's assault. Some buildings were halved between worlds. But to continue, Hester wasn't done with her attacks on the kin. She wanted humans to reign supreme in the world. She couldn't obliterate the kin entirely—our presence is necessary in many areas, part of the balance of life—so she granted us all half lives. One half of the year, we must live in the human world, where we're mostly prey, lacking much of our magic. Across the veil, in a full magical realm named Arcady, we can be our full, true selves, until our time is up." He ate more bread.

Solenn nodded thoughtfully. "Camarga horses exist throughout the year. You don't all leave and depart at certain times, then."

"No. For us, when we're young, our internal sense of belonging aligns with our parents. That changes as we age. We Camargas can actually stay in the human realm however long we wish, but if we try to overstay in Arcady, we eventually sicken, body and soul."

"So you could've eaten grass today, but didn't."

"I feel ill if I shift with food in my belly. Better to fast and avoid that." He finished his bread with considerable zeal.

"Do you eat meat at all?" she asked with blatant curiosity.

"I can, in human form. These teeth are made for that." He gestured to his mouth. "I usually don't, though. I prefer to know the circumstances of the animal, even when it comes to things like cheese." He hesitated a moment. "You mentioned salt meadow lamb at the dinner. Do you know how the lambs and their mothers are treated?"

"I don't think I want to know right now," she said, remembering what he'd said about gruffs.

"Sorry."

Solenn needed to change the subject. "Can all of your kin speak in Arcady?"

"Most of us can communicate through vocalizations to some degree, but not necessarily in human languages. We also build cities.

We practice trades necessary for our survival. Awake oaks walk upon their roots. Vandrossa eagles use their fine eyesight to construct vast homes of salvaged materials."

The epicurea she had eaten over the years, long digested, now haunted her. "Hester did this . . . how long ago? Is she still attacking the Coterie?"

"Thousands of years ago, and no. She expended herself in her assault on Ys and hasn't been seen since."

Solenn thought of what Erwan had said about how Gyst had physically visited her birth mother. "So the Gods really do take on solid forms, like in the old stories?"

"Of course." Aveyron seemed puzzled by the question. "Though this effort does tax them, which is a reason why they intercede with people so infrequently. It's easier for them to interact with us in Arcady, as the magic of our world is closer to their divinity. Hester never has, of course."

"You mean that Selland, Lait, Gyst, and Melissa can actually walk around there?" She gaped at Aveyron and thought of Selland with yearning. She had sensed him on occasion, but how incredible it would be to *see* him!

Aveyron smiled, amusement in his eyes. "They can, yes, but haven't in my lifetime."

The idea of lifetimes made her wonder something more. "Can Gods die?"

Aveyron's brow furrowed in thought. "That is quite a question. The Five were human born but somehow ascended beyond that. Lait is from the far side of the world—"

"Selland is from an island with no name," she interrupted, "in an ocean with a thousand names. Hester is from Verdania, which is why they favor her so."

"And why she favors them as well. Melissa came from high in the mountains, deeper into the continent, and Gyst—well, Gyst likes to be a mystery in every way." Aveyron shrugged. "I don't know if they can die, but they have lived for thousands of years. Since before Ys fell."

Solenn took a deep breath. "My mother taught me how to survive Lutecian court. Now, I'm thinking of her advice as I prepare to survive a new court entirely. Foremost, and pardon if this is in any way offensive, what *is* Queen Abonde?" She nibbled more cheese.

Aveyron cringed and looked around, as if afraid someone were listening. "That *is* a very personal question, and it's not my place to answer. What I can say is that she represents all kin under the Coterie and is thoughtful and wise. She won't kill you simply because you're human."

"But she may very well because I'm a nascent Chef and because I've eaten epicurea." She made herself swallow. "You keep mentioning the matter of if we get an audience. I assume we must pass inspection with her guards and handlers first? And that they may not be so wise and thoughtful toward me?"

"Yes," he said softly.

They were both quiet a long moment. The rain increased to a torrent, spatters ricocheting onto her right side.

"Full darkness nears. How far must we go to reach Arcady? Is there some . . . kind of doorway? You mentioned a veil, but that doesn't make sense to me."

"It's difficult to explain, but our worlds overlap, and in some places that overlap is thin enough to pass through. Dolmens are often such places, as they hold old magic."

Solenn recoiled in surprise. "The doorway is right *here*?"

"Not exactly where we're sitting, but yes, it's here. Arcady is always close to us, though. A few creatures can cross the veil at will, but most of us need doorways. Arcady is a smaller world than the human one, and the geography is . . . truncated. For example, to get to Braiz from Lutecia, using Arcady as a bridge, would take only about a day."

"A day! That makes me feel strangely better, as if home isn't that far away after all. Even if it's not my home now."

"Solenn." Aveyron hesitated. "You could still vanish into the wild, you know. I could help you establish a refuge where you might be free of the threats against you."

She envisioned a cottage of stone and thatch looking upon a meadow with lush woods beyond. A water pump near the back door, cleared space for a garden behind it. A little home fragrant with herbs suspended from the beams above, a small cellar Gyst-blessed for cheese and meat preservation.

A fantasy, a pretty fantasy. That was all it could be.

"I might be free of immediate threats, but I wouldn't be free of my guilt and obligation."

"It was worth mentioning again." His smile was weary.

"Aveyron. I'm sorry that you're in peril because of how you've helped me. I want you to know . . . I intend to speak on your behalf to the queen. Being what I am, I hope that doesn't make you all the more condemnable, but . . ."

"If anyone could successfully parley on my behalf," he said quietly, "it would be you."

His faith bolstered her. "Should we go, then?"

"Let's." They packed what little remained of their food. "I hope that I'm not going to get you killed."

"If this leads to my demise, I take full responsibility for that." Anxiety fluttered in her chest, but she still felt resolute.

They pulled up their hoods and entered the dreary downpour. He led her to the midpoint of the dolmen. There, rain had slicked a broad, flat black stone big enough to hold a wagon drawn by four horses, and flat in a way that didn't look natural.

"Stand close beside me. The crossing may make you feel disoriented and ill. The guards on the far side will move fast but will only strike if you pose a physical threat. Otherwise, we should both get some words in first."

"That's . . . not exactly comforting, but very well."

"I respect you too much to offer falsehoods."

She had a fleeting, frustrated thought of her parents and Erwan. "And I respect you as well, and I know you'll do what you can to keep me alive. If you can't . . . I absolve you of that guilt, understood?" she said with fierceness.

"Understood." Aveyron took a deep breath. His head tilted up to his left, as if he could see something that she could not, and his fingers began to stroke the air like a harp.

She was about to ask how this kind of magic worked when the world took a decisive hard tilt. A yelp escaped her, and then reality escaped too. Everything blurred as if she'd been dropped into a deep fog, but one that flashed the colors of the rainbow in ominous shades. Pressure squeezed her arm—Aveyron's hand, she could only hope—but she couldn't see him. She wouldn't have been able to see her own fingers in front of her eyes. Her body plummeted, and her stomach felt as if it were being wrung out like a wet towel. Hot bile rose in her throat.

And then she saw darkness. A normal nighttime sort of darkness, and trees. No rain fell, but musty dankness weighed the air. She was on her knees, which suddenly felt bruised. Had she fallen?

Gasping, she sat upright.

Cold metal tapped against her throat. "Move not, human," growled a deep baritone.

"I am Aveyron Silvacane de Camarga. I am bringing the human to treat with Queen Abonde." She couldn't see Aveyron and dared not turn her head.

"Camarga, you fool! You bring no humans here, *ever*."

Solenn glanced down at the broad halberd blade against her neck and followed the length of the pole to see it gripped by an ornately attired otter the size of an adult human. A silver breastplate contrasted with the bright riot of braided cloth beneath. A mustache of whiskers drooped from its furry brown face. The creature would have been adorable if not for its stabby nature. She could just make out another otter who had Aveyron under similar restraint.

"These circumstances are unusual," continued Aveyron in a level voice. "I ventured with my party to Lutecia to—"

"Don't care where you went and why. Humans have no place in Arcady!" The otter's passion caused the halberd to wiggle. Solenn was afraid to breathe.

"She must meet Queen Abonde! Ugh!" Aveyron grunted as if he'd been struck.

"Aveyron?" she croaked out. Speaking, for some reason, awoke nausea in her gut.

"The paperwork this is going to cause," grumbled the other otter. "Why'd this happen on our shift, eh?" The thick accent reminded her of the drawling patois of humans who lived and worked along the Senna River valley of Verdania.

"Don't even talk, human. Don't taint our fine air," growled her guard.

"We need an escort to Queen Abonde. Please." Aveyron gasped and wheezed. He was clearly being hurt in some way.

"You, Camarga, have a lot to answer for, so we'll keep you for a trial, we will. You may be a fool, but you're still one of ours. But this thing—" The metal pressed harder. A warm trickle oozed down her neck.

Enough. "I am Princess Solenn de Braiz." She projected her most regal tone. "Under diplomatic protocols, I demand an audience with Queen Abonde."

"What's that?" The halberd drew back enough that she could safely breathe. "A human princess?"

"I'm Princess Solenn de Braiz," she repeated. "I request that Aveyron Silvacane de Camarga and I be safely escorted to meet with Queen Abonde."

"The paperwork," moaned the other otter.

"You ever hear the like? A *human princess*," her guard muttered, then shouted, "Get the captain!" The gaze returned to her, black eyes narrowing. "You're causing a lot of fuss."

As much as she wanted to apologize for the aggravation and paperwork, she couldn't risk lowering herself in their regard.

"Aveyron, are you hurt?"

"I'm restrained, that is all." By the tightness in his voice, they'd done more than that.

"Speaking of restraints." Her guard motioned with the halberd. "Bind the human."

The other otter bleated in disgust as it knelt behind her. Her knapsack was tugged off. She felt a surge of panic at being robbed of her food and canteens, but she couldn't fault them for taking the bag. Erwan would have done the same with prisoners. Something sharp grazed her forearms. She stiffened, worried that the otter held a knife, then lost none of her fear when she realized she'd felt its claws. A rope twined around her wrists to bind them at her back.

"Up," said the guard.

Solenn staggered upright, dizzy, stomach burbling. The guard seemed to realize her plight and didn't prod her forward yet. The nausea tapered off after a moment. She gave the otter a tiny nod, and they both then waved her forward. Aveyron stepped beside her. He looked well enough, not bloodied or bruised.

They walked a hard-packed trail through dark woods illuminated by drifting bugs that somehow glowed. Only when the lights drew nearer did she realize they were some kind of fairy.

"Human! Human!" the lights shrieked as they descended on her. Solenn screamed and hunched her shoulders as if she could protect her face. The things slammed into her arms and cheeks, stinging her like hot hail.

"Get off," snapped the nearest otter, slapping them away. The fairies retreated, grumbling. They hadn't had time to do any real damage, but the cut on her throat hurt now, the trail of dried blood tugging at her skin.

"Sorry," Aveyron whispered.

She gave her head a slight shake. He'd warned her what the reception would be like.

The path led to a single-story structure of stone and mortar in a style more reminiscent of Braiz than Verdania, the roof high peaked and tiled in wood. She had a strange sense that they were out in the middle of nowhere. How long would it take to get to Queen Abonde?

Inside the building awaited an otter with fur and whiskers fringed in white, adorned in colorful regalia bordered in gold braid. This could only be the aforementioned captain.

The captain consulted with its subordinates, their low voices incomprehensible. Other guards came and went, doing a poor job of hiding that they had come to gawk at the human. After a few minutes, the captain stepped back, and the otter guards encouraged Solenn and Aveyron to exit through another door. A line of evergreens stood tall and thin, and beyond them loomed even taller silhouettes of gangly towers and steep rooftops.

"Wait. Are we in the city *right now?*" Solenn asked Aveyron.

"We are, and just beyond the royal grounds," Aveyron said with a slight smile.

"I just—we went from the middle of nowhere, and when we came through, I thought . . ." She shook her head. "I don't even know what to think anymore."

"That's the smartest thing you've said yet," grumbled an otter guard. "Coming here, a human like you, proves you've got some thinking problems, but no matter to me. S'your life, your end of mysteries, and you'll have those answers soon enough." They motioned Solenn and Aveyron forward with the halberd. "Come along. The queen'll see you now."

CHAPTER
TWENTY-EIGHT

ADA

If a cheese, during aging, cracks, this may allow Gyst's unknowns to penetrate the paste. The moldy veins that develop are called fleurs de bleu. We advise that people at least try this streak of blue, even if none was intended for this cheese. From there, it is your choice whether to indulge further or to discard. If you remove it, do offer it to Hester's fire. This may well be a special treat for the God, blessed by her peer Gyst.

—Excerpt from *Book for Cooks to Excel as Do Chefs*

A loud crash caused Ada to jolt awake. Her room was ebony but for a candle upon a table some five feet away. She could smell its smoke—and the heady presence of the two powders in her coat, which draped from the back of a chair at her bedside.

The events of the past day returned to mind. The Valmonts. Ragnar. She pressed a hand to her cheek, feeling not hungover but just plain addled. What time was it? This room had no clock, and the windows were still as black as Gyst's cloak.

Loud voices carried from somewhere distant. Noise at this hour could not be a good thing. She worked on her boots, flinching at the stiffness in her shoulder, and pulled on her powder horn and coat. She looked for her bag out of the habit of recent days, then remembered she had boarded it with her horse.

She mulled over whether to eat her last oatcake, then decided to let it be. Best to know what was happening first.

Leaving the candle behind, she crept from her room, slow not only to quiet her steps but also to let her eyes adjust to full blackness. She approached the rail that opened to the stairwell and foyer below. She peered through a gap. In the foyer, Ada could see Maman, Ragnar, Segal, and Mallory, lamps lit around them.

"Where is it? Where is it?"

She recognized the roar of Mallory Valmont. The sound of shattering porcelain echoed upward.

"Père!" That was the son, Segal. "There's no reason to believe your epicurea is here! Please, let's go back—"

"Someone was in my room! Someone took my new powder!"

Ada was too distant from Mallory to perceive the empowerment still within him, but by what she'd sensed earlier, she could surmise that he was starting to feel his vivacity fade.

"As your son observed, there's no reason to believe that your powder or the thief are within my residence." Maman sounded collected in the face of Mallory's hysterics. She still wore elegant evening attire.

"I'm sorry about this, Comtesse," said Segal. Mallory continued to huff and heave like an enraged bull.

"I hadn't attempted to sleep yet, at least." Her attitude was flippant. She obviously had no idea the danger she was in.

Ada suddenly regretted not shooting Mallory while she was close to him earlier. From where she was now, she'd require a musket for a reliable shot.

"You're ignoring the problem. You *are* the problem," growled Mallory. He stalked a circle around Maman. Ada could see through his thinned wheat-colored hair to the paleness of his scalp. Ragnar took a protective stance in front of Maman. He was easily a foot taller and thrice Mallory's bulk, but he didn't hold within him the embers of a God.

"Me, a problem, monsieur?" asked Maman, clearly amused.

"Yes. You. You don't understand how much I need this powder. It's keeping me alive!" He seemed to be on the verge of weeping.

"Père, please. You're straining yourself. We'll get more of the powder. I'll deploy a hunter first thing in the morning! They'll be back in two days." Two days? Hester's physical form was that close to Lutecia? "In the meantime, you can use your other powder."

The rupic. Also in Ada's pocket.

Mallory moaned, pulling at his hair. "No. It's gone too!"

"What?" Segal's voice was sharp. "All of it?"

"Yes, all of it. I'm no fool. I know where I store it."

"I take it these are not powders within our stock, then." Maman hedged for more information.

"Madame." Ragnar spoke with soft caution.

Mallory whirled to face Maman. "No. They are mine. *My* medicine."

"Medicine that is effective, considering your improvement this week. Perhaps we should consider making it—"

"No!" Mallory's sudden yell caused everyone to jump, Ada included. Her forehead bumped a post. "They are mine."

"Found using the hunters I pay, from the sound of it."

Ada softly moaned and butted her forehead against the post again, this time willingly. Maman, ambitious, oblivious, hearing only the future jingle of livre.

"Madame." Ragnar's voice was louder, more insistent.

"Hunters who operate under our guidance," said Segal.

"And they are too slow," muttered Mallory, the words barely discernible. "Too slow! My medicine will be worn off by the time they return. We'll go there ourselves. We have a map."

Segal uplifted both hands. "Père, we must attend to our affairs in the city, and in your condition, a journey into the wilderness would be—"

"We're going!" Mallory's scream was shrill. Ragnar rocked in place, a fighting stance.

"Père." Segal sounded shaken by his father's deterioration. "I must oversee the delivery in the morning. It's the largest order of the season, and the men are already—"

Mallory paced, wringing his hands in agitation. "I remember . . . yes, yes, the rendezvous would be out that same way. We'll deliver the goods, then ride to where the statue was found."

Statue. Ada could scarcely breathe. She trusted in the accuracy of her perception, but the verbal confirmation still sent a chill along her spine. Hester was indeed a cursed statue.

"Statue?" Oh, why was Maman speaking up again and drawing his attention?

"Madame, let them depart," growled Ragnar.

"A statue. Are you using *rupic*?" Maman continued as if Ragnar hadn't spoken, her tone more curious than aghast.

"Come along. You should get rest if we're going to depart soon," said Segal, tugging on his father's sleeve.

But Mallory remained in place, as unmoving as a statue, his gaze fixated on Maman, or what he could see of her around Ragnar. "You're going to come with us. You need to see the site yourself. What was described was extraordinary. The sample powder was only collected on a whim. The hunter had no idea if there was any intrinsic magic, but there is . . . oh, there is."

"I'm not going anywhere," announced Maman. "Heed your son. He's trying to take care of you. Ragnar, escort Monsieur Valjay from the premises."

Ragnar was as unmoving as Mallory. "Madame, I will do so, but I will see you safely in your chambers first."

"*Safely,*" snarled Mallory. "What does the comtesse know of being unsafe? So cosseted, so spoiled. She doesn't know suffering. She doesn't know *anything*!"

Mallory lunged forward with surprising quickness, fist extended. His frail form, bulked by layers of clothing, looked too slight to even swat a fly, but Ada felt rage-fueled power surge within him. Ragnar sidestepped to intercept the blow.

Mallory's fist met the center of Ragnar's chest. Under normal circumstances, Ada would have expected a near-comical scene of the fist bouncing off Ragnar as the man stood there, unmoved and stoic, but nothing about this moment was normal.

The fist collided with Ragnar and kept going, even as Ragnar stayed still. Blood splashed Maman, a horrible spattering sound echoing in the atrium as Mallory's hand emerged through Ragnar's back.

The large man looked down at his chest as Mallory withdrew his arm.

Ragnar tottered and collapsed. Maman held both hands to her face and screamed, other yells and cries echoing all around. Much of the house staff must have been roused by the commotion and begun spying on the confrontation. Ada stayed silent in horror, the rapid thud of her heart like a war drum.

Oh, Ragnar.

Not Ragnar.

Mallory stared at his blood-gloved hand a moment, then tilted back his head and laughed. Everyone stared. His son. His nearby men. Maman, her front splashed with gore.

"I never even did that in the war!" he said, then pointed at Maman with his bloody hand. "See, now you're without your devoted lackey."

Ada knew Maman spoke only because her head moved. Ada couldn't make out the soft words, but then, she was making slight noise herself as she began eating her last oatcake.

She would not let Mallory take Maman.

"Well, you'll have to cope without him now. Listen here!" Mallory projected his voice. Ada moved toward the grand staircase. She stuffed the last half of the oatcake in her mouth and chewed and chewed and chewed, the thin disk drier after several days. There was no time to wash it down with drink.

The last liquid she'd had was the wine shared with Ragnar.

Ada blinked back hot tears as she unsheathed her knife.

"House staff!" called Mallory. "I know you're watching and listening. You will not summon gendarmes. You will not loot this household, or my own. If you do, I will know. The comtesse will be absent for mere days. Carry on as you would if she'd gone to Versay."

"No!" screeched Maman. "Summon help! Get word to the queen that—"

A sharp sound indicated she'd been slapped.

Ada was almost to the ground floor.

"I will kill anyone who tells a soul beyond this household of what has happened here. Their families will die with them." Mallory posed this as fact. "Come, Comtesse." Ada had a glimpse between posts as Mallory shoved Maman into the grip of a mustached goon.

"Père, you truly intend to—" began Segal.

"Check the wagon's manifest and have our own bags packed. We leave within the hour." The Valmonts passed through the arched doorway, headed toward the basement passage.

"No!" Maman struggled against her guard. "Ragnar! Please, Antonin, you must let me—"

"Madame, he's dead." The mustached guard, Antonin, was not unkind in his tone.

Ada would not, could not, look at Ragnar as she reached the marble floor. The oatcake and Gyst worked fast; she was already hidden from sight. She advanced on Antonin and Maman in the doorway. They were too close together for her to even consider a pistol.

"His body must be treated with dignity as his spirit meets Gyst." Maman's voice trembled, the tone still imperious.

Antonin stood with his back to the foyer as he pushed Maman toward the doorway. "Comtesse, we must—"

Ada stabbed Antonin in the back, blade at an upward angle. She knew she'd struck true as Antonin deflated with a groan. A strike precise enough to penetrate the lung and heart to deliver instant death involved either dumb luck or skill; Ada figured this attack involved both. Antonin sank to the ground. Maman shrieked, eyes wide with new fear, frozen despite the loss of her captor.

Then Mallory returned, his skeletal form looming in the doorway, his gaze impossibly fixated on the exact place where Ada stood, reaching for Maman. Her fingers found those of her mother. Maman went silent, gaze softening in wonder.

"What is that?" barked Mallory as he yanked Maman away. Ada's fingers were left clutching mere air, and then Mallory lurched forward. The epicurea within him might have been fading, but he still stank like a town razed by fire. Ada dodged his swipe. He spun at her again as if trying to wave away cobwebs. She staggered backward, his blow missing her by inches.

"What is what?" cried Segal.

"There was something there, like a thin mist," Mallory snarled as he punched the air in her direction. An invisible force smacked her with the strength of a four-in-hand. The room blurred as she was propelled beyond the glow of lanterns, back beneath the darkness of the stairwell. She struck the floor with a soft wheeze and skidded to a stop. "Did you hear that?"

"Yes, it was a door; the staff is running away in fright!" said Segal. "By Hester's light, who stabbed Antonin? He's dead!"

"Antonin!" That came from the other Valmont guard, his grief evident in his wail.

Dark as it was beneath the stairs, the world felt terribly wobbly. Ada's brain seemed to have been jostled in her skull like gelatin in a mold. What had Mallory done? In his obliviousness, he'd managed a dreadful blow without making a physical connection, as if he'd summoned a mistral wind with his swinging fist.

"*I* killed Antonin!" crowed Maman. "I did it and threw aside the knife." The claim was ludicrous, but even so, bold.

Ada tried to sit up. The world spun around her. She pressed a hand to her mouth and sank down as she resisted the urge to retch.

"You most certainly did not kill him," said Mallory. "There was a misty figure, but now it's gone."

"Père, we must go. This mystery must stay with Gyst." Segal's voice rattled. Judging by his tone, he simply couldn't try to comprehend any additional strange happenstances tonight. "You want your medicine as soon as possible, don't you?"

"Yes! Yes, of course!"

That seemed to inspire the Valmonts to make a quick exit, Maman in tow.

Ada lay in darkness that grew darker still as her eyes closed, her head feeling like a log bobbing along on ocean waves.

To Mallory, she must have looked like the figures and things that she saw when she enhanced cat hair within food.

That made sense, she supposed, that he could see a trace of her. The Gods surely were aware of this world and others.

Mallory saw as a God did.

Like Ada did.

A revelation that would have carried immense impact, had she been able to hold a coherent thought as her consciousness faded to absolute black.

CHAPTER TWENTY-NINE

ADA

Quick-hare is an epicurean prize. As any hunter knows, normal hares are difficult enough to capture—imagine, then, one that is ten times faster! Drying the meat for jerky is the most simple and common preparation, but for a true treat, make jugged quick-hare. After basic preparations, braise the quick-hare in two bottles of red wine along with garlic and shallots minced fine. The resulting meat will be tender enough to eat with a spoon, and due to the inherent abilities of the hare and a Chef's touch, the diner will be imbued with the ability to run with speed and ease for many hours. This is a meal worthy of the king's messengers.

—Excerpt from *Manual for Tour Chefs*

Ada heard sobbing. Heaving, hiccuping sobs, and from more than one person. Along with this were baritone grunts and gasps, and the sound of a heavy, dense weight meeting the ground.

She wasn't sure how long she had lain flat on the marble floor. She had tried to sit up several times, only to quickly flatten again. She suspected she had dozed some but wasn't clear on that, either, though the world did seem to be regaining clarity at long last.

Squinting one eye open, she could see plants in large white pots. One had been knocked over, the small tree's gangly roots exposed to the air. She could actually count the pots now—they were no longer attempting sailors' jigs in the near darkness.

"We can't leave him here," said a soft, warbling voice. "We need to get him to a pentad. The curate needs to do rites."

"We explain the hole through his body how?" asked someone else.

"An industrial accident," came a deeper voice. "I seen such as a boy. Boards and pipes can fall off a fast wagon, go through someone like a spear."

Oh, Ragnar.

Ada squeezed her eyes shut, but that did nothing to stop the sudden flow of tears. Mallory Valmont had murdered Ragnar. He'd kidnapped Maman. They were going to wherever Hester's statue was hidden in the wilderness. She needed to stop them.

But Ada needed to help Solenn too. And Erwan. Erwan was still in danger if he'd left the palace—not like inside that compound was safe either.

She pushed herself to sit upright. Vertigo spun her again, but more gently now. She could stay up.

Ada scooted closer to the wall and bit her lip to hold back a groan as she stood, slowly. She felt ancient, decrepit. She glanced down. Oh, Five. She must have been immobile for twenty, thirty minutes, enough time for her last oatcake to wear off. The Valmonts were likely gone.

She found her knife amid chunks of soil from the upended plant and sheathed the blade as she staggered into the lantern light.

Not ten feet away, five domestics clustered over Ragnar. Two of the men had clearly tried to move his massive body, smearing a blood trail for several feet. A woman gasped, staring at Ada. "Where'd you come from?" she squealed.

Another woman in baggy night attire leaned back to better see Ada, who stood with her hands up to convey her lack of threat. "Oh, her! Mademoiselle Gray, yes? She and her grandmother were here a few days ago, doing work for madame."

Ada recognized her as one of the cooks. "Yes. Ragnar set me up in one of the chambers upstairs. My grandmother isn't with me now," she added.

At that, the men relaxed . . . until screams and yells broke out at the back side of the house.

"What the—" began the cook, the words ending in a screech as several newcomers rushed the room. Ada had just managed to grip her knife anew when she perceived the distinct waft of epicurea, but her sense of it was strange, as though the ingredients were in effect, not in a state of digestion. How much had Mallory's blow addled her brain?

As quickly as she'd assessed the invaders, they assessed her. A woman in silken attire stopped before her, a wickedly curved dagger in her grip.

"What do you have?" she hissed, looking Ada up and down. Two companions stopped beside her, one bearing a falchion, the other a pistol.

Ada kept her knife sheathed as she raised her hands again. She would barely trust herself to cut a steak on a plate right now, much less engage in melee with several opponents.

"Who are you? What are you doing here?" she asked in a level tone.

The strange woman bared her teeth, which were the exact same deep brown as her skin. "You carry foulness."

"What?" Was this stranger a rare empathetic Chef like her? The woman was young enough that Ada wouldn't recognize her from the Guild ranks.

More people, all with the aura of magic, entered the room. The staff shrieked and cried as they were herded away by the strange invaders.

"Don't hurt them!" Ada snapped.

"You say that, but who have *you* hurt? Who have you *eaten*?" snarled a gangly figure beside the woman. By their accents, they weren't native speakers of Verdanian.

A newly arrived man bounded up the nearby stairs five steps at a time, fast as if using quick-hare. Indeed, she caught a whiff of quick-hare, and yet . . .

Ada shook her head and immediately regretted the sudden movement, as it caused the world to dip and waver again.

Nothing about these people made sense in her perception.

A man of particularly noble bearing entered the foyer and, seeing Ada, stopped. His clothes were worthy of court, tailored purple silk with an embroidered vest, his ornate buttons polished to a sheen. He looked like a commander, complete with a walking stick in hand, the silver top molded into a gorgeous horse's head.

Ada gave a quiet snort. Leave it to her to make such an observation even as she faced grim odds against these invaders.

"Who are you?" he asked. His nostrils flared as he inhaled, as if he were perceiving something peculiar about her, too, which he then verified by asking, "What's in your coat?"

Six strangers surrounded her. Not one of them was a common thug, not with their dapper clothes and magical auras. Another invader escorted two domestics past at gunpoint. They looked scared but unharmed, clothes not disheveled. Not yet anyway.

"What are your intentions with the house staff?" asked Ada. Were these rivals in black-market epicurea, already aware of the power void and making a move at dominance? Had they learned to process ingredients in some peculiar new way?

"Do you reside or work in this household?" he asked. The nobleman was near her age, with sleek silver hair that looked to be natural in coloration.

"No. I'm a guest, staying here for the night. Where are you taking them?"

He paused to consider what she'd left unsaid. "They won't be harmed so long as they cooperate. For now, they are being herded together so that we might search the household. We'll begin with the contents of your coat. Keep your knife where it is."

Her fingers twitched with need for a ready weapon. "Will I be afforded the same treatment if I cooperate?"

"You'll be treated with honor." He had the accent of a person from the south coast.

"Meaning, I'll see the knife come to slit my throat?" Ada asked.

She earned a flash of smile. "Yes, and verbal warning as well so that you may prepare yourself for the end of all mysteries."

That aspect might not have been so unpleasant right now, aside from the death part. The leader waved another man forward. He reached inside her jacket, somehow knowing exactly where the rupic and Hester powder were to be found. The man also divested her of her knife and pistol as he retreated.

Could *all* these people sense epicurea? The man held on to the rupic, while he tossed the Hester powder to the noble, who grimaced as if he'd caught a handful of scat.

"Do you realize the import of what you carry?" he asked her.

How much dare she say? "Some idea. The man who lives next door, known as Monsieur Valjay, has been indulging in that as his 'medicine.' But you're already aware of that, aren't you?" she said, taking in their lack of reaction. "Did you visit his household before coming here? Was he already gone?" Ada couldn't keep the frustration and despair from her voice.

He considered her for a moment. "Yes, we missed him, but I've already deployed agents in his pursuit."

Even though these strangers might well kill her, she was oddly comforted that someone else was following Mallory Valmont. "I hope you warned them of his profound instability, of what he can do with a single fist." Without looking, she motioned to Ragnar behind her. She could smell the iron stink of his blood through the magical presences around her, and she blinked back a fresh swell of tears.

"Monsieur Valjay was said to have panicked due to the theft of his medicine. I am guessing that's what this is. What were your intentions?"

Ada read the tension among the noble and his comrades. Her answer would decide whether she lived or died, but she had no clue what the right reply would be for such an audience. Therefore, she went with the simple truth.

"To keep a man such as him far away from something as foul as *that*." She made her disgust clear.

He nodded with new understanding, but the tension didn't ease. "You're a Chef. An empathetic one, to perceive potential."

Most people referred to Chefs with some degree of awe. He said the word as if it belonged in a latrine.

"And what are all of you?" she retorted.

He inclined his head. "Not *who* are we?"

"Oh, I'm curious about your names and origins as well, but the 'what' is my primary concern. I may as well be blunt about it, since you can kill me at will. You all seemed to have sensed that powder in my coat."

"If you knew what it could do, you could have used it and fought your way through us," said the woman with brown teeth.

"Rupic powder is vile. That stuff is *worse*."

"The curse of empathy," murmured one of the group, not with sympathy.

She arched an eyebrow. "Curse? In a pentad, that kind of blasphemy would get a Chef forced into starvation penance."

"You speak from experience?" The nobleman's tone carried vague amusement. "Tell me what you perceive here." He held aloft the powder.

291

"Something incredibly annoying." When that earned her only a loftily arched eyebrow, she continued, "It's unlike anything I've encountered before."

The noble motioned to his comrades, then pointed at a woman in a floral-patterned damask gown. "The Chef here reminds me of someone. Can you please get a closer whiff and tell me what you think?"

The strange woman advanced. Her frizzy brown hair was barely tamed into a snood, her face beautiful with its wrinkle lines.

Ada perceived a gamy odor about her that made her think of beasts, but up close, the potency defied what she would perceive in a person who had eaten epicurea. No, it was more akin to a freshly slain beast, still furred and unbled.

Ada remained immobile as the woman circled her close enough that their sleeves brushed. She studied her through the power of her tongue, her eyes. The beast-woman moved in the languid way of a honed warrior, her daytime gown of a style that was contemporary at a glance but allowed for greater flexibility. She was a trained fighter for certain, but for what intent was she here today? The stranger's expression shifted from threatening to thoughtful as she completed her route and murmured her thoughts to the noble.

"What a curious development," he murmured.

The woman whispered to her companions as well, who likewise regarded Ada in a new light.

"A strange coincidence," muttered a young man. He'd drawn her attention when he bounded up the stairs minutes before, but now he maintained the strange stillness of a hare that had spied a predator. His unusually round eyes contained intense black pupils, his queued hair and trimmed beard the very brown gray of a leveret.

Ada's heart beat fast. They couldn't all *be* epicurea—or could they? Who was she to deny the possibilities of what may exist in the world, when she herself had held the remains of a God a short time before?

"There are no coincidences. The Gods are nudging us," growled the woman who'd sniffed at Ada. Unlike many in Verdania, she sounded none too happy about this divine intervention.

Ada shifted in discomfort. "I realize I haven't bathed in some time, but you leave me rather concerned about how I smell."

The noble dipped his head with a rueful smile. Ada wondered, What manner of being could he be? His silver hair had to be a clue, but his aura, in all its radiance, was more subtle than that of his companions. "I imagine you sense an odor about us as well." She didn't contain her surprise at his admission. "Along those same lines, which of the Gods do you recognize in this bag?" The small pouch swayed at his fingertips.

There was no point in playing coy any longer, then. "Hester. It reeks of her. Do you know the name of the man who's been using that powder as his medicine?"

"Valjay is what we were told, but I take it that isn't true."

"He is Mallory Valmont, once called—"

"The Hero of the Thirty-Fifth I followed his case with interest," murmured the noble. "He survived Mont Annod and never lost his predilection for cursed statues, it seems."

"How are you already aware that Hester is a statue?" Ada met the eyes of the group. "Back in my younger years, I found *one hint* that she was cursed, and the pentad then destroyed that ancient document. You lot don't seem surprised at all."

"We have tried to preserve what your pentads have attempted to obscure and destroy."

Your pentads? The kitchen-temples were found on every continent and isle of the world. She knew plenty of people who'd lapsed in their worship and were ignored by the Gods because of it, but never groups who scorned faith entire.

"We can't continue dithering," said Ada. "The Valmonts kidnapped Comtesse Esme Alarie and are riding into the wilderness to harvest more powder from Hester. They need to be stopped by you, by me, by someone, anyone."

"In this we agree. We hold no great fondness for Hester, but such sacrilege is dangerous for all."

A curious opinion on the favored God of Verdania. "You are traveling in pursuit, then?"

"Imminently. We must quickly resolve what must be done here."

"You never did mention why you invaded this household—or the one next door. I take it that you're not a rival in the epicurea business."

His smile was thin. "No, quite the opposite. We will return these ingredients whence they came. You have no plans to pursue the Valmonts yourself? Do you have more pressing concerns than stopping the man who dares ingest a God?"

"Are you suggesting a *Chef* come with us?" asked one of the strangers, his tone of disbelief. The noble silenced him with a wave of his hand.

"A few minutes ago, I wasn't certain I'd be leaving this spot alive," Ada said, "but yes, I have other concerns. People I love are in danger in Lutecia. I cannot abandon them."

"If you hesitate out of concern for Princess Solenn, know that she escaped the tower and the city entirely."

Ada gaped at him. "You—how did you—" She paused to look between the noble and the woman who reeked like a beast. "I smell like Solenn? You *know* her?"

"I've made her acquaintance more than once, and the impression she left upon me is . . . considerable. You share some resemblance, and a stronger similarity in scent."

Tears pricked at her eyes. "Do you know where she is? Is she safe?"

"I wish I knew her whereabouts, but no. What I can say is that she's in the company of my son, Aveyron. They have become unusual allies in recent days."

"Your son? Who *are* you?"

"Ah yes, this is an appropriate time for us to make introductions." He bowed, doffing his hat in an elegant motion. "I am Comte Brillat Silvacane. By what name should I call you?"

"Adamantine Garland. If you know Princess Solenn, do you also know a man in her company by the name of Erwan Corre?" Her heart pounded.

"I know of him. He is captain of the Braizian musketeer contingent and her guardian. I actually sought him out before coming here, but he was otherwise engaged in efforts to save his ward."

Ada nodded, ruminating. "If Princess Solenn and your son are together, would it be better to follow them—"

"As much as it pains me to leave them to their own devices, I must. We have our own mission. We must stop Monsieur Valmont's contin-ued sacrilege upon the body of Hester Incarnate."

What a strange turn this day had taken. "It seems our missions are aligned, then. There is power in numbers . . . if we can trust each other."

"I vow that we will tolerate your presence without subterfuge or violence, so long as you do the same," said Comte Silvacane. "We do request that you not use epicurea in our presence."

"What if I need to use something like unicorn tisane?" Her head still ached, but she could tolerate the pain—not like she had a choice. She'd used her tisane on Emone.

"We are not without medical expertise and resources of our own. So, can you reciprocate our vow?"

Could she place faith in him and his cohorts? She studied them, their somber faces. Could she possibly succeed if she pressed onward, solo? That, perhaps, was the most important consideration, and the likely answer to that seemed negative.

"Yes," she said to him, bowing. "We will ally."

CHAPTER THIRTY

SOLENN

One of Gyst's great mysteries is how he has endowed such disparate things as fig milk and the inner mucosa of a calf's stomach with the ability to coagulate milk into cheese.

—Excerpt from *Manual for Tour Chefs*

Solenn shared a look of panic with Aveyron. "Queen Abonde will see us right now?" This was the audience she'd wanted, but this was so disconcertingly sudden.

The otter guard sighed. "Not going to repeat everything for your lousy human ears, but yes, she'll see you now." More guards surrounded them, their whiskered faces fierce and halberds sharp. Solenn and Aveyron were herded along a path through the tree line. Past that were thick stone walls, beige and mottled. More guards, none of them otters, awaited them at an open portcullis. Beasts she recognized from illustrated books. They looked like wolves standing humanlike on hind legs, but in garb not unlike those of their Braizian and Verdanian counterparts. The other creatures, she couldn't name—massive birds, trees with ebony eyes, large lizards upright on two legs—but she couldn't ignore the animosity in their collective gaze.

"Don't make eye contact," Aveyron murmured, "with them, or with the queen. Especially the queen." He sounded scared, which didn't help her own rising terror.

"Any other etiquette I should keep in mind?" she asked.

"She'll know if you're lying, not that I'd expect such from you. Just . . . be true in how you present yourself."

Not knowing what else to say, she nodded.

Solenn expected to be taken to a throne room, but instead they passed through a series of baileys to enter a grassy meadow fringed by hawthorns and oaks. The canopy of still-bare branches stretched overhead to form a ceiling of dark lace against a sky sparkling with foreign constellations. Moist grass brushed her boots as they were marched into the middle of the field. There, the guards stopped.

"Turn around, let's get those hands unbound," said one.

"Oh." She couldn't contain a sound of surprise as she faced away. She felt a tug at her wrists, and then her arms were free.

"Hands and limbs and flippers and any such say as much as a tongue," said another otter, freeing Aveyron, who looked as surprised as she felt. But then, he'd likely never arrived at court in such fashion before. "You need to be able to speak freely." With that, the guards retreated, leaving them alone in the middle of the meadow.

Solenn hadn't detected a waft of epicurea from anything in Arcady, but suddenly she knew the heady presence of magic. It evoked no memories, no sensation on the tongue, but she recognized the weight of its might, like thick quilts piled atop her on a frigid night.

"I grant you this, human. You are audacious and brave to come here." The voice was soft yet contained steel. Aveyron knelt beside Solenn. She followed his example, gaze on the eerily vivid green grass.

"Majesty," Aveyron murmured. Solenn echoed him.

Solenn sensed how Queen Abonde moved toward her. "You identify as a female of your species?" Queen Abonde asked, to which Solenn
nodded. "Why do you dare to come here? Any number of our denizens
would gladly eat you, as you have eaten us."

Solenn didn't need that reminder. "So I understand, Majesty. I'm
grateful that Brillat and Aveyron Silvacane have opened my eyes to the
depths of my ignorance."

"You did not come here to apologize. You want something."

At least the queen didn't dither with inane political niceties, as
many people did in Lutecia. "I've come to treat with you for many reasons, Queen Abonde. I am Princess Solenn de Braiz." She felt the need
to say that, human convention though it may be. "I propose an alliance
with you and the citizens of Arcady so that we may stand together
against our mutual enemy of Albion."

Dead silence followed. Solenn could hear her own heartbeat.
Finally, the queen spoke. "Braiz is a minor entity within the human
realm. What can you offer us in an alliance against mighty Albion?"

Solenn thought of how her mother and father spoke in their own
negotiations. "Braiz is small but strong, Majesty. Our coastline and sea
provide a buffer against an attack from Albion, who is actively encroach-
ing on the continent at this moment. They arranged for Prince Rupert
de Verdania to be assassinated—by an epicurea native to Braiz—with
me set to take the blame, all to sabotage our imminent alliance. When
Verdania dissolves into civil war in the coming years, which is almost a
certainty now, Albion will take advantage, and their fight will be fueled
by epicurea."

Queen Abonde shifted closer to Aveyron. "Monsieur Aveyron
Silvacane de Camarga."

"Yes, Queen Abonde?" He didn't lift his head.

"Report on the status of your mission to Lutecia."

He did, in a level tone describing his retinue's infiltration of court,
their search for vendors of epicurea within the palace and the larger city,

and how Princess Solenn had aided their discovery of a major collector at court.

"Princess Solenn." Solenn almost jerked up her head to gaze at the queen but stopped herself in time. "Monsieur Silvacane is appropriately subtle when he speaks of you, and I would hear the admission from your lips. Tell me more about this poison attack on Prince Rupert."

Oh, Selland preserve her. There was no way to explain what had happened to Rupert without condemning herself, but still she spoke the truth. "There were two attacks, Majesty. The night of the first attempt on his life, my tongue awakened." She swallowed dryly. "I experienced his potential death in visceral detail. I spilled the wine to spare him. The second attack was done by a knife contaminated with singing mushroom. I tried to dump the tainted dish and failed. The prince died." Her fisted hands clutched at the grass. "I was set up to take the blame, and King Caristo saw what he wished to see. Monsieur Silvacane mentioned the vast larder of the Marquis de Dubray. What he didn't mention yet is that the marquis took me there to forcefully interrogate me via gabby jay egg. I fought back and killed him." Her voice quivered.

"For that act of self-defense, Queen Abonde, her own kind will judge her all the more harshly," said Aveyron. "I assisted in her escape as a matter of honor and gratitude."

"And then you revealed your equine form and crossed the veil with her," said Queen Abonde. "You brought her here, fully cognizant that you both would still endure judgment."

"Yes, Majesty. I trust in you more than any human court."

Solenn sensed Queen Abonde pacing before them. "Such a complexity. A human girl who is a Chef untrained and shadowed by Gyst."

Solenn blinked, befuddled. "I beg your pardon, Majesty. I don't understand what you mean by 'shadowed.' I thought Gyst had only touched my tongue?"

"*Only.*" Queen Abonde guffawed. "Your family, the Chefs, are all inclined toward him?"

"My birth mother and my maternal grandfather and great-grand-mother that I know of, yes."

"That is because your line descends from Gyst."

Solenn was a great-great-granddaughter of a *God*? How was that even possible? The ancient August Chef back home liked to tell tales of Selland as the mother and father of all beings of the sea, Braizians included, with the implication that Selland took care of his people as would a devoted parent. And now, Queen Abonde was saying Solenn was actually a descendant of Gyst's. Did that mean that Selland also had children? What about Lait, Melissa, and Hester? "I . . . I had no idea."

"Be that as it may, you are still thoroughly mortal, and you will die tonight," Queen Abonde said airily.

"What? But we—I—what about Gyst, you would kill the descendant of a—"

"We acknowledge that the Gods exist. We even respect them, to an extent. That said, expect no devotion from us, not with so many of our number slaughtered for food. And there is the matter of you, in particular." The queen loomed close, her presence stifling, suffocating. "You have been helpful to our kind, yes, but you have also eaten of our corpses and the products of our enslaved kin."

"I didn't know!"

"You think we should forgive you for your profound ignorance? The fact remains that you are a Chef. Even now, as I stand over you, your Gods-touched tongue recognizes me as *food*. Does it not?"

Queen Abonde bent closer, closer, and Solenn knew she couldn't look at her, so she bent lower, lower until grass kissed her lips. The close presence of magic practically scorched her tongue.

"Yes," Solenn whimpered.

"I'm aware that in Verdania, Chefs who don't submit to the will of the Crown are punished by the loss of their tongues. This is done, I hear, to teach Chefs that if they scorn their blessing, it will be returned to the Gods. A person can live a long, content life without their tongue. Bah."

Queen Abonde made a sound of disgust as she withdrew several paces. Solenn stayed down, tears streaming from her eyes. She didn't want to die. She was only sixteen! She never got to say a proper goodbye to Erwan—oh, he must be fretting so much by now. And her parents, they would only know she had escaped into the woods, never to be seen again. Verdania would be blamed for her death, and war would begin *fast*.

Solenn wanted to bring unity. Instead, because of her, everything would worsen.

She motioned to Selland, then paused. What if she appealed instead to Gyst—her kinsman?

"Gyst, hear me, help me," she whispered beneath her breath. "Queen Abonde is going to kill me. I don't know what to do. Please, direct me through this mystery."

As she whispered, Aveyron spoke up, his voice trembling. "Majesty, I'm sorry for my offenses. Please, please show mercy."

"Yes, please, show mercy upon Aveyron if not upon me. He was only trying to help," said Solenn.

"*Help.*" Queen Abonde savored the word in an unpleasant way. "By his own admission, he has uttered aloud truths intended for no human ears and changed form before your eyes. For this, he, too, must die, but mercy *will* be extended to Brillat Silvacane and the others in their retinue."

Aveyron made a tiny sound of despair that snapped something within Solenn.

"Gyst," she hissed under her breath, in all her royal authority, "*help me.*" Her tongue practically sizzled.

And then Gyst was there, like she'd flung open a locked door to let him through. He stood just to her right, black robes visible out of the corner of her eye. He had to be about her own height, had she been upright, his figure slight in the formlessness of his clothes. Had he been a person on the street in Nont, he would have seemed nondescript but for the crackling aura of his presence. He was like a fierce storm or bonfire contained in a man. He was . . . energy. Potential. An undeniable God. Could she look at him directly? Did she dare?

"Queen Abonde." Gyst had a voice like a laden wagon wheel rumbling over fine rocks.

"Most August Gyst." Queen Abonde's voice quavered. "What brings you here this day?"

"You are on the verge of executing a human of interesting potential, and you do so out of sheer pettiness." He clicked his tongue in chastisement. He reeked like the deepest, most dank corner of a basement combined with the sharp tang of burbling yeast and the fresh, grassy pleasantness of a ripe soft-rind cheese. "How you expect this action to benefit you and your kind, I don't know."

Gyst had actually come when Solenn called him. He said she had *interesting potential*. Relieved as she was to have his support, she was also shaken. Her trembling hands clutched the grassy earth as if she could grow roots and stabilize herself, physically and mentally.

"Most August Gyst," said Queen Abonde, "you haven't graced us with your physical presence for well over a thousand years. How are we to know the mind of the God of Mysteries?"

"How indeed?" His laughter was like the creak of rotting floorboards, gingerly trod upon. "First of all, let us resolve some mysteries for Princess Solenn de Braiz, shall we? I give her permission to look upon me. I advise you do the same. If you're going to murder someone, at least grant them the dignity to know their killer."

"Princess Solenn." Queen Abonde sounded stiff and forced. "You may sit up and gaze upon me. Aveyron Silvacane, I grant you permission as well."

Now that Solenn had leave to look, she wasn't sure she wanted to, but she sat upright nevertheless.

Some fifteen feet away stood Queen Abonde in a voluminous white dress, its multitude of layers as sheer as butterfly wings. Her skin was likewise white and scaled like a snake. Brassy, round eyes stared from a face that was as beautiful as it was frightening, her jaw elongated and nostrils flat.

Queen Abonde was a dragon.

This must have been her human form—or as human as she could get. No wonder the queen exuded such power. Dragons were about the oldest and most celebrated of epicurea, and now extinct or practically so everywhere in the world.

That bit of gawking done, Solenn studied Gyst.

His physical appearance was far less dramatic. His robe and cloak covered him from head to foot. The depth of his hood showed only blackness. He had no visible skin; his hem even obscured his feet. The more she studied him, the more that his clothes seemed to . . . move. Vibrate. With a start, she realized his clothes—his very form—was made of minuscule dark specks like mold spores, all of them billowing in place in the shape of a human figure. Why, he could probably be any shape or size he wanted to be.

I cannot stand here for long. She heard Gyst's whisper like the soft rattle of seeds in a dried gourd and somehow knew that she alone heard him. *Even in this realm of strong magic, I am taxed by direct interactions. Yet I will speak for you, if I may do so through you.*

"Through me?" she whispered aloud.

"What?" Aveyron whispered back, his eyes widening. "Wait. Is Gyst speaking to you? Solenn?"

Queen Abonde regarded Solenn and Gyst, lips pursed, expression contemplative. Eerie quiet draped the meadow.

The queen's mind is not yet changed, said Gyst. *And my power fades.*

"But you're a *God,*" she hissed aloud.

Gods are not almighty. His voice was fainter.

"Don't leave!" Solenn squawked. "I need your help!"

"Solenn—" hissed Aveyron.

Open yourself to me. Empty your thoughts, so that mine have room, murmured Gyst.

Empty her thoughts. *That* she could do. She focused on her breaths, and fear loosened its strangling grip on her mind.

Strange coolness draped over her body, as if she'd been covered by a deep shadow. She shivered.

"There," she said aloud with a content sigh, but didn't really say. The voice, the lips, were hers, but the word was not.

Gyst was using her body to speak.

CHAPTER
THIRTY-ONE

SOLENN

*The presence of Gyst is readily recognized by his dis-
tinct aromatics, but keep in mind that his odors often
do not match the flavors left by his touch. Consider a
cheese that's rank in the way of sweaty woolen socks, a
reek that can overwhelm a room or, indeed, a building;
however, the flavor of this same cheese may be mild,
reminiscent of mushrooms and refreshing dank earth
after a rain. Such is the complex nature of the God of
Unknowns.*

—Excerpt from *Manual for Tour Chefs*

Solenn tried to move. She couldn't. She felt weirdly immobile. And
something was draped over her face too. It had to be Gyst's hood, the
living "cloth" like fine tulle.

"Oh, Solenn," Queen Abonde murmured in a tone of dismay.
"What have you done?"

Shh, shh, all is well. Gyst's voice echoed in her mind. His assurance didn't assuage Solenn's anxiety. What had Queen Abonde meant? Solenn couldn't even move her lips to ask for clarification. *Because we're kin, you are connected to my power, and I to yours.*

That's why I can taste death as I do? Solenn replied as a thought.

Yes. Quite curious, how your aptitude developed.

You mean . . . you didn't make this happen?

We Gods are given far more credit than we deserve. He sounded dryly amused.

The old homily came to her mind: *"A person must buy the cow and know how to tend to and milk it. Only then can Lait—"*

"—encourage the milk to flow. A person must know how to make the cheese and how to store it in the right place and temperature, and only then can Gyst work his art." Yes, yes, this is truth.

"Solenn?" Aveyron leaned close, his expression pained.

"Solenn is here, as am I." Gyst used her voice, adding a small rasp.

"The God had a foot wedged in the doorway. Now he has been allowed inside." Queen Abonde's tone was level, composure reclaimed after her initial shock. "Such a thing has not happened in many millennia."

"Three thousand, one hundred, and twenty-three years," Gyst said through Solenn. *"It's good to see you through living eyes, Queen Abonde."*

The queen seemed unable to reciprocate, or unwilling. She instead offered Gyst—Solenn—a gracious curtsy.

Why is seeing through me so special? Solenn asked. She wanted to scream but couldn't even do that. She was reminded of the time when, as a young child, she had been scooped into the sea by a high wave. She'd been wearing an elaborate dress for a high holy day, and the layered skirt and long sleeves had pinned her limbs and dragged her downward.

Erwan had jumped in to save her and said that Selland had aided the rescue. Oh, Erwan. Oh, Selland.

A human body offers a range of sensations that can't be experienced otherwise. It means feeling alive. In my full form, my awareness is of decomposition, of the necessary degradation of all that is vital.

Then, using Solenn, Gyst spoke aloud: *"A body such as Solenn's is a rarity. Therefore you understand why I am perturbed by your eagerness to send her soul to me."*

"I did not understand how . . . invested you were, August Gyst. Your influence is known in all Chefs, after all."

"Indeed. You would be wise to be more invested in her abilities as well. She presented to you an offer no human has dared broach before. Don't dismiss it so readily."

The queen's scaled brow furrowed. "By human standards, she's scarcely a grown woman. Even more, she is female, and among the higher castes of her kind accorded neither equality nor respect. Even if she were given leave to think and speak, how would she work on our behalf without giving away the secrets that ensure our tenuous survival? I shouldn't need to counsel *you* on the ways of secrets, Most August Gyst."

Let me speak! Solenn raged at Gyst. *If you're arguing that I can do the job, then let me do the job!*

Very well, he said in a tone of idle curiosity. Her lips opened—she made them open—with a gasp.

"I would find a way," Solenn said aloud. A mixture of relief and amazement flashed over Aveyron's face as he recognized who spoke. "I would talk to you and find out how much I could say. I want to earn your respect, and that means respecting your secrets."

Once Solenn started speaking she didn't dare stop. "As for my age and that I'm female, I agree with you. I will need to fight for every shred of respect among humans, but I *will* fight." A small smile curved the queen's face at that. "I already had a taste of that when I was given charge of the recovery efforts after a terrible fire in Nont. I had men who asked to talk to my parents or my musketeer captain instead of me. I had people who expected me to dress up prettily and nod a lot, and not *do* anything." Her lip curled in contempt. "I was there to work. I wanted to prove myself to them, but more than that, I knew there were many people who needed help. I was the person in a place to provide that. I couldn't let them down."

That was well said, Gyst added in her mind. She felt a surge of pride, even in her anger toward him.

Queen Abonde considered Solenn with a tilted head. The jerky movement reminded Solenn of how birds maneuvered. "Braiz is still a lesser power politically and militarily."

"For now." Solenn raised her chin, indignant. "The power and numbers of the Coterie are diminished, too, but I wouldn't call you weak, Queen Abonde. The thing is, we're *all* weak compared to Verdania and Albion, but we'll be stronger together." She paused, brightening. "Think of the sea alone. All my life, I've heard tales about merfolk, and selkies, and the sheer power of krakens. Why, last month, a kraken sank an Albionish trade ship off our coast. What if the Braizian navy worked *with* krakens? Our cannons could blast foes atop the waves, krakens attacking from beneath!"

Solenn glanced at Aveyron and opened her lips to say more, but she couldn't. Her head turned toward Queen Abonde instead. *"If anyone can make such an alliance happen, it is Princess Solenn,"* said Gyst.

"And if she fails?" the queen asked.

Gyst made Solenn's shoulders shrug. *"She'll likely die along with her people, as your kind are also slaughtered, in an efficient, ruthless manner, orchestrated by Verdania and Albion. You've long known that you're in a war, Queen Abonde. Even more, you know that it's not going well."*

"You attempt to sell her attributes to me, but you are now part of this proposal as well. What of your own liabilities?" Queen Abonde's smile was frosty. "The very political dynamics of humanity are based upon the powers they obtain by enslaving and eating the kin. Hobbled as we are by Hester, we are all prey. You cannot undo that. You don't show us favor at all."

"You're right. I cannot undo what she did. Even now, the manner in which Hester tore Ys and the world's fabric asunder is difficult to comprehend. She broke not only the kin, but herself."

Gyst, this is my body! If I am to be an ambassador, I need to continue to speak. The Coterie needs to know I can do this. Solenn felt like she was banging on walls, only to be ignored.

Queen Abonde's lip curled. "I will not sympathize with Hester. She created her own problem."

"She did," Gyst said levelly. *"But she can still deliver great damage to your kind . . . and to everyone else in this world."*

"You know where she is and what she is doing?" asked Queen Abonde.

"But of course. I am the God of Mysteries and the Unknown. I watch and listen." His version of a grin was toothier than Solenn's normal smile. *"I've monitored Solenn closely, but she's not the only human of interest to me. Curious things may be happening quite soon, Queen Abonde. But then, you're already party to that secret, too, aren't you?"*

Solenn could feel his smugness. He relished in knowing more than most everyone, and he enjoyed his control over Solenn's body. He liked that she struggled to no avail. She thought of the acrobat, lording over his horse, and of Rupert, lording over the acrobat in turn.

This is my body, Solenn repeated. *Let me control myself!*

Gyst laughed internally. *You were born in this body, true. And yet—*

Solenn felt him nudge her very soul. For a span of seconds, it was as if she were dangling in space, like when she'd climbed to the palace roof. Then the pressure eased. She again felt grounded in her own self.

Why are you doing this? she asked. She would have wept, but she couldn't even do that. *If you want control of my body, why not throw me out entirely?* In hindsight, this wasn't something to challenge Gyst on, but she didn't know how to keep her feelings a secret from him. Yet.

I am a God with many demands upon me. A human body needs constant maintenance. Besides, your taking on this role of ambassador appeals to me. I am a distant grandfather of yours, after all. I have an interest in your success.

You—you're treating my body the way Verdanian nobles treat Versay, as their retreat outside the city.

Gyst laughed within her mind, then spoke aloud: *"Queen Abonde, have we done an adequate job of arguing for the sustained life of the Braizian princess here?"*

Not just my life! Solenn yelled. *Aveyron is in peril because of me. Let me speak up for him.*

Now, now, you were taught better manners than that.

Solenn wished she could grit her teeth together. *Most August Gyst, please let me speak on Aveyron's behalf, as you apparently will not.*

I choose to ignore your petulant attitude, for now.

She felt his grip relax, as if her body were being released from a mighty fist, though the whisper-soft feel of the ethereal robe was still very much there. She rushed to speak while she could. "Queen Abonde, please, show mercy upon Aveyron de Camarga. His love and respect for you and his kin should not be questioned."

Aveyron seemed cowed by the divine arguments around him and kept his head bowed.

"Even as I prepared to punish him, I did not question his devotion," said Queen Abonde. Solenn raised her chin—oh, she could raise her chin!—as she observed the queen's use of the past tense. "Aveyron de Camarga, I rescind my judgment upon you." He released a long breath, eyes partially closed. "As for you, Princess Solenn de Braiz, you will be granted a half year to negotiate an alliance between the Coterie and your people."

A half year. That had to be a very symbolic span of time for them, considering Hester's curse. "Thank you, Majesty." Solenn also genuflected.

And lost control of her body again as she straightened.

Where is the gratitude for my role? Gyst asked, tone airy. *You asked for me to act on your behalf, after all.*

She had. She couldn't completely regret his intercession, as his aid had saved their lives, but oh, she did know regret.

Thank you, Most August Gyst.

That's better. I know you were raised to treat with the Gods in proper transactional form, so you should be more—

You've taken over my body! This was worse than being excluded from her marriage negotiations, worse than being locked in the tower.

Your body exists because of me. Though he spoke mentally, he punctuated the sentence with a shrug. Her anger didn't disquiet him at all, but then he was a God, probably screamed at all the day long. *I'm always nearby. Should you have immediate need of me, call me by mind or voice.*

With that, the feathery-light pressure of the robe dissipated from her body at long last.

"Oh. He's gone." Solenn contorted her lips to prove she could control them, then realized she was making funny faces at the queen.

"Gyst is not gone," said Queen Abonde. "All your life, he has awaited this opportunity, and you've given it to him."

"My tongue only awoke days ago, Majesty."

Queen Abonde looked severe yet sympathetic. "The Gods can be patient and impatient in turns. You've provided him something he's awaited for eons."

"How can I regain my autonomy?" Solenn asked, afraid. Had she created a union even worse than marriage to Rupert?

Queen Abonde extended her arms, palms up. "I tell you truly, I don't know. Much knowledge of the origins of the Gods and the workings of their divine power has been lost to time. Even more, the kin are not close to the Gods as are humans."

"The Coterie has kept itself apart, with good reason," said Solenn. "I'm going to work toward a more positive, mutually beneficial relationship between Braizians and the Coterie. This . . . this means everything to me, Majesty."

"You have chosen a difficult task to make your 'everything,' Princess Solenn."

"Yes, but it is my choice." This felt especially important now since Gyst, when he decided to assert control over her, did so absolutely. There had to be means to stop him.

While she still had dominion over her own body and an audience with the queen, she needed to forge a true foundation for the work she had to achieve.

"Queen Abonde, I formally request refuge in Arcady."

Aveyron's small gasp verified the seriousness of her request, whereas Queen Abonde's brassy eyes widened before she burst out in laughter. Solenn channeled Mamm's most cool and regal pose.

"Oh, you *are* tenacious," said the queen with a sharp-toothed smile. "If I had continued to speak with you, perhaps you could have survived our parley without intercession from Gyst. Your directness is welcome."

"In this regard, I'd like to think I am pragmatic. The human realm beyond Braiz isn't safe for me now, and depending on what happens soon, Braiz may not be a safe refuge either." That acknowledgment made her tremble, but she pressed onward. "You've given me six months to start an alliance. I need a safe base to work from to achieve that. I also request that this agreement between us be put into writing—that I can read—as we may need to negotiate the finer points of our arrangement as well."

As Tad liked to say, "Nothing is official until it's in ink." The words and wisdom of her parents and Erwan had truly sustained her today.

"Princess Solenn," Aveyron said softly. "Among the kin, our word is our bond."

Worry twinged within Solenn. Had she just offended Queen Abonde? If so, Her Majesty showed no outward sign. Solenn pressed onward. "The queen has already demonstrated that her mind can be changed, for which I'm grateful. That's why legal documentation—and thorough documentation of revisions—is important."

"You are a curiosity for a youth of your kind," said the queen. Solenn tried to interpret this as a compliment, that she was demonstrating that she was indeed suited to be an ambassador. "Such documentation, as you say, can be produced soon. In the meantime, a public declaration will suffice." Her head tilted up. "Let it be known that Princess Solenn may live in safety in Arcady these next six months in accordance with the passage of seasons in the human world. She will be provided with a home and sustenance so that she may be comfortable. She is not to be harassed or harmed by any of the Coterie. At the completion of six months, her status will be reassessed."

Solenn was jolted by a soft chorus of acknowledging roars and rumbles from all around. By Selland's rake, had the surrounding woods been filled with observers?

"Thank you, Majesty," she said, bowing. "I intend to earn the trust of you and others during this time span."

"Queen Abonde." Aveyron's voice was steadier. "I request that, as my father's mission is near completion, I may assist Princess Solenn as she adapts to life and ambassadorial duties here in Arcady."

"I will allow it," said Queen Abonde, "with the understanding that your sire will be your consultant and superior once he is available." To this, Aveyron nodded.

"You'll be a better help for me than Madame Brumal," Solenn whispered to him, provoking a tiny smile.

"With this matter resolved for the time being, I declare this meeting at end. Attendant, see to the princess's needs." Queen Abonde motioned to one side. She turned away with a flare of her draped white sleeve and in an instant was gone.

Solenn blinked. Well, that was abrupt. In her relief, she almost sank into the lawn as if her legs had been rendered boneless. She'd survived.

She had a refuge, and a chance to build a new life for herself—and a new hope for Braiz.

And oh, she suddenly felt tired enough to curl up in the soft grass and be asleep within a minute.

A bark-skinned figure approached them. Aveyron offered Solenn his arm, which she was glad to take. "Let's get you to your domicile," he said softly. "This has been a long day."

Indeed. She let him guide her across the lawn, giving him the reins, as it were. That thought almost caused her to giggle aloud. She had fought against the control of a God but readily put her trust in a shape-shifting horse. Erwan would be unsurprised by her priorities, if he knew.

Her heart lurched at the thought of Erwan. He must be worried sick for her well-being. She could only hope and pray that he wouldn't do anything foolhardy in his efforts to help her. She made a small motion to Selland; in him, she would still place her faith. Not Gyst.

She shivered, her skin suddenly tickled by a so-brief return of that robe, as if she needed a reminder that Gyst was there, ever ready to assert his dominion.

CHAPTER THIRTY-TWO

ADA

Chefs-in-training are tested by having their tongues tainted by foul flavors, forcing them to perceive through more than divine perception. After all, a Chef is as susceptible as anyone to cankers and infected teeth that may contaminate the mouth; even an empathetic Chef may find their senses nulled or distorted by nasal congestion. The tongue is an asset, but it is not the sole thing that makes a Chef into an expert in cuisine.

—Excerpt from *Manual for Tour Chefs*

With incredible efficiency, the comte's crew emptied both households of their magicked ingredients as well as any and all relevant paperwork. The catalogs and maps of sources and lists of customers held immense monetary value, but for Comte Silvacane's comrades, this obviously meant something more. Ada couldn't help but notice that they handled epicurea with the reverence with which most people regarded the dead.

She considered this along with her other observations and perceptions. They were people, yet more than people. Essentially, epicurea that could walk and talk and feel as would any person in Verdania. That was disturbing, considering how much epicurea she'd indulged in and prepared over her lifetime. These people were an even greater mystery than the subtle magic practiced by cats.

Ada was granted a brief opportunity to speak with the domestics to ensure they were well. The staff of both households had been corralled together in a spacious parlor and provided with bedding and basic necessities for their captivity.

Her visit to them was not entirely philanthropic. She trusted them to know the city gossip from earlier in the day, and she wasn't disappointed: Princess Solenn had indeed made a dramatic exit from the palace and city.

"Monsieur le Comte, the staff told me that Princess Solenn escaped alone on horseback," Ada said as she joined him in the stable yard. They stood in parallel, saddling Camargas. The fact that he had equipped his entire retinue with such horses, notorious for selectivity in human companionship, raised him greatly in her esteem.

"Please, let us not engage in excessive formalities. Call me Brillat, as do the rest of my company." At that, she arched an eyebrow. Another curiosity to the tally. Every provincial noble she had ever known would never be so quick to shed their vestige of power. "My son joined her at some stage of her escape. I am unsure of when." He didn't look at her as he adjusted the girth. Dawn smudged the horizon in pink.

"How old is he?" She felt vaguely maternal asking such a question.

"Sixteen, as she is, and of stalwart, trustworthy character." At this, he made eye contact. "He will regard her person with the utmost honor."

Ada pursed her lips. She remembered the antics done beyond adult oversight during her distant youth.

They exited the château as the sun's full orb glared over the land. Ten of Brillat's retinue were in accompaniment, the rest having left to handle the epicurea.

"Tell me more of Hester's history," she asked as they rode through Lutecia. "What pentads didn't, and don't, want me to know." Around them, the city awoke with wagon wheel rumbles and cook smoke and scurrying pedestrians.

With some pauses due to the proximity of strangers, he explained that long ago, Hester had hated a great city and torn it asunder in her rage. No one had seen her physical incarnation in the centuries since. While she was most certainly alive and capable of doing her duties as a God, it had been presumed that she had exhausted the greater measure of her might, rendering her immobile.

Ada could hardly bear to be bedbound for a day. She could only imagine the frustration of a God, famous for her temper, stuck somewhere for centuries.

They stopped briefly at the gate to pay the requisite graft. Once outside the city, the Camargas entered canters as smooth as sweetened whipped cream, their goal to the northwest—a relay station near Rozny, where the Valmonts were to make their delivery to Albionishmen. Camargas were creatures suited for endurance and proved such as they continued through the morning. When Ada recognized Rozny, Brillat deployed three riders to scout ahead.

To Ada, it felt like it took forever for one of them to return. The man's eyes sparkled with eagerness. "The Valmonts have moved onward, but that wagon of theirs broke down and was left behind, and there's a battle taking place around it."

"What?" Brillat and Ada said in concert.

The man grinned, clearly relishing his role as storyteller. "The Albionishmen are fighting *Braizians*! That captain and his lot. They tracked the spy who set up the princess for murder. The woman is with the Albionish."

317

The words flashed like beacons in Ada's mind, her emotions likewise bright. "Captain Erwan Corre?"

The scout nodded. They wasted no more time talking, ascending to a gallop.

Of course Erwan had gone in pursuit of whoever had tried to frame Solenn. That was the best way he could help their daughter to clear her name. Ada felt a fierce surge of affection.

They thundered past the waypost, then turned from the main highway onto a narrow dirt defile through thick woods. One of Brillat's other riders waited in the road ahead. She directed them to the left, to a worn wagon trail. Shadows and coolness fell over the riders as they slowed. They passed through a copse with multiple still-smoldering campfires and farther into the woods.

The third scout awaited them, waving to Brillat. Their group reined up and dismounted, but Ada's heart continued to gallop—not because of the battle, but because of who she was about to meet. Beyond the scout, she could see the distinct blue cassocks of Braizians scattered amid the brush. Past them, a wagon sat lopsided in the path, a wheel clearly broken. Figures huddled behind it for shelter, musket barrels jutting upward.

Passing her horse to a man in the retinue, Ada followed Brillat toward the Braizians. There in the sheltered shadows, staring, was a strange yet familiar figure.

Erwan.

He hadn't lost his dignified stance, and oh, he could still wear that uniform as smartly as ever. He'd always been naturally slender and would still be considered so, though he had thickened some. His long, wavy hair was threaded by silver, his face clean shaven. That crooked smile of his still sent a hot jolt through her as it had back in the old days.

"Captain Erwan Corre," she murmured. "It's good to see you."

I've never stopped loving you; I have loathed our years apart; I am terrified to stand before you now. Her thoughts were a bittersweet mélange, but foremost, she knew relief. He was alive. He hadn't turned to stone or suffered other evident perils. Even if he looked on her with absolute indifference, she was simply glad that he was here and well.

He didn't gaze upon her with indifference, though, which was another tier of terrifying. Warmth—dare she consider . . . love?—glistened in his eyes.

"Adamantine Garland." His voice was a gentle, deep rumble. "It has been far too long."

She was as tongue tied as an innocent youngster meeting a would-be beau who had been giggled over from afar. Erwan. Here. Before her.

Brillat cleared his throat. Ada almost startled at the interruption. "I am Comte Brillat Silvacane de Camarga, Captain Corre. I'm aware of secrets between you two that I will not give voice to," he said softly.

If Brillat's group could smell the familial connection between Ada and Solenn, surely Erwan's bond with her was just as evident.

Erwan furrowed his brow in puzzlement. "His people are annoyingly perceptive," Ada added. "I can explain more later." She would get to talk with him more later. Despite their peril, she wanted to grin. He seemed to read her restrained giddiness, his expression softening as he smiled.

Brillat continued, "I understand that this reunion is of deep meaning to you both. However, we should address immediate concerns." He motioned to the woman with an aura of beast. "Patrol the area. Gauge the terrain and how we might best resolve this fight."

"I have a dozen musketeers with me, which looks about equal to your number, Comte Silvacane. It's good to confer with you at last," Erwan said. "Our enemy numbers twenty. We captured three and killed several as the melee began, and it was from our prisoners we discovered that half of their party pressed forward at the demands of a Monsieur Valjay, who had with him a prisoner, Comtesse Alarie." He acted like this had no special bearing for Ada, though he knew well their relationship.

"I'm here for another reason," Ada murmured. A shot rang out from the wagon, causing them all to shelter behind trees for a moment. She gripped her pistol, ready to defend Erwan however necessary, though he looked equally ready to fight, a hand to his rapier. When no cries or further gunfire followed, she continued, still tense with readiness: "The elder Valjay is truly Mallory Valmont. Yes, he is alive, and has been a recent business partner of Comtesse Alarie's. Together they created a successful commercial enterprise in epicurea, with Albion a major customer."

Erwan's mouth formed a grim line. "We came here in pursuit of the lady-in-waiting for my ward, Princess Solenn, daughter of Morvan and Katell." At this, he hesitated. As well he should have.

"I know who she is," Ada said, grief and joy and frustration and so much more in her voice. "Brillat Silvacane knows as well. As I said, he's disturbingly perceptive."

"You have heard, yes, of the princess's escape from the city?" Brillat asked. Erwan nodded. "What you did not hear is that she escaped with my son."

"I only heard she escaped riding bareback on a Camarga." Erwan tilted his head toward the Camargas ridden by Brillat and his party, just visible through the trees.

"Indeed," Brillat said airily. Ada scrutinized him. There were a peculiar number of Camargas around this man.

A pistol fired, not in the vicinity of the wagon, but behind them. Ada crouched behind a birch, her pistol in hand. Their companions had likewise taken cover, everyone wary of the woods around them.

One of Brillat's company crept close to report. "An armed man circled behind us, expressing too much interest in our proceedings. I questioned his intent. He responded by firing at me as he fled."

"Albionish?" Brillat asked.

"If he was, he wasn't dressed at all like them." She gestured toward the wagon. "Never spoke either."

"My thanks for your continued vigilance," Brillat said to the woman, who retreated to resume her post. Brillat looked between Ada and Erwan. "We have before us a dilemma. This wagon is of concern to both our parties. You want the erstwhile lady-in-waiting. We want the epicurea."

"For them epicurea is . . . personal," said Ada. She knew of no other way to word it. "Their intention is not to sell it."

Erwan nodded. "Princess Solenn spoke with young Silvacane on this very subject."

Ada experienced a surge of yearning. She wanted to hear more about Solenn. She wanted to bask in Erwan's deep, pleasant voice. The ongoing battle, however, acted as an annoying but rather important distraction. Two shots rang out from the vicinity of the wagon, husky voices shouting out in Albionish. She, Erwan, and Brillat took cover again.

"We have another vital concern," Brillat continued, gazing toward the wagon with wariness. "We must pursue the Valmonts. I think, perhaps, your word will carry more weight in explaining this complexity to him?" he said to Ada.

By the Five, she hoped so. "Mallory Valmont is with his son, Segal." Gunfire blasted around the wagon again, causing a brief fog among the trees. "Mallory has survived only because of continued use of rupic over the years, but he was near death in recent days—until he sampled a new acquisition." She took a deep breath. "Incomprehensible as it sounds, his new epicurea is derived from Hester, her actual physical form. She's somewhere in the wilderness out this way, and has been for centuries."

Erwan furrowed his brow. The wrinkles were deeper than they used to be, and quite attractive. "Hester is made of actual stone?"

"Yes. And the power it possesses . . . Mallory killed the comtesse's man Ragnar with a single punch through his chest." Her voice cracked, and sympathy flashed in Erwan's eyes.

"*Through* his body? Selland preserve us." He pinched his fingers. "What might befall us all if he grinds Hester to nothing?"

"If that happened, the comforts of home and hearth wouldn't completely cease, as they existed before Hester walked the earth," said Brillat. "But we would all become more acquainted with cold."

"Many people wouldn't last that long," Ada muttered. "And Mallory . . . he's already gaining powers like a God, and he hasn't even used the powder for long. Can he *become* a God? If he had enough, could he even turn to living stone? Rupic obviously hasn't done that to him, but this Hester powder is so much *more*." She shivered at the very memory of its terrible taste.

"There is much unknown about the Five and their ways," said Brillat. "I don't know what could become of Monsieur Valmont. I don't wish to find out."

On that, they could agree. Ada faced Erwan. "I found out about the Valmonts because the son sent mercenaries after me. I soon discovered that you and our companion officers were also targets. Most of us were intended to be turned into rupic for Mallory's dining enjoyment. Your sequestration in the palace made you difficult to access, thank the Five."

Erwan sucked in a sharp breath. "You . . . you were not terribly harmed? What of the others?"

"Didina is dead," Ada said softly. Erwan motioned an X, and Brillat furrowed his brow as he listened. "Petry fled. Emone's Golden Horse burned, but she escaped. Segal Valmont wanted her scorched alive rather than eaten." Describing such a horrid thing left her feeling dirtied.

"Oh, Didina. I had intended to visit the Golden Horse before I left Lutecia too." Erwan looked pensive for a moment, then nodded. "I must join you as you ride after the Valmonts. This matter is personal, and the greater threat involving Mallory and Hester will imperil Braiz as well. My second can take command here. How will you divide your forces, Comte Silvacane?"

"I alone will ride onward with you both so that we'll make good speed," he replied. "The rest of my contingent will remain here to help subdue the Albionish."

"Very well. Permit me a moment of conference with my company. Pardon me, madame, Comte." Erwan gave them a quick bow, then crept to join his musketeers.

Ada stared after him, her grief and rage an old familiar ache in her chest. Did he truly still feel something for her after all this time? Dare she hope? Regardless, she couldn't let her emotions distract her more than they already were. The ride ahead would be strenuous.

There was something else that distracted her too.

She faced Brillat. "You know I'm a Chef. As I've said before, what *you* are remains unclear."

"Indeed."

"For all that my tongue is said to be blessed by Gyst, I am truly exhausted of vagueness and mysteries."

"I can't say what I am without also endangering my comrades. You and Erwan know similar loyalties with your old company."

"We do." Ada sighed. "And despite what I don't know, I'm ready to trust you with my life."

"In spite of what I *do* know, I trust you with mine," he quietly retorted.

That answered her question well enough. Erwan returned, an expression of grim resolution on his face. He looked between her and Brillat, and they each nodded.

They were ready to ride.

CHAPTER
THIRTY-THREE

ADA

Honey diluted in water, exposed to the air, visited by unknowns: in this way, mead begins its fermentation, and it ends in delighting the senses of the imbiber.

—Excerpt from *Book for Cooks to Excel as Do Chefs*

Ada, Erwan, and Brillat rode as fast as they dared through brambles, glade, and hill. As they slowed to pick their way up a slope in the graying light, Ada gave her horse an affectionate pat on the neck.

Erwan watched her, smiling. "Solenn loves horses more than most anything else." Due to their speed, they'd barely had the chance to speak through the day.

"By the Five, but I want to know all about her, Erwan. My heart has broken time and again over the years, wondering if she was alive and well, wondering about you . . ."

She didn't know how to continue that line of thought, or if she had a right. When they had been forced to part, they had tried to handle matters like mature adults and agreed that neither should stay lonely or celibate. For Ada, though, moving on had meant sharing a cot with her grandmother more often than not, and working fifteen-hour days as a cook. She couldn't expect that same isolation from Erwan—he was still as handsome as ever, his heart good and kind. How could people *not* want him?

Brillat stopped his horse and hopped to the ground beside a pile of horse manure. He hovered a hand over the mound of nuggets. "Still warm," he said. "We've almost caught up."

"I wish they would set up camp for the night, but Mallory's mania probably won't let them," said Ada.

"He may be behaving like a crapulous individual denied additional drink as he craves more powder, but his body is still human and will have need for food and sleep," said Erwan. He rubbed at his jaw. He had developed some scruff, and knowing him as Ada did, it was probably irritating him immensely.

Brillat mounted again. He gave them both a look. "We'll need to take care in this low light. You two have much to say to each other. I'll grant you space." With that, he trotted ahead some twenty feet. Ada's horse snorted as if to laugh at his overtly noble act.

All these hours, Ada had stewed over what to say when she was finally alone with Erwan, and now she was at a loss of where to begin. Their horses resumed a quick walk in Brillat's wake.

"How did you discover Solenn's identity?" Leave it to Erwan to find words first.

"The formal announcement of Prince Rupert's death. I was in the crowd, with Emone. I saw Solenn, and I knew."

"You must have hated me in that moment, wondering how Solenn had come to be raised as Morvan and Katell's daughter."

"I had . . . questions, yes." Ada's understatement made them both laugh.

"Permit me the opportunity to supply you with answers, then," Erwan said, and explained past circumstances to her, along with what had happened in recent days. Ada was appalled at the strong nature of Solenn's empathetic gift.

From there, Ada explained her own recent travails.

"That leads us to now," Erwan said. "What is your take on the Silvacanes?" They both looked to the rider ahead of them.

"They aren't human," she said. Other people might have recoiled, exclaimed, or doubted, but Erwan accepted her judgment with a nod. "Neither are any of their companions," she added.

"Solenn sensed something peculiar about them from the first. She initially suspected their aura arose from the use of epicurea, and then she spoke with Aveyron and learned of his passionate distaste for magicked ingredients."

"The aura I get is that they *are* epicurea." Ada shook her head, discomfited.

"That would make their strident opposition to its use understandable."

"Brillat's boy, Aveyron. Is Solenn safe with him?"

"Safer than she'd be in Crown custody. He seems pleasant enough."

The crack of a musket pierced the quiet. Erwan tumbled from his horse with a surprised grunt. Ada spun her mount around, the Camarga quick and calm as she tried to locate their assailant amid the surrounding boulders. In the growing dark, though, she could only identify that the shot had come from their left. She leaped to the ground, reins in hand, and crouched over Erwan.

He stayed down. In the scant seconds that had passed, he'd loaded his pistol and positioned his sheathed rapier for ready draw. "The shot grazed my arm." He motioned to his torn sleeve, the blue fabric showing no blood, then pinched his fingers in gratitude to Selland. Gunpowder contained saltpeter and hence was in Selland's domain.

She likewise motioned to the Five. "There's a good boulder behind you, ten feet away."

"I can cover us," he said, levelheaded as ever.

Ada stayed at a crouch, leading her horse. Erwan crept backward across the uneven ground, his eye on a large set of rocks some twenty feet distant. A dense patch of woods backed them. Up ahead, she could just make out Brillat's horse behind another boulder. Erwan's mount had trotted a bit farther downslope behind another set of stones; his musket remained fastened upon the saddle.

"The Valmonts could've laid an ambush," Erwan murmured as he joined her. "But they had no reason to believe they would be followed."

Ada nodded without looking up. She had begun loading her gun the instant she had shelter. "This is too far from roads for highwaymen to lay a trap, too, not unless we're near a hideout." Her derriere bumped Erwan's as they positioned themselves to peer out opposite sides of their boulder.

"Surrender!" a raspy baritone yelled. The man fired again. The shot pinged off a nearby rock.

"You first!" Ada yelled back. By the Five, she wished she had a musket. Pistols were highly inaccurate at this range.

"I'll tell you what," the man called. "I'm only being paid for the Braizian. I don't want to fuss with you other folks. Why don't you continue onward? I promise I won't shoot you from behind!"

Ada and Erwan looked at each other, eyebrows arched. "Why would we believe you?" Ada shouted, then in a lower voice: "He's shooting to kill you."

"I noticed," Erwan remarked dryly.

"I'm just a man trying to make livre to get by," the man continued. "I've already been waiting nearly a week for a chance at this Corre fellow."

"Ah, well, if he's been waiting such a long time, we surely must oblige him," Ada muttered, rolling her eyes. Erwan snorted. "This must be the man Segal Valmont hired to track you down, but I thought he'd force-feed you stony owl, not try to kill you."

"I can't say I object to the change. I'd rather meet the bullet," Erwan said. "This man could well be the fellow who lurked around the wagon standoff."

The scuff of hooves on the rocky ground made her turn. Erwan's horse had plodded over, ears twitching, still incredibly skittish compared to Ada's mount, which clearly had more battle experience. At Erwan's look, Ada took a position to cover him as he rose slightly to grab his musket. Terrible as this situation was, she took comfort in that they hadn't lost their old battlefield chemistry.

A head poked up from behind the distant boulder. Ada fired. Through her smoke, she saw debris scatter as her shot hit rock.

"Were you contracted to kill me or nab me?" Erwan yelled.

"You'll soon find out." His tone was strangely chipper.

"If he was the man at the standoff, he must have forced epicurea on his horse to both pursue us and get ahead to waylay us," Ada murmured. "I don't like him very much."

"I don't fancy him either," Erwan said.

The man emerged again and fired. A shot pinged off the ground not five inches from her foot as she drew it in again. He was toying with them.

"He must be using Vandrossa to see this well in the dark. Valmont would've supplied it. Gyst take him," she spat.

Without need to articulate, they switched spots, giving Erwan a better vantage point to fire.

Ada glanced out in time to see the man aiming again. The three of them fired at once. A horse squealed at the same time that the man emitted a shriek of pain. Ada turned to find that Erwan's horse, not fully sheltered by a boulder, had taken the shot. Her own Camarga squealed as the other horse bolted toward the woods.

"The horse—" began Erwan.

"Yours. I couldn't see how badly she's hurt." She didn't need to state that it had been intentional. They both knew.

"This man will die." Rage shook Erwan's voice as they simultaneously loaded their weapons again. He had never tolerated soldiers who purposefully aimed for horses on the battlefield.

Ada laid a hand on his shoulder. He briefly leaned into her touch.

They pulled apart as another gunshot rang out, but at a distance. They kept their backs flat against the cold rock. In the silence, the jostle of Erwan's sheath against stone rang as eerily loud.

"He's dead," called Brillat.

"Well." Ada released a deep exhale. "Nothing like a quick skirmish to wake up a person again. Your arm. How is it?"

Erwan moved it around. "Barely stings. I was fortunate."

"Yes," Ada said, relief sparking tears in her eyes as she brought her lips to his.

Erwan's calloused fingertips brushed her jaw as he pressed into the kiss. His lips felt as they did in her memory, soft but somewhat chapped, the evening scuff on his upper lip not the slightest bit bothersome to her. A surge of heat traveled from her lips to deep down in her center.

They pulled apart, breathy.

"I remain fortunate." He smiled, studying her face up close. "You're still as beautiful as ever."

"Oh, shush. I'm older, I sag, I—"

"And I'm older in parallel with plenty of complaints of my own, but you're still beautiful," he repeated softly.

"We should go check on the dead man." Ada's eyes didn't shift from Erwan's.

"We should." His hand cupped her cheek. She let her eyelids mostly close as she savored the touch that had been too painful to even daydream of in recent years, then stepped back with a sigh of regret.

Ada and Erwan crept into the open, still wary. Ada leading her horse, they found Brillat cleaning his knife on the man's coat. His throat had been slit.

Brillat regarded them with open relief. "Good. You're unharmed. I'm going to check on the injured horse." There was an intensity to Brillat's voice that brooked no argument. He hurried away, leaving his own horse nearby.

Ada crouched beside Erwan as together they searched the would-be killer. She knew right where to find his epicurea—a pickled Vandrossa eyeball in a plugged jar, quick-hare jerky, and empress bee mead, along with the expected stony owl gut, still in raw form.

"What, did Segal Valmont give this man a sampling of his wares?" Ada asked in disgust.

"His other agents have failed. Perhaps he wanted at least one of them to see success," Erwan said.

"These would help many a soldier, to a point." She hefted the items in both hands, expression wistful.

"We *could* simply not tell Brillat about all of the epicurea," Erwan murmured.

"He'd know. Remember, he and his fellows can sense this stuff like empathetic Chefs. You should have seen how they tore through the comtesse's house." She gawked. "Is that musket *broken?*"

"Yes." Erwan nudged the weapon pieces with his boot. "The make was crude to begin with. It looks like it smashed against the rock as his last shot went wild as Brillat came upon him. The man had plenty of powder, though, but not many musket balls."

Ada grunted. Another musket and more ammunition would've been nice, but she couldn't scorn what blessings the Gods had provided. She glanced at Erwan's torn sleeve and shuddered.

They both stood to face Brillat as he returned. He carried Erwan's Braizian saddle and bridle, leaving no question as to the fate of the horse. Ada's Camarga keened softly.

"Oh no," Erwan said, drawing Gyst's X. "I pray she didn't suffer."

"I don't believe so," Brillat croaked. He took a breath to compose himself. "The man's mount is tethered in the woods there."

"As that horse will now be mine, I'll fetch it," said Erwan, taking his tack and going that way.

Ada faced Brillat, holding out the epicurea. "I imagine you want custody of this."

Brillat looked exhausted to the bone. "Such is my burden."

"We may need the advantages that these offer. Stony owl aside."

"No, we won't," he said with firmness as he tucked the items into his coat.

"Even the mead?"

"The mead is the least offensive of the lot, I'll grant you that. The bees are kept captive, not slain for consumption."

"Related to that . . . my condolences on the death of your Camarga comrade," Ada said softly. Brillat stiffened. "I know that I'm . . . repulsive to you as a Chef, but if I can help somehow, please let me know."

Brillat looked away. "I wondered if you sensed something about your horse."

"Nothing magical, no, though she is highly intelligent and attentive, like the few other Camargas I've known. My sympathy on your loss, as well," she murmured to both nearby horses, who bowed their heads in acknowledgment.

"If you might recall, my son escaped with your daughter," said Brillat. "Though he is not described in the narratives of her escape."

"No, only that she escaped upon a Camarga." Ada paused. The mathematics were simple, but not. Solenn left on horseback, yet also departed with Aveyron Silvacane. No young man was seen with her. Perhaps that was because he wasn't a man at all, at least, not at that moment. She barked out an incredulous laugh. "Your son . . . no. You mean, Solenn escaped *riding* him?" She had to cringe at the strange double-edged nature of the words; Brillat gave an abrupt nod. "You and your retinue, you can all change, then? You can assume forms other than human? Now what I perceived of your companions makes more sense, though I'm . . . greatly addled, to say the least."

As a Chef, she'd had the best education offered by the realm. Now she grasped enough to comprehend that everything she knew was wrong.

"Perhaps the ways of magic aren't meant to be understood by people such as you." He didn't say this in an unkind way. He suddenly pivoted around, staring into the trees. Both horses perked up as well. "A catamount is in the woods. I must intercept it quickly." Ada reached for her pistol and began to follow, only for him to wave her back with a scowl. "No. Bloodshed won't be necessary. I'll talk with it. I needed a messenger, anyway."

That he could parley with a catamount seemed among the least strange revelations of the day. "But if it smells the slain horse, it'll—"

"I'm very aware of why a predator has been drawn here, thank you, which is why I must speak with it promptly." He broke into a run.

Erwan, coming from upslope with his new chestnut horse, stared at Brillat's fading figure. "What's the matter now?"

"Would you believe he needed to speak with a catamount?" She frowned at Erwan's horse as her perception prickled. "Oh no. That fool forced quick-hare on his mount." Horses generally didn't eat meat, but desperate people would mash quick-hare with other feed to grant a horse temporary speed. Such cheating caused scandals in horse racing every few years. "That explains how he raced ahead of us."

"The poor thing's almost burned off the dose, at least, and by some miracle strained nothing in his exertion. No one will make you eat that stuff again," Erwan crooned to the horse, which kept quivering as if beset by invisible flies. "You'll be all right now."

His voice, his care for the horse, everything about him flared emotion in her anew. "By the Five, Erwan, but I never stopped loving you."

"And I, you." He took her hand and brought it to his lips. His touch induced a deep shiver, and not simply because of his warm breath upon her night-cooled skin. "Should we survive these travails, I would very much like to court you again."

Ada laughed softly. "To court again, after all this time. I suppose that's for the best. We're older now. We're different, our bodies are different . . ."

"I should like very much to discover the entirety of our differences," Erwan said with soft sincerity.

To her chagrin, Brillat returned at the moment, though she was glad he was none the worse for wear from his chat. "Are we ready to continue, then?" she asked.

"Yes," he said, in typical fashion, offering no further enlightenment on how things went. She gave her head a rueful shake as she mounted up again.

"He rather likes being a mystery, doesn't he?" Ada muttered to her horse, and found herself smiling as the Camarga bobbed her head in reply.

CHAPTER THIRTY-FOUR

SOLENN

To say someone "died like a marmot" is a grievous insult for the deceased. Marmots are large mountain rodents, floppy and lazy by nature. There is no pride in bagging one—no spirit of the hunt. A marmot can be captured while asleep, and remain asleep when dropped into boiling water. We may suppose, though, that such somnolent bliss can also be envied. Perhaps more of us should pray for such a quick, merciful doom on our way to Gyst's embrace.

—Excerpt from *Manual for Tour Chefs*

Tired as Solenn was, she assumed she would sleep soundly in the cozy cottage that the Coterie had provided her, channeling the enviable laziness of a marmot, but she kept awakening to the sensation of Gyst's clothes upon her shoulders and head, as if she suddenly donned them even through the thickness of blankets. With a start, she would try to shove back a hood that wasn't there, in the effort proving that she was still in control of her own body.

She finally gave up on slumber. Swinging her legs from the bed, she stretched. She still wore the same clothes from her journey; Queen Abonde's attendant had said a tailor would be sent to her in the next few days. Her knapsack had been returned to her as well. It rested against her bed's footboard.

In the kitchen's sole cupboard, she found a coarse loaf of bread, a butter crock, a small round of white mold-fuzzed cheese, and apples. She noted the absence of meat. Coterie predators had to eat nonmagical prey here, which meant there had to be meat available, but she didn't mind the absence. She had a bad feeling that when Aveyron told her more about how lambs and other nonmagical creatures were treated, she might be making more permanent changes to her diet.

She shoved down three pieces of buttered bread, the cheese, and an apple, and when she went for more bread, she found the offerings replenished and different—the new soft goat cheese was wrapped in moist walnut leaves, the bread round was full and of finer-sifted quality, and the apples had a roughly mottled yellow and green skin unlike any she had seen before.

She shook her head, awed. *Magic.* At least the food in her gut was real.

An oil lamp in hand, she stepped outside to take in her immediate environs. She'd been so exhausted upon her arrival that she'd maintained only a vague awareness of where she was.

The gray stone cottage was probably half the size of her apartment at the Lutecian palace, but she adored it. All it needed were more homey touches—curtains of Braizian lace, maybe that wood sculpture Aveyron had given her—to make it perfect. A matching stone wall encircled the building and a small edible garden that already budded with promise.

In the woods beyond the garden, an owl hooted, and several voices muttered.

"Hello, neighbors," she called. They went silent. She sighed.

"Solenn?"

A familiar voice from the darkness startled her. "Aveyron?" She held up the lantern to find him sitting on the moss-furry wall, legs crossed at the ankles. "What are you doing out at this hour?" She stepped over strawberry furrows to join him.

"I could ask the same of you." He looked about as well rested as she did, meaning haggard but mostly awake. "I was dozing in the woods nearby."

"What? I assumed you had a place to stay. Oh, Aveyron, I'm sorry! Wait . . . did you feel you needed to guard me, even though the queen declared—"

"No," he was quick to say. "You're safe here. I simply wanted to be nearby to help you around Arcady in the morning." He gave her a toothy smile. "Which I suppose it is now."

"You could have come into the cottage." To think, all he'd done to help her, and he was sleeping in the cold woods. "Oh, I know it's not proper, but you're a gentleman. A gentlehorse?" They both laughed. "I'll need to take special care with my words in my new employment. I'm used to language that centers itself on humans. I can only imagine how offensive that could be to various kin. I have so much to learn."

"You're right in that," he said. "Don't let the task overwhelm you yet. Braiz has a small population of kin by its modern human borders. You haven't the lifespan to understand the diversity of all of Arcady."

"Selland preserve me. What have I gotten myself into?" she whispered, glancing up at the stars. Strange as the constellations were, she found sudden peace.

"Why the smile?" asked Aveyron.

"The thought of Selland put me in mind of a ride along the beach near my family home last year. It was a cloudy day, and I rode my favorite mare, Maiwenn. A storm was coming in. When I flung my arms wide and opened my mouth, I could taste it. Not in a Chef kind of way," she added hastily, "but it made me feel profoundly close to

Selland. Even more, when I think back now, that moment was like the very embodiment of home." Through the memory, she could almost taste the brininess and wind and cold and *everything*. Her fingers twitched, longing for the feel of that sand in the actual place, not the scoopful kept in a box back in Lutecia.

"I understand what you mean. I've had moments like that on both sides of the veil that make me feel a nostalgic yearning for the other place. I love them both, in different ways."

"I don't think I ever could have come to love Lutecia."

That feeling of the cloak returned. She stopped walking, her hands brushing her face. The sensation dissipated. "Aveyron, I keep feeling Gyst's presence upon me. I think he's doing it just because he can." She spoke in a loud, clear voice. By canon, Gyst was more likely to hear a whisper than a shout. Nothing attracted his attention like a secret.

"The God of Unknowns craves to be known," Aveyron said, quoting a line that Solenn knew as well.

"I would very much like to keep some thoughts private." She paused, recalling the audience with the queen. "Actually, now that I think about it, he *didn't* have awareness of everything. We talked back and forth as if we were speaking, just not aloud."

"That makes sense. If he could read minds as readily as books, he wouldn't need secrets whispered to him as offerings. Did he say why he didn't just . . . take over your body entirely?" Aveyron shifted in discomfort.

"He did, actually. Human bodies require constant care, he said, and he has many demands upon him as a God. He did demonstrate that he could evict my soul, though, if he so desired." Solenn shivered, not because of the tickle of the robe, but from fear.

"What a lout," Aveyron muttered. "But if he can do that to you, that means you can do the same to him. Right?"

"I'll find a way," she said, balling her fists. "I'm sick to death of everyone wanting to use me. For Braiz—for Braiz I was willing to marry, but I never wanted that. I've never dreamed of being a wife, a mother, or even being a queen. I want to be respected primarily for my mind, not controlled because of it. I still don't understand what sets me apart from the other Chefs in my family. Why hasn't Gyst been able to see through human eyes for over three thousand years?"

"Well, I—" Aveyron went rigid, staring into the nearby woods. "A catamount?"

She looked in the same direction. "Are we in danger?" She held up her light again.

"One might say that danger is ever present," said a rumbly voice. A wildcat strolled into the lantern light. Twice the size of a standard house cat, the catamount had tawny fur lined by faint black stripes. It cocked its head at Aveyron. "By your scent, I know you as the colt of Brillat Silvacane de Camarga. I seek you and the human on behalf of Queen Abonde. You are to follow me." With that, the cat turned away with a flick of its thick black-tipped tail.

Solenn sent Aveyron a questioning look. He shrugged and started to follow the cat. "The queen doesn't like to wait."

Upon returning the lamp to the cottage, they departed.

The catamount escorted them into the city along a haphazard route amid crooked lanes and buildings of more sizes and makes than she could comprehend. Many structures were not buildings as she under-stood at all, but clustered trees with tiny doors and curtained windows, places that were undeniably homes. The cat seemed to take a purposeful route to avoid other beings that might be out and about, for which Solenn was grateful. Tired as she was, she wanted all her remaining wits preserved for this confrontation with the queen.

They entered the palace after a brief conference with the guards. The catamount guided them not to the meadow where court had been held earlier, but to a softly burbling stream draped by swaying willows. There, posed on a rock with her knees tucked near her chin, was Queen Abonde. She wore the same billowing dress as earlier.

"Come. Listen." She gestured to the rocks beneath her. Solenn and Aveyron sat. "I will share information with you both as befitting your new roles." Solenn took that as a good sign. "Brillat Silvacane has sent me messages today, the last coming through this helpful agent." Queen Abonde gestured to the catamount, who was nestling into a mossy spot beneath a hawthorn. Solenn wondered how and why the cat went about this role but saved such questions for later. "Monsieur Silvacane's quest has come to interesting results. Humans recently discovered the most sordid of ingredients: Hester Incarnate, which in their ignorance they have harvested. At least one human has ingested of her stone body as powder."

"She's similar to rupic, Majesty?" Solenn asked, brow furrowed, to which the queen nodded.

"Not even Hester should endure such sacrilege," murmured Aveyron.

"Agreed," said Queen Abonde, her thin lips in a moue. "Curiously, a Chef of empathetic ability had also become aware of this travesty and was seeking to undermine it. Brillat has partnered with this person, one Adamantine Garland."

Solenn jolted in place. "*What?* You mean, do you know—"

"The God of the Unknown is not the only entity privy to deeply held secrets. I know this person birthed you."

Aveyron looked between Queen Abonde and Solenn. "I plead for your pardon, Majesty, but you're saying that of all the people in the world, Solenn's birth mother has allied with my father? That seems . . . convenient."

"The Gods toy with us. This was made clear by Gyst's unusual manifestation and his manipulation of Princess Solenn."

"His manipulation?" Solenn asked, then thought back. Was this about more than Gyst experiencing what it was to be human again? "He asked to see through my eyes because being physically present taxed him."

"That is indeed what I suspect to be a manipulation of you. He should not have been strained, not in Arcady."

Solenn's jaw dropped. "You mean I didn't even need to open myself to him? He *lied* to me?"

Aveyron regarded her with sympathy. "Humans have largely forgotten that Gyst is also called the God of Untruths. After all, what is a white lie but truth decomposed?"

"You were vulnerable, Princess Solenn. He took advantage," said Queen Abonde.

"I'm still left wondering why the Gods would prod us this way. They must want us to help Hester, and yet . . ." Solenn mulled that for a moment. "Have the Four suffered since the destruction of Ys and the disappearance of Hester? Or have their existences actually been *better*? Hester is pretty hard to get along with according to the old stories. Maybe it's nice that she's lost so much power."

Queen Abonde was quiet for a moment. "That is a disturbing insight, Princess Solenn. You may find it enlightening to hear the recent message to me in full." The queen looked to the messenger. "Catamount, if you would please?"

The cat sat up with a knife-sharp yawn. "Truly? For the human and horse?" At the queen's chill expression, it sighed and began, "Brillat Silvacane de Camarga wishes to update Queen Abonde that his mission proceeds apace. A large shipment of epicurea has been intercepted in the company of Albionish. Brillat's retinue has joined with Braizian musketeers in a siege to acquire the goods and the person of Madame Brumal, the spy sent by Albion to sabotage the union of Princess Solenn and Prince Rupert." Tears sprang to Solenn's eyes. Her people had found Madame Brumal. "Brillat has continued his journey to Hester Incarnate in the company of Chef Adamantine Garland, and has been joined by Monsieur le Capitaine Erwan Corre de Braiz."

A wordless noise of shock and joy escaped Solenn. Her parents were together again? The cat scowled at the interruption, then continued.

"Brillat Silvacane de Camarga anticipates an interception with the sacrilegious humans in the morning, whereupon his company will do whatever is necessary to put an end to their offense. That is the message in its entirety, for Queen Abonde." The cat's tail flicked as it curled up in a tawny round.

"I thank you for repeating your message twice over," said the queen. "You're dismissed."

"This is a rather pleasant spot, actually. I believe I'll stay awhile yet, Majesty." The cat closed its eyes. Solenn gawked at the impertinence, but Queen Abonde showed no reaction.

"My father, working with a *Chef*." Aveyron shook his head. "Yes, there must be divine intervention."

Her parents were together again, about to meet a God known for her fiery rage. Fear doused Solenn like icy water. "We have to go there, Aveyron, and not because the Gods nudge us this way. Our parents are in terrible peril. We have to help them however we can. Right, Gyst?" She said the name with equal measures of boldness and fear.

Gyst's presence fell over Solenn in an instant, his cowl no longer ticklish but warm against the night's chill. *"Ah, what a lovely stream this is."* Solenn took in a hearty breath, the air fragrant of greenery and damp earth. *"Queen Abonde. Monsieur Silvacane. Another conference, so soon?"*

She sensed that he truly was oblivious to what they had been speaking of before he was called. Good. *Captain Erwan, Chef Garland, and Comte Silvacane are venturing to Hester Incarnate. Are they in peril?*

Do grapes make wine? he retorted. *Of course they are.*

A strand of hair dangled over her right eye. She instinctively tried to brush it behind her ear. She couldn't. *You don't have to dominate my body!*

Gyst made no verbal response but compelled her to stretch out her arms and to twirl around, head craned back to take in the starry sky through the black branches.

"Most August Gyst," Aveyron said stiffly. "We take it that you're aware of Hester Incarnate and that our parents will soon be in her proximity."

Solenn felt a surge of gratitude for Aveyron and that he'd made sure the subject was raised.

"*Yes, yes. That secret location is finally becoming known. And I 'take it' that you're both wishing to go and help them?*"

"Yes." Aveyron didn't quite meet Solenn's gaze. That made her wonder what he saw in her face that was so different.

"*Why would I encourage such a thing?*" Gyst asked. "*I just saved this body from death. Why place it in imminent danger again, so soon?*" His voice, through Solenn, sounded amused, like a professor asking rhetorical questions with the hope of stumping his students.

"Most August Gyst raises a concern you must be aware of, Princess Solenn," said Queen Abonde. "If you are terribly injured, Gyst cannot spare you from death. There is a point when a body must fail. However, through his manipulation of unknowns, he could drag out life in a merciless way."

"*This is true, Queen Abonde. I can also speed up death, if I so desire. I wonder about your own opinions on this matter. Would it be more convenient for you if the would-be ambassador met an early demise, sparing you the ordeal of working with me as well?*"

Queen Abonde tilted her head in consideration. "She *is* the one I will be working with as ambassador, Most August Gyst. Permit me to kindly state that diplomacy is not your strength." At that, Gyst laughed. "As to her demise being convenient? To that, no. If I wished for her to be dead, she would be. If you and I can agree on nothing else, Most August One, we can be unified in our appreciation of her bright potential."

Gyst nodded as Solenn spoke in her mind. *Gyst, did you and the other Gods prod us to be positioned as we are now? Aveyron and myself. My parents and Aveyron's father. Have you intended for us to unite and aid Hester in her moment of need?*

"Solenn has asked me questions, and for the benefit of all, I will answer aloud," Gyst said in a fake cheery tone that made Aveyron grimace. *"I have indeed worked with my sibling Gods to coax people and kin to be where they are now. The process has been much like herding cats. Quite unpleasant."* The catamount opened one eye, huffed, and closed its eye again. *"Together, we made cheese smell stronger, herded horses to go where they ought, and tried and failed in many other efforts. However, I would judge our efforts to be an overall success."*

"To what end, Most August Gyst?" asked Aveyron.

Solenn had wanted to physically *hear* herself asking that same question, but she was walled off.

Even a strong wall had weaknesses, though. Erwan and Prince Morvan often discussed such military strategies—the need to seek out seams and soft earth, to notice a divot that could become a crack.

"I fear what Hester will do in this next while if she's not stopped," said Gyst. *"I fear what the man taking in her power will do."* A surprising note of yearning and heartbreak came through in his words.

You love Hester? Solenn asked.

"Of course I love Hester," he said, answering her unspoken question aloud. *"The tales still say as much, don't they? That I soaked cheese in red wine so that she might slake her hunger with her favorite drink? That in the most bitter of winters, I caused mola to grow like fur and keep her warm? Those are acts of love."* He sounded airy and nonchalant as he spoke of this subject, as he did of all things. He was the kind of being who would shrug and laugh off most anything, she thought, excusing sharp insults as mere jests.

Such people were annoying.

She destroyed Ys so long ago. Why gather us together now? Why us? Why me? Solenn had to wonder.

If your souls and your powers could've existed before this time, oh, we would have acted sooner, but even the God of Unknowns contends with unknowns. At that, he sounded bitter.

Solenn took heart in that Gyst had limitations that frustrated him. "Unusual to hear a God speak openly of fear," said Queen Abonde.

"Well, as you *can never forget, I was born human."* Gyst made Solenn's grin too broad and toothy.

She pounced to ask the question that had perturbed her for a while. *How did you even become a God?*

Ah, that is the most unknown of unknowns. Sometimes things just . . . happen. His carefree voice sounded more strained. Was it so long ago that he didn't even remember?

Was it that way for Hester and the others?

Ah, Hester. She ate something and began to change. A disturbing thing, that, as epicurea didn't truly exist yet. Her body and soul were sensitive in ways like no one else. She eventually gifted all humans with epicurea in order to give them control over such awakenings of power, but I don't think that went as she anticipated. He sounded amused. *Poor Hester. She makes grand plans when she should let things be.*

At the same time Queen Abonde was speaking. "No, we dare not forget. Some of my kin have lived in these worlds longer than even you, Most August Gyst. We have not forgotten our existence as it was, and after all this time, neither have you ascended past your humanity."

"'Ascended past.' So judgmental, Majesty." He tsked, his focus on the queen, not on Solenn as she sputtered for attention within her own body. *"I've retained many human traits. I hate, I love, and oh, and I can be selfish, as Solenn is acutely aware of right now."*

So he *was* willfully ignoring her. *This is my body, Gyst!* She was sick of saying that.

As it will be, most of the time, he said to her with strained patience. *There will be instances when you call upon me in desperation and I don't answer. Perhaps those moments will teach you proper gratitude.*

Solenn felt his hold go slack, even as his cloak stayed over her. Despite that, she sighed in relief and said in her own voice, "The other Gods do want us to go help Hester, but more than that, I wish to go."

"As do I," said Aveyron. "Majesty, how do you gauge the time we need for travel?"

"The way is far by dolmen. You would need to gather supplies and depart with urgency that would tax your young bodies, tired as you already are."

To Solenn's surprise, Aveyron then faced the catamount, bowing. The brassy eyes squinted open. "Monsieur Catamount, could you please escort us by your waylines?"

Cats can cross between worlds at will, said Gyst with fondness, his presence reasserting itself in her mind. *Hence they make for helpful couriers and guides.*

Couldn't Queen Abonde order the cat to help us? She found Gyst tolerable when he acted as an encyclopedic helper. She finally brushed the strand of hair behind her ear.

Order the catamount to help a human and Camarga? He scoffed. *She wouldn't ask such of any of the Coterie.*

Solenn was discomforted by the reminder of what her humanity meant here, and the difficulties she would face in her forthcoming diplomacy, but she could also understand the perspectives involved.

The catamount stretched its front legs, long claws digging into the furry moss. "As much as I like variety in my diet, I'm not fond of people traipsing through my hills with their guns. Will this mission of yours, monsieur, stop these trespasses?"

Aveyron looked to Queen Abonde, who spoke up. "Now that we know where Hester is, yes, we will guard her against further encroachment."

"Pardon me, Majesty, but how is it you haven't known of Hester's place until now, since kin such as the catamount live close by?" asked Solenn, her tone curious.

"I can answer that, Majesty," said Aveyron. Queen Abonde gestured him to continue. "The ruins of Ys embody different miasmas. Some are positive, such as dolmen. Others reek with profound wrongness. No being of Arcady would willingly tread there."

"Indeed. The valley where she must reside is a place long known for its foul stench." The catamount stood, tail twitching. "I'll take you near it, mademoiselle, monsieur."

"Thank you, Monsieur Catamount." Aveyron bowed.

Solenn did the same. "Yes, thank you, monsieur."

The cat's amber gaze was cool. "Make certain Hester doesn't set my forest alight. If you fail and live, I'll eat you. If you fail and die in the valley, well, your bones must stay where they fall." The catamount sounded aggrieved by this potential lack of access. "You understand, mademoiselle?"

"I understand that I would be wise not to fail, for those reasons and many more," Solenn said, to which the cat gave a matter-of-fact nod.

CHAPTER
THIRTY-FIVE

ADA

Walk a cellar where the aging wine bottles have exploded in a violent cascade for reasons unknown, and know that Hester is not the only God who practices destruction.

—Excerpt from *Manual for Tour Chefs*

After conceding to a few hours of rest, Ada, Erwan, and Brillat continued their journey as the sun rose. The path left by the Valmonts took them into country pockmarked by steep craters, some closer together than others. The uneven ground and thick undergrowth made the going difficult.

"We'll be exposed at the crest," Erwan said. "Be wary." With guns at the ready, they stayed at a crouch as they finished the final stretch of a long, steep climb, but no ambush came. The Valmonts still had no reason to expect that they were being followed, thank the Five.

Only after Ada, Erwan, and Brillat had zigzagged down the path to find shelter behind some trees did they take the time to pause and study the valley below.

The place was like a pocket tucked amid sheer cliffs, colorful layers of rock exposed to the morning sun. The path they took looked to be the only one in and out. Tall, vividly green trees filled the gap below, but Ada caught glimpses of gray stones as well, a color that didn't match the paler rocks nearby.

It also reeked of magic with all the boldness of a garderobe on the hottest days of summer, and something about it felt distinctly like a warning. The Camargas shifted, ears back and hooves dancing, like they'd rather bolt back toward Lutecia. Ada felt like doing much the same.

Brillat frowned as he took in the scene. "The debris must have fallen hard, to cause such a crater," he muttered.

"Pardon?" Ada asked.

Brillat seemed to remember his company and shook his head. "Do you feel that strangeness?" he asked Ada.

"That miasma that makes me feel like I'd be an idiot to take a step closer? Yes."

"I sense nothing. I suppose that makes me a particular kind of fool," said Erwan.

"Ignorance isn't always bliss," said Brillat with a tight smile. He took the lead, leaving Ada and Erwan to fall into step behind him.

"He's right about that." Erwan looked sidelong at her. "I'd like to be less ignorant about the recent years of your life. Have you acquired any new hobbies?" He made an attempt to sound casual and carefree, even as they both gripped guns and tried not to slip down the scree.

"Long hours playing cook didn't give me much free time. I tried to maintain some of my fitness early on by sparring with Grand-mère, but we were limited in our exercises as we lived in apartments with thin walls."

"Petry will take good care of her, Ada." Erwan could still detect the worries she'd left unsaid.

"I know, but I can't help but worry. She's been my only family these last sixteen years, Erwan, and with the way her mind is starting to slip, I know she'll go to Gyst soon, and then . . ."

"She needn't be your only family from here on. The political situation has changed. I feel it safe to say that Braiz will not need to feign cooperation with Verdanian policies from here onward. Chefs may openly find new refuge there."

Mixed emotions tightened her throat. "I suppose we had best survive today, then, and see what awaits us tomorrow." The slope became more gradual, less pebble strewn.

"That's a sound plan." She loved the deeper crinkles around his eyes as he smiled.

A path had been hacked through the underbrush ahead, the defile wide enough for one horse at a time.

"These are coastal trees from Braiz," Erwan whispered. "Old ones. I rarely see them this tall or wide. How did they make it here? How have they survived?" The trees towered more than a hundred feet, their trunks thicker than a human with spread arms. The lowest branches did not even begin until some twenty feet up.

"The stones are from the coast too," Ada whispered. "Everything about this valley feels wrong, misplaced."

They entered the shade of the forest. A low, haphazard wall, coarse with age and lichen, was almost obscured by greenery. A horse whinnied in the distance, but their Camargas and Erwan's chestnut stayed quiet.

Brillat tilted his head to one side. "We need to leave the horses here," he murmured.

"Could they, perhaps, change? We may need more allies," Ada said, motioning at the Camargas. Even though she'd whispered with Erwan about how the horses could alter form, some words were still strange to say out loud.

"No," Brillat said. "They must stay as they are." The Camargas nodded, Ada's mount sighing as if in disappointment.

"I don't suppose you'll explain why that is?" Ada asked.

"No," he said. Ada released a frustrated sigh of her own. He added, "If we don't make it out, however, they will be able to carry a report of our actions back to my kin."

"That's no small thing," said Erwan, dipping his head in respect. "Let us pray this onerous burden doesn't fall upon them."

They found a place off the path where three high walls formed a protected, hidden space. They left the horses and crept farther on foot.

Past a line of trunks were more stone buildings, roofs long gone. They wound their way through. The height of the surrounding trees cast deep shade upon them, leaves and twigs thick underfoot.

Voices carried from up ahead. Brillat stopped at a high stone wall and peered through an eroded arched window. A small gasp escaped him. Ada moved to take position between him and Erwan.

"By all the salt in the sea," Erwan whispered with a motion to Selland.

Ada could only stare in speechless awe.

Her first impression was that a pit lay below them; then she realized it was more like an ancient amphitheater tilted at a slope. The side to their right heaved upward, the steps almost unrecognizable as stairs. Along that slope stood a statue easily fifty feet in height.

"She's *huge!*" blurted out Ada. Now she understood how Hester had made lakes with her footsteps.

"Her size was . . . not anticipated," said Brillat in a low, strangled voice.

The statue was formed of the granite common for hearths throughout Verdania. Eroded as the stone was, the carving was detailed and elegant . . . but no, it couldn't have been carved. She had somehow been cursed into being a stone giantess. Her tunic and breeches resembled those depicted in old storybooks, formed of numerous drapes and pleats. One knee touched the ground as if she had frozen in midfall, the other jutted up. Her hands dangled near her hips, limp as if in exhaustion.

And her face: it held a contemptuous sneer, her mouth open to show teeth and the obvious tufts of bird's nests.

No wonder the epicurea hunter had obtained only a small sample of powder from this place. This statue was too strangely large and grand to be the average rupic. The powder must have been procured on a whim.

From this close, Ada recognized that the aura of Hester matched that of Mallory's powder, evoking memories of hearth smoke, cooking meat, the contentedness of being home, but also a rage that arose from injustice and personal violation, a need to not only defend but offend.

About a dozen figures and horses stewed around the statue's base. Mallory Valmont was distinct at the statue's toes, his shoulders heaving with motion. He was filing at the stone. His son lurked a few feet away. She recognized the remaining lackey from the tavern, along with a few other household staff. Maman stood among them, her arms bound at her wrists. The Albionish were attending to the horses and nosing about in curiosity.

"We have the high ground for an attack," muttered Erwan, "but the theater is deep, much of the slope exposed."

"There are some large rocks for them to use for shelter, plus the statue itself," said Ada, "and pits farther back. Impossible to tell how deep they are from here."

"Can you hit Mallory Valmont if we position ourselves over there?" Brillat asked Erwan, motioning to a wall farther down.

"Perhaps, but that's a long shot." Erwan obviously knew not to propose using the Vandrossa.

"A shame we can't simply wait to ambush them as they depart," Ada said. "He enlisted those Albionishmen for a reason, though."

"Workers," said Erwan with grimness as Ada and Brillat nodded. "He likely promised them epicurean delights if they would come and grind down the statue. Those packhorses there look to be carrying empty bags and—"

"He's *eating!*" Brillat hissed. Indeed, Mallory had bowed forward, his head bobbing.

Ada gaped. "By the Five, he's gorging himself. That would be fatal, and fast, with raw rupic powder. Maybe he can only do this *because* he's had so much rupic?"

"Like an alcoholic who must drink more and more to become drunk," added Erwan. "Poisoning themselves in the process."

"I hold no love for Hester, but the wrongness of this is without parallel. We must act," said Brillat.

Erwan led the way downward.

They reached the stone-shielded outcrop below. Erwan balanced his musket barrel on rocks that acted as a low wall. Ada and Brillat loaded their pistols with quiet speed.

After a long moment of breathless tension, Erwan fired.

The trajectory was good, and yet—Mallory jerked upright as the musket split the air. Through the drift of smoke, Ada saw Mallory snap out a hand as if he were catching a fly. Yells rang out as people scattered for cover.

"Mallory caught the bullet. *He caught it,*" Ada whispered in horror. Erwan reloaded.

Mallory began to laugh. The sound was strangely loud and booming, nothing like the laugh of his younger, healthier years. He gazed up at where Ada, Erwan, and Brillat hid. He cupped his hands. A fireball bloomed between them.

"I see you," he sang, and he lobbed the fireball, which spun and grew in size as it neared.

"Mercy upon us," Brillat whispered, and they scrambled away.

Ada had made it about ten feet when the fireball exploded into the stones that had sheltered them. Debris pelted her back and legs, her hat sailing somewhere beyond sight. "Erwan!" she cried, her need to seek him more urgent than anything else.

"I'm fine," he gasped, rising to a crouch. Small trails of blood oozed down his filthy face, his hat gone as well.

Brillat crouched behind a stone nearby, similarly bloodied. "We need to—"

Another fireball smacked nearby, raining down more rocks and dirt. "We need to move, that's what," Ada snapped, rushing at a crouch behind a line of scraggly bushes.

"I can walk!" A delighted cackle punctuated the statement. Mallory's voice had taken on a higher pitch. "Centuries stuck in place, and now I can *move!*"

Ada and Erwan shared a look of horror, both pausing to look at Brillat. "He's . . . Hester—"

"This is without precedent," snapped Brillat. "Hester may possess him now, but it's only through the sway of the powder. His body remains human and vulnerable."

"If we may land a strike," Erwan added.

Chaos arose from below. Men yelled, a horse squealed, several shots rang out. Brillat glanced at the action. "The Albionishmen aren't keen on staying around. We can take advantage of the distraction as they fight each other." He vaulted over a boulder, scrambling down the slope.

Ada and Erwan followed.

Three Albionish soldiers writhed on the ground, screaming as they burned, victims of Hester's flames. Their comrades had scattered behind any available shelter.

Ada had a glimpse of a face emerging from behind a pillar, mouth gaped in terror. Brillat fired. The man retreated, dust rising from the impact feet away.

Two other soldiers took off running up the slope. The pair stayed so close that Mallory's next fireball took both men from behind. They fell, screaming as they blackened.

Mallory remained in the open fifteen feet away. Ada paused and fired. Distracted by his other kills, he didn't seem to have anticipated the blow. The shot took him in the shoulder. He whirled around, blood streaming from the wound.

"You." That singular word, in Mallory's voice. Ada half expected an instant fireball, but he lingered, staring, frozen as if by indecision.

Segal Valmont cowered on the ground before his father. He twisted to face Ada, his jaw slack. He seemed incapable of speech.

"Ada!" yelled Erwan, grabbing her by the arm to retreat behind a broken marble column that barely covered them both. A musket blasted, the ball thudding somewhere nearby.

"Was that a soldier that fired at me?" Ada asked, her back to the column as she reloaded. Erwan did the same.

"No, a man in house livery."

"Not everyone from the Valmont household is frightened witless by what their master has become, then." Despite the dangers all around, she grinned at Erwan. "Did you see? I made Mallory bleed!"

"He's still inhabited by an angry God. That's rather discouraging." They cringed as a fireball smacked the earth some five feet away, scorching the low green grass.

"I'll take whatever sunshine I can get," Ada said.

"Ada?" A tremulous voice drew Ada's attention to a large stone between her and Mallory. Maman huddled there, sheltered from the Valmonts but exposed to her daughter's side of the theater. She had a triangle-tipped rock wedged between her feet and was trying, with great awkwardness, to work through the thick rope that bound her hands in front of her.

"Stay there, Comtesse," Ada called in a low voice.

She heard Mallory speaking in a lower voice and peered out. He'd taken shelter behind one of Hester's feet.

She needed to distract him.

"Mallory!" she yelled. "Let's parley."

"What are your intentions?" Erwan murmured.

"We already know Hester's powder makes him feel better. I don't want him to have the chance to eat more or take other curatives."

Erwan glanced out. "Can you see who he's speaking with? It's not his son. He's on the other side of the statue, rather distressed."

"I didn't see anyone else go to that side of the statue. Brillat?"

The comte had stationed himself nearby behind a stout tree fringed by shrubs. He had an ear cocked toward Mallory. "Nor did I, but do you sense as I do?"

Hester's presence overwhelmed her perception, forcing Ada to close her eyes and truly focus to ascertain any details. Hester was like a bonfire, Mallory a small campfire alongside—no, that wasn't quite right. The greater might of Hester was dissipating by degrees, bolstering Mallory instead.

"Five . . . well, Four, help us. Hester's presence is getting stronger in Mallory. I still hear his voice, though. He's not constantly eating to take in her power that way." She sucked in a sharp breath. "That's who he's talking to."

Erwan motioned to Selland. "He's allying . . . with Hester? She's willingly helping him?"

"That cannot be good," Ada muttered. She liked it better when the Valmont household was being kept icy cold. "Hester! Mallory!" she yelled. "Let's talk." Ada stood, exposing herself to fireballs and gunfire.

"Ada!" Erwan hissed. "Get—"

"I need to interrupt their palaver." Though it may have already been too late. Mallory was fully aglow to her senses.

"Do you want to die?" Mallory leaned out to look at her, his tone amused.

"Not particularly. I understand you wouldn't mind me dead, perhaps ingested, but I'd like to know Most August Hester's thoughts on the matter. I've always held her in high regard."

"Adamantine Garland." Mallory's voice shifted. Hester was speaking. *"I have appreciated your devotions, this is true. You never resented*

offering me the best of your kitchen, whether acting as Chef or cook. You remembered me on my Days. I have reciprocated accordingly."

Amid everything, it felt oddly nice to be appreciated by a God. "Most August Hester, then why do you seem to be partnering with the man who would see me dead? Who is openly defiling your body?" She gestured to the very foot Mallory hid behind, the tip of the big toe absent.

"The defilement was done out of ignorance. He only learned the full truth of my nature minutes ago. The same cannot be said about the razing of my pentad in Lutecia." Hester's voice harshened. Ada blinked and needed a moment to remember what the God was speaking of. *"That place has long been acknowledged as the most holy of pentads within my homeland, and with reason—I built it!"*

Hester's rage quivered through the air. Ada was reminded of her own vulnerability as she stood there, exposed. It was a wonder that no one had shot at her, but then, the Albionishmen were probably amazed at her audacity and wanted to see what would happen.

"Oh. I can understand why that offends you, Most August Hester. I was disgusted when I heard—"

"And that king of yours, he had the impudence to order the stones that I moved be thrown into the river, saying that they are too old, too worn—"

Ada's own temper flared. "Caristo is *not* my king. You of all Gods know how he cost me my family, my very sense of home."

Erwan touched her knee. The pressure was gentle and felt through cloth, but it somehow defused her rage. For so many years, she had wanted revenge on Caristo, to make him suffer because she'd suffered.

She didn't want to care about Caristo anymore. Didn't want to hear his name. Didn't want to taste vengeance against him, no matter the recipe. She just wanted some semblance of her family back.

"And you as a soldier also know well that innocents, unfortunately, also must suffer in the course of war." Hester-Mallory said this as if in apology.

"War?" Ada echoed.

"This land is my home. In all the world, I've looked upon it with favor, but now—I have been forgotten, betrayed, dismissed, even though I, in my captivity here, still extended my precious power to aid those in need."

"This sounds like Ys all over again," Brillat said softly from behind his column.

Before Ada could inquire about this Ys he spoke of, Hester continued: *"I will not only withdraw my blessing from this land, but I will raze the earth. People will know my fire not for its coziness, but for its wrath and destruction. Verdania will not take for granted the love of the God of Home and Hearth!"*

The words were punctuated by a dramatic billow of fire. It wasn't aimed toward Ada, but she still felt the heat. She sank down again with a groan.

"Hester knows my own feelings about Verdania." This, spoken by Mallory. "She has my loyalty, my body. That means, Ada, that Hester regards you as an unfortunate casualty of war. Today will be your last."

"No!" A young, unfamiliar voice rang out from the far side of the statue.

Erwan gasped. "Solenn!"

Simultaneously, he and Ada looked out from either side of their shelter. Solenn strolled into the open to come around the statue. She wore a gray trouser suit in the style of court, the fabric mottled with wear and stains. Her black hair was pulled up, but loose tendrils bobbed with her confident stride.

Solenn, *here*. Tears stung Ada's gritty eyes. She wanted to hug her daughter, then shake her. What was she doing here? How had she even found this place?

Beth Cato

Then Ada caught a whiff of sour fermentation. Her brow furrowed as she focused to perceive more through the thick must of Hester. Ada knew that smell, that aura. Even more, as Solenn came into the sunshine beyond Hester's shadow, Ada could see a gauzy veil over her form.

"Oh, Gyst. *No*," she said in a breathless whisper. Erwan faced her with wide, fear-filled eyes. "Gyst is controlling her, just as Hester controls Mallory. I don't understand how or—"

That's when Mallory emerged with a roar and flung fire at Solenn.

CHAPTER
THIRTY-SIX

SOLENN

*The modern raised stove is a vital invention that spares
Chefs and cooks from many injuries, but Chefs begin
their training with hearth fires because this means of
cooking develops intense flavor and texture through the
power of Hester's direct touch.*

—Excerpt from *Manual for Tour Chefs*

The fireball loomed closer, closer. Solenn could feel its increasing heat,
but she couldn't move. She was as stuck still as the massive statue beside
her. At the last possible second, Gyst yanked her body to the ground.
She rolled across the scrubby grass and uneven stone, the fire sailing by
overhead.

That was too close! she yelled at Gyst.

"*Oh, Hester,*" said Gyst through Solenn, fondness in his tone.
"*Verdania still holds you as their favorite, but because of the slight committed by one arrogant man, you'd kill thousands upon thousands?*" Gyst

forced Solenn into a crouch. She couldn't even raise her hand to brush dirt from her breeches. *"You erred when you punished the kin and have suffered much ever since. Don't repeat your mistake."*

To think, the old man Hester resided in was the infamous Mallory Valmont, whom Erwan and Tad had often discussed across the years. The powder he'd eaten—ugh, how vile!—had obviously helped his health, but he still looked about ready to meet Gyst in the realms beyond. His cheeks were sunken, his red-veined eyes bulging. One of his shoulders bled profusely and must have been awfully painful, but Hester compelled him to stay upright, as if he were corseted.

"I punished the kin in order to help *humanity. Why, I gave people the greatest of all gifts—magic through epicurea. Do you remember what it was like for most people before we ascended to godhood, brother? Humans were so weak and could only gaze upon unicorns and dragons with awe and envy."*

One of the Albionishmen made a break for the long, broken stairs out of the basin. Hester lobbed a fireball his way and didn't even continue watching as the flames snared his coat. He hit the ground, screaming.

Why did she immediately attack us? Solenn asked. She couldn't think of any old stories that would explain such an assault on Gyst.

Oh, Hester is like that. Gyst used that fond tone again.

No, I won't accept that answer. I've heard too many women dismissed along those lines. Her body moved to shelter behind a low wall as Hester continued to stalk.

Let's ask her, then. Aloud, Gyst spoke. *"Hester, my hostess wonders why you've promptly attacked me."*

Hostess! Solenn inwardly bristled. She would throw a fireball at Gyst if she could too.

"I absolutely detest you," snarled Hester. *"You're obnoxious, arrogant. All these years, I've been here alone, and you show up now, when I finally can achieve freedom—"*

"Freedom for you means suicide," Gyst said loudly enough that most everyone around the arena could hear. *"The sheer quantities of rupic that Mallory Valmont has ingested have altered the unknowns within his body. That means he can also eat your powder now without promptly dying and, by doing so, absorbs more and more of your power. As that power settles into him, your lingering soul will fade, until he—"*

"Oh, certainly, tell everyone!" yelled Hester. *"What does it matter? They'll all be dead by the end of the day. You're in no place to judge me. You haven't endured what I have. I'm the God of Hearth and Home, and I've had neither for centuries. I'm tired, Gyst."*

"I know." Gyst made Solenn's voice soft, sympathetic.

She's been that isolated here? Solenn asked. *You Gods can't talk to each other, like how we're talking right now?*

We cannot speak directly through our minds. We only experience a brief awareness of each other when our powers intersect.

"You 'know.'" Hester mimicked Gyst's words and paced around Solenn's hiding place. *"No, you don't. You're never alone, you with all your little unknowns. You relish in it. You love what you can do."*

"So did you."

"That was a long time ago."

Solenn felt a surge of sympathy for Hester—to be the defender of homes, and yet be locked out like a person standing in the snow, staring through window glass at a cozy family inside.

No wonder the God wanted her misery to end, but surely a way to achieve that could be found that didn't involve Hester's death.

"And your host there, Monsieur Valmont," said Gyst. *"He's fine with this arrangement? With becoming a God in your stead?"*

"He doesn't want to suffer or to die. He won't be stuck here, as I am. He can do as he will with the power. For a while, I will be able to live viscerally through him, as I am now." Solenn could hear the smile in Hester's words. *"I'm reminded of how, in Verdania, rogue Chefs are given*

the opportunity to choose their last meal before their tongues are sent to me. This period will be like my own last meal."

If he assumes her place as God, does that mean he'll become a statue, too, and a giant? Solenn asked, horrified.

Out of the corner of her eye, Solenn saw Aveyron dashing behind rocks, columns, and trees to work his way closer to his father. Somewhere along the way, he'd picked up a musket. More than anything, she wished she were with him right now, going to join Erwan and Adamantine. Solenn hadn't even had a proper view of Adamantine yet, only heard her voice from afar. How much did they look alike? Move alike? She wanted to know, wanted the chance to know. Tears welled in her eyes, and her body automatically blinked them away.

Hester became stone through other means, and grew in size as a vessel to accumulate power to attack the kin. As to how his body will change, that entire process is a mystery even to me. Gyst brought up an arm to point at Hester as he made Solenn lean out to make eye contact. He said aloud, "On behalf of our siblings, I implore you, let us help you. We have been Gods together for thousands of years, keeping this world and its people in good order." The Coterie would staunchly argue against that statement. "We wish to keep you with us, not him."

In response, old-man Hester lunged toward Solenn, both hands enrobed in flame.

Solenn jumped atop a boulder and from there leaped across a sequence of large rocks. Hester followed with a snarl. Almost circling around, Solenn landed behind Hester to scamper away again.

We're taking Mallory Valmont farther away from the statue, Solenn observed.

She sensed Gyst's pleasure at her intuition. She hated that his approval still meant something to her even as he held physical control. *Yes. We make for a temporary distraction, but a necessary one.*

He's burning power through his movement and use of fire.

Yes, which will eventually give us an advantage. Gyst scampered to dodge another fireball.

An advantage? With what goal? Kill Mallory Valmont? Then what? Hester remains in abject misery?

She made her own prison.

The wrongness of this forever punishment galled her. *Let me speak with Hester—and with Mallory Valmont.*

What, you would be a diplomat to the Gods as well as the Coterie? Gyst sounded dismissively amused.

She wished she could scream out her frustration. *Where are the other Gods? Can they help us?* Could Selland intercede? Or was he fine with her being used by Gyst like this? That very idea made her despair.

Gun blasts rang out from the vicinity of Erwan, Adamantine, and Brillat. She would have cringed and glanced that way if allowed, but it was probably best she didn't, as Hester had flung more fire at Solenn. Gyst dropped to the ground, sheltering behind a jagged rock.

The other Gods have been involved, remember. You and the others wouldn't be here otherwise.

Hester changed angles and flung fire again. Solenn leaped, rolling to one side. Grit ground into her shoulder, the impact with the stony ground shoving air from her lungs. She sat upright to face a surprised Albionishman, the right sleeve of his leather coat blackened by blood. Gyst brought up Solenn's hand to slap the man across the face. His stunned expression was almost humorous, and then the change began. He grunted, twitching, his gaze darting from his arm to Solenn, his jaw gaped in terror. His skin shriveled like fruit past its time. Red veins, like vines, extended up his neck to his jaw to his face. The lines darkened. A wheeze escaped him.

What did I just do? she screamed in her mind, in Braizian. *How did my touch do that?* The death of the enemy soldier didn't offend her—she didn't doubt that he would have killed her, given the chance—it was that her own skin had acted like a toxin.

Her body leaped up in time to avoid another attack by Hester.

His arm would have killed him within the week. I sped the process to keep him from attacking you. Gyst responded in her language, with a mocking undercurrent.

You sped the process, but through me. My touch! My touch did that. Solenn felt the urge to look at her hand, to study it as if she could comprehend how it had betrayed her.

Solenn. Gyst's tone revealed impatience. *I'm engaging in this fight not only so that you survive this but also so that Adamantine, Erwan, Aveyron, Brillat, and perhaps some others may also see tomorrow. I'm your ally.*

An ally, yes, because she was useful for his purposes. *But are you really fighting? If you can do* that, *why have we been dancing circles around Hester like this?* As if to illustrate, they again hid to avoid a fireball.

As you yourself noted, I extended power through your direct touch, Gyst said with strained patience.

That was true, and yet, Gyst was the God of Unknowns. Mallory had a seeping shoulder wound. Solenn thought of what Queen Abonde and Aveyron had said about Gyst and his decomposed truths.

As awful as his control of her was, he wasn't wielding his full power. Otherwise, this fight would already be over.

They rounded a cluster of hardy pines that had grown through the rocky ground. There in the shadows was another hidden figure—Mallory Valmont's son. He had to be some five years older than her. His face was pressed to his knees. When he recognized her, he gasped, his expression one of horror. He scooted back on his derriere, no weapon in hand.

"You—you're the one he—stay away!"

Gyst, don't— Solenn began.

What, you think I kill everyone I meet? This man isn't my enemy. Not even his father is my enemy, truly. Then to the young man he said, *"I'm not here to fight you."*

The laugh in reply was small and nigh hysterical. "Good. I trained to duel, but here, now, what's even the point?" Sunlight filtered through the branches to illuminate the tears that streaked his face. "My father, my life has been devoted to his aid, and now, now . . ."

"You want the man, the father. Not a God." Gyst made Solenn's voice gentle. The man nodded, unable to speak. *"You must understand that he'll die today, one way or another. Either he becomes a God, or he stops the powder that has kept him alive this week."*

"I know," he whispered, pressing his face to his knees again. Vulnerable, broken. "I know."

Footsteps scuffed nearby. Gyst propelled Solenn to scamper away, rounding the trees to the return to the more open stage. She mulled what she'd witnessed. She'd known that the Gods were complex, that they were people, but Gyst continued to confound and surprise her.

Gyst, why did you— she began, her mental dialogue ending with a scream aloud as fire lashed the fronts of her thighs. Pain sent black dapples across her eyesight, the terrible odor of burned meat filling her nostrils.

While you were stunned by my capacity for compassion, I lapsed control of your body, and this is what happened. You didn't even see that attack coming, did you? Gyst scolded. He made her move again, the agony up her legs like nothing she'd known before. *Your musketeers provided you with some defensive training, but you're not a fighter, Solenn.*

Why did you do that? Why?

Gyst didn't answer. He didn't need to.

He wanted her to need him.

She let him continue to maneuver her because she knew that otherwise, she would sink to the ground and sob in sheer agony. He'd released his hold on purpose. He was trying to train her to rely on him utterly, or to suffer. Like the equestrian acrobat, beating his horse.

And like that mare, she could take the blows, but that didn't mean she was defeated.

CHAPTER THIRTY-SEVEN

ADA

A Chef intimately knows the anatomy of a knife: The point, to slash pastry or flick seeds from a lemon. The lower cutting edge, the belly, useful to slice open fleshy bellies. The opposite side, the spine, as necessary for balance and strength as your own spine. The side, to smash garlic. The sharp edge nearest the handle, the heel, where it is best to dice harder items such as nut meats. The tang, metal obscured in the handle that binds the two pieces together at a place called the return. The bottom of a handle, the butt, to tenderize meat and grind coarse salt. The tongue is our direct conduit to the Gods, but practiced knifework is a connection as well.

—Excerpt from *Manual for Tour Chefs*

Solenn's scream sliced through Ada as if she'd been stabbed, but she didn't hesitate as she reloaded her pistol.

Erwan's hiss told of his own agony. "Mallory swiped her with fire. A glancing blow to her legs, but bad enough." He peered over the broken column, his musket ready.

"Can she walk?" Ada asked, ready to run across the open floor if the answer came in the negative.

"Yes." This came from Brillat behind his tree. "She acted strangely distracted for a moment. A dangerous lapse."

"Solenn is resisting Gyst," Erwan murmured. "She must be."

Ada caught another glimpse of the only other being, beyond the sparring Gods, to move across the battlefield right now—Brillat's son, obvious by his strange silver hair. He was gradually working his way closer to their position.

To their right, a man's head popped up from behind rocks. The Valmont lackey. He watched Solenn with far too much interest. He was beyond range of Ada's pistol.

"Erwan," Ada said.

"I see him." She really hadn't needed to say a thing. Erwan was already aiming. The man fell with a plume of blood. "I'm low on musket balls."

"I am as well," said Brillat. "And none of the downed fighters are within reach." The closest other person was Maman, and she had no arsenal to offer.

"Brillat, we may need to resort to—"

"No." Brillat inferred her meaning immediately. "We will not use epicurea."

"The mead alone would help us. Please."

"The honey for this mead was harvested by a hive kept captive, the empress herself—"

"A terrible thing, but not equal to the Vandrossa eagle killed for its eyeballs," she snapped.

"It is still exploitation of my kin," retorted Brillat. Noteworthy, that he made no effort to hide his inhumanity now. Maybe that was unconscious, arising from the pitched fever of battle, or maybe he'd accepted that they would soon meet Gyst on the far side, and so there was no point in hiding the truth anymore.

Ada had no desire to meet Gyst here or there. She just wanted the chance to know her daughter at long last.

She wanted her family back.

"Père." A soft voice came from behind them. Aveyron hopped a low wall and crept to join Brillat. The two embraced, heads pressed ear to ear. Aveyron carried a musket, powder horn and pouch swaying against his chest. "Heed Solenn's mother."

Ada sucked in a small breath. *Solenn's mother.* Such a strange, welcome phrase to hear. Erwan seemed to catch her reaction and brushed her leg with his hand, his smile for her brief as he again focused on the battlefield.

Brillat recoiled. "Aveyron, what? You know not what you—"

"I comprehend some things that you do not." He tilted his head toward Erwan and Ada. "How much do they know about us?"

"More than they ought." Brillat sounded weary. "But speak with care."

"I took Solenn *home.*" Brillat flushed with quick anger, but Aveyron motioned him to silence. "She proposed an alliance between Braiz and our kin, to stand against our mutual enemy of Albion."

"This must have had some measure of success as you both survived the journey." Brillat's voice was tight.

"We did, and she earned a half year to prove her value as an ambassador. I'm to assist her, as are you."

Erwan cast Ada a questioning look, to which she shook her head. The subtext was beyond her as well.

Aveyron answered more questions at a fast clip, with pauses as more volleys were exchanged.

"How is Gyst able to control Solenn in such a direct way?" asked Ada, thinking of the many times she had sensed Gyst's presence, even heard him speak. Could he have done the same to her?

"You are of the same family line as Gyst, madame," said Aveyron. "That's why your tongue connects so strongly with his. Solenn's bond with him is unusual, though. The God of the Unknown said he hasn't been able to embody a person in over three thousand years."

"The same family line? *Three thousand years?*" echoed Ada. She was the distant granddaughter of a *God?*

Erwan fired his musket and muttered at the miss. In response, two shots sang their way, none striking close. "The God could have been lying," he said over his shoulder.

Aveyron paused to consider his next words. "He may have lied about other things, but those with me didn't doubt the truth of that particular statement."

Ada wondered about the burden of an ambassadorship being placed on a sixteen-year-old, even under ideal circumstances, but she didn't give voice to such a tangent. "That means it's all the more important that we go on the offense, Brillat. We'll soon be out of ammunition. We cannot camp here." She furrowed her brow. "I don't even understand why their fight is dragging out. Mallory Valmont is fragile, though he can fling fire, and Gyst is the God of Unknowns. He could use them to attack. Is he wanting to drag out the fight?"

"You may be right in that," Aveyron said. "Gyst wants the full experience of what it is to be human again. What makes a person—and indeed, my kin—feel more alive than to risk death?"

"With Solenn as his puppet." Erwan made an urgent motion to Selland.

Aveyron faced his father, expression fierce. "Our kin need an alliance with Braiz to not only stand against Albion, but Verdania. Therefore we must help Solenn fight against Hester, and Gyst."

Brillat scowled. "We cannot acquiesce to our kin being—"

"We must compromise, not simply to survive this battle, but to coexist in the future, Père."

"If Solenn is an ambassador on behalf of Braiz, then I, as her musketeer, ask to be recognized as her servant, Comte. I officially plead for the advantage that epicurea will provide us in this battle," said Erwan.

Brillat reached inside his coat with a weary sigh. "A compromise, then, but neither of us will indulge." At that, Aveyron readily nodded. Brillat checked the security of the stopper, then shoved the flask along the slight slope to Erwan.

As soon as he touched it, Ada knew how the mead would gloss his parched tongue in semisweet relief, the honey heavily floral, originating from near the Braizian border. The liquor was as potent as the sweetness, relief to be welcomed in its own right. The rogue Chef who'd overseen distillation knew the craft well.

"The time Mallory takes to grow fireballs is comparable to loading a firearm," said Ada. "We can use that to our advantage."

Brillat pursed his lips. "A multipronged attack will be best. We move at once, from different directions. That will make it more likely we'll be able to find shelter as we approach."

"We'll need to address those remaining Albionishmen as we go," murmured Aveyron.

"I must first see if I can get the comtesse away from the middle of the battlefield. Her cover won't protect her from a direct fireball," said Ada. "I'll go straight from her to Solenn."

"Who is my foremost goal," added Erwan.

"You will be the advance, and we will provide what cover we can as we follow," said Brillat. Ada understood he didn't promote them out of cowardice on his part. Soldiers enhanced by epicurea most always had the vanguard.

Ada faced Erwan. "Be careful out there," she said softly. "I just found you again. I don't want to lose you."

"The same." Erwan's thumb brushed her jaw, his touch coarse and gentle at once. "My love for you never ceased, Ada. Please do your utmost to avoid injury and death."

"Don't I always?" she asked with a rakish grin. "You do the same, Erwan. I love you." She tapped a small mole amid the scruff of his jaw, a farewell and good-luck gesture she had almost forgotten about after so long. His grin of recognition created broad creases in his face. "Here, you drink first." She pushed the mead at him.

As the liquid slid down his throat, Ada called to Melissa in her mind. *Melissa. I haven't forgotten your kindness in sending a horse my way. I can only wonder if you intended me to get this far so that I could calm Hester's rage, as you did in old stories.* Ada sensed the God's sudden attention, like the aftertaste of sugar beet molasses. *Please, I plead to you, heighten the powers already latent in this mead.* Ada couldn't waste time listing the ways she'd demonstrate her gratitude to Melissa later, if she lived, and sufficed with envisioning sown fields of clover and wildflower.

Melissa's answer was immediate. The magical potency increased fivefold. Ada could only liken it in Hester-like terms, as if the door to a furnace had been flung wide open. Pleasant yet not overbearing sweetness filled her mouth. Erwan swallowed his drink and gasped. She detected his increase in vigor and speed.

"Well, that's something," he said, an understated and proper Erwan reaction if ever there was one. "My gratitude, Melissa." He wavered his fingers to symbolize the flight of a bee, then passed the flask back to Ada.

She drank down what remained with a tilt of her head, the physical mead as delicious and divine as she had perceived. Melissa was no less generous toward her. Power tingled to Ada's extremities, her tongue practically buzzing like a hive. She and Erwan shared a final resolute look, and then at the same instant, they sprang from their shelter.

Ada sprinted across the open stretch toward Maman, while Erwan angled out toward a nearby plinth. As she reached a low rock, a bullet sang overhead. She dropped flat; without the preternatural speed granted by the mead, she knew with certainty she would have been hit.

A sequence of shots rang out to her right, the direction in which Erwan had dashed. She glanced over but couldn't see anything from her low vantage point. Bringing her feet beneath her, she sprang upward and ran the remaining distance to Maman. She flung herself down, making herself as flat as possible.

Maman greeted her with a small cry. "Ada. I knew you would come, I knew it!"

Never in Ada's memory had her mother expressed that kind of joy in her arrival. The tears in the woman's eyes were strange too. She had never seen Maman cry before. In her past cynicism, she had wondered whether her mother was capable of it.

"You couldn't—are you unharmed?" Without moving much, she scanned Maman for visible blood, and she found filth and torn cloth. Maman's hair was frizzed out, many of her pins gone. Maman's effort to cut through her rope had made little progress, with reason; the sharp rock she'd been using rested near Ada's knees, the tip broken.

"Of course I could believe you'd come. You're my daughter, the Chef. In my house—Antonin—that was you, wasn't it?"

She was *not* going to discuss the powers she'd utilized to do that. Her mother would shave every cat in Lutecia. "Maman, did the men hurt you?"

"Beyond pushing me around, no. The Albionishmen might have done more, but Messieurs Valjay were not entirely uncouth. Tell me, what has happened to Monsieur Valjay?" She spoke with absolute faith that Ada knew what was going on.

Ada leaned to her immediate right, finding one of the pits she'd seen from her initial high vantage point over the bowl-like theater. The pit varied from about five to ten feet in depth, but it was hard to accurately gauge due to thick grass within the basin.

"His epicurea has some unpleasant side effects," Ada said.

Grief flashed over her mother's features. "Ragnar."

"I'm sorry, Maman," Ada said softly.

"Yes, well." Maman tried to recover some of her austerity. "We'd best leave."

As if that clever idea were all her own. "We can't. In case you missed it, Monsieur Valjay is throwing around fireballs, and the remaining Albionishmen are willing to shoot at anything that moves. You need to stay down."

Panic flickered in Maman's eyes. She nudged Ada with her bound hands in a not-so-subtle hint to be freed. "No, we should really go. It's not safe here."

Ada released a long exhalation and thought on what Ragnar had told her. "Maman, do you respect my experience as a Chef and soldier?"

"Yes," came the resolute reply.

"Then heed what I say. There's a pit here." Ada motioned with her head. "Stay there. It'll provide better cover than this rock."

"No! Ada, please!" This Maman was a stranger, clingy and terrified. Ada felt a surge of anger. All the years she'd wanted Maman to need her for more than her skills, and now Maman's very life depended on those skills.

Ada shoved her mother into the pit.

Maman fell down feetfirst, screeching. She hit the grass and rolled down the slight slope. With muffled rage, she wiggled her body around so she could glare up at Ada. Her tied arms bobbed up and down.

"Adamantine! You could at least have—"

"No," she hissed, taking Maman's spot behind the rock. "I don't trust you to stay down otherwise. You're a manipulative harridan, but I don't want you to die here. You're my mother even if you've never acted like it, and I love you against all sense and logic. So stay put."

Maman stared, wide eyed with shock. "I will. I love you, too, Ada. I'm sorry."

She was sorry. Here and now, she was sorry. She'd confessed her love. It came across like an opera script, a neat and tidy resolution, too neat and tidy to be reality. Ada closed her eyes for mere seconds to withhold the urge to scream out decades' worth of frustration, then took a steadying breath.

Whatever happened today, Maman could not learn that Princess Solenn was her granddaughter or a Chef. Ada would not see Solenn manipulated as she had been. She would not let herself be manipulated further either.

Ada had once said farewell to Erwan out of immense love. She would do the same to Maman.

When it came down to it, Maman was her mother, but not family. Family was Grand-mère, and Petry, and Emone, and Erwan—always Erwan. And Solenn . . . Ada wanted to be her mother, not simply by blood but by heartfelt support.

Ada scanned the area where she'd so recently camped. Brillat peered from the shelter that Ada and Erwan had just used. Ada motioned to him that she was about to move. He nodded.

Ada pushed herself up and ran toward the circling figures of Solenn and Mallory, every stride propelled by magicked mead and desperation and love.

CHAPTER THIRTY-EIGHT

SOLENN

"Never eat cheese in the dark," as the old saying goes. Heed the colors of the molds that arise from Gyst's touch upon your cellared cheese. White and blue are often safe, but not always. Be chary of unexpected colors, textures, and odors. Gyst often warns us when his blessing turns to a curse, and if we are inattentive, it is to our folly.

—Excerpt from *Book for Cooks to Excel as Do Chefs*

Gyst continued to use Solenn's body to evade Hester, and Solenn used that time to think. Gyst had intended to use pain to subjugate Solenn; instead, it grounded her in the urgency of the moment.

She would break free of his control.

Back in Queen Abonde's court, he had told her to let her mind go empty so that his presence could have room. As she focused, she found she could sense him, not simply by the ethereal garb over her body but within her mind, as if she were asleep and just knew that someone stood over her, even if not making a sound. His presence had her boxed in.

He formed the walls that kept her from controlling her body, but she reminded herself: walls have vulnerabilities.

Just as this day had proven that Gods have vulnerabilities.

Minutes passed as she simply observed the Gods continuing their dance. For all Hester's vitriol, Solenn suspected the God was actually enjoying this fracas—and that was what this was. Not a real battle; she'd grown up around soldiers and knew most fights were resolved in mere minutes. No, this was a sparring match, two Gods enjoying the movement of human forms they hadn't known in centuries. The injury to Solenn's body didn't even seem to have dampened Gyst's mood. She had a sense he felt invigorated by her pain. He *felt*.

By a horrible smell, she knew she was near someone who'd been burned by Hester's flames. Even so, she couldn't contain her shock when Gyst compelled her to shelter behind a low, eroded wall. The unconscious, mustached man sprawled there wore luxurious house livery—at least, he still did above the waist. His legs were blackened by fire. Solenn didn't want to look, but Gyst made her gaze linger for what was truly a ludicrous amount of time during a fight.

Please don't— she began as Gyst reached to touch the man.

Not even I wish to touch such terrible burn wounds. Gyst laid a gentle hand on the man's unblemished cheek. *His life would drag on for hours, agonized hours, without my direct intervention. His mysteries can be resolved now.*

Solenn understood that this was intended as a demonstration of Gyst's mercy, and his power. But instead of dwelling on the horror and the awe of the scene, she focused on *how* he wielded this ability. Those walls around her shifted. They were diaphanous, like his clothes. Power flowed like a draft of air.

And just as with a draft, she understood that the flow arose from a larger source. Gyst had said that he didn't want to control her body all the time because he had other concerns. As Gyst's power fluctuated, she had a brief sense of that larger well, just out of reach.

I'm glad this man will no longer suffer, Solenn said, knowing the comment would please Gyst.

This man's death wasn't visible and dramatic, as with the Albionishman, but even so, she had an intrinsic understanding now of how it had happened. The man's innards had been poisoned and overwhelmed by the extent of his injuries, and Gyst had sped the full failure through his—her—touch.

This power wasn't simply coming from Gyst. It was inherent *in her.* That was why it was so easy for him to kill using her touch and for him to reside in her at all. Now that she thought about it, he'd appeared in the Coterie's court because she'd ordered him to do so.

She had compelled the God to come to her aid—drawing from the same pool of power he himself used—and yet he had her convinced that she was in debt to him.

She'd been no supplicant to the divine. She *was* divine.

"*Gyst, where are you hiding?*" yelled Hester through Mallory Valmont.

Solenn's body moved, staying at a crouch behind the crumbled wall. Gyst was going to let this drag on longer.

Mallory Valmont is slowing down. We can sneak up behind him and end this! she yelled in her own mind.

Soon. The single word was smug.

The longer this continues, the more likely it is that the people I care about will be hurt too. You said you don't want that to happen, so prove it.

Solenn, that tone is hardly diplomatic.

Don't patronize me.

Why not? Aren't . . .randfather of some remove, as well as a God? Who would be a better patron than me? You don't need to fight me, Solenn. You already know that my control isn't permanent. Put your trust in what I can do here. To use terminology you may better comprehend, give me free rein.

She was so tired of being told to be agreeable and trust in the opinions of men who knew better. Marry this boy! Know your place! Cut his food for him! Smile, don't speak!

Solenn let out a wordless mental scream.

With an inward sigh, Gyst made her stand up straight just as a fireball sailed her way. Jarred by the change in elevation, it took her several seconds to realize he'd released all control of her body.

She dived to one side, over mounded rocks and grass, and didn't find level ground on the far side. Instead, she'd found the old edge of the amphitheater stage, and a pit thick with rubble and shrubs. She screeched as she rolled, harsh rocks scraping her shoulders, back, and ribs. It was all she could do to tuck her arms against her head. The world blurred and flashed between gray and green and bright-blue sky, and then she found the bottom. She heaved for breath. The burns on her thighs seared with new ferocity. Both elbows stung, weeping hot blood, along with other bashes and bruises beyond measure.

Well, that was one way to evade, Gyst said.

Still in control, she pushed herself to sit. Rocks and something prickly dug into her backside. About fifteen feet up a very uneven slope, Mallory Valmont stood at the crumbled edge. Anger twisted his face in a sneer, mirroring the expression on the giant statue behind him.

"Solenn!" Erwan and Adamantine yelled her name at almost the same instant from different directions.

Mallory's fists clenched and unclenched. "My old peers. I need justice."

Solenn was jolted as she recognized that Mallory had been allowed to speak for the first time in a while and that he wasn't talking to her. He apparently couldn't engage in mental dialogue as she did with Gyst.

"I suppose this is a good time to get that done." His voice shifted as Hester replied. *"You're not going to try to leave, are you, Gyst?"* Hester called down to where Solenn sat. Mallory Valmont turned away.

If Erwan Corre and Adamantine Garland die, it's your fault, Gyst said to Solenn in an almost bored tone.

Rage left her stunned for several seconds. *No! Let's go stop Hester—Mallory Valmont—we can—*

This isn't a negotiation. You aren't an ambassador here. In this place, in this battle, I'm in charge.

She tried to move. Gyst kept her frozen in place. She wanted to kill him—no, she wanted him to hurt in ways he hadn't been able to hurt in centuries. She wanted him to feel her revenge like a hundred salted splinters beneath his toenails.

Instead, she knew his satisfied superiority as she made no progress. He was like a big brawny man, keeping her pinned, just as Marquis Dubray had tried to do.

She had killed Marquis Dubray.

This wasn't a time to flail. That was what was usually expected by an arrogant, physically mighty opponent. She needed to drop her weight, strike where it wasn't expected.

While projecting her outrage, she probed the walls around her again, tempted by the possibilities beyond. Could these weaknesses be a trap? Her intuition told her no. For all Gyst's awareness of secrets and unknowns, he didn't know her. He had underestimated her, for now. If Gyst understood what she'd sensed, he could draw in more power and build better walls. She couldn't give him that opportunity.

She willed her consciousness to follow the breeze back toward the source.

She found the well of the divine.

In her sight, everything around her writhed as unknowns became known. Every rock, every blade of grass, the very surface of her skin. With her human eyes, she couldn't make out the tiny dots, but she *knew* their potential for growth and change and sickness and death.

She suddenly understood that like Mallory Valmont, she, too, could become a God, but she had been born with that potential. That was why Gyst was able to use her body as he did, and why he was try-ing to keep such a tight grip on her. He wanted to break her, make her obedient. Like a good wife. A good granddaughter.

She'd always been a bit of a rebel, never afraid to take charge. This opportunity to assert herself carried incredible consequences, however.

If Solenn immersed herself in the well of the divine, she could oust Gyst to become God of Unknowns.

Which would kill her.

And yet, this would not be a complete death. She would lose her body and enter a constant condition of voracious decomposition, her wayfaring soul cloaked in unknowns that would then be fully known to her.

Gyst was so very powerful, but his powers weren't absolute; she knew that intimately now, through her vague awareness of his scat-tered attention in thousands of other places across the world at this very moment. People spoke languages she didn't know but intrinsically understood, asking for his blessing upon their beer, their liquor, their cheese; for their unicorn tincture to save a loved one fighting gangrene; for Gyst to guard them as they engaged in the hard, dangerous labor of draining a privy. He lurked in cellars with floorboards pockmarked by whey acidity and within cobweb-shrouded firkins and the very skin of distant grapes.

She had the sudden idea that Gyst was like a cat who had before him an entire flock of hundreds of resting birds, his attention flicking between each. Even though she was the nearest, plumpest prize, he had to watch the other birds as well, as any and all could take flight in an instant.

Several guns fired in sequence. The sound brought Solenn's full awareness back to the here and now. Mallory Valmont no longer stood on the cliff.

"Ah, Erwan," mused Gyst.

What? What about Erwan? Frantic, Solenn reached into the well of power again, but she was too human, too alive, to extend her consciousness to the next realms.

What happened? Is Erwan dead? she asked Gyst.

His mental shrug was blatantly manipulative. *Why should I tell you? Perhaps you need some time to sit and consider the consequences of your actions. Erwan may be in danger, but look at yourself.* Her gaze was forced down to consider her battered condition. Holes and threadbare sections flecked the sleeves, the flesh of her burned thighs a visible angry, bubbly red. *You could get terrible infections. What then?*

You don't want me dead. She now understood that, unlike Gyst, unknowns felt no malice, not like humans or kin. Theirs was a simple existence of eating and reproducing and dying and birth.

Of course I don't want you dead, but perhaps some pain and suffering would put things in perspective for you.

Please, climb up so that we can see if Erwan and the others are safe! She raged in her paralysis, and when he brooded in silence, she reconsidered the futility of her position. He liked feeling superior and in control; it was how he treated Hester as well.

Hester wasn't going to succeed in besting Gyst through physical blows or her grandiose plot. Solenn would fail only if she followed in Hester's sizable footsteps. She had to play and win through different means.

Please, Most August Gyst. I'm sorry. She could smile and feign obedience as a proper Verdanian princess should, as instructed by Madame Brumal, even as she also remembered Mamm's lessons on surviving court. She would be underestimated. She would be empowered by that.

Oh, Mamm. Tad. She wanted to see them again. Selland preserve them.

Oh, I suppose we can go up there, as you've now remembered your manners, Gyst said. Solenn's body began a crawling climb up the slope. Her burned thighs bled as the muscle and skin flexed. *You're incredibly special to me. I don't like resorting to such measures, you know. My family line has recently diminished, along with their most-blessed tongues. You need to live many years more.*

She caught his meaning. *You want me to have children.*

That is typically how one bolsters a family line.

As a girl, a woman, a noble, she'd been told childbearing was her greatest of duties. She'd been shamed in the past for even suggesting otherwise. She'd been treated as if there were something wrong with her for feeling as she did.

But now, racked by pain, fully aware of her power and vulnerability both, she had to say the truth. Why lie, to the God of Lies?

I don't want children.

We don't always get what we want, said Gyst.

She perceived what was unsaid. He could control her body. He could make certain she did as he willed.

She also understood, with cold, hard certainty, that she would rather die first.

And by "die," she meant become a God.

CHAPTER
THIRTY-NINE

ADA

To make gelée d'orange, first soak the isinglass, this being the bladder of a sturgeon, in some quantity of water. Grate the peel of four oranges and two lemons, then squeeze the juice of two oranges and one lemon. Place together the zest and juice and strain it into a quarter liter of water. Boil until it is almost candy. To this add a quart of isinglass water, then boil again. Strain it and let it cool somewhat before pouring it into a mold to set—and thank Gyst with secrets when it does, because nothing grieves a cook like unset gelatin.

—Excerpt from *Book for Cooks to Excel as Do Chefs*

"Adamantine Corre."

She glanced out from the cover of a plinth. Ada could tell by his voice and stride that Mallory had been given charge of his body again. That probably didn't bode well for her, but better for him to come after her than Solenn, or Erwan.

She shot another desperate glance to where she had last heard Erwan engage in a gun battle, followed by a clash of rapiers. There had to be at least two Albionishmen in his vicinity. As much as she wanted to run to help him, she couldn't. Luring Mallory from Solenn had to take priority. It was what Erwan would want too. It was what she would expect of him, were their circumstances reversed.

On his behalf, she gestured to Selland, her right hand ready with a loaded pistol.

A glance confirmed that Mallory was almost on her. Ada bounded from her hiding place, mead bolstering her speed.

Mallory chuckled. "You're not getting away from me this time, Ada. Hester has given me leave to eliminate you. A small reward, for which I'm grateful."

She dropped behind a low rock, pivoting on her hip to emerge on the other side, facing him. She fired her pistol. He sidestepped away, matching her speed. She knew she'd missed and ran, zigzagging with purpose, trying to draw him farther from Solenn, and closer to where Brillat and Aveyron should be coming into position.

"You used to prefer gelée d'orange for special occasions," she called out as she sheltered again. That was a fine dessert if ever there was one; the use of isinglass had required the blessing of Gyst.

Mallory laughed. "I had forgotten about that! It's been so long. I should seek it out again."

"It may be difficult to enjoy such fineries when you're razing the realm."

"I will destroy with discretion." That old Mallory Valmont arrogance was there. "The God of Home and Hearth must still cultivate worship and adoration. That's how power grows. That's how *my* power will grow, even as I take in Hester's remaining might."

Mallory Valmont had embodied natural charisma back in his youth. He probably wouldn't have trouble cultivating adulation again.

The threat of immolation would provide people with additional encouragement.

"You were supposed to die years ago," she said. His pursuit had quickened, his smile brightening. He was enjoying this. He'd been like that on the battlefield, too, the kind of person who took perverse delight in being a predator.

"Mont Annod couldn't kill me. You won't kill me, either, Ada. Why, you haven't even had a chance to reload."

She probably had only one or two bullets left, anyway. Dropping that gun, she unsheathed her knife. They were five feet apart. She walked backward, still facing him. Fire arose from his hands. No fireball for her, then—he wanted to feel her die beneath his touch.

Well, as his taste preferences went to ground stone, maybe he wouldn't be tempted to eat her if she was cooked meat.

Her knife had no range to be effective, but she could wound him with her pity. "For all that you've endured, you haven't changed, Mallory. You only became the Hero of the Thirty-Fifth because you murdered and cannibalized people. You couldn't have achieved that status on your own, just as you couldn't become a God on your own. No, you're ascending to that role because you're yet again eating ground-down statues." She shook her head with blatant disgust; his smile faded. "Gelée d'orange would taste so much better than that, especially if it was made by a Chef."

"Die!" His lips curled in a sneer as he lunged forward.

A musket blasted from her right. She had a fleeting glance of the shooter—Erwan! The ball struck Mallory between the ribs. Red bloomed through his shirt. Mallory's flames faltered as he glanced down, a stunned expression on his face.

The next bullet came from behind, as Aveyron Silvacane leaned from behind a tree. If the bullet had passed through, it could have struck Ada as well, but it didn't. Mallory took the blow with a gasp that sprayed blood from his lips.

The third shot split the air to her left—Brillat, who struck not Mallory but an Albionishman emerging from a gap in a broken wall.

But Mallory still didn't fall. The fire over his hands flared anew. He and Ada stood too close for anyone to shoot again.

"Why can't you just die?" yelled Ada.

Mallory's gap-toothed grin was feral as he loomed over her.

"No!" came a scream from behind him.

Solenn. Ada gazed past Mallory, desperate for a final sight of her daughter. Solenn stood some twenty feet away, bloodied legs braced wide. Gyst's cloak covered her like fine tulle.

"We end this," said Mallory. He swiped at Ada. She dodged thanks to the mead, then brought the knife down in an arc. He sidestepped, bringing around a fist to strike her forearm. To her surprise, she didn't catch fire, but the blow felt like she'd collided with a marble column. He'd utilized rupic-like might. Her jarred arm released hold of the knife. It struck the ground and spun away along the slight downslope that glittered as if it had been sprinkled with salt.

CHAPTER FORTY

SOLENN

Salt makes boiled vegetables brighter in color, helps whipped cream lighten, and cures fish and meat. It adds to the rise of bread. It makes most everything taste better with a mere sprinkle. Such is Selland's might. He does much, through little.

—Excerpt from *Book for Cooks to Excel as Do Chefs*

Solenn's scream left her throat and soul raw. As much as she loved Mamm, she yearned for a chance to know this woman, the one who had loved Solenn enough to send her away with hopes that she could live a better, freer life.

That could still happen. Adamantine's sacrifice didn't need to be in vain.

Gyst had locked Solenn in place with a view of the confrontation between Adamantine and Mallory Valmont. *See, because of your insolence, Adamantine is now in a precarious place—*

Solenn delved into the well of the divine. Around her, millions of unknowns squirmed as if to wave in greeting. She couldn't help but be amazed by how they coated everything from the dirt to the rocks to the body of Mallory Valmont. His multiple wounds were like open doors, confirmation that Gyst could have ended this fight from the moment they arrived.

Adamantine's knife rested near her feet. Solenn comprehended more unknowns than even Gyst.

Gyst. Stop.

She mentally found the ethereal cloak. She *tugged.*

She didn't steal his mantle. More like, she truly stepped beneath its shelter, as if to hide from the rain, but there was no hiding from anything, not here.

Before, she had only tasted the presence of death as caused by epicurea. Now, she directed death into the portals created by the fresh bullet wounds in Mallory Valmont.

Infection. Gangrene. Putrescence. Decomposition of one life while thousands of others blossomed and thrived.

Mallory Valmont stopped with a gasp. His fire withered. *He* withered. His body huddled and shrank within his layers of clothes, his hair falling free as he collapsed to his knees. A wheeze escaped him like air released from a child's bladder-ball. He struck the ground face-first.

Solenn felt him die, that new vacancy created by his departing soul. Hester's presence in him was gone too. Snuffed in an instant, like a wet blanket had been tossed atop a stubborn glow amid ashes.

Solenn! Gyst sputtered in her mind. *What—how did you—you're a mere child, how—*

"I'm sorry, Hester," Solenn said aloud for the God bound in the statue to hear. Tears slipped down her cheeks. She felt Gyst recoil as he realized she'd fully severed his control. "I understand why you're angry. I don't want you to be trapped here forever, but neither can you be free to carry out your vendetta. I'll search out a way to help you, starting with a means to communicate with you that *doesn't* involve eating stone."

"Solenn!" Erwan emerged from his cover, unabashed relief across his features. She'd never seen him so grubby and scruffy.

"Solenn." Adamantine said the word with softness, as if still testing it on her tongue. Maybe she was. Solenn would have been a nameless babe when they'd parted ways.

Solenn. This is deep power you're playing with. Gyst sounded smooth, but she knew he was unnerved. She felt him try to marshal more of his power here, through her. Her tongue tingled, a conduit alight. She couldn't hold him off for long, and once he had control again, it would be absolute. She needed to make her own move now, but, but . . .

Solenn didn't want to be a God, not of unknowns, not of anything. She wanted—she wanted to help Braiz. To live. To ride horses, to go to her favorite beach again, riding bareback, the gray skies heavy with rain like a sway-bellied cat near ready to birth kittens. Solenn's favorite place, her favorite memories, set to the music of pounding hooves, with Selland's presence evident by the brininess of the stormy sea upon her tongue.

Even through the intense presence of Gyst in her mouth, she tasted Selland again at that moment, and knew. He was with her even here.

Of course he was. She was a daughter of Braiz.

The taste of the sea was very much like the taste of tears.

Solenn smiled at Adamantine, who gazed back with outright longing. "I don't even know you yet, but I love you," Solenn said to her, then turned to Erwan as he approached. "And I love you, Erwan, as I always have."

She gestured to Selland. "Thank you for seasoning my life with such joy," she whispered to him.

With that, she grabbed the knife from the ground, stuck out her tongue as far as she could, and sliced it off.

CHAPTER
FORTY-ONE

ADA

There are a thousand recipes for revenge, and every one of them tastes like scat.

—Verdanian Chef proverb

There was blood. So very much blood. Ada had been forced to witness rogue Chefs subject to this punishment during her tour days, but never up close, never experienced by someone she loved. Ada and Erwan carried Solenn to the shelter of a boulder, one of the girl's gray sleeves ripped off and balled into her mouth to try to stanch the flow. Even so, they had to angle her face to the ground so that she wouldn't choke. Solenn, mercifully, had fallen unconscious from the pain.

Aveyron stood guard over them, his glances at Solenn fearful. Brillat stalked the rest of the amphitheater to eliminate any remaining soldiers.

Tears trailed down Erwan's face. "Was there any other way she could have been free of Gyst?" he asked softly.

Ada thought for a long moment before shaking her head. "I don't know. I don't think so. This . . . this option never even occurred to me. It was too terrible, I suppose."

"Whatever will she do now?" A tear slipped from the tip of Erwan's nose to splotch on a flat stone.

"The same as she would have done before." Aveyron spoke with quiet conviction. "She's going to represent Braiz among my kin. Terrible as this injury is, it will only increase her esteem among us."

Erwan nodded in sudden understanding. "She's no longer a Chef."

"More than that, it was a willing sacrifice," added Ada.

"Yes. Solenn will gain new respect for this act." Brillat rejoined them, holstering his pistol. His breath escaped in a hiss. "She's still bleeding too much. Aveyron, what gate did you use to get here? Is it close?"

"We had a guide. The messenger you sent." Aveyron's eyes widened. "I can find the catamount again—"

"Yes. Go."

There was no need to tell the boy to hurry.

"We have potent healing items that are not epicurea. Nor must they be ingested by mouth," Brillat said. "I have accounted for everyone who came here. Segal Valmont is bound and gagged nearby. He offered no—" He stopped speaking as Solenn awoke with a whimper.

"Shh, shh, take it easy, we have you," murmured Erwan. Solenn turned her head enough to see Ada, Erwan, and Brillat. Her cheeks twitched as if to smile, only for her eyes to fill with new agony.

"Can you sense anything of Gyst?" Brillat asked.

Solenn gave her head a slight shake, a muffled noise coming from her throat.

"I'm going to get you something to write with," Ada said, touching Solenn's knuckles as she stood. Their hands were almost the same size and coloration, but Ada's were scarred from martial training and years in the kitchen.

Her daughter had lost her tongue. She'd cut it off herself. Grief and horror rose anew. Ada blinked back tears as she walked the immediate area.

"Aveyron has gone to fetch you medicine," Brillat said, his voice unusually kind as Ada returned with a sharp stick. "In the meantime, we should discuss strategies regarding—"

"With respect, Comte," Erwan said through gritted teeth, "Solenn has just sustained a grievous wound after being possessed by a *God*. Extensive planning will be necessary, yes, but such matters are currently superfluous."

Brillat genuflected. "My pardon. Of course."

Ada knew that their deliberations must include the delicate matter of Comtesse Esme Alarie. She remained hale within her pit, according to Erwan. Ada hadn't checked on her, and would not. She had already decided that it would be for the best for Maman to think she'd died here today.

"I hope your son returns quickly," Ada said to Brillat. "Solenn's sleeve will soon be saturated. We should probably start boiling cloth in the meantime, though the fire will be reluctant, I'm sure. And Gyst . . ." She stopped herself there. Solenn didn't need to hear Ada's speculation about how Gyst may attack through infection.

"We have made enemies of two of the Five," Erwan said quietly, sharing in Ada's fears but with more tact. "What can we do?" He spoke to more than the party present, his fingers pinched in an appeal to Selland.

Solenn's brow furrowed as she bent to scratch in the dirt. *Those odds still favor us.*

Ada couldn't help a dry laugh. Her daughter had inherited her humor, it seemed.

Erwan's smile depicted a more strained reaction. "How can we best help you?" he asked Solenn.

She wrote her answer. *Want to go home.* Tears fell along with blood droplets.

"That's exactly where you should go," said Brillat, causing Solenn to gaze at him in apparent surprise. "What, did you think you would get to prompt work in your new role as ambassador?" He clicked his teeth in chastisement. "No one will expect such a thing of you. Our medicine will alleviate your immediate suffering, but your injury remains severe. Recuperation in a safe, familiar place will be best."

War is coming. Solenn's fervent concern came across in her forceful writing. Ada's heart ached. Solenn was so very young to take on such burdens.

"It is," said Erwan. "Which is exactly why you must recuperate *now*. Grant yourself permission to rest, as you would help a horse to rest after a hard gallop. What happens if you push a horse to run again too soon, hmm?" Solenn's brows twitched in a signal of a faint smile.

"In Braiz, what will be your destination?" asked Brillat.

"Malo," said Erwan.

They quickly hashed out a plan: Solenn would ride with Erwan to the musketeers at Rozny, where the Braizian contingent would divide: Erwan to Lutecia, to settle diplomatic matters; Solenn to Braiz, to refuge.

Solenn tapped Ada on the hand and then wrote, *What about you?*

"What about me?" Ada rephrased as she read the words. She had been so focused on Solenn that she hadn't let her mind wander to her own predicament. "I need to go to Rance. Your great-grandmother is there in the care of a dear old friend of ours."

Bring her to Malo.

"Malo? But I can't, Braiz—" Ada stopped, remembering. "Rogue Chefs won't be extradited to Verdania now."

"You and Eglantine can go to my parents' château," said Erwan. "Solenn would be a ten-minute ride distant."

"Our mother-and-daughter relationship could be recognized," Ada said.

Solenn considered this for a moment, then gave her head a slight shake. "I agree," added Erwan. "People see in Solenn the similarities to Katell's kin. However harsh the gossip has been over the years, it has never questioned her parentage. And now, the whispers will focus on what has happened in recent days.' He grimaced.

Solenn wrote a single word and then squeezed Ada's hand. *Please*.

That settled it. "Yes," Ada whispered, throat tight with emotion. "I'll come." Her daughter wanted her in Malo. No further justification was required. As Solenn had noted, war was coming, and soon. If her family was reunited in Braiz, they could confront whatever came next together.

Together, no matter the threats against them, there was hope.

ACKNOWLEDGMENTS

This book challenged me like none before. I'm grateful for the constructive criticism of Cécile Cristofari, Ember Randall, M. K. Hutchins, Lisbeth Campbell, J. Kathleen Cheney, Deborah L. Davitt, and Rebecca Roland. The crew at Codex Writers has motivated and supported me for more than ten years now. Thank you, friends.

I've been honored to work with a great team at 47North, including my editor, Adrienne Procaccini, and developmental editor, Clarence A. Haynes. Their insights produced a much stronger book, for which I'm grateful.

My agent, Rebecca Strauss, has been my champion on good days and bad. Thank you, thank you, thank you.

My husband, Jason, has earned a caramel apple pie whenever he wants one. My son, Nicholas—I am so proud of the young man you have become. My kitties are my stalwart companions through my writing hours; my gratitude to Sun Cities 4 Paws for saving my cats so that they could save me.

ABOUT THE AUTHOR

Beth Cato is the Nebula Award–nominated author of the Clockwork Dagger series and the Blood of Earth trilogy. Her short stories and poetry can be found in hundreds of publications, including *Fantasy Magazine*, *Escape Pod*, *Uncanny Magazine*, and the *Magazine of Fantasy & Science Fiction*. Beth hails from Hanford, California, but currently writes and bakes cookies in a lair west of Phoenix, Arizona, that she shares with her husband, son, and two feline overlords. For more information, visit www.bethcato.com.